7.11.10

12
BJ
JO
AV
FC
HG

27.12.12.

DE
SC
TA
HI
MC
NIXON

BI

ES
HA
JO
HG

CM
WO

DE
BC

CC
CM
HA
AS
ER
SC
CC
PC
HG

A SILVER FLOOD

Taller and more intelligent than most of the men in Mousehole, Charlotte Trevennan is seen as different from her neighbours, and is further isolated when she is bequeathed a new fishing boat from Charles Polruan. William Trevennan is a powerful lay preacher but a lazy fisherman and when he denounces his daughter from the pulpit for refusing to let him captain her boat, no man dares work for her. But when she rescues Kit Hargreaves from a drunken brawl, Charlotte's fortunes begin to change, for Kit recognises a remarkable woman when he sees one. Especially when she looks like Charlotte...

A SILVER FLOOD

A SILVER FLOOD

by

Janet Wright Matthews

Magna Large Print Books
Long Preston, North Yorkshire,
BD23 4ND, England.

British Library Cataloguing in Publication Data.

Matthews, Janet Wright
    A silver flood.

    A catalogue record of this book is
    available from the British Library

    ISBN   0-7505-1492-2

First published in Great Britain by Judy Piatkus (Publishers) Ltd., 1998

Copyright ' 1998 by Janet Willcock

Cover illustration ' Len Thurston by arrangement with P.W.A.
International Ltd.

The moral right of the author has been asserted

Published in Large Print 2000 by arrangement with Piatkus Books
Limited

Magna Large Print is an imprint of Library Magna Books Ltd.

Printed and bound in Great Britain by
T.J. (International) Ltd., Cornwall, PL28 8RW

To the Cornish fishing industry that has served
the county so well for so many centuries –
long may it survive!

And to Norman – as ever.

Chapter One

'You can't do this to me!'

Charlotte Trevennan jumped swiftly backwards as a gnarled fist thumped onto her desk, sending a fountain of ink splattering across the entries in the leather-bound ledger.

She jerked her long skirts out of the way of any stray drops, her heart beating nervously, aware of her vulnerability. She was the only one left in the usually bustling offices except for the angry fisherman. Outside, even the busy road along the cliff at Newlyn was empty and lifeless, with not even the common trip-trip of a donkey cart along the cobbled street to break the silence.

But to show her fear would be to lose even the small vestiges of the authority left to her. She took a deep breath, forcing herself to act as she would have done in the past when she had been able to rely on the complete support of the owner of the firm.

'Mr Angarrack!' She grabbed a piece of blotting paper and mopped frantically at the ledger, trying to rescue her records before the ink dried, hiding them for ever. 'We both know that you were responsible for the loss of those nets and–'

'Both!' the fisherman broke in angrily. 'There's no *both* about it. What does a girl understand about fishing? I want to speak to some man who knows what he's talking about. I'm not going to

9

have me money docked by no blasted woman.'
The scorn in his Cornish voice vibrated through
the room, making the oil lamp hanging above her
desk swing, throwing leaping shadows through
the room.

Charlotte hoped that he could not see her
nervousness. 'It was Mr Polruan himself who
made the decision.' Her voice sounded as firm as
ever, despite her feeling of insecurity. 'I am
merely the agent.'

'Oh, yes?' He leaned across the high desk,
thrusting his weatherbeaten face into hers. He
was the same height as she was but far heavier,
his muscles developed by long days at sea. 'Tes
easy to blame him, a dead man who can't answer
for himself. And you with not even the decency
to go to his funeral.'

His answer tore at her raw nerves, multiplying
the ache in her heart until it was a physical pain,
until she could bear it no longer. Twenty-one
years of training to be a polite, self-effacing
woman, twenty-one years of learning to
subordinate herself to a man – any man –
suddenly these were swept away in a flood of hurt
and anger.

Careless of the danger of reprisals, she reached
out, catching the man by the lapels of his dirty
coat, pulling him even closer to her. 'Then why
did *you* come here, when you knew his funeral
was on?' she demanded furiously. 'Why aren't
you there now, paying your last respects? He was
your employer as well.'

The fisherman's face changed and he pulled
away from her grasp. 'I'm not staying here to be

insulted.' His voice was angry but she could see the doubt in his face. He moved away, grabbing for his greasy black hat. He rammed it onto his head and made for the door, then turned, his belligerence growing again.

'I'll get my rights,' he threatened. 'I'll make sure in future that I deal with a man, not some great lump of a girl who can't even find herself a husband. And I'll tell your boss how you treated me, you – you *hussy!*'

He stormed out, slamming the door behind him and Charlotte could hear the thump of his leather boots as he stomped heavily down the bare wooden stairs.

Quickly she moved across the room, stooping so that she could peer out of the small window. Through the thick, distorting panes she saw him pause briefly outside the office, glancing up at the lighted window with a malevolent sneer before hurrying off through the rain, his footsteps ringing on the shining cobbles.

Charlotte let her breath out with a relieved sigh and smoothed her long black hair with shaking hands, tucking a wayward tendril back into her neat bun. Polruan & Son was a composite business, mainly trading in fish which they bought from the local fishermen before selling it 'up country'; they also owned a few drifters. Although she had worked in the office since leaving her school in Penzance, Charlotte had never had to cope with an aggrieved fisherman before; Charles Polruan had always protected her from that sort of unpleasantness.

She stared out across the choppy waters of

11

Newlyn harbour to the luggers pulling and backing at their moorings, bucking like active ponies before the capricious April winds. It was difficult to believe that she would never see him again, ducking his head under the lintel with an automatic action, never hear his cheerful greeting: 'All well, little one?'

She bit back a sob. No one else ever called her that, no one else ever would. She was a great gawk of a woman, taller than any of the men in Mousehole, still unwed, uncourted even, at twenty-one years old. No one would ever marry her, so different from the dainty image of young womanhood, personified by the Queen at her romantic marriage to Prince Albert. And even though now, after the birth of eight children, the Queen was no longer the slim girl she had once been, the ideal remained unchanged. No, only a giant like Mr Polruan would ever dream of calling her 'little one'.

Charlotte clamped her lips together to stop them trembling. He had been so much more to her than just an employer. Almost, he seemed one of the family, and now he was dead.

And she had been forbidden to attend his funeral.

A step on the stairs warned her of another visitor and she moved quickly back to her desk, bending again over the ink-stained ledger as the door swung open.

'The light of my life!'

Despite her misery Charlotte began to smile. It was impossible to be angry with Carlos Da Silva. The little Portuguese scarcely came up to her shoulder but he always made an extravagant play for her, throwing out the most outrageous compliments.

Now he kissed his fingers to her. 'My beautiful one! The lady of my desires.'

'Are you hoping to persuade me to accept some very low prices for very good fairmaids?' Charlotte smiled at him. He was one of Polruan & Son's best customers, buying all the hogsheads of salted pilchards, locally known as 'fairmaids', that they could sell.

'Me?' He raised his dark brows, his plump figure thrusting against the tight-fitting frock coat, then he frowned. 'Bela! Are those tears on your lashes?'

'No.' She turned away, dashing a hasty hand across her eyes. 'You are mistaken. I have a cold.'

He came round the desk to her, reaching for her hand. 'But why should you not be sad? The good Senhõr Polruan, dead, and so young. Less than fifty.' He clasped her fingers in his warm, plump hands. 'An accident?'

'His horse was frightened by some boys fighting.' She cleared the tightness from her throat. 'He fell and struck his head.'

He tutted. 'You Cornish. When you are enjoying yourself you are mad. Mad! Fighting and throwing things, jumping out at people.' He shrugged. 'It is because you are Protestants. Always, you try to be good and then, when you have fun – whoosh!' He threw up his hands. 'All the evil comes out.'

'It isn't like that.' As the daughter of a Methodist local preacher she couldn't let the slander pass. 'We have standards...'

'Standards!' He snorted, putting more meaning into one sound than most Cornishmen could into a dozen sentences. 'We Portuguese, we too have standards but we know that people cannot always behave. So we give them ways to enjoy themselves without hurting people. We have carnivals, we enjoy wine, we love beautiful women...' He ogled her.

She knew how her father would condemn her for listening to such talk, but it was impossible to take the little Portuguese's protestations seriously. He scarcely came up to her shoulder and she knew that he had a wife and large family at home. He always carried miniatures of them in his case and would display them to anyone who showed the slightest interest. Besides, she was grateful at present to anyone who took her mind off her troubles.

Charlotte moved to the desk at which she stood every day and began to turn the pages, looking for his account. 'Can I help you with anything, Senhõr?'

But he was staring in bewilderment around the empty office. 'Why are you alone? Where is everyone?'

Again, it hurt to say it. 'At – at Mr Polruan's funeral.'

'It is today – now? But why are you here? Why are you not there?'

She couldn't bring herself to tell the truth. She lowered her glance to the ledger, her shaking fingers playing awkwardly with the thick pages. 'Someone has to stay here.' Even she could hear the roughness of unshed tears in her voice.

'But why you?' The little man was honestly bewildered. 'You were his favourite, the one he liked, the best clerk. Never when you do the invoices is there a mistake. And I tell him so. I say "She is the only woman but she is the best," and he agrees. And now...'

The lump in her throat was choking her and tears burned at her eyes. Unable to look him in the face, she forced the words out. 'Mr Frederick Polruan told – asked – me to stay, to mind the office.' A tear forced its way past her defences and plopped onto the ledger, raising a blister on the thick paper. She rubbed at it clumsily, trying to hide the evidence of her weakness. 'He is the owner now that his father is dead...' The sob came from nowhere, cutting off the rest of the sentence.

He moved immediately to her side, putting his arms around her. 'My little one.' At any other time the expression from such a short man would have amused her; now, echoing as it did Mr Polruan's pet name, it was the final straw. She sobbed again, the tears welling up uncontrollably, and he thrust a silk handkerchief, the size of a small tablecloth, into her hand.

'I see how it is.' Carlos Da Silva moved away from her, pacing angrily around the office on his thick legs. 'He is jealous of you, that lazy, no-good son. Never does he get my order right, never does he perform his sums correctly. Pah! What father would be proud of a lump like him? While Senhõr Polruan was alive, he was afraid, but now...'

15

'Please,' Charlotte protested, mopping her tears, 'you mustn't say such things.' But the man's words only echoed her own thoughts. She had always known that Frederick disliked her, but never until he had forbidden her to attend the funeral had she realised how deep his jealousy ran.

The Portuguese turned to her. 'You must find another office. A woman like you, with your skills...'

'Won't get another job,' Charlotte broke in. 'This is Cornwall, Senhõr. In London, perhaps I could have found work, but not here.' Her voice was bitter. 'Mr Polruan was the only man in Cornwall who would have employed me. Down here, the only proper career for a woman is to marry – and who will marry a gawk like me?'

The fact that he did not come back with one of his flowery compliments showed Charlotte more than anything else how worried he was. 'But what else can you do? Your father...?'

She shook her head. Although nominally a fisherman, her father's energy and time all went into his work as a local preacher. For the last few years it had only been her wages that had kept the family from starving. And now, with his mind set on becoming a proper Methodist minister, he would bring home less than ever.

'I could always be a jowster,' Charlotte said bitterly, referring to the small army of women who hawked fresh fish around the district, going as far as Land's End, their wares carried on their backs in a cowal, a special basket suspended from a band that ran around their forehead. 'With my

16

height and strength, it was probably what God intended me to be anyway.'

Da Silva's instinctive denial was cut short by the noise of hooves coming down the cobbled street – a horse, not one of the ubiquitous donkeys, Charlotte registered automatically. Silently, she and the Portuguese stared at each other as the horse came nearer, then clattered to a halt outside the office.

'If it is the young Senhõr Polruan I tell him what I think.' Da Silva moved swiftly towards the door.

Charlotte reached out frantically, clutching at his coat. 'Please, don't say anything,' she begged. 'It won't do any good.'

'I tell him,' the small Portuguese insisted, dragging himself free and standing before the door, his arms folded belligerently across his chest as Charlotte watched in an agony of trepidation.

But to Charlotte's relief, the man who ran up the wooden stairs wasn't her new employer but someone completely different. Although she knew the face, he was so out of context in these offices that she had to struggle for a few moments before she could put a name to him. 'Mr Brightman.' She couldn't hide the shock in her grey eyes as she recognised Mr Polruan's attorney from Penzance. Surely Frederick Polruan wasn't so frightened of her that he would send his lawyer to sack her?

He bowed to her, his bright eyes travelling warily over the foreigner. They were both short and round, and the similarity to two robins eyeing each other aggressively was so marked that, despite her concern, Charlotte had to bite back a smile. Hastily, she introduced the two men.

The lawyer bowed politely. 'Senhõr.' Then, turning to Charlotte, 'I have a communication to make to you, Miss Trevennan. A private communication.'

The Portuguese hesitated. 'If you need me, Senhõrita—'

'If there is no urgent business that you require, perhaps you had better go, Senhõr,' Charlotte broke in quickly. Whatever the attorney had to say, her position would not be helped by so volatile and interested a defender as Da Silva.

Politely but firmly she saw him out of the office, making sure he had left the premises before she returned to where Mr Brightman was waiting for her, her heart beating leadenly in her chest.

Whatever he had to say to her, she could only think that it would be bad news.

'I'm telling you, you'll marry her and lump it!'

James Hargraves was on his feet, his face scarlet with fury.

'And I'm telling you I won't!' Kit Hargraves roared back.

He hunched his broad shoulders and stared at his father across the huge mahogany desk inlaid with brass that dominated the modern office of the owner of Hargraves & Son. It was almost like looking into a mirror, except that there were grey threads in the mass of fair curls that covered James Hargraves' head and the laughter lines that

18

surrounded his blue eyes were gouged more deeply. Not that either of them was laughing at the moment.

'You'll marry her,' James insisted, 'or you'll not get one penny of my money. Do you understand?'

'And do you understand, I'm not going to sell myself to the highest bidder just to satisfy you and your snobbish pretensions,' Kit snarled back. 'I will *not* marry a woman I don't love.'

'Oh "love" is it?' The sneer was manifest. 'Well, who should know about "love" better than you? Been "in love" with half the strumpets in Hull, you have, yet when I find a decent woman for you, a woman with money and breeding, what's more, all you do is turn your nose up at her.'

'Look, Dad.' Kit made a belated attempt to keep his temper, 'All I'm asking is the chance to choose my own wife, the way you did with Mother, not have some female I don't know and can't like foisted on me in this way.'

James Hargraves thumped the desk. 'When I married your ma I was a poor man.' As he got angrier his voice thickened, the original Humberside accent getting stronger. 'I weren't like you. You've got an education, a future. You could marry whom you like. Yet all you want,' he concluded bitterly, 'are women off the streets with no learning and no money.'

'That's not true.' Kit could feel himself growing heated again, despite his best intentions. 'Just because I don't fancy the mealy-mouthed bloodless bits of la-di-da you keep producing doesn't mean I go out with tarts.'

'It means you won't do the one thing I ask you!'

Fury suffused the older man's face with purple. 'You're my only son, for heaven's sake.'

The words fell like particles of ice between the two men and Kit felt his face grow stiff. If his father were throwing that in his face…

But the older man seemed unaware that he had gone too far. He pounded the table again. 'I'm telling you, Christopher, you marry that girl or not one penny of my fortune do you get. Ever.'

The hated name, which was never used except when his father was trying to coerce him, was the final insult. Kit felt anger surge through his veins in a red tide. He had tried to be reasonable but it hadn't worked.

He leaned forward, resting clenched fists on the gleaming wood. 'That's it!' he shouted. 'That is the last straw! You don't want a son – all you want is a puppet, a creature to live out your stupid, snobbish dreams, to do your bidding and drag the family the last rung up the social ladder which you can't climb yourself.'

He straightened. 'Well, you can forget it.' His voice was suddenly deadly cold. 'I don't need you or your money. You made your own way in life and I'm as good a man as you, any day.'

He moved to the door, his long legs covering the room in a couple of strides. 'Keep your damned money – buy some other cat's-paw,' he snarled. He hauled the door open and turned, briefly, in the doorway. 'I'll live my life my own way. I don't need you and I don't need anything you've got.'

Kit Hargraves slammed the door behind him

and strode swiftly through the outer office. Serried rows of clerks, standing at their high desks under the watchful eye of the Chief Clerk, bent industriously over their books. Too industriously. Even the panelling that lined his father's office could not have kept out the sounds of this latest row.

Well, what did it matter? He reached for his hat and jumped the marble steps leading down from the front door in one athletic leap. This was the last time; he had had enough of his father's attempts to run his life for him. This time the old man had gone too far.

Kit stood for a second, considering his options. The first thing was to get away from here, as far away as he could. The destination did not matter.

The cold wind blew on his heated face, bringing with it a spatter of cold rain, and he tasted the salt from the North Sea on his lips.

That was it. His mind made up, Kit turned on his heel and headed for the port. He'd take the first boat out of this damned place. And he'd never come back.

Suddenly, just outside the village, Charlotte could contain herself no longer. The need to tell her news, to speak to someone sympathetic, was too great. Picking up her skirts to free her long legs, she began to run, wishing, not for the first time, that her father would allow her to wear the new metal crinoline frames that were so much lighter and less restrictive than her voluminous petticoats.

She was much later than usual. The spring

21

evening had already fallen and low, scudding clouds hid the stars and dropped a thin drizzle that stung her face as she ran.

The path was rough but this close to the sea it was never really dark and there was light enough to see and avoid the stones and holes that littered the road between Newlyn and Mousehole.

It was even a relief to run, to be able to release all the pent-up feelings which she had had to suppress ever since she had heard of Mr Polruan's death. And at the end of her journey, she knew that she had the comfort of the cottage, the warm fire, her mother's presence. She breathed a sigh of relief as she remembered that her father had arranged to go out fishing that afternoon. The weather was cold and blowy but not bad enough to keep the hardy Cornish fishermen in harbour if there was a chance of getting a catch.

As she passed the first outlying cottages Charlotte slowed, panting. It would never do to run here, where she could be seen. Someone would be sure to tell her father and then there would be trouble – even more trouble than she was already in. He expected higher standards of modesty and decorum from her than from the other village women, and to be seen acting in such an unrestricted manner could only lead to a reprimand. Automatically she straightened her bonnet and wrapped her shawl more securely around her shoulders.

It was darker in the village than on the open road. The windows of the low, granite cottages glowed yellow, lit by the small lamps that burned the evil-smelling oil called 'train' that was pressed from pilchards, but they did little to illuminate the narrow passages.

Carefully she made her way down the steep streets, the rounded cobbles, picked from the rocky beach, slick under her leather soled boots. In the small harbour she could dimly see some movement, possibly a fishing boat just landed, but she was in too much of a hurry to investigate.

Eagerly, she hurried through the empty streets, her longing to unburden herself growing stronger the nearer she got to her destination. If only her mother could advise her; if only her mother would tell her what to do...

And there the cottage was, in front of her, right against the side of the harbour, the window glowing with the promise of refuge.

With a surge of relief she thrust the door open, automatically bending her head to duck under the low lintel. Warmth and light surrounded her, the smell of fish cooking over the fire for dinner, the yellow oil light reflecting softly off the whitewashed walls and the blackened beams, saved long ago from forgotten shipwrecks.

At the entrance her mother turned round, a welcoming smile on her thin, pale face. 'Charlotte, my dear...'

But Charlotte could bear it no longer; the need to tell what had happened was a physical weight on her heart. Impatiently, she broke in, her louder voice drowning her mother's weak bleat, the words tumbling from her. 'Mother, Mother, you'll never guess what's happened!'

There was a swift arrested look on her mother's

face, as if she were suddenly afraid. She opened her mouth to speak but Charlotte interrupted. Her news was too important, too overwhelming.

She burst out: 'Mr Brightman, Mr Polruan's attorney, has been to see me – and what do you think he said?'

Charlotte gazed excitedly at her mother but the older woman did not respond. Only her mouth moved, opening and shutting speechlessly for a few seconds, the little colour she had draining from her thin face as she stared at her daughter with wide, frightened eyes.

Chapter Two

Charlotte moved swiftly across the stone-flagged floor towards her mother. 'What's the matter? Are you ill?'

A tremor ran through the older woman, leaving her face white and drawn. Her tongue flicked across bloodless lips. 'My sins!' She began to shake, burying her face in her red, work-roughened hands. 'I am a great sinner!'

'No, you're a good woman.' Charlotte led her mother gently across to the wooden settle that stood by the fire and pressed her down into it. These attacks of conscience were easily dealt with, as long as her father wasn't around. She pulled the older woman against her, stroking her hair, once golden, now faded and streaked with grey and strangely damp under her fingers. 'You are a very good woman and God has rewarded you.'

The head lifted, the pale eyes stared at her with curiosity. 'Rewarded?'

'That is what I was going to tell you.' Charlotte could feel the excitement rising inside her again and her hands tightened unconsciously around her mother's chapped fingers. 'That is what Mr Brightman came to say. I have been left something in Mr Polruan's will.'

'Money?' The voice was breathless with the dawning of impossible hope. Money would mean

25

so much – warmth, comfort, ease.

Charlotte laughed, her silver-grey eyes dancing. 'As good as. Maybe even better.' She could not stay still any longer; her excitement coursed through her so that she had to walk around the small room, throwing off her shawl, hurling her bonnet carelessly onto the white scrubbed table. 'Mother, I've been left a boat and some seine nets.'

The expression of disbelief on the older woman's face made her laugh again, throwing back her head, her white throat vibrating unselfconsciously. 'A boat, Ma. A boat!'

Charlotte dropped onto her knees beside her mother, reaching again for her with hands that shook. 'It's a good one, too – the *Faith-Lily*, a drifter. Do you know how many shares an owner gets?' Her voice raced on, rising as she contemplated the richness awaiting her. 'Ten nets, if it's mackerel. And Father only gets six as a crew member. That means we more than double the amount of money coming into the house. And that's without the seine nets or my pay at Polruan's.'

It was riches beyond belief, freedom from the constant worry of poverty, of illness, of making ends meet and keeping up appearances. It meant the difference between existing and enjoying life. Charlotte could feel her happiness expanding within her like a flower in bloom, colouring her whole view of life. 'Even if Father doesn't get ordained we shall still be better off; we shall still be safe.'

The word reverberated round the low room.

Safe. No danger now of the workhouse, of living on charity, of losing one's self-respect. Safe. Charlotte could feel tension she had never noticed before dropping from her. *Safe.*

'Oh, thank the Lord.' Bertha Trevennan looked as if she would collapse with relief. 'Dear God, thank You. Thank You.'

Charlotte had no time to spare for her mother's prayers. Restlessly, she strode around the small room, automatically swinging her skirts out of the way of the stools and chairs. Only the respect for her father, beaten into her since she was a small child, had stopped her from saying what she knew to be true, that the money from the boat would be almost three times what her father brought in.

It was true that he hadn't been reared as a fisherman. He had been an agent on an estate the Polruans had owned in North Cornwall until he had married the smart and attractive lady's maid who waited on Elizabeth Polruan. It was only later, when he had converted to Methodism, that he had left his work on the estate and taken to fishing.

'If it was good enough for Our Lord,' he would state, his voice rich with belief, 'then who am I to do otherwise?'

But Charlotte had realised, as she grew older, that if the disciples had done as little actual fishing as her father, they would soon have starved.

She whirled around and sped back to where her mother sat, reaching out for her.

'Do you understand what this means?' Charlotte's voice shook with suppressed energy; it was impossible to sit still. 'We will never have to worry about money again. It doesn't matter that I'm too tall to get a husband. It doesn't matter that Father–' she hesitated, changing the sentence. 'It's all right if he devotes his time to preaching. We can survive.'

The feeling inside her grew, expanded until she felt as if she could hardly breathe. It took her a few moments to identify the feeling, it was so seldom that she felt like this. Then she realised. It was happiness. Pure, unadulterated, complete.

She pressed her shaking hands against her flushed face, letting the emotions wash over her, letting her thoughts pour out without the habitual restraint.

'This means freedom, Mother, freedom for us all. It means independence.' It was almost a frightening thought. Always, she had been dependent, on her father, on Mr Polruan's employment. Now, she was in charge of her own destiny; she was no longer bound by the shackles of poverty.

She drew in a deep, unsteady breath. Her changed circumstances brought responsibility too, of course; as owner she had to make sure the boat was maintained and properly crewed, but that was no problem. It was already part of her remit at Polruan's, to ensure these things. She knew the crew of the *Faith-Lily;* George Angarrack, the man she had seen today, was the captain. Involuntarily, her mouth twisted with distaste; he was trouble but she was the owner. Surely she could deal with him?

And even now, the *Faith-Lily* was anchored offshore at Newlyn, awaiting her annual refit or 'paying up' as it was called locally before the start of the summer mackerel season. Within a week, she would be ready to sail again, catching mackerel, bringing in money – money that would make all the difference to the Trevennans' lives. And, in the summer, there might be pilchards. The shoals were growing smaller every year and some years they did not appear at all, but if they did...

'Praise be.' Bertha Trevennan fell to her knees on the stone floor and her heartfelt thanks rang out unusually loudly, startling Charlotte with the difference from her usual hushed tones. 'The Lord has been merciful to me, a sinner.'

'Yes, dearest.' It was a welcome change from the usual self-abasement but just as dangerous in its own way. Once her mind was set on religion, Bertha Trevennan could go on for hours. It was best to turn her mind to something practical as soon as possible.

'Shall we have some tea?' Charlotte suggested, reaching out to help her up. Under her hands the older woman's clothes felt damp, as had her hair. 'You've been out?' she asked, concerned.

Bertha's face paled, her eyes widening so that the whites showed all round the faded blue pupil. 'I – I–' she seemed to crumple in Charlotte's arms. 'I had to go, I *had* to.' Her voice rose hysterically and she began to tremble, her thin body vibrating tautly.

'Yes, dearest,' Charlotte soothed, stroking her gently, trying to conceal the worry she felt. Her mother had always been nervous, excitable; she hoped that her mind wasn't weakening. 'But where did you go?'

'I – it was–' Bertha swallowed, then forced the words out in a rush. 'I went to his funeral. Just to watch,' she added quickly, 'just from the road. I didn't intrude.' Her eyes closed again and tears spilled slowly down her sunken cheeks. 'I wasn't in the way.'

'Of course not.' Charlotte was puzzled by her agitation but now was not the time to question her. She tightened her arms about the older woman. 'I'm glad you went, glad. One of the family should have been there, to say goodbye. Mr Polruan was always very kind to us. And you used to work for him once. It was right that you should have gone.'

'You think so?' The thin face stared up at her, hungry for approbation. 'You think I did right?'

'I know you did,' Charlotte said warmly, 'and so will Father.'

'Don't tell him.' The change in her mother was frightening. The fingers bore painfully into Charlotte's arms and her mother's face was white with desperation. 'You mustn't tell him, Charlotte.' Her voice was a pleading whisper. 'Please.'

'I won't tell,' Charlotte began, but she could get no further.

With a crash the door of the house was flung open and she whirled around, hearing her mother's frightened gasp behind her. Framed in the doorway, black against the lighter backdrop of the night sky, a man stood, arms outstretched

30

against the doorframe. 'Blessed be this house and those that dwell therein.'

Tension swirled back in a dark miasma, ousting the feelings of happiness and comfort. Bowing her head dutifully, Charlotte murmured, 'Good evening, Father,' and heard the repression in her voice.

Behind her, she could hear her mother's frightened voice. 'Supper will be ready shortly, husband.' Bertha scurried mouselike to the pot simmering on the range, head lowered, seeming thinner and paler than she had when Charlotte had arrived.

The contrast between the trust and closeness that had vibrated through the small cottage only seconds ago and the feeling of restraint now was so great that Charlotte felt her stomach roil with shock. Suddenly resentful, she stared at her father with stormy grey eyes. 'I thought you were at sea tonight.'

He entered the cottage slowly, his prematurely white hair gleaming in the subdued lamplight as he pulled off his black bowler hat and hung it on the peg behind the door. 'I saw a vicar walking the cliffs above Lamorna.' He moved towards her, pulling her body close to his in a long embrace. 'Are you not pleased to see me, daughter?' His beard scratched the sensitive skin of her face and her nostrils twitched at the smell of fish and tar that clung to his clothes.

'Of course.' But he had ruined her happiness. Abruptly, she pulled away from him. 'You said that you saw a vicar?'

He turned to look at her, his blue eyes gleaming

in the tanned face. 'On the hill above Lamorna. Of course, we couldn't go out, not after that.' He sighed. 'It was only a glance. I called to the others but by the time they had turned he had already disappeared. Still, the ways of God are strange. Now I shall be able to attend the meeting with the Superintendent tonight.'

It sometimes seemed that God was determined to make her father an ordained minister. So often, when there was a chapel meeting that he felt he ought to attend, something happened that prevented him from going to sea. In her head, she heard again Charles Polruan's laughing voice, saw the cynical quirk to his eyebrows. 'If all the vicars who were seen on the cliffs were really there, every church would have ten incumbents.'

The sudden loss of her feeling of happiness had upset her normal equilibrium, and instead of accepting his words as she had so often before, Charlotte was horrified to hear herself say, 'You need not have told them; you could have stayed silent. Captain Peters needs money desperately now that his daughter is ill.'

Her father raised his fine brows, so much darker than his white hair. 'And risk the lives of all on board? For mere money? Would you really want me to have that on my conscience?'

She blushed, turning away to hide her confusion. 'No, of course not.' And it was true; all Cornishmen knew that to go to sea after catching even a fleeting glimpse of a vicar would be to risk a shipwreck. And her father was a good man, a local preacher, admired and respected through-out the whole of Penwith. He would never lie about such a thing, would he?

The thought was so shocking, so impossible that she felt her face flame with guilt. Hastily, she tried to make amends. 'Dinner is ready, Father, so you can have a meal before you have to leave.' She reached into a drawer under the table for the knives and forks and began hastily to lay the table. 'I was late tonight so we can all eat together.'

'Late?' He turned to look at her, knowing well that it was very rare for her to be kept after hours at the office. 'Why was that?'

Charlotte was aware of a strange reluctance to tell him her news. She knew it was stupid; there was no way that she could keep her inheritance a secret from him, even if she wanted to. Once the men on the boat knew who their new owner was, it would be all around Mousehole in a minute and William Trevennan, as a local preacher and *de facto* village mayor, would be amongst the first to be told. But she wanted to hug the secret to herself for just a few hours more, to savour it without having her father draw lessons on the goodness of God from it, to revel frankly in the mercenary benefits without being reminded of her moral obligations.

Head down, she concentrated on placing the cutlery in exactly the correct positions while she made up her mind what to say.

'Actually–' she began.

But he had caught her by the shoulder, swung her round. Startled, she raised her eyes to his. 'Father?'

'Do not tell me, daughter.' His voice was a rasping groan. 'Do not tell me that you have been

33

dallying with a man?'

The idea was ridiculous. There wasn't a man in Penwith who would be interested in a woman like her, too tall, too clever, one who did a man's job. A bubble of laughter rose in her, choking her. 'Of course–' she started but he interrupted her again.

'Ah, God, that it should come to this. That my daughter, my own daughter, should feel the stirrings of lust in her loins, that she should feel the burning white heat of passion in her virgin body.' He clutched her closer to him, pulling her against him. 'You can tell me, my daughter. You can confess to me. Did he, have you–'

Charlotte tried to pull away but he was too strong for her. His arms held her close. 'Tell me, my child.'

Amusement turned to distaste. Behind her, she heard a clatter as Bertha dropped a ladle onto the stone floor and then her mother's voice rising on a hysterical note. 'A sinner. Oh God, I have been such a sinner.'

It was too much. With a final effort, she thrust him away with such force that he staggered back then she turned, hurrying to her mother's side, trying to calm her before the hysteria drove her beyond reason.

'You are totally wrong,' she told her father firmly. 'I was late only because I had a meeting with Mr Brightman that went on longer than expected.' She held her mother against her, calming her by the closeness of her body, by the gentle way she stroked the greying hair.

She had to say it, she realised. It was the only way to stop him ranting at her in this ridiculous

34

fashion and upsetting her mother.

Taking a deep breath, Charlotte said, 'If you must know, Mr Polruan has left me a drifter and a pilchard fishery in his will.'

The silence spread through the small room. Even her mother's sobs had stopped and her father stood motionless, his head back, his eyes closed. For long seconds, all that could be heard was the splatter of rain against the window and the low rumble of the waves washing against the harbour walls just outside the cottage. Then her father spoke.

'Daughter, God has blessed you.'

Charlotte felt the glow of pleasure begin again. How could she have doubted him, even for one moment? You had only to look at his flowing white locks, the sturdy, honest body, his eyes that could glow with religious fervour; you had only to listen to his voice, deep, full, reverberating, to know that this was a man blessed by God.

She smiled happily at him. 'Indeed, Father. I am aware of it.' She gave her mother a final hug and helped her to her feet then moved back to the table. 'It will make such a difference to us. We will be getting the benefit of sixteen shares of the catches now, what with yours and the boat's.'

She was immersed in sorting out the knives and she almost missed his comment in the rattle of the cutlery. Unsure that she had heard aright she paused, staring at him. 'I beg your pardon?'

'Twenty shares,' her father repeated, with a satisfied smile. He moved towards her, his hands outstretched. 'You will not deny me the position of captain on your own boat, will you, Daughter?'

The ship hit the rolling waves of the North Sea, heeling over as the wind caught her sails.

Deep in the crew's quarters Kit Hargraves grimaced as the first spasm of nausea caught him. He was a good sailor, could stand any weather – after the first twelve hours were passed. But he had to get through those twelve hours first, and nothing about this situation would help him.

'Move yer arse. You're not on your yacht now, you know.'

He stood aside as a sailor pushed rudely past, giving him an angry stare. It had been a mistake to come straight to the dock, Kit knew that now. It would have been better to have called in at a pawnbroker's and bought some nondescript clothes that would have allowed him to fit in, but fear that his father would catch him up or have him followed had driven him straight here. He had taken the first available boat out.

That was his second mistake. A Cornish boat, for God's sake! What had possessed him? And there wasn't a man on board who came past his shoulder, so he couldn't even borrow or buy a change of clothing. Instead here he was, dressed like a gentleman and living in conditions he wouldn't keep a dog in. And with a lot of murdering Cornishmen!

The ship lurched again and he felt the sweat break out on his forehead. Then a bellow of *'Hargraves!'* brought his head up.

'On deck, Hargraves. Get a move on. You're not here for your health.'

Kit swallowed and made his way up the

36

companionway. It was only for a couple of weeks, then he would be in Portugal, with money in his pocket and out of reach of his father. That was worth any amount of discomfort.

'Well, 'tes your choice girl. There's no other can bid him nay.'

Charlotte poked uncertainly with the toe of her boot at a corner of one of the stone flags that covered the floor of the small, damp room where the Jelberts lived. 'But he's my father,' she protested weakly.

Granfer-John Jelbert raised his head and stared at her. The net he was making hung limply from a rope strung across the corner of the room, and the harsh smell of the new twine made Charlotte's nose twitch. 'Well, I reckon...' He paused deliberately to set another mesh and Charlotte waited anxiously for his opinion.

Granfer-John had been one of the best fishermen in the village in his youth. She had heard men say that he could bring his boat back in fog so thick that the bow was invisible from the stern, knowing where he was just by the sound of the echoes of the conch shell thrown back by the surrounding cliffs. Now he was old, crippled by rheumatism, supporting his orphaned grandson and himself by the pittance he could earn making nets, but he still knew more about fishing than anyone else in the village. With her father out at the meeting with the Superintendent, it had seemed the ideal opportunity to ask advice about her inheritance from one who knew all about fishing.

He tugged the knot tight and glanced back at her with rheumy brown eyes. 'I reckon your da's the sort of man to navigate by a candle.'

'What?' She had never heard the expression before.

From the table where he was eating his meagre dinner of mackerel and potatoes Boy-John broke in. 'I do know what it means.' He grinned cheekily at Charlotte, showing the gap where he had lost a front tooth, a black eye almost hidden under his untidy thatch of fair hair. 'It do mean he's the sort who'd get up in the morning and hold a candle out of the window. If it blows out 'tis too windy to set to sea and if it don't then there's too little wind. I'n't that right, Granfer?'

'You keep your mouth for eating yer dinner,' advised the old man crossly. 'I'm the one doing the talking round here.'

He turned again to Charlotte. 'Reckon the lad's got the right of it, though. If you leave your da to captain her, she'll bring in only a quarter of what she should get.'

'But how can I stop him?' Charlotte wailed. 'I can't tell him I won't let him captain my boat.'

The old man spat. 'What can he do to you if you does tell him that?' he asked.

She paused. 'Oh, I don't know.' Surely she was too old now for the kind of physical chastisement he had meted out when she was a girl. Or was she? She shivered, not so much at the thought of the pain but the humiliation. But she could not confess to that.

'I suppose,' she said slowly, 'he could pray over me.'

The snort of derision from the two Jelberts showed how little they thought of this as a threat. The eight-year-old even laughed cheerfully, swinging his bare feet under the ragged edges of his cut-down men's trousers. 'He told me I were past praying for,' he announced proudly. 'That was when he give me this black eye.'

Charlotte glanced quickly up, shocked out of her misery. 'My father hit you? But why?'

Boy-John shrugged. 'Dunno. He always does hit me, just about. Perhaps he don't like me or something.' He shovelled another forkful of potatoes in his mouth and chewed manfully.

'I expect you did something to deserve it.' Charlotte sank back into her thoughts. How much would it matter if her father did pray over her? It was embarrassing and boring, but she couldn't let her one chance of independence be ruined because she was afraid of standing up for what was rightfully hers.

And it was hers. Absolutely. Mr Brightman had explained it. As she was over twenty-one, as long as she stayed single her inheritance was hers. He had warned her that if she married it would then become her husband's property, but Charlotte had dismissed that. No one had wanted to marry her before, so tall as she was and so ugly with her strange silver-grey eyes and wide mouth, and if anyone asked her now she would know it was only her inheritance they were after. No, this boat was hers and she had to make the best of it because her future depended on it.

Whatever her father did.

Chapter Three

'Daughter.'

The soft rap on her bedroom door as she was brushing her hair for the night made Charlotte jump. She hadn't even heard her father come in after his meeting in Newlyn with the Superintendent of the Circuit on which he was a local preacher.

'Daughter.' Louder this time. Charlotte grimaced. She had only just got her mother off to sleep and it would be bad for her to be woken again after the excitements of the day. She glanced down at her plain, white cotton nightdress with its high, square neck. It wasn't considered correct for a young woman to greet even her own father so improperly dressed, even though the neckline was far higher than that worn by fashionable young women. Instinctively, Charlotte moved towards the cupboard where she kept her shawl.

'Daughter.'

Still louder. No time for the shawl, not if she were to prevent her mother from being woken. With a quick step Charlotte crossed the tiny bedroom and threw open her door. 'Yes, Father?'

'Child.' He brushed swiftly past her then turned. 'I have been speaking to Mr Borlase this evening.'

He made no attempt to lower his voice and she

hastily pushed the door shut, anxious that Bertha should not be woken. 'You said that you were going to see him this evening,' she reminded him. Mr Borlase was the Circuit Superintendent, a frail old man now but well respected and he had always been kind to Charlotte when she was younger.

'He has said that he is recommending me for ordination.' Her father's voice quivered with excitement. 'He says that even though I have not passed my examinations he feels that I have special qualities that make me suitable for the ministry.'

'I'm very happy for you.' Charlotte knew that this was what he had longed for, had worked for since she was a small child. And it was true, he did have very special qualities. His sermons could move strong men to tears and since he had been preaching, the number of converts in Mousehole had risen amazingly. With such gifts, it was not surprising that the Methodist Superintendent should decide to overlook her father's very limited education.

'He says,' William Trevennan went on, 'he can see the influence I have in the village and that it marks me out as someone they need.' He began to walk around the small room, crossing it from wall to wall in a couple of strides, his energy and enthusiasm too strong to let him stand quietly.

'I am glad that they appreciate you, Father,' Charlotte said. It was cold in her room and she crossed her arms to hug what warmth she could to her as she watched her father, puzzled.

He came towards her, his face lit with a

beaming smile. 'Yes, appreciate me. You have it right, daughter.' He moved to her and caught her by the elbows, staring down at her.

Charlotte was suddenly aware of the thin cotton of her nightdress, of her black hair, still loose, covering her shoulders and falling to her waist in one long, shining sweep. She folded her arms more tightly across her body as if for protection. 'Perhaps tomorrow would be a more suitable time to discuss what this means to you – to us all,' she suggested, trying to hide the uneasiness that was growing within her.

'I needed to tell you now,' William Trevennan insisted. 'It's so important, you see. There must be no mistakes now.'

'But if Mr Borlase is supporting you...' Charlotte began.

'Yes, but it is not as if I had passed the exams,' Trevennan insisted. 'I am older than the usual candidates, a working man, uneducated. All that I have going for me are my own gifts, my preaching, the authority which I can exert on those with whom I come into contact.'

He stared down at her, his blue eyes dark in the flickering light of the solitary candle that lit her room. 'And that is why, Charlotte, you have to let me captain your boat.'

'No.' Her response was so automatic that it came out before she could stop it. Then she felt him recoil, saw the anger that suffused his face and tried to put things right.

'If I do that,' she explained, 'Mr Angarrack will lose his position and that will not be fair on him, especially as you will have to give up the sea once you are ordained.'

The memory of George Angarrack today, directing his anger and scorn at her just because she was doing her job crossed her mind but she forced the thought from her. He might not like her but he was a good captain despite his recent problem with the nets, and a good fisherman. With him in charge, the *Faith-Lily* would keep them all comfortably, whereas if her father was captain, especially now that he could see the possibility of ordination before him, she knew that the boat would seldom be at sea.

'If you do not,' William Trevennan said, 'I will not be ordained.'

'That's not so.' With a twist of her shoulders Charlotte pulled away from him, stepping quickly backwards to put as much distance between them as she could. 'You are a great preacher, a good influence on ordinary men. It is unimportant whether or not you are a captain of a boat.'

'It is important if my own daughter does not trust me enough to let me captain her boat,' Trevennan insisted. 'It will seem to the Superintendent that I do not have the exceptional qualities necessary.' He reached out a hand, caught at her arm, pulling her towards him. 'My daughter, reconsider.'

Charlotte bit her lip. It was so difficult to say no, to refuse him this thing. He had been her guide all through her life, was the guide and counsellor of most of the village. How could she refuse him? But if he were to captain the *Faith-Lily*, she knew that the boat would have to be sold within a few months as he would not earn enough to keep her afloat.

She turned away, her head in her hands. It was so difficult. Her one hope of security and he was asking her to throw it away, to give him a chance of being ordained.

He spoke again. 'Once I am ordained we will all be supported by the church.'

She knew what he was saying. The boat would be unnecessary then; all their futures would be secure. But supposing he *wasn't* ordained? Supposing something happened to prevent it – then what would happen to them all?

He moved up closer behind her; his arms crept around her waist, he buried his mouth in her hair. 'Think, Daughter, think. If you do this thing you will be doing God's will.' His arms tightened, pulling her back against his strong, thickset body. 'After all, it must be right otherwise I should have been at sea today, not at the meeting with Mr Borlase. It was God who put that vicar on the headland so that I could turn back.'

The words brought back the suspicion that had crossed her mind earlier, that he had invented the mysterious vicar. She hated herself for distrusting him, for thinking such evil thoughts. He was a good man, wasn't he? He was her father.

As if he sensed her hesitation, William gripped her more tightly still. She could hear his breathing, strangely harsh and quick in the quiet of the tiny bedchamber. 'Daughter.' A shiver of unease at his closeness ran through her, forcing her to make up her mind.

With a gasp she reached down and pulled his

arms from her waist, stepped away from his embrace.

'No.' She loathed herself for saying it, but she had to do so. 'I am sorry, Father, but I just don't believe that it will make any difference at all. You will be ordained if you are worthy, and whether you are the captain of the *Faith-Lily* or not will have nothing to do with it.' She took a deep breath. 'I will not let you captain my ship.'

His usual mellifluous voice rasped in a way she had never heard before. 'So you won't do God's will? You will bow down and worship Mammon but not God?' His anger, his hurt, seemed to fill the room in a rising tide, suffocating her.

Twenty-one years of religious teaching warred within her but she could not do it, she could not throw away the one chance she and her mother might have. She avoided his eyes and her voice shook when she spoke but the words were distinct and decisive. 'I'm sorry.'

'Then on your own head be it,' he snapped and was out of the door in a second, slamming it shut behind him. The sound vibrated throughout the tiny cottage and she heard her mother's voice, sleepy and plaintive, but Charlotte had no time to worry about her now.

She let out her breath in a shuddering sigh and leaned against the bed trying to compose herself. Her father was angry but she was sure she had made the right decision. He would be ordained on his own merits, not because of his position. There was no need for her to put their security at risk.

And after all, what could he do to her?

The *Faith-Lily* was lying on the sandy beach below Newlyn, her crew busy unloading the ballast of huge rounded rocks prior to giving her her annual overhaul.

William Trevennan watched them silently for a few minutes, considering his approach and it was only when George Angarrack saw him and shouted down a greeting that he came nearer. 'Morning, George. Paying her up?'

Angarrack nodded, carefully lowering one of the great rocks in a hoist that they had set up. 'Mr Polruan said we were to do it now because we hadn't done it last winter.' He spat over the side. 'Well, he's dead now, God rest his soul, but she still needs paying up and Master Frederick hasn't said nothing against it so I thought we'd just keep on.'

So he didn't know! Trevennan had to struggle to keep the smile off his face. He nodded. 'You get on well with the Polruans?'

'As well as can be expected,' the other man confirmed. 'They're fair enough usually but a bit hard like all bosses.' He climbed down and leaned against the tarred side of the drifter ready for a break and a chat. 'Mind you, I don't approve of them having a woman in their offices, even if she is your daughter. It isn't right, that it's not, having a woman telling a man what to do.'

'Against God's will, you think?' Trevennan prompted. 'God made Eve to be Adam's help-mate, not his superior.'

George Angarrack's face cleared. 'That's it exactly, Cap'n,' he said, giving Trevennan the usual Cornish title of respect. 'You do always know the right words to say, that's why I enjoy your sermons.' He spat again. 'Brem moving, they are.'

The compliment pleased Trevennan but he did not allow it to move him from his path. 'So you don't like the idea of working for a woman?'

'Work for one?' The other man's voice rose in horror. 'I'd never do that. Bossy they are and never know their own mind. Well, can't be expected of a woman, can it? Even your girl – well, she's hardly a woman, being so tall and all, but she's still not the boss, thank the Lord. She may act like she was but, when all's said and done, I work for her employer – and he's a man.'

Trevennan could feel satisfaction expanding inside him like a hot-air balloon. 'You've not heard how Polruan left the drifter in his will, then?' It was an effort to keep his voice calm and matter-of-fact.

'Don't tell me she's to be sold?'

'No, no, nothing like that.' Trevennan rubbed a hand against the barnacled hull of the drifter as if he were judging her condition but his eyes never left Angarrack's face. 'She's been left to someone other than Polruan's son.'

Angarrack massaged the bristle on his chin with a horny hand. 'So that's what you've been getting at, is it? Mr Polruan's left her to his wife?' He thought for a moment, eyeing the towering sides of the lugger as he debated the matter in his own mind. 'Well, Mrs Polruan's a real lady and she's never been involved in business so I don't reckon she'll start now. She'll leave it all to that gert son of hers. I can live with that.'

'Not Mrs Polruan.' Trevennan could hardly keep the smile out of his voice. 'He's left your boat to my daughter.'

There was a long silence then Angarrack swore. 'Bloody hell, I'm not having that.'

'Against God's will, you think?' Trevennan prompted, deciding to overlook the blasphemy this once.

'Against everything,' Angarrack snorted. 'She'll be interfering all the time, telling me when to go out and where I should be going.'

'Acting just like a man,' Trevennan put in.

'She's bad enough already.' Angarrack hammered one fist into the other palm. 'Tried to fine me yesterday, she did. A woman! What do *she* know about fishing?'

'When has that ever stopped a woman?' Trevennan asked softly.

'You're right, Cap'n! You're bloody right!' Angarrack turned and shouted at the crew who were lowering another rock. 'How're 'ee doing?'

A weatherbeaten face peered down at him. 'Just done, Cap'n. 'Tes the last one. She's empty now.'

'And she can stay empty,' Angarrack snapped. 'I'm not working on no bloody ship owned by no woman.'

Trevennan shrugged. 'It's not as if she's the only ship around, either. I heard that Polruan has another one being built.'

'Yeah. And she's nearly ready.' Angarrack's eyes gleamed. 'Wonder if he's got a crew for her yet?'

'I believe not.' William patted the wooden hull again. 'I should think he'd be glad of an established crew like yours to take her on.'

'That's right.' There was a pause. 'I suppose I ought to tell your girl, though.'

'Tell her now.' Trevennan pointed across the sand. 'She's in the office today. Why wait? The sooner you're free from her, the sooner you can offer your services for the new drifter.'

'That's true.' He cast a glance up at the ship's tarred sides. 'But what about her?'

'You can't leave her here,' Trevennan said quickly. 'Why don't you just get her back to her moorings. She'll be safe there.'

Angarrack looked worried, a fisherman's instinctive care for a ship coming to the fore. 'She's got no ballast in. What if there's a storm? She'll smash herself to pieces.'

'Looks clear enough to me,' William Trevennan said, eyeing the sky, 'and anyway, that'll be the responsibility of her new captain, won't it? Whoever that is.'

Frederick Polruan stood at the door of his private office like an avenging angel ready to clear Eden of intruders.

Even with her head bent over the columns of figures that marched across the ledger Charlotte was aware of him, and aware that it was on her that his furious glance most often rested.

She knew that he had never liked her, had always been jealous of the way she was better at her job, was the favourite of his father, but now, after the reading of the will, his dislike was palpable.

She sighed, totted up another column and,

dipping the steel pen nib in her inkwell, inscribed the total in clear, neat copperplate at the bottom of the page.

All around her the other clerks worked in unaccustomed silence but she could tell by the cautious way they had greeted her this morning that they knew she was out of favour. Now they ignored her, bending industriously over their desks whenever she approached, separating themselves from her as far as possible.

The sound of footsteps on the stairs was a welcome relief. Anything that broke the oppressive silence in the dusty office was welcome at the moment. But at the sight of the stocky figure that shouldered his way through the doorway, Charlotte's heart dropped even further.

'Mr Angarrack.' It was an effort to appear her normal cheerful self; the last thing she needed today was someone complaining about her. Frederick, she was sure, was only looking for an excuse to sack her. She flickered a hopeful glance across the office but he was still there, his cold grey eyes watching her as if she were some poor felon who had been dragged up in front of him in his position as a Magistrate rather than a trusted employee.

Charlotte hastily turned her attention back to the captain of the *Faith-Lily*. 'How can I help you?' She hoped fervently that he had forgotten the contretemps of yesterday afternoon.

'Help me?' At the contempt in his voice her spirits sank. 'There's no way a woman like you can ever help me.'

She heard the soft scratch of nib on paper cease

suddenly as each clerk turned his attention to the scene being played out in front of them. The knowledge that they were gloating over her discomfiture roused Charlotte's anger. She had done nothing wrong; there was no reason for her to be ashamed of anything. She raised herself to her full height, her grey eyes full of scorn. 'You have a complaint, Mr Angarrack?' Her voice was as cold as the winter sea.

For a second he seemed to quail, glancing round at the interested eyes that surveyed him but then he rallied. *Perhaps he has sensed Frederick's antagonism,* she thought as he spread his feet apart in a fighting stance and leaned towards her, his fists clenched.

'I do have a complaint,' he snapped. 'I'm a good Christian man I am, converted by your own father as you should know. And I don't believe 'tis right that women should be put in a position of authority over men.'

Charlotte raised her dark brows enquiringly. 'It must have pained you all these years then, to have had to live in a country ruled by a Queen,' she remarked, her voice honeyed with sarcasm.

He wasn't used to women using logic and her words threw him. With a faint smile she watched him cast desperately around for an answer to her. 'That idn't the same,' he said, finally. 'The Queen, God bless her, was set there by the will of God, but,' he pointed a red, gnarled finger at her, 'that don't apply to you nohow.'

'You are still angry about the fine we spoke of yesterday?' She might as well get the problem out in the open.

51

'Fine? *Fine?*' His voice, loud and harsh from years of shouting over the noise of the wind and waves, made the rough floorboards under her feet vibrate. '"T'aint the fine that I'm upset about, 'tes that there boat. The *Faith-Lily.*'

Charlotte was aware of her heart beating leadenly in her breast. She had not anticipated this. 'And what is the problem with the boat?' She was proud that her voice did not betray her concern.

'She bain't got no cap'n, that's what's the matter with she,' he announced, his voice growing more Cornish as his self-righteous anger expanded. 'I ain't going to work for no woman and that's that.'

She swallowed but her eyes did not waver. 'Then I will get one of the crew to sail her. They are all good men.'

He leaned forward until his breath fanned her cheek, his voice rising in triumph. 'Aye, they *are* good men. And they've got their pride, all of them. None of them aren't going to work for no woman and that's that.'

'You mean, I haven't a crew *at all?*' Despite herself her voice rose uncontrollably.

'Not one. And that there lugger of yours is offshore now with no ballast in her so you'd better find one quick – unless you want to lose her in the first bit of blow we do get.' He turned to Frederick Polruan who was still standing in the doorway to his office, taking in the scene. 'Mr Trevennan said that you were looking for a crew, sir. For a new lugger that was being built, he said.'

'But...' Charlotte turned to him but he wasn't looking at her. For the first time that morning a smile crossed his plump features.

'That's right, Angarrack. Do I take it you are interested?' He moved back. 'Why don't you step into the office so that we can discuss this – privately,' he added with a look at Charlotte.

As the door closed behind him she stood motionless, her hands clenched until the nails bit into her palms. Her father! Her father had done this! Dry-eyed and furious, she stood silent, struggling to understand the depths of his betrayal. How could he? How dare he!

A mutter from one of the men brought her back to herself. She blinked and made herself stare down at the meaningless jumble of figures in front of her as she tried to come to terms with what had happened.

Chapter Four

Charlotte stood poised on the old battery position where for years cannons had been trained out to sea for use against the Turkish pirates. In front of her the massed fleet of drifters crowded into the protected area of the sea off Newlyn known locally as Gwavas Lake.

Although it was only early afternoon, almost every boat was already at her moorings. The fiercely religious Cornishmen would never have dreamed of putting to sea on a Sunday and she knew that before night fell every fisherman in the district would be at home, preparing for the Sabbath.

Even amongst the mass of boats she could easily pick out the *Faith-Lily*. The lugger rode high in the water without her ballast, bobbing wildly even though the winds were light and the sea calm. It didn't take a seaman to tell that she would fare badly if the weather worsened.

'Admiring your new possession, Daughter?'

Charlotte jumped and swung round nervously, her heart thumping. 'Father! I didn't hear you come up.'

'I saw you ahead of me and hurried to catch you up. I hoped to be outside the offices to meet you as I know that you leave work early on a Saturday, but I was detained on chapel business.'

The bitterness that had been festering inside

54

her ever since George Angarrack had spoken suddenly burst out. 'Not just chapel business either.'

He took her arm, his strong fingers urging her along beside him. 'And what does that mean?'

She cast a quick glance over her shoulder, taking courage from the sight of her boat. 'Mr Angarrack came to tell me that he would not captain my boat.' She looked sideways at her father, unable to make up her mind about him. He was a good man – surely he would not have deliberately made trouble between Angarrack and herself? She turned away to stare out across Mounts Bay. 'I wonder how he knew?' Her voice was deliberately cool.

She was relieved when he answered immediately: 'I told him.' Surely if he had done this deliberately, her father would not have admitted it openly?

'Yes,' he continued, 'I thought that the news would get out quickly enough and that it would be better, being so closely involved, that he should hear it as soon as possible.' He turned to her. 'You do not object to my taking on a duty like that, as the owner, should by rights have been yours?'

Again, she felt that he had cut the ground from under her feet. 'Not at all. But he says he will not work for me.'

Her father shook his head sadly. 'He does not agree with women being in a dominant position.' He sighed. 'A good, Christian attitude, of course. There is much support for such a view in the Bible.'

Charlotte said sharply, 'It is lucky that such an opinion is not more widespread. I can think of six or seven boats that are owned by women, but they seem to have no trouble getting crews.'

Trevennan sighed again. 'Yes, but in your case, there is the scandal.'

'What?' She stopped dead, dragging her arm out from under his. 'What do you mean? What scandal have I ever been involved in?' She stared at him, her eyes wide with shock. 'I have done nothing,' she insisted. 'Nothing.'

'I know it, Daughter. And so I say, but...' he shrugged. 'The other women are widows; the crews worked for their husbands, everyone knows why they have been left their boats. But you...'

She couldn't breathe. Outrage burned in her veins, firing her brain. 'And what about me?' she demanded through gritted teeth.

'Well,' he made a dismissive gesture and she was reminded suddenly of the way he could move the whole congregation of a chapel to his will. 'A man leaves you a valuable boat, a man, unrelated to you, fit, virile – a man with whom you have spent many hours alone.'

'We were working!' she insisted. 'He was my employer!'

'But that merely makes it worse.' He smiled sweetly at her. 'Why should a man in that position employ a young woman? No other firm does. You must see that to some people it could seem to smack of...' He let his words trail off.

'No!' The word seemed to echo round the bay. Charlotte took a deep breath, trying to compose

56

herself. 'No one thinks that,' she said hotly. 'They couldn't.'

He shrugged again. 'I do my best for you. And, as my daughter, you are to some extent protected by my position in the community.'

She stood still, gnawing her lip, fighting for calmness. She would not let herself get carried away.

'You must be mistaken,' she said stiffly. 'If people thought that – if that were so – no one would speak to me, no one would respect me. But they do! They shake my hand, they are my friends. No one believes that awful lie.'

'It is simply because of my position,' he told her again.

Finally, it sank home. She turned to him, her grey eyes blazing. 'This is all a ruse, isn't it?' Her voice quivered with disgust. 'This is just a plot to make me let you captain my ship. You are just trying to frighten me by telling me these stories, by linking my reputation to yours, so that I will do as you want.'

She drew herself up to her full height, her cheeks burning with indignation. 'Well, I won't do it, Father. I *won't* be coerced like this! I am sure of my position here in the village, as sure as you are of yours. These people know me, they trust me. You may have turned one person against me, but that doesn't mean that everyone will follow. I am calling your bluff. I will get a crew to sail my ship, never fear.'

She swung round on her heel. 'Tell Mother I shall not be in for lunch,' and she set off down the road back to Newlyn, glad to be able to work off her fury in physical activity, her long legs carrying her swiftly away from her father.

But not so quickly that she didn't hear his parting shot. 'I shouldn't be so sure of that, my girl.'

Kit's nightmare ended as it always did. Far below him, greenly wavering in the pale light, Jonathan's face faded, the mouth and eyes still open as it slid forever into the darkness.

'No!' Gasping, struggling, he reached the surface of the sea and woke knowing instantly that something was wrong.

Here, in the bowels of the ship, there was always noise; the creak of timbers, the constant movement of men coming on or off watch, the snores and groans of the other tired seamen, sounds he had become accustomed to in the last few days upon the trader.

Now, suddenly, there was a small pool of stillness, quite close to him. The stillness of someone trying not to make a noise.

Kit lay motionless, his breathing slowed to a sleeping rhythm, his eyes closed as he probed his surroundings with his hearing.

There was the mutter and disturbance of a sleeper the other side of the small cabin before he sank again into regular snores. And, closer, there was the faintest whisper of someone moving within their clothes.

Softly, the evil miasma of unwashed male stole over him, another rustle, then the disturbance, so gentle, of a hand sliding under his pillow, feeling for the gold watch that Kit had placed there for safety.

His hand came up, catching the other's wrist, squeezing it until he could feel the bones move under his gripping fingers. The thief gasped and tried to pull away but he was too late.

Using the other man's body to lever himself up, Kit swung at him. One enormous fist hammered into the thief's nose and there was a gush of blood as the bone shattered under the blow.

The man's cry of pain woke the other seamen. For a few seconds they stared across the tiny cabin, stupefied with the shock of their awakening, then strong hands grasped Kit, holding his arm back from yet another bone-crushing blow.

'For God's sake, man, do you want to kill him?' The Cornish voice was harsh with anxiety.

'Suits me,' Kit said furiously, attempting to throw off the restraining hands. 'He tried to rob me, to thieve from a fellow sailor. Death's too good for the likes of him.'

He pulled himself a step or two nearer the cowering sailor but others had come down now, more arms held him back. He was far taller than the Cornishmen who made up the majority of the trader's crew, but they all had a stocky strength and in the grip of so many men he was powerless.

The injured thief stared at him balefully from hands cupped protectively over his broken nose. 'You're not one of us.' His voice was thick and distorted by his injuries. 'You're a bleeding toff, you are. Coming here with yer pockets full of silver, playing at being a working man.'

Kit struggled forward a few steps despite the best efforts of the three men holding him back. 'I've pulled my weight,' he shouted furiously. 'I've done double watches ever since I came aboard this tub. I've climbed to the crow's-nest, aye, and covered for you when you slept.'

'You're a toff,' the other repeated. 'Say what you like, you're just here for a bit of adventure like. Then you'll get bored and it'll be back to the big house and the fancy women.' He spat, blood and mucus mingled. 'You're not one of us and you never will be. You're just trouble on a ship like this.'

Kit struggled again but the seamen had his measure now and he could not move. Slowly, he stared round at the others. Their faces were closed and watchful but it only needed the painfulness of their grip to tell him what he needed to know. Their sympathies lay with the thief.

His face twisted into a bitter grin. He should never have come on this ship, he knew that. No good ever came of mixing with bloody Cornishmen.

The small chapel at the bottom of Raginnis Hill was full to overflowing. Charlotte sat by her mother with the other women on the sea side of the building while the men sat together on the right, against the hill.

She had to admit that her father looked impressive, standing in the pulpit, head bowed as he collected his thoughts in preparation for the sermon. Even though she still burned with anger

60

at the memory of their last talk, she could still admire his presence in the pulpit.

Besides, she was winning; she had achieved her aim. It had taken her until late last night, but she had finally done it; she had found a man who had agreed to sail her boat for her.

She smiled secretly to herself. Kemyal Davey was a good man who had worked on several of the Polruans' boats. A thickset, serious young man, he was a chapel-goer and a hard worker. He would get a good crew together and do his best to make the boat successful.

Not that she should take an unchristian delight in besting her father, she reminded herself. But what he wanted was dangerous, dangerous for the whole family. Of course he would be ordained. No one who had ever heard him preach – who knew about the dedication with which he attended and held prayer meetings and services – could ever doubt that, but just in case something happened, she and her mother would be safe.

As if Bertha had picked up her thoughts, she leaned over to Charlotte. 'I'm glad your father was on time,' she said, her soft voice almost lost in the rustle of low-pitched whispers that ran around the congregation. 'Going off like that this morning. It would have been dreadful if he had been late, with the chapel so full and all.'

Under lowered lashes Charlotte glanced swiftly around the crowded room. Her mother was right, the chapel was packed, but that was not unusual when her father was preaching. The Cornish Methodists loved a good sermon, full of

61

fire and oratory, and William Trevennan was acknowledged to be one of the best speakers. People would come from miles around to hear a sermon by their favourite preacher. And it was common knowledge now, that he aspired beyond being a lay preacher, that he was aiming for the Ministry. It would be safe to assume that this sermon would be even more fiery than usual as he sought to impress the congregation with his powers of oratory.

There was a stir as her father got to his feet and moved to the front of the pulpit. 'Friends.' The deep, resonant voice rolled out, and an expectant buzz ran through the congregation.

William Trevennan raised his arms until they were outstretched, almost in parody of the crucifixion. Charlotte thought, then forced down the thought. That was blasphemous. But her father did look like an Old Testament prophet with his white hair waving back from his high forehead and his thick, white beard.

'Friends.' Head back, eyes closed, he faced the congregation, holding them still with anticipation as they awaited his next words.

His throat tightened above his black coat and the words exploded in a thunderclap of denunciation. 'Honour thy father and thy mother. That is the Commandment Our Lord gave to us. Honour thy father and thy mother.'

He lowered his head, holding the congregation motionless in the mesh of his blue gaze. 'But there is a sinner amongst us, my friends. An unregenerate sinner. A woman who defies all morality, all exhortations, even the commands of

Our Lord Himself.'

He paused, then his arm shot out, his finger pointing straight at Charlotte. 'Behold that sinner!'

Chapter Five

This time there was no neighbourliness; this time there was no friendship.

Alone, a leper in the midst of humanity, Charlotte walked from the chapel.

She moved in the centre of a shifting circle of silence, aware that all around her were staring and whispering but in her immediate vicinity there was only the blankness of turned backs and averted eyes.

Shame burned through her, flaming in her cheeks, twisting her stomach into knots. Only pride kept her moving, pretending not to see how much skirts were whisked away from her as if her very touch carried the plague. Holding her head high, she stalked away from the chapel into the village, forcing her long legs to keep to a decorous pace so that it should not seem that she was fleeing the scene.

Behind her, she heard the conversation break out, louder and even more animated than usual. She could envisage them all, discussing her, shaking their heads over her, lamenting her behaviour. And her father would be at the door of the chapel, shaking hands, as ever, with his congregation, accepting their compliments on a powerful sermon while she...

She closed her eyes momentarily. What had she done that every boat-owner in Cornwall had not done? Only tried to get the best possible crew for her boat. And because of that she was ostracised, branded a sinner, a breaker of the Commandments.

Her shaking fingers tightened on the handle of her reticule and her breathing became more ragged as she stormed sightlessly through the village. It wasn't fair! No one blamed her father, even though it was partially his fault; if he had been even approximately capable she would have let him captain her boat, and welcome. But he wasn't, and what was more, all the villagers in Mousehole knew it. Yet somehow, because of the power of his words, everything had been twisted around, so that she was in the wrong and he was in the right.

'Watch it, Lotty.'

The shrill voice was almost under her feet. With an effort, Charlotte pulled herself together, forcing herself into the unpleasant present. The urchin was crouched on a rock by the side of the road, a slice of bread and dripping in his hand.

'Boy-John.' The one person who would not yet have heard about her infamy. The Jelberts were notorious in the village for attending neither church nor chapel. She smiled tremulously at him. 'Sunday dinner?'

'Same as every other day's dinner,' he snorted, eyeing her inquisitively over the thick piece of crust. 'Why's your face all red, Lotty?'

'Just something silly.' She tried to laugh but her voice cracked and broke. 'Nothing to worry about,' she insisted, biting her lower lip in an attempt to control herself.

65

'So why are you out here, then?'

'Out here?' Then she realised. In her blind hurry to get away from the others she had walked all the way through the village to Penlee Point. She grimaced. The village had been empty because she had been the first to leave the chapel, but to make her way back would mean coming face to face with the others of the congregation. The village streets would be crowded, the men walking home from chapel, the women hurrying to the bakehouse to collect their Sunday dinner. And all knowing about her disgrace, discussing her. They would stare at her, not meeting her eyes, mutter about her after she had passed, condemn her. Her heart shrank from the ordeal.

Wearily, she sat on the stone beside Boy-John. It would mean another telling off if word got back to her father, but what could he say that was any worse than what she had already heard? She reached for the small child, giving him a quick hug, grateful for the feel of his young body in her arms.

'My father has been telling everyone how bad I am, for not letting him captain the *Faith-Lily*.'

He snorted. 'So, what's that to get upset about?'

'Nothing, to you, you limb of Satan,' she answered, tightening her grasp. 'People say worse than that about you every day. But, well, to hear it from the pulpit...' Her voice tailed off as she relived the cold horror that had run through her at the denunciation.

'He preached at you from the pulpit?' Boy-

John's blue eyes were wide with astonishment. 'Cripes, Lotty, everyone'll think you're as wicked as me now.'

She looked at him tenderly. 'You're not wicked, Boy-John, just always up to your neck in trouble.'

'And now you are.' He wriggled away from her, taking another mouthful of bread and dripping. 'What are you going to do?'

Misery sank cold fingers into her chest. 'Give in, I suppose.' She shivered despite the warmth of the April sun which made the day almost springlike. 'What else can I do? I – I never thought that it would come to this.' She stared bleakly out across the blue sea, her eyes narrowed against the blinding glints and flashes as the sun caught the waves.

'The *Faith-Lily*'ll finish paying up in a few more days, they've already got the ballast out of her. Then Peter-Jack Carey could take her out mackerelling. I thought – I thought that once we had some money coming in, Father would see I was right.'

She wrung her fingers miserably together, the tight gloves twisting under the pressure of her fingers. This was the end of her dreams of freedom, of the chance to run her own life. She had fought her father and lost. And once he had the boat, it was only a matter of time before the whole family was back where it was now, with just enough money to keep respectable, to keep their heads above water, with no cushion against the ravages of fate. And she would spend her life toiling in a dark office, knowing that every penny she earned would be spent on essentials, that she would never have pretty clothes or good food or the luxury of not worrying about her mother.

Overcome with misery, she burst out: 'I can't see why Father minds. He isn't even interested in fishing. And he's going to be a proper preacher – why should he do this to me?'

Lost in her unhappiness she had almost forgotten that she had an audience, and Boy-John's rude snort made her jump. 'My granfer says it's nothing to do with the money at all. He says your da is afraid them chapel people won't think so much of him if his own daughter won't let him captain her boat.' He squelched his bare toes in a patch of mud left over from the last rain shower. 'My granfer's clever about things like that.'

'But why should anyone care?' Charlotte asked, bewildered. 'Besides, now that he's preached about it, that's what everyone will think.'

'And you're feeling so bad about it you're going to let your da do as he wants,' Boy-John broke in. 'So he wins. And you've lost.'

'It isn't like that,' she protested. 'It isn't a case of winning or losing. It's – morals or something.'

The boy snorted again. 'I ain't never been to chapel but we did religion at school and I never heard of no Commandment that said you had to let your da ruin you.'

His words brought back the sermon she had just sat through and her stomach churned painfully. 'I can't do it,' she said miserably. 'God knows, I don't want my father to captain the boat, but if I don't...'

She knew what would happen. She would be an outcast in the village, even worse than Boy-John and his grandfather, worse than Peggy who had had a baby out of wedlock and who now lived a miserable existence in a hovel in Newlyn, visiting sailors her only companions. She would be shunned, stared at, whispered about. And her father would have the chance, every Sunday, to twist the screws, to tell the world what an undutiful daughter she was, what a sinner. She couldn't bear it. Just the thought made her feel physically sick.

The sound of footsteps made her head jerk up. The gossiping crowds outside the chapel must have split up at last and some of the congregation were making their way back to Newlyn.

She jumped to her feet in a panic. 'I must go.' But there was nowhere to hide. The footsteps came closer and Charlotte shrank back against the hedge, her face flaming with embarrassment as two men hurried up the road towards her. With a sinking heart she recognised them as Kemyal Davey and Peter-Jack Carey – the man who had agreed to become the master of the *Faith-Lily* and his probable third mate. They must have been at the service, she realised but she had missed them in the crowd.

Even through her all-pervading shame she felt a brief doubt. They were both Newlyn men who always attended the chapel at Newlyn Trinity. Why had they come to the service in Mousehole today? She couldn't remember ever seeing them there before.

With shaking hands, she busied herself with her

bonnet, unnecessarily retying the strings, half turned away to allow them to pass her with the minimum of embarrassment on both sides.

But the footsteps moved towards her, paused. Swallowing anxiously, she glanced up. Kemyal Davey stood over her, his brick-red face set in a look of disgust.

'I just wanted to say,' he began abruptly, 'I can't captain your boat no more.'

Shock widened her silver-grey eyes. 'But...' It was what would have happened anyway; if her father was captain then she would have had to have sacked Davey, but the sudden announcement threw her off-balance. She took a breath, trying to steady herself so that she could explain her decision but he went on, 'Nor can Carey here work on your boat, nor any of the other men.' His mouth twisted. ''Twouldn't be right, working for a woman what goes against God's commandments like you do.'

Fury enveloped her. She raised herself to her full height, staring him straight in the eyes.

'I shall get someone else then,' she said furiously. 'There are others around who would be glad to work on a good boat like the *Faith-Lily*.'

Kemyal Davey shook his head. 'I reckon you're wrong there, Miss Trevennan. There isn't a man-jack around who would want to work for no woman who breaks the Commandments, see. We come here today to hear what your da had to say and now we've heard we know our own minds.' He spat energetically. 'I don't reckon none of the men will work on your boat, not when they've heard what we have to tell 'em.'

70

Anger flooded through her, spurring her brain to analyse what she had been told.

'You knew what my father was going to say today! You came especially.'

He didn't bother to deny it. 'A powerful good speaker, your da,' Kemyal Davey said heavily. ''Tis a pity he hasn't got a daughter worthy of him.' He turned and began to plod off down the road but a small figure erupted in front of him, clutching at his hand with grimy fingers.

''Ere, you can't do that.' Boy-John's voice was shrill with dismay. 'That there boat hasn't got no ballast in. It's bobbing like a cork. And there's a storm coming, my granfer says so. That boat'll be dashed to pieces like that! You can't just let her go.'

Kemyal Davey pushed the child roughly out of the way. ''Tisn't my responsibility,' he said. 'I don't work for the owner no more. 'Tes up to her to get the boat payed up – if she can.'

'But if she can't you're as good as killing that boat!' There was all the horror of a seaman's respect for the means of his livelihood in the child's wail. 'You can't do that.'

He reached out and caught at Carey's sleeve but the fisherman brushed him aside like a fly. 'She do deserve it,' he said. 'Damn gert wench. What right do she have to own a boat and tell men what to do? That's men's work, that is. 'Tisn't natural, a woman like that. 'Tes against the word of God.'

Charlotte reached out and grasped the boy's hand. 'Let them go, Boy-John. It won't do any good.' In silence the two stood together watching as the men disappeared around the bend in the road.

Boy-John glanced up at the woman beside him. 'What will you do now, Lotty?'

She stood motionless in the bright sunlight; only the flame in her cheeks and the angry light in her eyes showed her feelings. It was seconds before she spoke.

'They knew.' She almost spat the words out, her voice trembling with suppressed anger. 'They came because they knew what my father would say. They all knew! That was why...'

She was silent, remembering the unusually full chapel, the strange sense of anticipation that she had felt before the sermon. How many of them had known beforehand? To how many had her father dropped a hint?

The depth of the betrayal appalled her. He was her father! He was a good man, a Christian, a Methodist! And he had done this to her. And for his own ends.

The boy pulled again at he hand, trying to get her attention. 'You'll have to give in now, Lotty.' There was great regret in his voice but also acceptance. He had learned too early in his young life when it was hopeless to fight.

'No!' The word exploded out of her. 'I won't do it. I won't give in.'

She glanced down at him, her eyes burning with anger. 'If I give in now – that's it. He won't just be captain, he'll be owner as well. I won't be able to make any decisions. If I try to disagree with him, he'll bring all this up again and I'll have to do what he wants. He'll have my inheritance –

and I'll have nothing!'

'But what can you do, Lotty?' Boy-John stared at her doubtfully.

Charlotte's lips tightened. 'Mr Polruan left me that boat for my own use. *Mine.* And it's going to stay that way if I have to sail her myself.'

And she turned and strode back to the village so fast that Boy-John had to run to keep up.

'Is that you, Frederick?'

Frederick Polruan sighed and changed direction towards his mother's sitting room. The softly spoken enquiry was, he knew, a command.

As always, her room was stifling. Despite the springlike warmth of the day outside, a fire leaped high in the grate, reflecting off the gleaming brass of the fender. The crimson cloth draped over the table and the cerise wallpaper made the room seem even hotter, reflecting the heat one to the other.

Elizabeth Polruan reclined on her couch; the black-edged lace handkerchief weighed down her thin hand as it lay on the black crepe of her dress. 'Was it a good service, dear?' Her weak voice quavered sorrowfully.

As always, her presence made him feel like a hobbledehoy, looming gigantically over her faded frailty. He began, 'A very good service, Mama,' but his voice seemed to boom around the crowded room and he hesitated as he saw her wince. He cleared his throat awkwardly and tried to speak in a lower tone. 'A great many people expressed condolences about Papa.'

Now he sounded as if he had a sore throat but

at least Mama seemed to brighten a little. 'And the new sidesman?'

He was on safer ground here. 'Mr Tregarrick, from Kerris. Not a patch on Papa. No...' He paused, trying to think of a word that would please her. 'No grace.'

A faint smile played around her thin lips. 'Your Papa was always truly a gentleman. There is no one else attending at Paul Church who could ever equal him.'

Including himself, Frederick knew. He forced the thought away. 'People asked after you.'

The smile was replaced by an expression of suffering. 'It is so unfortunate to be such an invalid, unable to go out, unable even to have visitors.' She sighed.

He knew that she could go on in this vein for hours and broke in quickly. 'I hope that you can partake of the beef today. Farmer Matthews delivered it specially, a bullock he had been keeping his eye on, just for you.' He smiled down at her. 'He swears that even the most delicate stomach would enjoy it and it certainly smelled good as I came in through the hall.'

Her hand moved fractionally. 'A cup of weak tea only, dearest. If you could ring the bell.'

He moved around the couch and tugged on the woven pull which hung only inches from her hand. Father had managed to keep his mother interested in life, amused even. Frederick could remember times when her silvery laugh had joined Charles Polruan's, when she had sat up on the couch, talking animatedly as he brought her the latest gossip from Penzance and the surrounding villages. But this was just another way in which he knew that he would never match up.

Irritated, he swung away, staring out through the window. On the far side of the ornamental gardens studded with tropical palms, the ground dropped steeply away. Far below, he could see the clustered roofs of the village of Newlyn and beyond it, cradled by the twin peninsulas of The Lizard and The Lands End, the blue waters of Mounts Bay glittered and flashed like living sapphires. Against the green mass, St Michael's Mount rose in a dramatic black pyramid, and nearer, bobbing lightly just off Wherry Town, a small fleet of boats.

At the sight of them a harsh grunt escaped his throat, catching his mother's attention. 'Are you ill, Frederick?'

Impossible to lie, impossible to turn and let her see the fury that he knew had reddened his plump cheeks. 'That boat.' The words seemed to burn in his throat. '*Her* boat.'

'It's a crying shame.' The unusual animation in his mother's voice brought him round. She was sitting up on the couch, the lace handkerchief crumpled in claw-like fingers, a tinge of colour in her pale cheeks. 'Your father should have thought of us. It isn't right, exposing us to rumour and ridicule like this. Leaving a boat to a woman, indeed. It's ridiculous.'

'And such a woman.' Relief made him expansive. 'A great gawk, as tall as me. What sort of a woman is that?'

'And no relation either. People will talk. I don't

care what you say, people will talk. They'll want to know why and they'll invent reasons. I know it.'

He moved closer, enjoying this rare moment of unanimity. 'He said she was a good clerk, good at figures. I ask you, is that a feminine accomplishment? Is that what a woman should be expected to do?'

She was sitting bolt upright now, hammering her thin fist onto her knee. 'It isn't right! You're his heir; he should have left it to you. What right had Charles to do this?'

She paused as there was a knock on the door and the maid entered. 'Ah, Phillips. I will be down for luncheon after all. If you will tell the butler.' She glanced quickly at her son as the door closed. 'I think I feel a little better, all of a sudden.'

There was a brief silence after the maid had gone. Frederick moved heavily to the window, playing with the fringes on the scarlet curtain as he struggled with his feelings. It was so unfair. Papa had always preferred *her*, always treated that Charlotte Trevennan as if she were someone special. He had even paid for her to go to school in Penzance, as if she was the daughter of a proper lady, not just the offspring of a part-time fisherman and a lady's maid. And then, to employ her! To give her a proper job, to call everyone's attention to her cleverness, to use her to show up his own son...

Lost in his thoughts, he could not at first make out what his mother had said. 'I beg your pardon?'

'I said,' she repeated caustically, 'that I blame the mother. I never did trust her when she worked here. Sly, I remember, always with her eye on the men. I'd have got rid of her years before she left but your father wouldn't have it. Just because she'd come down with me from Bristol. He said it wouldn't be right to throw her off in a place like this.' Her face darkened and she hammered her hand lightly on the arm of her couch. 'I know where I'd like to throw her.'

'You and me both,' he said, feeling more at ease with her than usual. 'You had to put up with the mother, I've got the daughter under my feet all day.'

He thrust his hands deep into the pockets of his best Sunday suit, dragging the material in great creases from his shoulders. Bloody woman, he thought, frowning furiously down at the leaping flames in the fireplace. If she *was* a woman! Taller than him, dark as sin, what had his father ever seen in her? He kicked irritably at the brass fender with a plump foot.

'But you don't have to put up with her.'

'What?' Startled, he raised grey eyes to his mother. She was on her feet now, her back as straight as a young girl's, her mouth pulled into a tight line.

She smiled thinly at him. 'I said, you don't have to put up with her.'

Realisation spread over his plump features. He had forgotten that he was the boss now, that he had the right to sack her.

If he could pluck up the courage.

''Tedn't kind, that's what I do say.' Granfer-John sucked on his empty pipe and stared at Charlotte with rheumy, troubled eyes.

She tugged off her bonnet, dragging her fingers through her hair, careless of the dark tendrils that pulled free and curled springily around her angry face.

'I don't care what it is, I'm not going to put up with it.' Her voice was quiet but vibrated with fury. She swung round, turning to the old man. 'Do you think that a minister should have done that? To his own daughter?'

The old man looked uncomfortable. ''Tes no good you asking me about ministers. I haven't been next nor nigh a chapel since my Sarah died, nor will I till I know the truth.'

Charlotte whirled around, turning to stare out of the window across the small harbour. It was peaceful today; the double-ended boats pulled gently at their moorings. Her boat would have been here in another week or so, newly tarred, with ropes and nets dark with preservative. Instead of which...

She swung back. 'But you're just agreeing with me!' She dropped to her knees on the hard flagstones, looking up at the old fisherman. 'Sarah was your daughter and she – well, we all know she wasn't very clever. But you supported her, even when you discovered she was going to have a child.'

''Tweren't her fault,' he broke in forcefully. 'She was an innocent, one of the Lord's lambs. She didn't know what she was adoing of no more than a kitten does. But *HE* knew, the man what done it. He knew and he led her astray and left her.'

His face was mottled with remembered fury and he pointed the stem of his pipe at her. 'It says in the Bible about tempering the wind to the shorn lamb, but God didn't temper no wind for my Sarah. She were ruined and all they good Christian folk,' he spat disparagingly, 'they condemned her, that woman who knew no more than a child what was going on. And they condemn my Boy-John, just because he was born a bastard.'

He stared at her, his brown eyes faded with the years but full of hurt. 'That's Christianity for you. I were glad when she died in childbirth – yes, I was – because I didn't want her to suffer no more in this sinful world. And I done my best to bring Boy-John up proper. But we'll neither of us go next nor nigh a chapel until God tells me who the man was, and then I swear I'll kill him! I'll kill him with my own hands!'

Charlotte was silent. After such a tragedy her problems with the boat seemed suddenly small. She reached out, catching the old man's hand. 'I'm sorry, bringing all my problems to you like this. But–' her voice shook suddenly 'there's no one else.'

'And I'm brem sorry, too.' His twisted fingers stroked her hair back from her face. 'But there's naught that I can do for you, maid. If I were ten years younger I'd captain the boat for you myself, but as it is...'

'I know, Granfer-John,' Charlotte smiled at him, using the name from her childhood. She

79

stood up and shook her skirts straight, tucking the straying tendrils of hair back behind her ears and reached for her bonnet.

'So you've made up your mind, then?' he asked, but there was no hopefulness in his voice.

She nodded. 'It was finding out about Father that did it.' Her mouth tightened determinedly. 'It looks as if I'm going to lose the boat whatever I do, but at least this way I'll keep my self-respect.' She sighed. 'And you never know. There may be someone who'll sail her for me. A church-man perhaps.'

'They'll all stick together,' he said gruffly. 'Anyway, you may not have time to find another crew.'

She paused, her hand on the latch that opened the tarred door, her head already bent to duck under the lintel. 'No time?'

He shook his head. 'I'm brem sorry to tell you, maid, but there's a storm coming. A bad one.'

His old brown eyes stared at her sadly.

'If your boat is off Wherry Town beach tomorrow night with no ballast and no crew to fend her off, she'll be in pieces by Tuesday morning.'

Chapter Six

'What are you doing here, Lotty?'

Charlotte swung her head around nervously then relaxed as she recognised the small figure. 'Thinking, Boy-John.'

'But it's brem near night-time.' He moved beside her where she lay face down on the short grass, staring through the dusk out across the bay. 'You did ought to be home.'

'I don't want to go home yet.' She returned her gaze to the sea. Already, the storm that Granfer-John had predicated was almost on them and the bay was filled with the white tops of the small, choppy seas. Soon, she knew, the waves would get bigger, rolling in from the Atlantic on the wild southwesterly winds and that would be the end of her boat, of her dreams.

All day, at work, her eyes had turned constantly to the boats dipping and pulling at their moorings off Newlyn beach. The *Faith-Lily* had been easy to pick out, riding high as she was with no ballast. Even with all the fishing boats still in, in expectation of the storm, she stood out.

Worry about the boat had taken precedence over everything else. Even the cold looks that Frederick Polruan had been giving her all day had not caused more than a fleeting concern.

In a storm, empty of ballast, the fishing boat would be thrown around like a cockleshell. She

81

might break free from her moorings but, more likely, according to Granfer-John, she would simply tear herself to pieces. It happened to even fully ballasted boats every year.

Throughout the long day, automatically adding up columns of figures, the worries had gone round and round in Charlotte's head. Should she risk the boat sinking? Was her struggle with her father worth that? She knew that he would be at home, as all the fleet was in. If she got a message to him, if she gave in, would he manage to get a crew together in time to save the vessel?

But her pride would not let her. He had tried to cheat her to obtain the position he wanted, and then he had humiliated her. Whatever it cost, she would not give in to him now. If she lost the boat tonight she would be in no worse position than she would have been in a few months' time, had she allowed her father to act as captain. And she would have her pride.

But she could not face him, sit down to supper across from him, pray with him in the family prayers. The thought of him asking God to forgive her sins stuck in Charlotte's throat, nauseated her. Abruptly, she turned her attention to the boy, trying to take her mind off her own worries. 'What are you doing here, Boy-John?'

He grinned, showing his broken front teeth. 'Poaching.' He held up three rabbits. 'Brem good eating on they.'

'If you get caught they'll thrash you,' she warned, her eyes already turning back to the ships now hidden in the gloom.

He stood beside her, following her gaze. 'It'll be a brem bad blow tonight, Lotty. What are you going to do?'

She shrugged. 'What can I do? I can't go out there myself and look after the boat.'

'I'd help you,' he said eagerly but she shook her head. 'You're only eight and far too small. Anyway, it's time you were home. Granfer-John will be thinking you're in the cells in Penzance if you don't get back soon.'

He stood on one foot, awkward in his cut-down trousers, swinging the rabbits from one hand, the spots of blood at the end of their noses shining like berries in the gloom. 'Even if the boat does sink, Lotty, you've still got the seine nets.'

She knew that he meant it kindly but he was simply making things worse. Bitterly she tore a handful of grass from the cold earth and shredded it with angry fingers. 'And what good will that do?' she demanded. 'The drifters are breaking up the pilchard shoals, we hardly ever get any off Mousehole now. And even if we do,' her voice quivered despite her best intentions, 'it won't do any good. I'll need men to work the nets, women to salt the fish; do you think my father will put up with that?'

She threw away the grass and the rising wind caught the pieces and whirled them out of sight into the growing darkness.

The boy paused, trying to think of a way to comfort her. 'Come with me, Lotty. Granfer can give you supper if you don't want to go home.'

But she shook her head, deliberately turning her back on him. All she wanted was to be left

83

alone with her thoughts.

The last few drinks had been strong ones and Kit weaved slightly as he made his way down the slope to the quay. He hadn't expected to be given shore leave and had made the most of it. The boat had only called in for fresh water although, with the bad weather approaching, she would probably stay in Mounts Bay until the storm had blown itself out. But he had assumed that, as it was a Cornish boat, making her last call before Portugal, it would have been the local men who were allowed off, not a resented stranger like him.

Still, it had given him a chance to buy a few old clothes which would be more suitable for working on a ship than the good tailcoat and top hat that he had with him. It had taken most of his money, but what did that matter?

He peered through the gloom. The quay at Newlyn was a small one, with room for only a few boats. Surely he hadn't drunk enough to miss the trader's rigging, even in the poor light? But there was no sign of her.

The wind tugged at his fair hair and he grimaced. Of course. She would have moved to safer anchorage to ride out the storm. The locals would know. He caught hold of the first man he saw. 'The *Isabelle*, where has she anchored?'

The wind snatched the words from his mouth and he had to repeat them, shouting louder. The other man shook his head.

'The *Isabelle?* She's gone, Cap'n, left just after the turn of the tide.'

Kit's brows lowered. 'For safer anchorage?' he insisted.

Despite the darkness he could see the gleam of amusement in the other man's eyes. 'Gone, mate. They only called in to pick up the captain's brother and they was off. Thought they could make the Scillies before the storm hit but I reckon they're cutting it a bit fine, myself.'

Kit stood bareheaded in the darkness, his fists clenched as he realised that he had been duped. No wonder they had been so happy to take him on. This must have been their plan all along. Just take a man on until Newlyn, and then dump him.

He dug his hands deep into his pockets but he knew what he would find. Just a few shillings. He had walked out of his father's office with scarcely any money on his person. A trip to Portugal and back would have given him some pay and time to work out what he was going to do with the rest of his life, but now he was denied that. He had even been denied the pay he was owed for the trip from Hull.

To be had like that, as if he was a greenhorn! He felt his face flame with self-disgust. And, to make matters worse, he had already drunk most of the money that remained after buying the clothes. And all while he was supposedly waiting for the ship to be made ready to sail. He snorted.

The other man looked at him warily. 'You all right, mate?'

'I'm a bloody fool, that's all,' he said bitterly. He jingled the coins in his pockets. He could pay for cheap lodgings, of course. Or he could go back into the Swordfish inn, have a few more drinks and see what he could pick up there. He had received some interested glances from the young females who hung out in the public house. One of them, Peggy, had already made her interest known. But he would have to pay her, he knew that as soon as he had seen her thin, tired face, already marked by the bitterness of a thousand insults. He would have given her the money, for nothing, just to help her out of here, away from this dead and alive hole where she was a marked woman, despised and derided even by the men who used her, but he had not even had enough spare cash for that.

Still, there had been others there. It was possible that for the price of a couple of drinks he might get a free night's lodging and some fun; with his tall, strong figure and fair hair it was not unknown for such things to happen. And he was discreet; he would never allow a woman to suffer from his friendship.

Almost before he knew that he had made up his mind, he was pushing open the door to the public house and the warmth and noise and light enfolded him welcomingly.

She was cold now, shivering uncontrollably in the April night. Even huddled into the lee of the high Cornish hedge the wind still cut through her and it was beginning to rain. As yet it was still only the occasional spit but soon, she knew, it would begin to pour down.

Charlotte made up her mind. She could not go home, she could not face her father, not see him looking at her, knowing that even as their glances met her boat was being destroyed – and all because of him.

And if her boat was gone, then gone too were all her hopes of a better future. She had told no one of her dreams but the images had flickered through her mind. A better house for her mother – warmer, more comfortable. A maid to take some of the heavy work off her, even (Charlotte had to force herself to admit this), even some new clothes for them both – pretty clothes, fashionable, with crinolines and even the newfangled drawers that her father had forbidden, considering that they were unhygienic and encouraged lust.

Had William Trevennan guessed? Had he known that deep inside his daughter there was this flame of rebellion, this longing for all the things he preached against? She lifted her head, suddenly struck by the thought. For as long as she could remember she had had this desire for something better, something beyond what life had given her, a desire encouraged by Charles Polruan. All her life her father had punished her for not being the person he wanted her to be, for running when she should have walked, laughing when she should have smiled, joined in boys' games when she should have sat quietly. Had he been afraid that if she had a little money she would escape from his influence?

A memory, long suppressed, came to her, of the last time he had beaten her. It had been because she had challenged one of the village boys to a sculling race around Mousehole Island – and she had won. She had come home, laughing, exultant, proud – to meet with punishment, reprisals, control. And no more laughter.

Suddenly, she could bear it no longer. That boat was her one chance of a good life. If she couldn't have that, she would rather die. She could scull, she could get herself out to the *Faith-Lily*. And once there, she could do as well as a man; she was taller than most of them anyway, and strong for a woman. And if she failed – if the boat sank with her on board, then so be it. She would have died trying.

Almost without realising it she was on her feet and hurrying down Paul Hill towards Newlyn beach and the fleet of fishing boats.

If she could save the boat, it would be the first thing in her life that she had achieved by herself – and against all the odds. Those qualities for which she had been criticised all her life – her height, her strength, her taste for boyish activities would have enabled her to save the ship. And she would need all her strength, mental as well as physical. Her humiliation yesterday, her concerns about the boat had resulted in a sleepless night. Already, her eyelids were heavy with lack of sleep. It would take all her willpower even to stay awake through the coming night, let alone survive the hard physical work she would need to do.

She broke into a run, her boots kicking against loose stones as she pelted at a breakneck speed down the narrow lane. Why had she always thought of those qualities as bad? She realised now, it was because of her father. The thought brought another energising burst of anger flooding through her. He spoke so much about

God and God's gifts, then criticised her for the very gifts that God had given her.

It was another example of the power of words, and she slowed automatically while her mind grappled with these new ideas. The wind was stronger now and the rain had softened the ground so that her boots made no noise on the damp earth. The group of men, fighting and struggling on the ground, were not even aware that she had approached.

For a moment she was tempted to move on – a respectable woman would never even acknowledge a fight between drunks – then her newfound freedom of thought made her reconsider. Who was she to walk by on the other side?

The religious connotations of the thought brought back her memories of her father and the power of words to change things. Well, why not? What did she have to lose?

She took a deep breath. 'Is this the way to behave?' Despite her nervousness her voice rang out clearly above the noise of the wind. 'Is this how Cornishmen are expected to act?'

It was probably the sheer amazement at the unexpected sound of a woman's voice that stopped them as much as anything. The grunting tangle of arms and legs on the ground sorted itself out into four male bodies, four faces staring at her, gleaming palely in the darkness.

And she recognised three of them and could put a name to one. 'Pentecost Trelawny.' She poured contempt into her voice. 'What will your men think of you? How can they respect a

89

captain who brawls in the street like a vagabond? And your wife and little boy.' Pathos, now, full of throbbing emotion. 'What will they think when you come home, bloodied and dirty? How can they look up to you?' She stared around at the four faces. 'Any of you?'

The three familiar faces were beginning to look downcast but the stranger, a fair-haired man as far as she could tell from under the mud and blood, seemed amused more than abashed. The faint smile that played around his cut mouth simply roused her to greater efforts.

'Look at you all. I've seen dogs behave better.'

There was a growl from the middle of the group. "T'weren't our fault. He were chatting up our Sarah-Elizabeth.'

Charlotte knew the girl concerned, attractive but with an eye for any good-looking man. But the words identified the second man. 'And you decide to attack him, do you, John Grose? And you think that it will take three of you to teach him a lesson?' Her voice rose. 'And where's your precious sister now, who you care so much about? Is she home, with her mother? Did you see her safely indoors before you decided to beat up this stranger? Or did you leave her in the public house, that den of iniquity, where she can flaunt herself at any other man who offers her the price of a pint?'

They were picking themselves up now, and their hang-dog expressions were as good as any her father had ever brought to his sinning congregations. John Grose retrieved the cap that had fallen from his head and brushed it with a muddy hand. 'I'll go and get her now, miss.' He bobbed his head at her, a courtesy she could never remember receiving before, and hurried off in a haze of beer fumes.

They had all been drinking, she realised; that meant they were unlikely to be strict Methodists who abhorred the stuff as the tool of the Devil. And in that case, perhaps she could achieve even more. If any men would defy her father, it was the hard-drinking ones.

She eyed them carefully. The stranger was still sitting on the ground, mopping the blood from his face and watching her with a faint smile that she found strangely disquieting. She turned away from him to the other men, pulling her wet shawl closer around her shoulders. 'And you two, why aren't you out looking after your boats?'

The local men gazed at her surprised. 'There's a storm coming, miss,' Pentecost Trelawny explained awkwardly. 'Our drifter's moored up safe come morning. We'll not go anywhere till tomorrow's second tide now.'

She had known it, of course but it gave her the opening she needed. 'Then you could spend the night more profitably than in a public house,' she said quickly. 'I have a job for a good man in a boat and I am prepared to pay well.'

There was silence, then they shuffled backwards. Just the look of them told her all she needed to know; the story of her disgrace had spread even to those who were not chapel-goers; not even they would risk angering her father.

It was Pentecost Trelawny who found the words. 'Not tonight, miss. My missus isn't well.'

'Nor my boy,' the other broke in. Within seconds they had faded gently backwards into the darkness and she was left alone with the stranger. Who was laughing.

'That's the best way I've ever seen of getting rid of people,' he said, his voice sounding strange without the soft Cornish accent, and Charlotte realised that he had known all along that her talk was mere rhetoric, and had thought her final appeal was all part of the act.

She opened her mouth to explain but the words died unsaid. He had got to his feet and she could see that she had done the men an injustice in accusing them of setting on a stranger three to one. He was enormous, even taller than Mr Polruan had been, and Charlotte only reached just past his shoulder. He was a gentleman, to boot. Even in the dim light she could see the distinguished cut of his coat, hear the signs of education in his voice. She could only stare in silence up at him.

He bowed to her with a flourish, his fair hair gleaming in the darkness. 'I have to thank you for your eloquence, madam.' His voice shook with suppressed laughter. 'I had misjudged quite how strong Cornishmen can be.'

She found her voice after a struggle. 'And you had misjudged quite how available Cornish-women are, as well, I believe,' she responded tartly.

He threw back his head and laughed. The forbidden scent of alcohol made her nostrils twitch. 'Oh, I got the availability right,' he said cheerfully. 'It was just that she had offered herself for rather less than her brother thought she was worth.'

Charlotte blushed rosily, unused to such openness and he smiled at her, wiping the last of the blood from his cut lip. 'Are you out without your maid, madam? Can I escort you home?'

For a second she suspected him of making fun of her, then she realised. In the darkness he had mistaken her for a proper lady. The education in Penzance that Mr Polruan had paid for, combined with her parents' background, had given her a speech and manner at odds with her financial situation. And throughout her haranguing she had deliberately forced herself to sound assured and confident, just like a real lady.

It was all she needed to complete her dis-comfort. She stammered awkwardly, trying to find the right way to explain that he had misunderstood the situation, that she was not the sort of woman to have a maid – but the words would not come.

Her half sentences were suddenly broken off. A gust of wind, stronger, more violent than before, caught at her skirts and sent her staggering sideways. Automatically he reached out an arm and she found herself suddenly enveloped for the first time in a stranger's grasp.

Her heart jumped and it was suddenly difficult to breathe. She swallowed nervously, stepping quickly backwards, away from him. Memories of her father's prayers and sermons, concentrating on the lustful desires of the flesh came to her mind, upsetting her further.

And then there was the man himself. When he

realised that she was only a common woman, he would despise her utterly – and she had had too much humiliation in the last couple of days. With a gasp she pulled herself together and turned away from him.

He was still looking down at her, his hat in his hands. 'It is too windy for you,' he said. 'It isn't safe. If I may see you home...'

There was no easy way to say it, no polite expression to pass over his mistake with grace. Her words came out in an ill-considered rush.

'I'm not going home,' she said, her voice suddenly high with embarrassment. 'I'm not a lady. I'm a boat-owner.'

Chapter Seven

His laugh made her hot with embarrassment, wishing she could recall the awkward words. Then he said, his voice still quivering with amusement: 'Don't boat-owners count as ladies, then?'

'Not when they're...' she bit the rest of the words off just in time.

But he had made the connection. 'A boat-owner. So the offer you made those men wasn't just a way of making the workshy layabouts run?'

Her lips tightened in the darkness. 'It was genuine,' she said shortly, and pulled her wet shawl more closely around her as the wind gusted suddenly.

'Then the least I can do is offer myself in their place.'

'You!' Surprise jerked her head up so that she was staring into his face from only inches away. She could see his eyes and teeth gleaming in the dim light. 'But you – you're a gentleman!'

'Oh no,' he protested calmly. 'If a boat-owner isn't a lady then a sailor can hardly be a gentleman, can he?'

'But you're no sailor.' It was unthinkable. His looks, his manner and, now that she was closer to him, his clothes, all refuted his words.

He grinned again, his teeth white in the darkness. 'I have sailed in all sorts of vessels since

95

I was a boy. Why don't we go and look at this boat of yours, then I can tell you if I can handle her?' He reached down, picking up a bundle from the ground. 'Shall we go?'

His calm assumption that she would do as he suggested had her moving towards the beach where the *Faith-Lily* was moored before she had time to think, then she stopped. 'No.'

'You don't believe me?'

'It isn't that,' she said wretchedly. 'But – she might sink.' It was one thing to risk her own life, another to risk the life of a stranger.

He glanced up at the sky. 'It's not that bad a night. She can't be very good if she can't ride this out.'

'But she's got no ballast,' Charlotte explained miserably. 'She'll smash herself to bits if she isn't fended off from the other boats. Maybe even if she is,' she finished.

His brows, darker than his hair, drew down over his eyes. 'And the rest of the crew?'

'There is no rest of the crew,' she said baldly. 'There's only me.'

There was a long moment of silence and she stared unhappily at her boots, waiting for him to take back his offer but instead he asked softly, 'You were going to do this all by yourself?'

She nodded dumbly, afraid to trust her voice.

'You've got courage.' She could hear the admiration in his voice, then he leaned forward, picked up his hat and set it carefully on his head. 'Come on.'

'What?' She stared up at him.

'Your boat,' he said shortly, as if it was the most

natural thing in the world. 'We should get to her, and the sooner the better.'

Relief and guilt made Charlotte want to cry. After the problems of the last week, to have someone help her, someone to show her kindness was suddenly overwhelming. She walked beside the stranger in silence, struggling with her emotions as they made their way to the sandy beach off which the fishing boats were moored.

'We can take any of the punts,' she said as they reached the sea edge, already fretted white with foam. She pointed to the *Faith-Lily*, easy to see by her high profile amongst the dark hulks of the other drifters. 'That's her.' Despite the situation she couldn't help but feel a thrill as she saw again the boat – *HER* boat.

He stood, hands on hips, surveying the scene, his eyes narrowed against the splatter of rain in the wind. 'The other boats are fully equipped?'

She nodded and he moved to the nearest punt, bracing himself to heave it across the wet sand. 'Then I can borrow oilskins from one of them.'

She pulled the punt alongside him, turning her head from the gusting wind that threatened to snatch the words from her mouth. Her long dark hair blew loose from its pins and whipped around her cheeks as she pushed the punt into the waves.

He reached out a hand and touched her shoulder. 'You're not coming.' His touch seemed to burn even through her clothes.

Irritably, she turned to him. 'It's *my* boat,' she said assertively. And before he could remonstrate she had lifted her full skirts high above her ankles and climbed swiftly over the gunwale of the punt.

Despite the darkness, she was aware of his eyes following her movements, taking in the glimpse of her long legs as she swung them clear of the punt's sides but all he said, with a faint quiver in his voice, was: 'I do like a woman with a good understanding.'

She was busy with the oars, slipping them in the rowlocks, digging the blades deep into the waves to hold the punt steady as he pushed it out into the choppy seas before making a quick, easy leap over the side – and it wasn't until he had taken over the rowing that the full meaning of the remark struck her.

'You – you...' words failed her.

He laughed, cheerfully. 'A woman should always look after her possessions, that's what I say.'

'Then you're different from all the men down here,' she answered tartly, remembering her father.

'I'm not sure that many men agree with me either where I come from,' he admitted, his broad shoulders working the oars easily even in the heavy seas.

'And where's that?' she asked curiously, and then added, surprised, 'I don't even know your name.' It was amazing that she could feel so at ease, so trusting with this man she had only just met.

There was a long pause before he answered, 'I'm Kit Briars, from Bristol.' Then, eagerly, as if he wanted to stop her asking him questions, 'Which ship shall I get the oilskins off?'

The pause made her suspicious. She did not want to doubt him, and under the circumstances she had no right to interrogate him – but she felt a cold shiver between her shoulderblades. It was an effort to answer, 'Any one,' in the appropriately careless tone of voice.

He glanced over his shoulder and headed for the nearest fishing boat. 'Is there anything else I should borrow off them while I'm there?'

'I don't know.' She felt rather ashamed of her ignorance. 'I've never been on the *Faith-Lily* before.'

'Never...' She could feel his surprised glance in the darkness and hurried to explain.

'I've only owned her for a few days.'

It was difficult to believe that her life had changed so much in such a short time. She remembered again the premonition of bad news she had experienced when she had seen the attorney in the office. How right she had been. And now, she was in a punt in heavy seas, planning to spend the night alone with a strange man on a small boat.

She had a feeling that this was another irrevocable act.

'Where is she then?'

Bertha Trevennan quailed before her husband's furious stare. 'I – I don't know.' She cast round nervously for something to placate him. 'Perhaps she's working late.'

'Working late!' William strode round the tiny kitchen, his leather soles sounding crisply on the stone flags. 'When did she ever have to work until this time? She should have been home hours ago.'

Bertha bowed her head, silent under his scorn. Not even her love for Charlotte would enable her to stand up to her husband when he was in this sort of mood.

At the far side of the room Trevennan turned, throwing his arms wide in a dramatic gesture. Against the whitewashed wall he stood out, preternaturally large and black, like a bird of prey – or a demon from the Pit. At the thought, Bertha gasped and turned away, horrified that even secretly she should think of her husband, the man joined with her in front of God, in such a way.

'She's defying me.' His voice rang out, large enough to fill a chapel. 'She is angry with me, her father, merely for showing my congregation that she has sinned. She did not come home yesterday until I had left to preach at Penzance and now she is late again. She is avoiding me.'

'Surely not.' She had to think of something, she *had* to. 'Perhaps – perhaps she is with old Mr Jelbert.' Her husband disapproved strongly of Charlotte having any contact with that family, and Bertha usually tried to cover for her daughter when she went there, but seeing the Jelberts would be a far lesser offence in his eyes than actively defying him. Bertha felt a brief dawning of hope well up inside her. 'Shall I go and look for her, husband?' Anything, anything to get out of the house, away from his barely controlled violence.

'She is not there.' His voice was cold with displeasure. 'I visited that house of sin myself and they had not seen her.'

Bertha swallowed. 'It could be...' Desperation put the words into her head. 'It could be that she has repented of her ways, that she has visited the Superintendent to ask for his advice.' Not that it was likely. While Charlotte had always attended Chapel and all the prayer meetings that her father insisted upon, Bertha was sure, in her own mind, that her daughter was not deeply religious. But if the thought could satisfy her husband... She glanced longingly at the door, praying for Charlotte to come in, praying for something to avert the scene she knew was building up.

He moved towards her, slowly, menacingly. 'You know where she is, don't you? You know what she is doing.'

She backed away, her mouth dry with fear. 'I know nothing, husband.' Her voice was a mere whisper. 'Nothing.'

He ignored her, coming nearer, nearer. She was backed up against the wall now, her thin hands clasped together until the knuckles showed white. 'You know!' His voice was loud enough to fill a chapel; it hammered at her. 'It has happened at last, the call of the flesh, the lust of the body. At last, despite all my teaching, all my prayers, she has succumbed.'

He reached out, grasping her by the shoulder; his blue eyes blazed down at her. 'And you know this, don't you?'

She shook her head. Her knees were shaking so much that they would barely support her. 'No!' It was more of a mew than a word.

His fingers tightened, digging painfully into her flesh; his eyes seemed to grow bigger, brighter.

101

'You know! After all this time, all my efforts! Blood will out! Even now, the heat of lust is burning in her loins. She is sinning, as her mother sinned before her.'

The world had shrunk until it contained nothing, nothing except the pain from her shoulder, the blueness of his eyes. Bertha's knees gave way and she sank to the floor, tears pouring down her cheeks, and as if from a long way off she heard a voice she hardly recognised as her own, wailing, 'A sinner! I have been so great a sinner!'

Dawn was no more than a light streak beyond the flat horizon of The Lizard when the bottom of the punt grated softly on the sand. 'I don't like this.' Kit Hargraves sounded worried as he handed Charlotte carefully out onto the beach. 'It isn't right that a lady should walk alone like this.'

If she weren't so tired, Charlotte thought, she would have laughed. 'Please, Mr Briars, there is no danger.' She glanced out at the fleet, dimly seen amongst the tossing waves. 'The *Faith-Lily* is in more danger than me, I assure you.'

'Not for much longer. The wind has dropped and the sea will be calmer soon.' He still held her hand in his, his fingers warm around her cold flesh. 'I have nothing to do tomorrow; the ship I should have sailed on has gone. Shall I put some ballast in the lugger? Otherwise you will have the same problem again next time you have a bit of a blow.'

She hesitated, gnawing her lower lip. The offer

was tempting but... 'Thank you, but I shall have to get her payed up,' she said regretfully. 'She should have been done months ago and without a new coat of tar the hull will rot soon.'

She pulled gently at her hand but he still had hold of it. 'If I had some help...' he began.

'You'd do it?' She peered through the darkness at him. 'But you are a gentleman!'

His voice quivered, as if he were laughing. 'I must say, you have some funny ideas about ladies and gentlemen. First you insist that boat-owners can't be ladies, and now you tell me that I can't pay up your boat.'

She paused. 'I was going to try to employ someone,' she admitted.

'Then that's all right then.' His voice was relaxed and carefree. 'You can employ me – providing I have someone to tell me where to get the tar and paint.'

'I can do that.' The Jelberts would be pleased to help there; Granfer-John was not up to heavy work himself but he could certainly help Kit by arranging for supplies.

She tugged again at her hand. 'Mr Briars,' she made her voice as serious as possible, trying to disguise the sudden happiness that flooded through her. 'I have to go. I have to be at work at eight o'clock.'

She wasn't sure if she was pleased or regretful when he released her. 'I still don't like the idea of you walking two miles by yourself like this.'

'I do it twice every day,' she reminded him. 'Besides, I can look after myself. I am no delicate lady, whatever your kind words say. In fact, I am taller than any of the men around here.'

'I daresay,' he agreed. 'I expect Snow White used to say the same thing. But that didn't stop the Prince wanting to look after her and kiss her, did it?'

'Kiss!' The beach was suddenly bereft of air. Charlotte could feel the world turning on its axis, then her common sense asserted itself. She was his employer now. He was probably only trying to get into her good books. But it was an entirely improper thing to say, even if that was the reason.

She stepped swiftly backwards, suddenly afraid that he might actually put his words into action. 'Good – good night, Mr Briars.'

'Good night, Miss Trevennan.' As she hurried at an unseemly speed up the beach she was almost sure she could hear the quiver of laughter in his voice, but when she turned the punt was just visible in the growing light, already on its way out to the lugger.

The words kept repeating themselves to her as she walked home. Snow White, indeed! She gave a sudden snort of laughter, startling an early sea-gull, pecking at something by the roadside. Still, it did make her feel better about the Cornishmen who so obviously found her too tall for their taste when she thought of them as the seven dwarves.

The village was still sleeping as she hurried through it, the sound of her boots echoing crisply off the thick walls of Cornish granite. Then she rounded the last corner and her heart sank as she saw the gleam of lamplight in the window of her cottage.

She took a deep breath to calm herself, then pushed the door open, ducking swiftly under the low lintel. 'Good morning, Father.'

He rose like an avenging angel, his thick eyebrows drawn over his blue eyes, the big Bible clasped in his hands like a weapon. 'Whore. Harlot. Sinner.'

The words startled her and she gaped at him, taken aback. 'Wh – what are you talking about?'

He pointed a quivering finger at her. 'That the daughter of this house should be so wanton. Writhing in lust like a bitch on heat.' His voice shook with passion. 'On your knees, woman. On your knees and pray for forgiveness.'

Her eyes were red with tiredness, her body aching after the long, hard night she had had. Normally, she would have spoken politely to him, defended herself, true, but with due deference to his position. Now, she was just too tired.

Dragging her bonnet from her head she threw it onto the table. 'You stupid man!' Her voice seemed to be speaking of its own volition. Deep inside her weary body she heard the words it was saying and quailed, but the voice took no notice of her, went on regardless.

'Look at my skirt.' She spread the material with one hand, pointing to the salt stains that marked it with the other. 'Does this look as if I've been with a man? Do I look as if I've been indulging in a night of lust?'

She dragged her wet shawl from her and threw that in a damp heap in the corner of the room. 'I've been on my boat,' she said, and her voice rang with contempt. 'The boat that you made sure would have no ballast in if a storm came.'

Her lids were heavy, so heavy. She turned to the stairs; her tired legs felt as if they were filled with lead. At the foot of the stairs, she turned. 'It may interest you to know that she is still afloat. And I still have no intention of letting you sail her.'

Slowly, she began to climb the steep stairs.

'Wait.' Her father's voice rang through the house. 'Are you telling me – do you swear that you have told me the truth?'

'Yes, of course,' she said wearily.

'And you haven't been with a man?'

Her honesty was habitual. She prepared to answer him. Then stopped.

If she told him the truth he would twist it, use it against her. Worse, he would harangue her, probably for hours. And she had to go to sleep even if it was just for a few hours. She could never cope with another day at the office without even a couple of hours' sleep.

'I was all alone,' she said, and disappeared up the stairs.

Somehow, she pulled off her still-damp skirts and petticoats and tugged her corset free, not caring that she broke the laces. Exhausted, she threw herself onto the bed. She made a vain attempt to get her stockings off but the tied garters defeated her and she simply crawled under the covers with them still on.

Which must surely have been the reason that she fell asleep hearing in her head an amused voice saying lightly: 'I do like a woman with a good understanding.'

'Did Lotty send you to help or hinder?' Kit enquired caustically, pulling Boy-John away from the fire for the fifth time in as many minutes.

Boy-John grinned. 'Reckon she were that tired she didn't know what she was asking us to do, just told us to come along so we did.' He reached up a hand and patted the black sides of the *Faith-Lily* towering above them on the beach, standing solid on her sea legs on sand left dry by the retreating tide. 'You did a brem good job, saving her like that, what with the wind and all.' He gazed at Kit, wide-eyed. 'Here, do you think that there bridge the Queen's going to open next week up Plymouth way could have blown down? It'd be brem funny if she turned up and there weren't no bridge, wouldn't it?'

'No way, lad.' Even in Hull they knew of the great bridge Isambard Kingdom Brunel was building across the Tamar. 'That bridge will outlast both of us.' He bent and thrust the wad of old nets attached to the end of a pitchfork first into the barrel of tar and then into the fire until it was blazing. He turned to the boy. 'Now are you going to help or do I have to do it all myself?'

When Granfer-John Jelbert returned they were working amicably together, Kit holding the blazing pitchfork against the side of the boat, burning off the old barnacles and smearing a layer of melted tar onto the wood while Boy-John used a brush on the end of a pole to work the tar well into the ship's sides.

Kit threw a glance over his shoulder. 'Have you sorted it out?'

The old man spat. 'No trouble. You didn't do

107

no more than any other man here would have done in the same position. We all borrow from each other in an emergency. It were just because it were Charlotte's boat I were afraid there might have been trouble.'

Kit brushed the melted tar onto the boat's sides in silence for a few seconds. 'Why don't they like Charlotte?' His voice was carefully neutral.

But not neutral enough. Boy-John turned to him, his small face red with anger. ''Tedn't Charlotte!' he insisted. 'She's a brem lovely great maid. 'Tedn't her!'

'Watch what you're doing, lad.' Kit grabbed at the pole in the boy's hand. In his anxiety to defend Charlotte, Boy-John had let the brush get too close to the burning tar and the bristles were blazing.

With a quick twist, Kit ducked the brush in a bucket of sea water standing ready for just that emergency and the flames expired in a cloud of smoke and steam.

Granfer-John chuckled. 'My da used to wallop me when I did that. Reckon you got off lightly there, lad.' He turned back to Kit. 'But, as the boy says, 'tedn't Charlotte that's the problem. 'Tes her da. He's a brem powerful man in Mouzle, aye, and Newlyn too, come to that – and when he says no one's to help her – well, no one will.'

'So no one will man her boat for her?' Kit moved a few steps further along and attacked a fresh part of the hull.

'No local men. And that's what you need, fishing around here. Without local knowledge you're wasting your time,' the old man agreed.

Boy-John broke in, 'If she lets her da sail the boat, she might as well have let it sink last night. He'll never make any money out of it.'

There was a silence between the three of them for several minutes as they concentrated on making the hull of the boat seaworthy again. Deep inside, Kit felt his anger burn like a slow fuse. Fathers, they always seemed to cause problems. First his and now Charlotte's lives were being ruined by their respective fathers. He, at least, had managed to get free; because he was a man he had been able to escape the suffocating influence of his father.

He had made the decision as he had walked out of the office in Hull, and the only regret it had caused him was when he had had to lie to Charlotte last night about his name and background. James Hargraves was not a man to give up easily; once he finally realised that Kit wasn't coming back he would send out men to hunt him down, and Kit had no intention of being found.

It was a pity Charlotte had no such easy option. She was an attractive woman, and last night he had been astounded by her courage and the way she had used every ounce of her strength to save the boat. Under other circumstances he would have been delighted to get to know her better and he was sorry for her problems, but he had troubles of his own. He couldn't ruin his life for the sake of an unknown woman, however attractive.

Boy-John suddenly turned to him, grinning

broadly under the untidy thatch of his hair. 'I got an idea.'

'Oh? And what's that?' Kit demanded, knowing in his heart what it would be.

Boy-John spread the tar over another bit of the hull while he chose his words. 'It seems to me,' he said, 'that you could sail her. And Granfer here could tell you all you need to know about the fishing hereabouts.' His face brightened. 'I can work as ship's boy, too. I'll be good at that.'

Kit dipped the end of the pole into the melted tar. 'Sorry, lad, but that's just not on.'

'Oh!' The boy's mouth was a disappointed circle around his broken tooth. 'Why not?'

Kit's usually good-natured face hardened as he remembered the way he had been treated by virtually all the Cornishmen he had met. This was a dead-and-alive hole. There was nothing for him here, nothing that would enable him to make his fortune, to show his father that he could be a success without the older man's money and influence.

'Well, lad,' he said, and his voice was grim. 'I'm only doing this because your Charlotte has promised to pay me for the work. But once I've got the money,' he glanced out across the bay, out to sea and the wide, beckoning world, 'then I'm out of here on the first boat. And I'm not coming back.'

Chapter Eight

'See, Lotty's rich, ain't she?'

In the early morning sun Boy-John leapt and spun around the space between the ancient granite pillars that surrounded the open court-yard. ''Tes a real pilchard palace,' he exulted, his bare feet soundless on the sea-rounded cobbles.

Kit slapped his hand against the wall, admiring the strength and size of the building. It looked very old; it could almost have been a relic that survived the burning of the village by the Spanish in the sixteenth century. Lofts covered by thatched roofs surrounded three sides of the yard, providing shelter for the women who would work there when the pilchard shoals arrived. 'Palace?' he queried with a laugh in his voice as he followed the gutter leading to a sunken hole and peered down it cautiously.

''Tes what they call un.' Boy-John came closer and pointed at the hole. 'They put a barrel down there to catch all the blood and oil and such.' He whirled away again but his foot slipped on the dew-slicked cobbles, and if Kit hadn't grabbed at his collar he would have disappeared down the hole himself.

'All the rubbish, in other words,' he grunted, heaving the boy back on his feet again. 'No wonder you seem set on joining it.'

'Not rubbish.' Boy-John grinned happily,

111

recognising the good humour behind the remark. 'She could sell it for – oh, lots of money.' He glanced up at Kit, his small face suddenly solemn. 'If you were to sail the *Faith-Lily* for her, Lotty might marry you, then you'd be rich too.'

'I've already told you, I'm not going to captain that boat,' Kit snapped. 'Nor am I the sort of man to marry a woman for her money!'

'Course not.' Boy-John skipped swiftly out of the way. 'But it would be nice for her. You're the only man round here who's taller than she.'

The boy's rationale was so ridiculous that Kit couldn't help grinning despite his dislike of the subject. 'Cut it, Boy-John. A gentleman doesn't talk about such things.' Not that the boy would ever be a gentleman.

As he had expected, the child was unabashed by the reprimand. Running to the doorway, the boy called, 'And she's got the seine boats and all. Come and see.'

Kit followed more slowly, glancing carefully around him as he went. The cellar was certainly impressive but an evening with Granfer-John Jelbert, before Kit had accepted the offer of a bed for the night, had made him realise Charlotte's true position. Being owner of all this would be of no use to her if she couldn't get anyone to help, should a pilchard shoal come in near the shore. And even that was unlikely, these days.

No, however impressive the legacy seemed, Kit knew that it was almost worthless in real terms. With the pilchards coming less and less often to this coast, Charlotte would probably find it very hard to sell the business, even if her father hadn't made her an outcast.

It was a pity. He had been attracted by the tall woman with the strange silver-grey eyes and wide mouth. Normally, she looked so quiet, so meek but when she was amused her whole face changed, her eyes danced. Once, on that stormy night they had spent together on the boat, she had even thrown back her head and laughed, a deep, throaty laugh that had stirred his blood. But he was not staying here, Kit reminded himself. He had to prove to his father that he could be a success on his own terms, and there was no way that he could do that here.

He followed Boy-John out of the fish cellar – a strange name for it, he mused, as it was above ground. But then, most of the net-lofts in Mousehole weren't in the roof either; words seemed to have a different meaning in this part of the world.

It was high tide, and they still wouldn't be able to get to the *Faith-Lily* for another hour so Kit had no objection to strolling around the village in the spring sunshine, indulging his curiosity about the people who lived there.

Boy-John's racing figure had already disappeared in the direction of the harbour when there was a clatter behind Kit; he swung quickly round. A thin woman in the drab black skirts that all the village women seemed to wear was leaning against the rough wall of a cottage, her face contorted with pain. It was easy to see what had happened; her foot had turned on the rough cobbles, the sprain made worse, no doubt, by the two full buckets of water that she carried.

113

She was not old, her face relatively unlined though the once-blonde hair under her bonnet was streaked with silver, but she looked too slight for the burden.

Kit's easy-going chivalry rose at once. 'Allow me.' He was by her side in a couple of paces, his strong hands reaching for the buckets.

She glanced up at his great height and a brief colour flooded her pale face. 'No, really, I can manage. It was just a stumble.' Her voice was clear and low, not a lady's voice but lacking the soft Cornish accent to which his ear had already become accustomed.

'What?' His voice was horrified. 'Don't you think I am strong enough?'

'No, it isn't that...' she began, then the realisation that he had been teasing her slowly dawned and her mouth trembled into an uncertain smile.

'Then let me carry them.' He pulled them easily from her weakened grasp. 'I have time to spare – and the strength.' He walked on and she moved beside him, her steps uneven as she favoured her turned ankle. He slowed his pace, glancing at her out of the corner of his eyes. Despite the common dress and tired face there was an elegance about her that was missing from the other women he had seen in the area – except for one.

'Do you have to carry water far?'

She glanced up at him, half frightened. 'No, only – only from a little way up Raginnis Hill.' Her voice was breathless and subdued.

'Well, at least you only have to walk downhill

with full buckets.' He followed her down a flight of granite steps and past the ancient Keigwin Arms, the pillars in front looking out of place before a public house. The harbour was just ahead of him; an ancient slipway, paved with local stones, disappeared under the lapping waves while on the water black-hulled double-ended luggers jostled together in the sunlight, their rigging dark with the brown of drying nets.

She reached out. 'I'll take them now.' He opened his mouth to object but the worry in her face got to him. A jealous husband, perhaps, though it seemed unreasonable to mind such a public and minor service. He handed the buckets over. 'You've not got far to carry them?'

'Oh no, sir. I'm almost there.' She flickered a brief, nervous smile and hurried off.

Kit wandered down to the harbour already dismissing the happening from his mind, his blue eyes searching for Boy-John. The huge stones that made up the old quay, softened by their coat of golden lichen, dwarfed the men leaning over the rail to eye the work of the fishermen preparing to sail. Everywhere the air was full of the shouts of men, happy in their work. He watched as one lugger manoeuvred easily through the narrow opening, admiring her lines as she caught the wind and heeled over, the water creaming along her hull as she left the lee of the rocky island that protected the harbour mouth and set out to sea.

It confirmed what he had thought from the first moment he had set foot on the *Faith-Lily* – that these boats were well-built, perfectly designed for the conditions they had to meet. Now that he had seen one in action, he could believe Granfer-John's story about the *Mystery* – a thirty-three-foot lugger that had sailed to Australia a few years earlier.

Slowly, he wandered back along the quay. Still no sign of the boy. He grimaced. It was almost time to leave for Newlyn; the *Faith-Lily* would be aground soon, ready for them to start painting the decks. He lengthened his stride, anxious to find the boy as soon as possible.

In his concern he almost ignored the running man who came panting along the quay, the sudden knot of frowning men. Only one word came to him, after he was already past, and he swung quickly around, touching the shoulder of the nearest man. 'What was that about the *Isabelle?*'

The sailor swung round. 'Lost with all hands off the Scillies. God help them.'

'God help them,' Kit murmured, automatically doffing his hat. He should have been on that ship – would have been if they hadn't cheated him, leaving him ashore in Newlyn while they took on another man – the captain's brother, he remembered. Dear God, two from one family! Despite his unhappy experiences on the ship his heart still ached for the loss.

The news was spreading through the village; he could see people running together, talking, the men doffing their caps, then a woman's voice rising in a sudden, spine-shivering wail – someone for whom the loss was closer, more tragic. His blue eyes found the small figure, her apron over her head as she gave herself up to despair and felt his own heart contract with pity. Then another female came up to her, slight, with silvered-blonde hair, and he recognised the woman he had helped earlier with the buckets. Across the harbour he saw the two move away together, the closeness of their bodies providing the only comfort that could reach the poor creature in her misery.

Kit shook himself. It was no good brooding about the loss – all men connected with the sea learned that. Life had to go on, and he had to find Boy-John. He turned away from the harbour, past the pilot lookout station and the blacksmith's shop decorated with lucky horseshoes, and there he was. The small, untidy figure in the cutdown trousers was clambering over some rowing boats, pulled up above the high water mark. Presumably Charlotte's seine boats. Kit drew a deep breath to shout to him.

But before he could let out the bellow that was rising in his throat, another figure appeared. From behind a granite pile a thickset man in a rusty black coat came up behind the boy and his hand shot out. Even at that distance, Kit could hear the *thwack* of the blow as it caught the child across the ear. The small body rose from the hull with the force of the cuff, his ear-splitting yell tearing the air even before he sprawled, froglike, on the surrounding pebbles.

Even while the child was in the air Kit was running, anger flaming through him at the injustice of what he had witnessed. 'Hey, you!' His shout cut through the morning air, but the man was already turning, alerted by his pounding feet.

He stood, bare-headed in the sunshine, awaiting Kit's arrival, his white hair a halo around his head, but there was an alertness and a slight crouch to the body that told Kit that the man would be a good fighter. 'Yes, my boy?' The words were mild, the tone reproving, totally at variance with his actions and stance.

Kit slithered to a halt on the pebbles. He was taken aback by the greeting but, in any case, whatever the provocation, he could not have brought himself to attack a man so much older and shorter than he was. 'Why did you hit that child?' He reached down and helped Boy-John to his feet.

The white eyebrows rose. 'Am I not allowed to protect my property from thieves and vandals?'

'I ain't no thief,' Boy-John protested loudly, involuntary tears cutting their way through the dirt on his face. 'And it idn't your boat, 'tes Lotty's!'

So this was Charlotte's father. 'Quiet, young un,' Kit ordered, handing the child a clean handkerchief as he carefully eyed the man in front of him. Everything about him spoke of respectability, even holiness, from his windblown white locks to the worn Bible clutched in his hand, and if Kit hadn't seen for himself the undeserved assault on the child he would never have believed this man capable of such an action.

His silence seemed to unnerve the older man. 'You mustn't believe everything this boy says.' His voice was calm, measured, authoritarian. 'We have done what we can for him but with such a background...' he cast a look of dislike at Boy-John and lowered his voice '...a bastard.'

But the boy had heard it. ''Tweren't my ma's fault,' he broke in hotly. 'She were simple, everyone do say so. She wouldn't have known what she were doing.'

The trained voice of the preacher easily drowned out the shrill piping. 'As he says, simple. And, of course, her child...'

Kit fought to keep control of his temper. 'Whatever the mother did, the child is not to blame,' he said hotly.

'But, my dear sir!' The man lowered his voice again. 'Inherited moral degeneracy,' he murmured. 'And mental, of course.'

The ridiculousness of the claim would have made Kit laugh under other circumstances. 'If you think that the child is simple...' he began furiously.

'Oh, only where morality is concerned.' It was said with breathtaking authority. 'I am sure he is capable of earning his own living. Though with his background, of course, the workhouse is the most likely destination. As I am certain you will agree, sir.'

So, Trevennan didn't know who he was and had been taken in by his manner and his clothes. Well, Kit had no wish to set him straight. 'The only way that child will end up as a criminal or a beggar,' he said coldly, 'is if people like you think of him in such a way. He is as bright as a button and more truthful than many lads his age.'

'Yeah,' broke in Boy-John. 'That'll teach you!

Think you're as good as gold, you do, but Kit here's the *real* gentleman, he knows what's what. And what's more,' he added, getting carried away by the power of his own oratory, 'he's going to sail Lotty's boat for her, and that'll teach you and all.'

Kit would normally have set the facts straight but after extolling Boy-John's truthfulness he found himself in a dilemma. 'Well,' he began carefully – but William Trevennan broke in.

'Sailing her boat?' His voice rose. 'You would be ill-advised to do that, young man.'

His pompous tone made Kit's hackles rise. 'And why would that be?'

'You must know that as her father *I* am the proper person to decide who should be in charge of her boat.'

'Really?' His anger was a burning fire in his belly now, but only the glint in his blue eyes betrayed him. 'I hadn't realised that she was underage.'

'She is over twenty-one,' Trevennan admitted, 'but–'

'And she seemed of sound mind,' Kit mused.

'She's brem clever!' Boy-John broke in hotly, his words followed by the preacher's more reasonable, 'She is, of course, of average intelligence.'

'So why doesn't she have the right to decide who will sail her boat?' Kit demanded.

Trevennan shrugged. 'My dear sir, a female – and a young one at that. It's not as if she had a husband to guide her,' he added disparagingly. 'Too tall, you know, too unattractive.'

'So, because she is a woman she is to be condemned as useless!' His hatred of injustice broke down Kit's slender hold on his temper. 'In the same way as this child is to be condemned to a life of crime because his father didn't have the decency to treat his mother with the consideration that was her due.'

Trevennan's face was mottled with rage. 'Who are you to query my decisions?' he demanded. 'As her father–'

'As her father you have no rights over her any more.' Kit was in no mood to put up with another overbearing parent trying to ruin his child's life. 'She is of age and of sound mind and good character. When our Queen was years younger than your daughter she was ruling this country, and we haven't had a better monarch since the days of Good Queen Bess.'

Swinging on his heel, Kit began to stride back to the village. 'Come, Boy-John.'

The child followed, pausing only to turn when he was out of reach and shout back to the furious preacher: 'That'll teach you! That'll put you in your place, you old snodderwig!' Then he ducked his head down and ran after Kit as quickly as he was able.

'Here you are, Kit, here's your knacking.' He held up a grimy square of cloth which it took Kit several seconds to recognise as the clean handkerchief he had handed the boy a few minutes earlier. He repressed a shudder. 'Keep it,' he said shortly.

Boy-John slowed, his head drooping. 'Are you mad at me, Kit? Because of what I said?'

The genuine remorse in the lad's posture caught at Kit's heart. He reached out an arm, pulling the small boy to his and gave him a hug. 'I forgive you, Boy-John, but you shouldn't have said it. Especially after I'd told the man how honest you were.'

The boy looked up at him, his blue eyes bright with mischief. 'And did you mean it, Kit? What you said about helping Lotty?'

For a second Kit hesitated, his desire for freedom, for the chance to prove himself to his father, warring within him, then he glanced at the boy, saw the bruise already beginning to disfigure his cheek, and changed his mind.

William Trevennan was a bully, riding roughshod over anyone he could. The small people in the village, like Granfer-John Jelbert and Boy-John and Charlotte needed someone to fight for them. And it wouldn't be for long. 'I'll help her get her boat ready,' he said, 'but that's it. I won't sail her, Boy-John, whatever I said to that pompous bully back there.'

After all, it would only be for a couple of days. He could pay up the boat, get the ballast in, make her safe, then he could be off.

And let's hope, he thought fervently, that Miss Charlotte Trevennan doesn't get any silly ideas about why I'm doing it. I escaped from Hull because my father wanted to marry me off, and I don't want to have to escape from Cornwall for the self-same reason.

William Trevennan stared after the retreating figures, his body shaking with anger. He was an

122

important man in the village; what he said went. To be disobeyed by his daughter and that young heathen – it wasn't supportable! It would undermine all his authority.

And what about his chance of becoming a proper preacher? What would the Methodists think of him if he couldn't even keep his own daughter under control? And now she had that young giant supporting her, encouraging her in her wilful ways. He ground his teeth. It didn't take a mindreader to see where *that* would end. He was a good-looking young man. Before she knew where she was, Charlotte, *his* Charlotte, would be seduced, corrupted, led astray. The man was after her money, of course, but that wouldn't stop him having his way with her. William Trevennan shivered in the April sunshine, his hands clenching as he imagined the scene.

'Mr Trevennan. Sir.'

Slowly he dragged himself out of his self-induced trance. He focused groggily on the fisherman beside him, turning his filthy cap round and round in his hands. 'Yes?'

''Tes our Mary-Jane, sir. 'Tes terrible news. The *Isabelle* is lost off the Scillies with all hands and her boy was on her.'

Now that he could attend, he was aware of the cries and wails coming from the harbour. 'Mary-Jane Spargo, and her daughter, Susan, too?'

'Aye, sir. Susan be trying to comfort her ma but she's scriching like a whitnick herself and your wife can't do nothing with them.'

'I'll come at once.' The summons had calmed

123

him. He was still in charge of Mousehole, of course he was. It would take more than a stranger and a disobedient daughter to unthrone him. Luckily, he had his Bible with him; that would show the villagers how religious he was.

He glanced down and saw that in his fury he had clenched his hands so tight that he had bent the Bible up inside them. Now the covers were curved, the back coming away from the sides. Damn that young man with his fair hair and superior smile, damn him to Hell!

He pushed his way through the silent crowd to the two women at the centre. 'Children.' He shouldered his wife out of the way and reached out his arms, enfolding the bereaved women in his embrace. 'Do not weep for your son, your brother. He is at peace. After the toils of this hard world, he sleeps on Abraham's breast.'

Moved by a connection of thoughts, he tightened his grasp on the younger woman until he could feel her own, soft breasts, pressing against his chest.

But even through the pleasure he got from the touch of her young body, his mind went back to Charlotte and the stranger.

He would have to teach them a lesson.

Chapter Nine

'Why, Charlotte?' Richard Spargo's handsome face was drawn with grief. 'Why do these things happen?'

'I don't know.' She refused to give him the usual platitudes about God's will; her father had been here all day and he would have said that more than once.

She smoothed back her dark hair from her forehead with a weary hand. A drowning sent a shockwave through the whole community. Everyone had relations at sea, and although they all knew and accepted the dangers, the loss brought back to everyone the knife-edge on which their lives were lived. A slip of the foot, a misjudgement, a rope breaking at the wrong moment, and any house in the village could be mourning as the Spargos were now.

The only comfort that anyone could offer was their presence, their concern. As well as her father, the other villagers had come to sit quietly, to cry together, to bring a small gift of food, each in their way offering a small shred of comfort.

They would all be at the prayer meeting now, begging God to help these poor people. Only she was left behind, a black sheep, to help them through the evening.

She said gently, 'Your mother is sleeping now, she'll be able to accept things better tomorrow.'

'Aye,' the heavy-set young man sighed. 'Accept that she's one step away from the poorhouse.' He slapped the bandages and splints that held his broken left leg out at an angle, supported on a cushion placed on a crab pot. 'And me not fit to go to sea for weeks, at least – months maybe. Where's the money going to come from, that's what I want to know.'

Charlotte took up the old brown teapot from its resting place by the fire and poured him out another cup of tea. 'Phil Trevelyan will have you back on his lugger as soon as you're fit. And no one in the village will let you starve, you know that. We look after our own.'

'For now,' Richard snorted. 'But what about when I go, eh? Two sons and a husband my ma's lost. There's only me and Susan left now, and what will happen to them if *I* drown?'

Charlotte heard the harsh, uneven intake of breath that presaged another hysterical fit from Susan and moved swiftly to the girl's side, holding her shuddering body close to her own.

'You're talking rubbish,' she said firmly. 'You sail with Phil Trevelyan and we all know he's the best skipper in Mousehole, even if he was born a miner. And as for Susan here,' she tightened her grasp, 'she's so pretty that she'll be able to marry who she pleases in a year or two. Already I've seen the boys coming round courting. Haven't I?' She shook the girl lightly, trying to turn her mind away from her brother's drowning.

The pale lips broke into a tremulous smile. 'One or two,' she whispered.

'More like five or six,' Charlotte broke in

robustly. 'And you only fifteen. And it's not just fishermen, either, that I've seen. Wasn't that Farmer Matthews' younger son that came calling the other day?'

The pretty face blushed furiously, and the girl squirmed away, trying to hide her face. Charlotte patted her on the shoulder. 'Richard will have to stay home to fight them off for you, at this rate.'

'That I will.' Charlotte was relieved that he had realised what she was trying to do and joined in with a show of cheerfulness. 'Thinking of auctioning her off, I am, to the highest bidder. I reckon I'd have all the single men in Penwith trying to get her for a wife.'

'There you are.' Charlotte smiled down at the blushing girl. 'You'll have the handsomest husband and be the richest of all of us before you know where you are.'

'Mind you,' Richard said thoughtfully. 'I reckon that it's not just Susan here that's got a follower.'

'I don't know what you mean.' Charlotte, in turn, could feel herself blushing.

'That there young giant that they tell me is paying up your boat for you,' Richard grinned. 'Some gert bloke he is, by all accounts.'

'And he's not poor.' Susan was pleased for a chance to turn the tables on Charlotte. 'Boy-John showed me a handkerchief he had lent the boy. Silk, it were and with an *H* embroidered on the corner and all.'

H? But he had told Charlotte that his name was Kit Briars. Where had the *H* come from? She leaned over, pretending to feel the heat left in the teapot so that they could not see her face as a

127

cold shiver ran up her spine. In the intervening days she had thought a lot about Kit, remembering with gratitude the way he had helped to save the *Faith-Lily,* with efficiency, even with humour, so different from the seriousness of her father.

Now she remembered the hesitation, the constraint in his voice when she had asked his name, the pause before he had said that he had come from Bristol. Charlotte closed her eyes briefly as she fought down a sudden shock of realisation. Kit had lied to her.

Richard went on: 'They say he has an eye for the ladies, too. And he drinks. What's your da going to say when he knows you've got an admirer like that, Charlotte?'

The words ran through her like knives. She knew that not everyone felt about alcohol as her father did. Richard himself was a drinker, even though his mother and sister were both staunch supporters of the chapel. But she had been brought up in a home where alcohol was seen as a work of the Devil. It had never occurred to her that Kit might be a drinking man, and as for Richard's remark about women... Hadn't it been because of a fight over women that she had first met him?

She swallowed, forcing herself to hide her dismay and confusion. Ostracised as she was by the rest of the village, she had heard nothing of the rumours going round about Kit. Proudly, she raised her head, meeting Richard's eyes with an effort. 'My father will say nothing,' she said flatly, 'because this is all a fairy story. I don't have an admirer. All Mr Briars is doing is paying up the boat and he's doing that for money.'

Money which he would almost certainly be coming to collect the following day, she realised with a sinking heart. She had seen the *Faith-Lily* at anchor in Gwavas Lake, a safe anchorage off Newlyn as she had walked home that night and it had been obvious that the work had been completed. Charlotte had even been able to see the thin white strip or 'straike' around the lugger's bows, denoting a death in the owner's family, and knew that she had Granfer-John to thank for that.

'Then what was he doing carrying the water-buckets for your ma this morning?' Susan said triumphantly. 'I know because I saw them. It was just before...' her voice wavered at the memory of this morning and her carefree happiness before the news of her brother's death.

Richard broke in quickly, trying to divert his sister's mind from their troubles. 'Come on, Charlotte, admit it. You've got an admirer.'

Dear God, if her father heard these rumours, if Kit did... She rose to her feet, shaking out her skirts, tidying back the stray wisps of hair with trembling hands. It was several seconds before she had control enough of herself to try to speak, and when she did her voice sounded higher than usual and her lips felt stiff.

'You're wrong, it's all a mistake. There will never be anything between Kit Briars and myself.'

William Trevennan ended the prayer with a

resounding 'Amen!' and lifted his eyes.

All around him, the faithful of Mousehole finished their private prayers and sat slowly up. The small dark room off Duck Street, in which the weekly prayer meeting was held, filled with the rustle of clothing as figures that he had held silent for the last two hours began to move again as if coming back to life.

As he watched them he could not help a thrill of righteous pride. There were sixty here, sixty! And a quarter of those had been converted by him. He moved to the door and shook hands with the congregation as they passed slowly out: Thomas Penhale, who had been a drunkard and a fornicator until he had seen the light, thanks to William's preaching; Phil Cornish, who had frequented illegal fist-fights and mixed with other low company. Both now good Christians and good Methodists – because of him.

But here was one who had always been one of the saved. He took the mittened claw gently in his hand. 'Miss Makepeace, so good of you to come.' He smiled into the thin face half-hidden by the brim of her bonnet.

'A wonderful meeting, my dear Mr Trevennan, wonderful.' Her faded blue eyes were raised to his. 'I could feel God in my heart – in my heart, Mr Trevennan.' Her free hand pressed against the black silk of her jacket as if to stop that organ from getting too excited.

He squeezed her hand. 'Ah, Miss Makepeace. If only the others were as near to God as you!' She was the daughter of the squire of Paul and far above the rest of the village in breeding and status. Yet she admired him, looked up to him! He felt again the thrill of nervousness run through him.

If he were turned down by the Methodists, if he were not accepted for ordination, he would lose all this. No more admiration, no more reverence, no more acceptance by those who were socially his superiors. And it could all so easily happen. If they saw that Charlotte was defying him, if she made him look small in the eyes of the villagers, then all this could be taken away from him. *It must not happen.*

He dragged his mind back to the present. 'To have the approbation of such as you, dear Miss Makepeace...' He smiled warmly into her blue eyes, small and sharp behind metal pince nez, and saw an answering gleam. No, he would not risk losing this – not for anybody. He would carry out his plan.

She smiled thinly. 'Your dear wife isn't here again, I see.'

'She is worn out helping those poor Spargos,' Trevennan said shortly. He disliked having Bertha present if Charlotte wasn't there to look after her. Each year his wife's emotional state grew worse. When Charlotte was present she could be trusted to prevent her mother from leaping to her feet, confessing her sinfulness, but Charlotte was comforting the Spargos and without her it was better that Bertha remained at home.

The thought of Charlotte reminded him that he had another call to make tonight and he mustn't be too late. He gave one last squeeze and released the hand. 'I have to hurry away, I'm afraid. Duty calls.'

She nodded understandingly. 'Those poor Spargo women.' She automatically leapt to the desired conclusion. 'Of course you must comfort them in their bereavement.' She sighed. 'The Lord gives and the Lord taketh away.'

'Exactly so, Miss Makepeace.' He bowed to her. 'Mrs Spargo is fortunate in one respect. Her youngest son, Richard, should have been at sea but due to a broken leg...'

Miss Makepeace clasped her hands. 'The ways of the Lord are strange, my dear Mr Trevennan. Who would think that a broken leg—'

'Strange indeed,' he intoned, anxious to hurry her away. Even stranger was the fact that the boy had broken his leg falling into the harbour when rolling drunk out of the Ship Inn one night. *Not* one of the saved. But perhaps after this, when he saw the comfort that William Trevennan brought to his widowed mother and the delectable Susan, Richard Spargo, too, might be converted. But Trevennan knew that would not happen if he were made to look a fool by his own daughter.

It seemed an age before he finally handed the voluble spinster out of the door, but once she had gone the others were easier to get rid of. They were too in awe of him to initiate long conversations, and in a short time he was locking the door of the meeting room behind him and preparing for the steep pull up Paul Hill.

The Star Inn pulsated with noise and heat. The rank smell of unwashed skin combined with the

132

harsh scent of the beer in the great barrels lined up against the wall and the ever-present tang of fish that permeated the whole of Newlyn.

Kit Hargraves sat against the wall, his empty glass in front of him. It wasn't the public house he would have chosen, but drinking in Mousehole was an experience he never wanted to repeat.

No matter that the Methodists were all teetotal and would never enter an inn, no matter that the drinkers were consigned to hell by William Trevennan; the truth was that even in the smoky recesses of the Ship Inn or behind the solid granite front of the Keigwin Arms his influence could be felt. The sudden silence when Kit entered, the backs ostentatiously turned, the slow, unwilling service – all had shown him that William Trevennan's anger could be felt even there, where he never set foot.

In Newlyn the preacher's edict ran less strong. Already Kit had learned that there was little love lost between the two villages, and although men here might acknowledge Trevennan's spiritual influence, they were also inclined to enjoy cocking a snook at anyone from Mousehole so that, although he wasn't exactly welcome, Kit was at least served with a modicum of respect. And besides, he needed a drink. He had worked hard on the *Faith-Lily* and the Star Inn, at least, was close to where she was still moored.

But it was time to be going. Tomorrow, he would see Charlotte, tell her he was moving on, collect the money that she already owed him. As he got to his feet, the door opened and he saw

133

Peggy May pushing her way out into the rain. Under her tawdry finery she looked thin and cold and his heart went out to her.

He had a place for the night with the Jelberts and had had enough to drink. The poor creature could do with the few shillings he had left in his pocket. He set out after her, dodging round the clusters of riotous drinkers, ducking under the low beams, half-seen in the dim and evil smelling oil lamps that threatened to knock him out.

The wind had got up again while he had been inside, and Kit was thankful that he and Granfer-John had put the ballast back in the *Faith-Lily*, using huge, rounded stones from the shore, raised with the help of a sling they had cobbled together. At least she would ride out this blow without any help.

The woman's figure was almost out of sight on the dark road, just the faint glimmer of her white petticoats showing where she was. Kit hurried after her, feeling in his pockets for his loose change. 'Peggy!' She came to an immediate halt, turning to him with an eagerness that betrayed her desperation. He held out the money he had left. 'Here. It's all I've got.'

She stared down at the pitiful handful of coins in his palm. 'I've only got a small room, sir, but you're welcome – for a short time, that is.'

'No.' He could feel himself growing hot with embarrassment. 'That isn't what I meant. This is for you. To keep.'

'Charity, you mean, sir.' Her voice was dubious, trembling between want and dignity.

'Charity, my arse,' he said coarsely. 'You earn it,

living here with this sanctimonious crowd.' She stood in front of him, thin, bowed down and suddenly his anger erupted.

'For God's sake, girl,' he took hold of her shoulder and shook it lightly, 'get out of this place. Go somewhere else where you can start again.'

'And what could I do, sir?' There was a world of weariness in her voice. 'I've got no skills, no money. And after what I've done for the last few years – well, you can see my history in my face. No one would ever give me a respectable job now, sir. I've got no future.'

Her acceptance of her lot infuriated him. 'But there must be something – someone...'

'No one, sir. But thank you.' She leaned forward and kissed him lightly on the cheek and he could smell her sour breath and unwashed clothes. 'If you want to come along, sir – well, I reckon I could do you an all-nighter for the same money.' She shrugged in dumb acceptance. 'There'll be no one else on a night like this, anyhow.'

The cane slashed between them, cutting her across the shoulders, lancing pain across Kit's arm. 'What the hell?' he demanded, swinging around.

'Whoring again, Peggy May?' The voice was educated, fat with complacency. 'It really is time I sent you to the House of Correction for a good, long time.'

'What the devil do you mean?' Kit squared up to the half-seen figure. 'How dare you hit that woman!'

135

The man stared at him. Even in the dim light Kit could see that rich soft sheen on his top hat. 'Annoyed that I have ruined your evening, my man? But she is a very low whore, you know. You could get better.'

Kit gritted his teeth. 'I am not looking for a whore,' he said furiously. 'I was just talking to this woman and you assaulted her.'

'Talking?' The other man reached out and caught the girl's wrist, twisting it so that the coins she was holding flew from her fingers, scattering to the darkness, bouncing melodiously off the cobbles before they disappeared. 'I thought that was evidence that you had paid her.'

'Then you thought wrong,' Kit snarled. He reached out, catching the man by the collar, pressing him back against the wall. 'Apologise to the lady.'

'What lady?' The other voice had lost its arrogance now and sounded truculent with fright. 'She's just a whore.'

'Whatever she is, she doesn't deserve treatment like that.' Kit was aware of Peggy May scrabbling in the darkness at his feet, trying to find the money she had dropped. 'Get up,' he said shortly. 'Leave it.'

'But it was good money.' There was a brief flash of light as the door of the Star Inn opened to let out a reeling crowd of men and she dived for a coin as it gleamed momentarily.

'Get up,' Kit insisted harshly. 'This – *gentleman* – will make good your loss.'

That pulled her to her feet. 'But he's a Magistrate,' she said, horrified.

'Then he will be able to afford it, won't he?' Kit's fingers tightened on the other man's collar. 'Pay up.'

The newcomer squirmed but could not break free. 'Let me go.' There was panic in the voice now. 'I'll have you up for this. I'll have the police onto you. I'll have you locked away.'

'And *I'll* have that money off you first,' Kit said implacably. 'Now pay up.'

There was a clatter of feet on the damp cobbles as the men from the inn approached, their ribald comments dying away as they recognised the participants in the little tableau. Silent as a herd of curious cows they watched the scene in front of them.

Under their interested gaze the man struggled harder but Kit merely tightened his grasp on his collar until he was choking. 'Money for the lady.'

Faced with the silent interest of the crowd, with the ever-tightening grip, the man gave in. He fumbled one-handed in his pocket. 'Here.' His voice was a strangled gasp.

'Give it to the lady,' Kit directed, and grinned secretly at the flash of gold. A sovereign. Peggy May had done well out of this transaction tonight.

'Now go.' He released his prisoner with a push that sent him staggering through the surrounding men, who moved swiftly out of the way. 'Are you all right?' He turned to the girl who was staring down at the coin that lay in her grubby palm.

'Oh, sir.' She raised eyes huge with astonishment to him. 'All this.'

'You deserve it,' Kit said shortly. 'That bastard

137

had no right to hit you.'

'But he's a Magistrate.' There was awe and acceptance in her voice.

'That was even more reason for him to behave like a gentleman,' Kit snapped.

He looked at the girl, still gazing in delight at the coin in her hand and he reached out and closed her fingers over it. 'Go,' he urged her. 'Use the money to get away from this place.'

She opened her mouth but he laid a finger across her lips, silencing her. 'I know what you're going to say, but this *is* a chance for a new beginning. There might be a new life for you away from here. Take this as an omen and go.'

She nodded. 'But what about you, sir?'

'Me?' The others had moved on now and the two of them were alone. 'What do you mean?'

She nodded towards the road that her assailant had taken. 'Well, him. Mr Polruan. He's a Magistrate and he has a lot of power in Newlyn.'

'And you think I should be afraid of him?' Kit broke out into a genuine laugh. 'Let me tell you, lady, he's the second so-called important person I've upset today. And both of them together won't cause me to lose a moment's sleep.'

He looked down at her, quirking an eyebrow. 'Whatever do you think Mr Polruan could do to me?'

Chapter Ten

'There's a – person – to see you, sir.'

Frederick Polruan turned angrily on the butler who had opened the door to him. 'Well, I can't see him. I can't see anybody.' He let the man close the heavy front door and handed over his hat and cane with hands that still trembled. He stood for a second in front of the looking-glass that hung over the hall table, straightening his dark hair.

The woman had been a prostitute, plying her trade in front of him as brazenly as could be. And when he remonstrated, when he had acted quite correctly to stop her evil traffic, that man had attacked him. Him! A Magistrate! Not to mention making him look a fool in front of all those men.

He wiped the sweat from his brow with a large handkerchief. It wasn't right. He shouldn't have to put up with this. His father had never been treated in this way. Even though he never stood on his dignity, always had a laughing word for any Tom, Dick or Harry that he met in the street, his father had always been respected, while he, who acted like a gentleman...

He became aware that the butler was speaking again. 'What?' he demanded irascibly. 'What did you say?'

'The – person – said that it was very important

that you should see him. Important for you,' the servant repeated. Frederick looked at him doubtfully. Under the correct exterior there was a hint of excitement. He felt the butler knew more than he was saying. Had he been gossiping with this man?

He wanted to tell the butler to send him away; he was anxious to think what he should do about the way he had been treated; send a servant for one of the seven policemen who manned Penzance? Issue a warrant? But the size and assurance of his adversary concerned him. He wasn't one of the usual fishermen who could be intimidated by Frederick Polruan's name and position. What if he argued his case? What if he made Frederick appear in the wrong?

He gnawed at his bottom lip, trying to reach a decision. 'Who is this man?'

'A Mr Trevennan, sir. A local preacher.'

And the father of that blasted woman in the office. Had *he* come to complain on her behalf about some imaginary slight? Frederick hesitated, tempted to instruct the butler to send the man away. But Trevennan had mentioned that what he had to say was important for Polruan. Oh, why was life so deuced difficult?

He wavered a few more seconds, still mopping his brow then came to a decision. 'Send him in,' he said abruptly, 'and bring in some brandy.' God knows he needed it after that scene. Who would have thought that any man in that position, caught handing over money to a prostitute, would have been so brazen as to complain about her entirely proper correction by a Magistrate?

He thrust open the door of the library so that it banged back against the wall, then seated himself behind the shining protection of his father's – no, *his* desk. Around him, the tooled leather bindings gleamed softly in the lamplight, though some were marked with use. It always annoyed him that certain of the books showed these signs, but that was another area in which he and his father had disagreed. 'Do you expect me to buy all the new books and not read them?' His father had hooted with laughter. 'What a dolt you must think me to be.'

Well, they were *his* books now, and the most recent additions, ordered by his father, had just come back from the binders. He could read their titles as they stood in the mahogany, glass-fronted bookcases in their unsullied glory. *Tom Brown's Schooldays, Barchester Towers,* even that book there had been all the fuss about – *Origin of the Species.*

Suddenly diverted, he moved across and opened the door, pulling the book free, just as the door opened.

He hurried back to the protection of his desk. 'Mr Trevennan, you wished to see me.' He paused for a second then decided against offering his hand. The man was only a fisherman, after all; it did no good to let these people get above themselves. Instead he busied himself by aligning the book squarely with the edge of his blotter. 'What do you have to say?'

Without waiting for an invitation, William Trevennan moved forward, pressing his broad, red hands onto the shining wood of the desk.

'There has been an injustice done, an abomination in the sight of God. I demand that you should help to rectify it.'

More than one abomination, Frederick thought, remembering his recent run-in with the stranger. He eyed the fisherman's hands nervously. He had no right to lean on his desk, it wasn't respectful, but somehow William Trevennan's voice, his very presence, exuded such authority that Frederick couldn't reprimand him.

He swallowed and compromised. 'Won't you sit down and tell me the problem.'

'Problem?' The rich voice vibrated with scorn. 'Problems are for men to deal with; what I have to complain about is sin.' The very air seemed to shake with horror as the word rolled off his tongue.

'Well, what is it?' Frederick asked weakly. The man still hadn't sat down and he didn't like to insist. It was a relief when the library door opened silently and the butler appeared with the brandy.

All conversation was suspended as the man trod slowly to the desk and deposited the tray with its precious burden at Frederick's elbow. Polruan stared at it longingly, his mouth dry with anticipation. He needed that drink, God knew; first the confrontation in the village and now Charlotte's father. He barely waited until the door had closed behind the butler before his hand reached out for the decanter.

Do not touch that poison.

The voice roared out suddenly, making him

142

jump, his fingers instinctively darting back from the glass. It took him a couple of seconds before he could bring himself to bluster, 'This is my home, you know. You have no right to tell me what to do.'

'I have every right.' William Trevennan pointed a thick finger at him. 'I have the right of a God-fearing citizen, I have the right of a preacher, I have the right as an honest man.' His self-righteousness seemed to clothe him in an invincible armour which Frederick didn't feel able to break through.

Frederick pulled his hands back into his lap to hide their trembling. 'Very well, as you are a guest here I will bow to your – wishes.' He regretted that he had not the courage to call them 'vagaries' but feared another explosion. He cleared his throat. 'You still haven't told me what you want,' he reminded the man.

Trevennan moved away and lowered his thick body into a chair, to Frederick's relief. 'Your father made what I can only describe as a regrettable provision in his will. He left my daughter a drifter.'

It was such a relief to meet someone who shared his views of the subject that Frederick felt himself warming to the man despite his odd behaviour. 'Believe me, you can regret it no more than I do,' he said earnestly.

The blue eyes surveyed him coldly. 'I doubt that,' Trevennan snapped. 'You have merely lost a small part of your large inheritance; I am in danger of losing the respect of my congregation. And all because my daughter will not allow me to

143

captain her boat as she is bound to do by the Scriptures.'

His face darkened, the cheeks, already reddened by the salt air, assuming a purple hue. 'Instead, she is going to allow her boat to be sailed by a stranger!' His voice shook with anger. 'A man without character or background.' He leaned forward, lowering his voice. 'I fear – I very much fear that she has been led astray by her animal passions. All that this young man has to recommend him are his height and looks.' He shook his head. 'That a Christian woman, brought up as she has been, should be tempted so easily! It is true that sin is everywhere, and that no man or woman is safe unless he puts his trust in God.'

But the description had caught Frederick's attention. 'A young man, very tall, with fair hair, well-spoken?' he asked.

'If you call anyone well-spoken who calls not to the Lord as he should,' William interposed morosely. 'But you know the man?'

A small surge of triumph lightened Frederick's features. 'I caught him just now entering into a transaction with a known prostitute,' he said.

'A lecher.' William Trevennan's face contorted abruptly. 'My poor daughter. But it is ever the same; like calls to like.' He sighed. 'But now that I know, I am forewarned. I can pray with her, help her to resist the lures of the flesh, the terrible burnings in the loins, the lecherous longings sent from Satan.'

He continued earnestly: 'It is even more necessary that you should help me assert my

144

paternal influence, separate my child from this man, save her from a life of sin, reinstate my authority in the village and the Church to whom I have given my life.'

'But what can *I* do?' Frederick Polruan asked, bewildered.

Trevennan rose to his feet. 'Stop leading her into temptation,' he said. 'It is because she has worked like a man that she has forgotten her duties and position as a woman. Take that away from her, let her be dependent again on her father as an unmarried Christian woman should be, and all these crotchets will disappear. She will forget her caprices, learn again to honour her parents, and she will once more humble herself as she should before the desires of her father.' He thumped the desk with one of his large fists. 'Sack her,' he demanded, his voice suddenly harsh.

Frederick had to fight to keep a foolish grin off his face. He had been tempted to sack Charlotte ever since he had heard about the will; he was only waiting for a good opportunity. If even her father wanted the woman sacked… But for the sake of appearances, he had to put up some show of reluctance. 'What about–' he began.

Trevennan held up one hand, stopping him. 'I know what you are going to say; that we will miss the money she brings in. But what is money compared to a woman's virtue?' he demanded rhetorically. 'Where the disciples could be poor, should William Trevennan desire to be otherwise? Besides,' he went on, in a more normal voice, 'once I become an ordained minister I shall, in any case, earn more than enough to make up for the loss of her salary.'

Ordained minister! Frederick had never met anybody less suitable, but that wasn't his concern, thank heaven. He was a good Anglican and as such, he knew enough not to let religion take over his life. He rang the bell for the butler to show Trevennan out then sat, thinking deeply.

Tomorrow was only a half-day. In celebration of the opening of the bridge across the Tamar, the Town Council had proclaimed a half-holiday, and there would be a procession of local dignitaries from the railway station to the Town Hall in which he, as a Magistrate, would have to take part. But that would still leave him plenty of time to sack Charlotte tomorrow morning. She was only his employee – and a woman to boot, he reminded himself as his heart lurched nervously at the thought of the scene ahead of him. There was no reason to be afraid of her. If she caused a problem he could always get the other clerks to throw her out.

The decanter of brandy caught his eye but such was the power of Trevennan's influence that it was several minutes before he could pour himself a glass – and then only after he had made sure that the Methodist had left the house.

The knock on the door seemed to reverberate through the tiny cottage. 'Oh, no!' Charlotte stood motionless in her bedroom, her shawl in her hands, head cocked as she strained her ears to hear who it might be. She mustn't be late for work. Frederick Polruan was already angry with her because of the will, she didn't want to upset him any further.

'Oh, Mr er…' Her mother's voice, troubled and uncertain, and then a voice she couldn't mistake.

'Mrs Trevennan – how pleasant to meet you again. I hope you have recovered from your recent accident?'

Charlotte grimaced. She had hoped to avoid Kit until this evening. After the revelations yesterday of his drinking and womanising, she needed time to decide what to do – and time was exactly what he was not giving her.

'Charlotte! Charlotte!' Her mother's voice sounded excited now. Surely she couldn't think that Kit was a 'caller'? Taking a deep breath, Charlotte made her way slowly down the narrow, steep stairs into the kitchen.

Even though he had been constantly on her mind she had forgotten how big he was. His head seemed to brush the dark, twisted beams – remnants, like most of the wood in the village, of some ancient shipwreck. His fair hair gleamed in the early-morning light streaming in through the thick, distorting glass of the window.

Charlotte ignored the sudden erratic thumping of her heart. I am a businesswoman, she reminded herself firmly. This is my employee. She bowed her head briefly. 'Mr Briars.'

For a second he looked disconcerted and she felt a stab of sadness as her thoughts of yesterday were again confirmed. He had lied to her about his name. Then he smiled brilliantly, moving easily forward. 'My apologies.' He seemed as comfortable as if he were an old family friend. 'I have become so used to hearing you spoken of as Charlotte that it seemed strange for a moment to hear you so formal.'

The ease and speed with which the spurious reason came from his lips only confirmed her suspicions that he was a reprobate. Unable to meet his eyes, she stared past him through the window to the small harbour, almost empty now as most of the fishing boats had left on the morning tide. 'I owe you your money, Mr Briars.' Her voice sounded bleak and empty in her ears.

He gave an easy grin. 'It would be very welcome. I have been staying with the Jelberts since I saw you last and I should repay them for their kindness.'

She hadn't even known that! Her father had kept her in almost complete isolation all week, lecturing her as he accompanied her to work, praying over her every evening. Last night had been the first respite she had had, and then she had learned enough from Robert and Susan to know that all her preconceptions about this man had been wrong. She had looked on him as her saviour and he turned out to be seeped in sin.

She turned away quickly in case her feelings showed in her eyes. 'I shall get the money I owe you.'

Her small store of savings was hidden under a loose floorboard she had discovered as a child. Then she had kept in it her secret treasures – sweets called 'clidgy-nicies' that kindly villagers sometimes pressed on her, magic stones with a hole in that she had found on the beach. Now it contained a pair of earrings that Charles Polruan had once given her and which she had never dared to wear and, more useful, the bonuses all the staff had received at Christmas or whenever the firm had done particularly well.

She knew that she should have handed these over to her father as she had given him her wages each week, but he had never known of their existence and she had never told him, hiding them from him as if they were a guilty secret, knowing that this might at some time be all she and her mother could rely on.

Now, this small store of money might be enough to let her work her own boat. She counted out the sum they had agreed, feeling furtive and guilty as if her father were likely to walk in at any moment. The payment, small as it was, made a noticeable dent in her savings. She pushed the coins back into their hiding place with a heavy heart.

It was ridiculous to feel cheated and resentful; Kit had kept his word, payed up the *Faith-Lily* as they had agreed. He deserved the money he had earned. So what if he was a drinker and a lecher? He was merely her employee. How he spent his time after he'd finished working for her boat had nothing to do with her. Nothing.

She hurried downstairs. 'Here.' She knew that she was being ungracious but she didn't care. She held out the handful of coins towards him.

He raised his eyebrows, so much darker than his fair curling hair. 'Is that all you are going to say?'

She just wanted him to go, leave her alone. 'Mr Briars,' she said hastily, 'I have to go. I am already

149

late for work.'

'I'll accompany you,' he said calmly. 'We can talk on the way.' He moved to where Bertha stood by the fire, fiddling uneasily with some pans, made nervous by the presence of a stranger. 'Goodbye, Mrs Trevennan. It was pleasant to meet you again.'

To Charlotte's surprise her mother dropped a curtsey, strangely elegant after the bobs with which most of the village women greeted a social superior. For a second, under the faded looks and drab clothes, Charlotte caught a glimpse of a smart young lady's maid her mother had once been. 'Good morning, sir.'

'Now then.' Kit turned back to Charlotte, offering her his arm. 'If you will do me the honour...'

What would all the villagers think if they saw her walking arm-in-arm through the streets with a young man? What would her father say when he heard of it? Charlotte threw an anxious glance at her mother, but Bertha seemed to have regressed to her youth, to a time when young ladies did not walk without an escort. She smiled reassuringly at her daughter and Charlotte had no option but to accept the offer.

The startled looks that followed them as they climbed the steep streets did nothing to ease Charlotte's mind. She had become accustomed, in this past week, to being ignored, to seeing men and women who had known her from a child, turn from her and she accepted it even though their actions tore at her heart. To have a stranger witness her disgrace merely added to her misery.

But, even before her father had branded her a sinner in front of the whole congregation, the sight of the towering Miss Trevennan with a young man would have aroused interest and gossip. Now, her status as the black sheep of the village simply added to their interest. And what did they know of Kit? Charlotte worried as she walked by his side past unspeaking, staring villagers. How many others, apart from Richard Spargo, knew of his drinking and womanising?

During their walk through the village, Kit kept up a polite easy conversation about the weather and the history of the area as though he was unaware of the villagers reactions – although she could tell by the rigidity of his grip on her elbow that inside he was less relaxed than he seemed. It was only when they had passed the last house – a ramshackle cottage with a badly dipping thatched roof – that he turned to her, his face set with anger.

'Granfer-John told me about the way the villagers were treating you, but I didn't believe it.' His voice rose. 'Damn it, they've known you from a child. How can they treat you like this?'

Her shame was too great to let her meet his gaze, but some remaining loyalty to the people amongst whom she had grown up forced her to defend them.

'They are good people. They are following what my father told them, only doing what they think is right.'

'Right? *Right?*' The grip on her elbow grew fiercer. 'How can they think it right? What have you done differently from what any of them would have done? You only want to find a way of making your boat as profitable as you can.'

Hearing someone else echoing her own thoughts made her want to cry. She swallowed, grateful that she was not the only one in the world who thought as she did. 'But I am disobeying my father,' she whispered.

He snorted. 'A sanctimonious prig if ever there was one! He only uses religion for his own ends.'

She could not allow that to pass. 'He is a very good preacher,' she insisted, half surprised, half ashamed to be defending him in this way. 'He may soon become a Methodist minister.'

'Him?' Kit swung round to stare at her, his blue eyes frosty in his tanned face. 'A man like that? A man who abuses his position to try to further his own ends? He'll never be appointed.'

The very thought made her stop in amazement. Of course her father would be appointed – and if he weren't, it could only be her fault. As if he had read her mind, Kit squeezed her arm, smiling reassuringly down at her. 'The Methodists are decent people, you know, and they're not fools. They will only choose men for their Ministry who they are sure of. And they are only concerned with the man himself, not with his family so you don't need to worry about that.'

His easy assumption of superiority infuriated her. Pulling herself up to her full height, Charlotte said coldly, 'Neither I nor my father need your reassurance, Mr Briars.'

He grinned down at her. 'Won't you call me Kit? It's far more friendly.'

'Far too friendly,' she rapped out. 'I would have

152

you remember that I am your employer.'

This made him laugh outright. 'And you told me that a boat-owner wasn't a lady!' His blue eyes were brilliant in the early-morning sunshine. 'Yet, here you are, putting me down as if you had been born into the aristocracy.'

Charlotte felt herself blushing. All her life she had tried, as her father taught, to be properly modest and humble yet Kit could drive her to acting in ways she despised. Unconsciously, she quickened her pace, trying to reach the end of her journey as quickly as possible. 'You had better leave me now, I must hurry or I shall be late.'

He pulled a great, gold watch from his pocket and flicked it open. Charlotte stared at it. The soft gleam of gold, the ornate chasing around the monogram, all told her that this watch was worth a lot of money. What was a man with a watch like this doing working on her boat for a pittance? Who was he? Even as she stared, Kit snapped the watch shut and for a second the sun caught the monogram so that the entwined letters stood out clearly. *CH*.

'You have plenty of time.' He caught her startled gaze and pushed the watch swiftly back into his pocket. 'Tell me, will you be going to the procession this afternoon?'

She stared at him. She had forgotten that today was a half-holiday to celebrate the opening of the railway bridge across the Tamar – by order of the Mayor. Although the railway line had been installed from Penzance to Truro seven years earlier and although trains ran from Plymouth to

153

London, there had never been a rail-link between Truro and Plymouth.

Goods sent 'up-country' as the Cornish called it, had to be unloaded from the train at Truro and put onto a stage-coach which was then driven north and ferried across the Tamar before being reloaded onto the railway at Plymouth.

But now Mr Isambard Kingdom Brunel had built a bridge across the river and today it was due to be opened by Prince Albert himself; the Penzance Corporation had ordered a half-holiday in celebration.

She paused. 'My father wouldn't let me.' The words came out instinctively.

He stopped, swinging round to look at her. 'Your father is at sea.'

That made no difference. 'He will expect...' she began.

'Are you going to spend your life doing what your father wants – or are you going to do what *you* want?' he demanded.

No one had ever encouraged her to open rebellion against him before. The thought was suddenly exhilarating. And if Kit was going to invite her to accompany him... Despite her doubts about him she felt a thrill of excitement. 'Well...' she began.

But his face was dark with anger. 'Your father...' He stopped, staring at her then raised his hat. 'Goodbye, Miss Trevennan. I'm afraid I have to leave you here.'

The disappointment was overwhelming. 'But I thought–' She caught herself in time. He was no good, anyway. A liar, a drinker, she wouldn't have dreamed of going to see the procession with him. She raised her head proudly. 'Goodbye, Mr Briars. Don't let me keep you.' Her voice was icy.

She turned and walked swiftly off without waiting for an answer. This was the best way. Pay him off, forget him; he was nothing to her, nothing at all. At the next corner she just happened to glance behind her but he was already out of sight.

Chapter Eleven

'That's all very well, lad, but you don't know "A" from the track of a duck, not where fishing's concerned.' Granfer-John pulled his evil-smelling pipe from his mouth and pointed the chewed end at Kit.

Kit frowned at him across the small room, barely lit by the bright sunshine outside. 'I know how to sail a boat, and I can learn.' Now that he had reached a decision he was in no mood to let anything turn him from his course.

He hit his knee with a clenched fist. 'I will not let that – that sanctimonious bastard treat Charlotte like that. I will not let him win.' His face was set, his eyes blue chips of ice. 'I don't care what I have to do, I'll sail that boat and teach him a lesson. I'll damn well *learn* how to fish!' He took a deep shaking breath. 'How dare he treat her like that!'

Granfer's face was sympathetic but life had made him severely practical. 'You can't teach nobody a lesson if you can't fish,' he pointed out. 'And who do you think you're going to larn from? Not from any of they louts you'll get to crew for you, not if you pick them from around here you won't.' He spat. 'They don't know nothing, most of them. They wouldn't even recognise "Royal Purple" in good light, let alone from the smell.'

Kit glanced up. 'Royal Purple?'

'There. What did I tell 'ee?' Granfer-John asked triumphantly. ''Tes when there's a shoal of pilchards under the surface and all the sea has gone purple with the oil of the millions of them, and the smell...' He grinned reminiscently. 'In my day I could smell the fish but today the youngsters don't know nothing! Even Phil Trevelyan can't navigate from the echoes off his foghorn like what I could as a lad, and he's about the best, I reckon.'

'Then I won't be any worse than they are, will I?' Kit said impatiently.

'Nay,' Granfer-John continued, 'it won't do, lad. You do know how to sail a boat, my handsome, but you've got to know the weather, you've got to know the tides, and you've got to know the fish and the fishing grounds.' He took another deep pull on his pipe. 'There's none o' that can be learned in a week or even a month.'

Kit stared down the long length of his legs to his feet. His socks had worn through and there was a hole in one heel; he poked at it while he tried to think of a solution. There was no way he was going to let that bully of a local preacher win in this. The *Faith-Lily* was Charlotte's boat, and Kit was determined that she should get the full benefit from her.

'You'd better give that there sock to me and I'll crafe 'en home for 'ee,' Granfer said. 'You don't want to be walking far with no gert tatey like that in yer hosen.'

Kit looked up, his face breaking into a sudden grin. 'You?'

'Well, and why not?' the old man demanded crossly. 'I may be old as Methuselah but I still got all my faculties.'

Kit paused in the act of removing his sock. 'That's true,' he agreed. He glanced up at the old man from under his brows. 'I bet you know as much as any of the men out fishing now.'

'They?' The old man's eyebrows bristled furiously. 'I've forgot more than they'll ever know, the gert lummocks.'

Kit was still doubled over, his fingers playing with his holed sock. 'And you're a hale old man for your age.'

Granfer-John sat up abruptly, staring at Kit disbelievingly. 'Here, your wits have gone begging. You're not thinking I could work on that there boat, are you?'

Kit straightened, the sock in his hand. 'I was, actually.'

'Then you're as daft as a brush!' the old man said forthrightly. 'Me, with my rheumatics an' all – you expect *me* to work on a drifter at my age!' He spat into the dying fire. 'I couldn't no more work they nets than I could walk up Paul Hill on my hands.' He shook his head. 'It idn't on, lad. You need five or six strong men to work they boats, as you'd know well enough if you'd ever done it. There's no place for an old un who can't do his share.'

'But you could do mine,' Kit suggested.

'I don't get you.'

Kit was sitting upright now, his blue eyes blazing in the flickering light of the oil lamp. 'As I understand it, each man on the boat gets a

158

certain share of the catch.'

'That's right.' Granfer-John nodded, his white beard shining softly in the dimness. 'The men get six nets each, the captain and the owner ten each.'

'So, as the captain, I get ten nets,' Kit insisted.

'That's if you catch anything.' Granfer-John wasn't going to be sweet-talked into anything. 'You'll be lucky to come home with half a dozen bully-heads, with what you know.'

'But if we share the ten nets between us?' Kit rose to his feet, his fair hair almost brushing the low beams that crossed the ceiling. 'If I do the hard work and you provide the knowledge, we should do all right.'

'You'd give up half your share?' The old man's voice rose incredulously. 'That'll give you less than the men.'

'You, too,' Kit pointed out. He grinned at Granfer-John. 'But you'll be more than earning your share. You'll not only have to do all the navigation, you'll have to teach me as well.'

He watched as the old man puffed slowly at his pipe. 'You'll need more men than just us two, even if you are tall as Paul Church tower.'

'No one will work the boat from this village or Newlyn,' Kit admitted. 'But there must be somewhere round here where Trevennan's word doesn't hold sway.'

'The Barbican in Penzance is the only place.'

Kit grimaced. Even in his short time in the area he had heard of the place. It was by the Battery rocks, only yards from the sea but the atmosphere there was as noisome as any slum in

Hull. Only those who had sunk to their lowest would live in conditions like that. 'There are fishermen there?' He could not keep the doubt out of his voice.

'Men who were fishermen live there,' the old man corrected. 'They don't fish much now. Drink, mostly, or women.' He spat. 'There are many ways to fall lower in this life and brem few to get back up again.' He put down his pipe. 'Here. You'd better give me that sock to mend or you'll be getting chilbladders, standing around on the stone flags in your naked feet.'

Kit held out the sock then hesitated. 'I'd better wash it first,' he said doubtfully.

Granfer-John snorted. 'If we'm going to live together on a drifter, my lad, we'm going to have to get used to worse smells than that.' He reached out and plucked the sock from Kit's hand. 'And no matter how bad we smell, I reckon they varmints from the Barbican will be riper than ever we'll get – and that's before we've left harbour.'

Kit grinned. Suddenly everything was settled. 'That's what you think,' he laughed. He stretched, his hands brushing the cobwebs that festooned the ceiling. 'I wonder what Charlotte will say when I tell her this afternoon.'

'Miss Trevennan, where are the accounts for Bailey's that I asked for?'

Charlotte raised her head from where she was kneeling on the floor, searching through dusty boxes of invoices. 'But I thought that you wanted to see the old Smithson papers, Mr Polruan?' she said wearily. Frederick Polruan had been driving her crazy all morning asking for records that no one had used for years. She hadn't even had time to think about the scene with Kit. It was a good thing Polruan was due in Penzance for the procession this afternoon or she would be exhausted.

She heard his heavy footsteps and glanced up as he appeared at the door of this office. 'Are you saying I don't know what I want, Miss Trevennan?'

It was exactly what she thought, but the tone of his voice warned her and she scrambled stiffly to her feet. 'No, of course not. Sir.'

Despite her best intentions her tone expressed her feelings and his face hardened. 'This isn't good enough, Miss Trevennan.'

Don't argue with him, she told herself, he's just looking for an excuse. 'I am sorry, sir.' She lowered her eyes submissively, ducking her head so that she should not annoy him further by looming over him. 'I have looked through all the boxes that have been kept. Perhaps some records have been removed elsewhere for safekeeping?'

Frederick Polruan shook his head, his pink cheeks wobbling slightly. 'Surely you should know. After all, the men have outside work to attend to; you are only employed in the office.'

Charlotte gritted her teeth, knowing that she did not only her own office work but also a lot that should have been done by the men. It was easier to offer to take the clerical duties from them than to try to correct their errors afterwards. 'Your father never thought that I shirked my duties.'

As soon as she said it she realised it was a mistake. She saw him draw himself up, puffing out his chest in an attempt at manliness.

'My father, may I remind you, is dead.' The word seemed to reverberate around the small office and Charlotte was suddenly aware that even the slight scritch of the pens of the other clerks had ceased as they watched the scene unfolding before them with fascinated eyes. Frederick breathed in, drawing himself up. 'I am the owner now.'

She knew what was coming and bit her lips lest they trembled and gave her away. 'Yes, sir.' Despite her best efforts, the words sounded derisive rather than submissive.

He was working himself up, trying for anger to protect himself from her. 'I will not have a lazy clerk, do you understand?'

'Yes, sir.' Her breath was catching in her throat. Fear flooded through her, fear of the future, of poverty, of degradation. But it was all so unfair. She was better than him, a better clerk, a harder worker – and they both knew it. He was only taking this opportunity to get his own back on her. He would ruin her life for the sake of his petty self-importance.

Suddenly, her anger blazed. He was going to sack her anyway so what did it matter? She might as well tell him, just this once, what she really thought of him. She raised her head, her eyes blazing, and took a deep breath. 'It seems to me, Mr Polruan, that if you think I should be doing more, then it is ridiculous of you to have me

162

wasting my time searching through all this rubbish for something I am sure never existed.'

He stepped backwards, almost as if she had hit him, and she saw a fleeting expression of panic on his face. It was all the encouragement she needed. Now she had no reason to bother about making herself appear small and meek. She had burned her boats and might as well enjoy it.

She moved towards him, head high so that she made the most of her height. 'You're jealous!' Her voice vibrated with scorn. 'You keep putting me down because I'm a woman, but all the time you know that I'm a better businessman than you, better at figures, better at getting on with people – and more intelligent!'

He almost ducked as she spat out the last word and she laughed. 'You're even jealous because your father left me a boat.' She pointed a finger at him. 'What is that worth, Mr Polruan? You are supposed to be a businessman, so proud of your new lugger – can you tell me what it is worth?'

He didn't answer and she laughed again, triumphantly. 'Two hundred pounds. Two hundred pounds, Mr Polruan. Together with a set of seine nets and boats that may be worth nothing because we so seldom get pilchard shoals in Mousehole now. And what did you inherit? The mansion you live in, a couple of farms, this business and the five boats that it controls. What sort of value would you put on that?'

She moved towards him and he backed away, his plump cheeks mottled. 'And you are jealous of me!' Her grey eyes burned with scorn. 'Mr Polruan, you are a *little* man, little in mind and little in soul. You aren't fit to black your father's shoes.'

He was around the other side of his desk now and she leaned across it. 'I despise you.' Her voice trembled with the strength of her emotion. 'I despise you utterly and completely. You are beneath contempt!'

He managed to find his voice. 'Get out of here.' He pointed at the door with a shaking finger. 'Get out of here and never let me see you again, you – you overgrown *trollop*.'

'I'm going.' Now that she had had her say Charlotte couldn't wait to get out of the office, away from the staring faces of the other clerks, the dusty dimness of the room, the closeness to him. She swung round, her dark skirts billowing around her and stalked to the door, grabbing her shawl and bonnet from the bentwood coat-stand as she passed.

In the entrance she turned and loosed her final salvo. 'I wonder how well this firm will do now, with *you* at its head?'

Then she spun round and left the office for ever, letting the door slam behind her with a force which she knew would shake dust down from the aged beams onto the precious ledgers.

At the front door she halted and dragged her bonnet over her head, tying the ribbons with shaking fingers. She knew that, when she was cooler, she might regret what she had just done, but for now she was glad! Glad! He was going to sack her, anyway. At least she had taken her chance to tell Frederick Polruan what she thought of him.

164

But the future stretched ahead of her, cold and bleak. What would she do without her pay every week from Polruan's? What would her mother do? How could they survive on her father's earnings?

'Light of my desire.'

Her head came up, her mouth curving into a smile. 'Senhõr Da Silva.' Hope suddenly sprang into her mind. He was a man who had contacts all over Cornwall, he might be able to help her.

She moved forward, hand outstretched. 'Senhõr–' but he took it, breaking in swiftly.

'I was coming to see you, to say goodbye.'

Her heart lurched. 'You're leaving? But…'

He nodded. 'My wife. She is ill. The fever, you understand. I must go back. My place is by her side.'

'Of course.' She ruthlessly suppressed the disappointment she felt. She knew how much he adored his wife. 'You must go immediately, Senhõr. And I pray that all will be well.'

'Bela,' he pressed her hand. 'You are so good. And I will be back, God willing.' He raised her hand to his lips then he was gone, his short legs taking him down the hill with fast, bobbing steps.

Her hand on the doorpost Charlotte stared after him. Another disappointment. So far it had been a dreadful day.

'Charlotte.'

Lost in her thoughts she hadn't even seen the tall body lounging against the wall until the sound of her name made her jerk her head up. 'Mr Briars.' She couldn't believe he was here, not

165

after the way he had left her this morning.

He grinned down at her, his teeth white in his brown face. 'I didn't know what time you would finish work so I came early.' He swept his hat off in an orate bow. 'I hope madam will condescend to allow me to accompany her to see the procession in Penzance?'

She had never even considered it before but the idea was suddenly tempting. After all, she had no job to go to and as for her father, he would doubtless be angry with her when he found out but she was beginning to find his anger less frightening than it had been. 'Yes,' the smile was suddenly real. 'I'd like that. Thank you.'

Kit replaced his hat and she noticed that he had made an effort. His hat and coat were brushed and he had attempted to shine his shoes although it was impossible to get the salt marks off the leather. She felt a flash of guilt when she remembered that he had ruined them the night they had met, when he had helped her to save the *Faith-Lily*.

She had expected him to offer her his arm, but his keen blue eyes were fixed on her face. 'Are you well? You seem – different.'

'I'm fine.' She wasn't going to let him know her business. 'Just a little tired. I've had a – hard morning.'

She wasn't sure that he believed her but he did not argue, merely taking her arm and walking by her side. 'I'm glad of that because there's something I want to ask you.'

She raised her dark brows. 'Oh?'

He stopped and turned to her, and for once

166

there was no sign of the laughter that sprang so easily to his face. 'Would you let me captain the *Faith-Lily?*'

The feeling of distrust deepened. She had learned that night on the lugger that he knew nothing about fishing and had no intention of staying in Cornwall for any length of time. Had he changed his mind because he saw her as easy to dupe? Or as a reasonably well-off lonely woman who would fall easily into his arms? The thoughts made her feel suddenly alone.

'From what you told me, Mr – Briars,' she said cautiously, 'I did not think that you knew anything about fishing – or Cornish waters.'

She saw a hurt look in his eyes and modulated her tone. 'I don't think it would be fair to expect you to act as a captain in such circumstances, do you? I doubt that either of us would get the return we would like on our time and money.' She finished more mildly.

'Would you be interested in learning that I have found a way around those difficulties?' He raised an enquiring eyebrow.

Despite herself, she felt her attention caught. In her present circumstances it was even more necessary that she should get the lugger at sea, but Kit – she knew nothing about him except what Richard Spargo had told her yesterday. How could she let a complete stranger sail her boat? He might simply sail the *Faith-Lily* up the coast and sell her. Charlotte had to have someone she could trust.

'I might be interested,' she said slowly, 'if you really have found an answer.'

From the corner of her eye she saw him nod, but 'Granfer-John,' was all he said.

'You cannot be serious!' She swung round to glare at him. 'Granfer-John is an old man,' she snapped. 'His health isn't good, he could not possibly pull in those heavy nets, yet you dare suggest–'

'Calm down.' The authoritative words cut through her anger and she gasped as he caught her shoulders, shaking her lightly. 'Of course I don't expect a man his age to work on the boat as you suggest; it would be unfair and unkind.'

He released her and she stepped quickly away from him, her heart thumping erratically. Not because of fear, she knew instinctively that he would not use violence against her, but somehow his very touch made her pulse race.

Gazing down at her, Kit went on, 'What I have to recommend depends on you, both as the owner of the lugger and as a neighbour of Granfer-John's.' There was no trace of the humour usually seen in his face, and she had to force herself to meet his blue stare. 'I know how to sail a boat, though I have never sailed a Cornish lugger or fished in this area; Granfer-John knows the ship and the fishing grounds like his own hand. I suggest that he is employed as a second captain while teaching me what he knows.'

It was a possibility, a way out of her problems and she was desperate. The memory of her small store of coins rose before her. She had to get some money in – and soon.

She cleared her throat. 'And supposing I go

168

along with this, who is to pay the wages of two captains?' she demanded.

'It won't be you,' he assured her. He caught her arm, urging her to walk beside him. 'We'll divide the captain's share between us. You may even do well out of it as I shall help with the nets, and so there may be one less crew member needed. Your responsibility lies in another area.' He glanced down at her. 'Boy-John.'

'No,' she said swiftly. 'I'm sorry, but I refuse. You cannot take a child of that age fishing.' For a second she had wavered; the plan seemed to meet all her objections, even her lack of trust in Kit. With Granfer-John aboard there was no danger that he would steal her ship. But Boy-John was too young to be allowed to live on board ship. Fishing was dangerous enough for adults; to risk the life of an eight-year-old was unacceptable.

She turned to him angrily. 'You must be mad to even think of such a thing!'

'But I didn't.' He stared down at her, his face solemn. 'There's no way I would take that child on ship, but we can't go to sea and leave the boy at home with no one to look after him. Granfer-John says that no one in the village would take him in – even if he could be persuaded to stay with them, which I gather is unlikely. If Granfer goes to sea there's only one person who can look after the boy – and that's you.'

'Me?' She was genuinely bewildered. 'But what can I do? My father wouldn't let Boy-John stay in the house. He even objects to me talking to him and I have to see the Jelberts behind his back.'

Kit snorted. 'If you think that Boy-John would even consider living in the same house as your father, you don't know the boy as well as I thought you did.'

'So what can I do?' she asked, genuinely bewildered.

'You can stay at the Jelberts' with him while Granfer-John is at sea with me.'

The very idea took her breath away. It was unheard of. Of course, single women did move away from home, but it was usually to go into service where the mistress of the house or a housekeeper would act as a careful parent, ensuring that they did not get into trouble. For a single woman to move into a house by herself, with only a child for company, was tantamount to admitting to immorality. She would lose her reputation; no respectable man would think of marrying her. But then, Charlotte reminded herself bitterly, no man would ever think of marrying her anyway. No one wanted a great gawk like her when they could have a pretty, soft little creature like Susan Spargo.

But it was a big step to take, she realised that. Once she had left home there would be no going back; ever.

Her thoughts ran round and round like a rat in a cage as she walked beside Kit. Her whole future depended on this decision. Respectability or the possibility of financial security, that was what it came down to. Unconsciously she let her stride lengthen as if by the actions of her body she could lessen the turmoil in her mind.

Lost in her thoughts, she said slowly, 'It's so

much to ask.'

'Believe me.' His voice was quiet and sincere now, and more serious than she had ever heard it before. 'If there were another answer I wouldn't ask it of you.'

Still she hesitated. He had answered one of her problems and faced her with another. How could she defy all convention and move out of her father's house, even if she was unhappy there? It was impossible.

But it was her only chance.

Chapter Twelve

Penzance was alive with excitement. Everywhere children ran and screamed, diving between the legs of adults, playing hide-and-seek around the wide skirts of the women. Arches of evergreen, decorated with flowers, met across the narrow streets and the town band played, almost unheard except for the thud of the drum that vibrated the soles of Charlotte's feet.

'I didn't know it would be like this!' She gazed around, wide-eyed at the throngs of people. The feeling of excitement was contagious, it even drove out of her mind her concerns about the future. She could feel her cheeks flush with enjoyment and turned laughingly to Kit. 'I've never seen so much–' she cast her arms wide, searching for the right word '–so much *life!* It's breathtaking!'

He smiled down at her. 'What? Overset by a small town's minor celebrations? What about when the railway was first opened, can't you remember that?'

Her face darkened. 'I wasn't allowed to come. My father...'

He pulled her arm through his, pressing it against his side. 'Don't let the thought of that man ruin your day. You're here to enjoy yourself and I shall make sure you do.' His eyes lingered on her face. 'I see too little of that lovely smile of yours, and as for your laugh – I'm amazed you haven't forgotten how!'

She smiled back at him, trying to ignore the blush she could feel on her cheeks. 'I think I'll make up for that today.' Then her face fell again. 'But what my father will say...'

He turned to her, laying a finger across her lips. 'No.' He was suddenly stern. 'We won't talk of him, we'll only talk of happy things.' Then, with a mock groan, 'I spoke too soon.'

Her heart thudded nervously. 'Not my father?' She turned to follow his gaze then her face relaxed. 'Boy-John, I didn't know you'd be here.'

He grinned around the blackness of his lost tooth, hitching up his cutdown trousers. 'Wouldn't miss this for the world, Lotty! A brem find do this'll be, what with the Mayor and all.' He glanced down the crowded street. 'Shall we go and see the train come in?' His eyes widened with pleasurable anticipation. 'If that there wind hurt the bridge, maybe it'll collapse with the train on it and all.'

'Boy-John, you are a disgrace! You can't want people hurt,' Charlotte protested.

'Well, just a little. It's a brem bad place for a bridge, anyway.' He set off down the terrace that ran down one side of Market Jew Street, casting a quick look over his shoulder to check that Charlotte and Kit were following.

Kit raised an enquiring eyebrow. 'What's so bad about this bridge?'

'Oh,' she shrugged, 'it's not even a bridge; it's a viaduct the train goes over between here and Marazion. The trouble is, it's wooden and built

173

along the sandy beach so if we get bad weather there's always a danger of it washing away. It's actually happened once, just after it was opened, and it's fairly common for trains to stop at Marazion in bad weather because the drivers won't risk crossing it.'

He frowned thoughtfully. 'They'll have to change that now, won't they?'

'Why?' Charlotte stared up at him. 'It isn't really as dangerous as all that. It's only Boy-John and his dreadful imagination. He's always hoping for some disaster.'

Kit grinned sympathetically. 'Well, the poor child doesn't have a lot of excitement in his life. But I meant, now that the bridge across the Tamar is opened, people will expect to be able to travel the full distance to London every day, not have to stop partway because of the weather.'

'But they can't anyway,' Charlotte broke in. 'We have different-width lines down here. Everything still has to be unloaded at Truro and loaded onto another train that will go on the wider tracks from then on.' She grimaced. 'I don't know what all the excitement is about today, really.'

Kit grinned. 'Oh, like Boy-John, they're all looking for a bit of fun,' he said tolerantly. 'But I suspect the opening of that bridge is going to make a bigger change than you've dreamed of. Just think about it–'

He stopped suddenly, staring at the frontages beside them. 'That's a smart building.'

'That's Blacklock's Bank.' Charlotte was always pleased to show off the advantages of the town. 'Actually, it isn't because he went bankrupt, but the new owners still kept the name.'

'A banker going bankrupt!' Kit snorted with laughter, his blue eyes dancing. 'Talk about the biter bit. Still, he didn't have far to go for help.' He pointed at the board over the next shop. *McAlister & Sons* it proclaimed in ornate gold writing while, above the Terrace, a wrought-iron arch held the three balls that identified his trade. 'And he's a man who's got an eye for business. I noticed he hasn't closed his shop early.'

'He'll have good business later,' Charlotte said sadly. She had heard more than enough sermons from her father about the profligacy of men who drank away their earnings and then had to pawn their jackets or work tools.

'He'll have some business now.' Kit patted her arm. 'You go ahead; I'll catch you up later.'

'But...' Charlotte caught herself with an effort. She couldn't remind him that she had given him more than enough money this morning to keep a single man for at least a week.

Surely he couldn't have spend it already? And if so, what on? He was quite sober. Not – surely on a woman? She stood still in the middle of the Terrace, unaware of the busy crowd that jostled and barged around her, horrified by her thoughts.

She had been enjoying herself so much, lost in the whirl of life and excitement of the town, forgetful, for a few moments, even of Kit's proposition, and now, suddenly, all happiness was washed away in the ugly flood of suspicion.

She tried to argue with herself; after all, they had been together on the *Faith-Lily* all night and he had never made an unwelcome advance to her, but that was easily explained. The weather had kept them busy and besides, why should he fancy a great gawk like herself any more than the Cornishmen did?

'Charlotte, my dear.'

She blinked, dragged from her unwelcome thoughts by the sound of an unexpected voice. 'Mr Borlase,' her mouth curved into a pleasant smile. 'Are you feeling better? It's lovely to see you out and about again.'

The Superintendent of the Methodist Circuit in which her father worked beamed up at her. 'God has seen fit to grant me the strength to come here today.' His short-sighted eyes blinked dimly at her. 'It is good to see you, too – and young Boy-John, if I am not mistaken.' He reached out a shaking hand, the papery skin wrinkled and dry, and patted Boy-John's tousled hair. 'Growing into a fine young man, aren't you, my lad?'

Boy-John lowered his head, staring up at the old man from under his brows like an aggressive bull-calf. 'I don't go to no chapel,' he stated belligerently, laying his cards on the table. 'My granda and me, we don't believe in such things.'

Mr Borlase shook his head. 'That's sad.' His old voice quavered slightly, but there was still a smile on his lips. 'You are missing so many good things. But there are more ways to come to God than just through chapel, you know.' His trembling hand reached into his pocket. 'Here, boy. It's a day of celebration. Why don't you buy yourself some clidgy-nicies.'

Charlotte could feel the child's stunned amazement. 'Cor, a penny.' The grubby hand reached forward, hesitated as if he couldn't believe his luck, then the pink fingers grabbed, closed and with a breathless, 'Thank you,' thrown over his shoulder the child was off, his bare feet silent on the stone Terrace as he raced for the nearest sweetshop.

She turned to the Superintendent. 'That was kind of you. He loves those sticky sweets.'

His laugh was a wheezing rasp. 'Me, too, when I was his age.' He paused. 'It is good of you to take the trouble to look after him, Charlotte, when you have so many other things to do.'

She glanced up, nervously. Was this a veiled reference to the fact that she refused to let her father sail her boat? But the old man obviously knew nothing about that. He laid a shaking hand on her arm. 'You take after your dear father in your concern for the unfortunates amongst us.' His face lit up with enthusiasm. 'He is a wonderful man, my dear, wonderful. He will be a great asset to the Church. An outstanding preacher and a great Christian. I am proud to have such a man on my Circuit and prouder that I can recommend him to be ordained so that he may follow the work of Our Lord full time.'

Charlotte did not know what to say. She dared not disagree with him, but her father's behaviour in this last week had started her wondering about him as she never had before. The old man patted her arm gently. 'I see my friends, my dear. God bless you,' and he was off, helping himself along with the aid of a stick.

Guilt overcame her. Everyone seemed to think her father was wonderful except for Kit, and she was not sure about his standards. Was she right to go against him in this way?

'Lotty! Lotty!'

The persistent shaking of her arm brought her back to the present. She blinked down at Boy-John, grateful for anything that would take her mind off her unpleasant thoughts.

'Come on, Lotty. We don't want to miss the train.' Boy-John's cheek bulged with the sweet he was sucking and his words were slurred from the effort of forcing them past the sticky mound. He began to run down the Terrace, dragging her by the hand. 'Hurry up, Lotty.'

'I can't run, Boy-John, it isn't nice,' she protested. 'People will notice.'

He swung round to stare at her, his mouth wide with scorn. 'Oh, gusson! Who's going to stop their horse from galloping to look at you?' He set off again, dragging her after him. 'Come on, Lotty, come on.'

Unwillingly, she allowed herself to be pulled into a run, dodging and ducking around the slower-moving pedestrians. Most moved out of their way with surprised looks but one, a towering, red-faced man, planted himself firmly in their way and stopped Boy-John's headlong passage with an iron arm.

'Well, look what we've got here,' he slurred, and Charlotte could smell the beer on his breath. 'Two sinners for the price of one. The bastard and the bitch.'

'Not much call for this sort of thing down here.' The pawnbroker scrutinised the watch through his jeweller's lens, turning it slowly so that the ornate chasings caught the light from the window. 'Not many could afford a watch like this around these parts.'

'You can always sell it on up-country.' Kit leaned against the high counter, his ankles crossed, apparently relaxed. He knew that to get the best price for his watch would take some time but he was prepared to enjoy the bargaining.

He had become so used to the watch, it had been so much a part of him ever since his father had given it to him on his twenty-first birthday, that he had ceased to be aware of it except when he wanted to know the time. It was only when the seaman had tried to steal it aboard the *Isabelle* that he realised it had become a liability, and Charlotte's startled glance at it this morning settled the question. A gold watch did not go with his new persona. Anyway, he needed the cash. A captain had to provide his own nets and he needed money to buy those, more money than he had earned by working on the *Faith-Lily* for the last few weeks.

'Ten pounds,' the pawnbroker said at last with a weary sigh. 'It's the best I can offer.'

Kit held out his hand. 'I'll take it back then. It will pay me to go to Plymouth or Falmouth and sell it there; the extra money I get will more than cover the expense.'

Mr McAlister moved the watch back from his clasping hand. 'I wouldn't want to have to put you to all that trouble.' He peered again through

179

his eye-glass. 'It would be worth more if it didn't have initials on it,' he pointed out. 'Not many people with those initials round here.'

'And you couldn't erase them?' Kit was sympathetic. 'What a pity. With just a modicum of jeweller's skills you could probably double your turnover.'

The pawnbroker ignored the slight on his abilities. 'Then there's the chasings.' He peered closer. 'Can't erase them or the watch will lose all its value but, of course, they cut down its worth.'

'I know.' Kit's voice dripped regret. 'And they are all engravings of ships, too.' He raised his eyebrows. 'I suppose, being a port, no one in Penzance has an interest in ships.'

For a second he felt a qualm. He had been so proud of that watch. On the day his father had given it to him he had taken it out to admire a hundred times. Not only was the watch itself a beauty but the gold case had been specially designed and, hidden amongst the acanthus leaves that coiled across the case were the ships that had made his father's fortune, the fortune he had promised, on that day, to leave to Kit and Jonathan. And now Jonathan was dead and he...

He hardened his heart. It was his father's fault that he had left home. No man would stand for the sort of control James Hargraves wanted to exercise over him. He had a right to choose his own bride, and a right to decide how to live his own life. And he would. He'd make his fortune and show his father that he was as good a man as he had been any day. After he'd helped Charlotte, of course, he reminded himself. She wasn't like him, able to travel the world, make her own living; there was no way she could escape from that brute of a father. Well, he would see about that. First he'd help her to break free. Then he'd go and make his fortune.

'Fifteen pounds, then.' The voice of the pawnbroker broke across his thoughts.

'Oh, come now...' Kit happily prepared to beat him up still further.

'She's not a bitch!' Boy-John stepped forward, his small fists bunched, staring up at the huge man through the yellowing marks of a fading bruise.

'Boy-John.' Charlotte caught his arm. 'Come away. He's – he's not himself.'

Polite euphemisms had no part to play in Boy-John's life. 'Just 'cos he's drunk, it don't mean to say he can call you names, Lotty.' His shrill voice rang down the crowded street. Around her, Charlotte could see people hurrying away lest they get embroiled in a distasteful scene.

She tugged again at his arm. 'Come away.'

He twisted with practised ease, pulling away from her grasp. 'He shan't call you that, Lotty, he shan't.' He lashed out with one bare foot, catching the man on the shin. The hurt must have been minimal but the man reacted immediately, swinging a blow at the boy which caught him on the side of the head and sent him flying across the Terrace to crumple into a heap on the ground.

'No!' As the man prepared to kick the small body, Charlotte intervened. 'No, you won't hurt him.'

181

He looked her up and down, his bloodshot eyes filled with insolence. 'And I suppose you're going to stop me?'

Her heart quailed. He was even taller than Kit and he looked a vicious brute, but Charlotte knew that none of the crowd of respectable people around would intervene until it was absolutely necessary, and by that time she could be badly hurt. But Boy-John had been attacked merely for standing up for her and she could not let him down.

Charlotte took a deep breath. 'I shall stop you if I have to.' She spoke extra loudly to try to give herself courage. 'But it would be better for everyone if you were to simply apologise and help that child.'

'Apologise?' He guffawed, throwing back his head so that she could see his teeth, black with decay, then he pointed a contemptuous finger at her. 'I've heard about you, I know what you're like. Refusing to let a respectable man like your da sail your lugger. You're a disgrace to the name of woman, you are.'

Her jaw tightened with fury but when she spoke her words were honied. 'I am amazed that you know anything at all about anyone respectable. I am surprised that you even know the meaning of the word.'

Out of the corner of her eye she could see Boy-John's small body begin to move. Silently, she willed him to get up, crawl out of the way. A kick from one of the man's thick leather boots could easily break the child's ribs, crushed as he was against the granite wall of a shop.

As she had hoped, her words kept the man's attention on herself. His eyes narrowed. 'Oh, hoity-toity,' he mocked. 'That's good, that is, coming from one as bin the mistress of her boss since I don't know when.'

Shock took her breath away. She could only stare at him, white-faced. Around her, she was aware of a ring of silence spreading out, with herself at the centre. Surely people didn't really think that?'

When she finally managed to speak her voice came raggedly. 'Mr – Mr Polruan was my employer.' She glanced round at the ring of spectators, praying for someone to come to her assistance, to back her up but no one moved, no one met her eyes.

She cleared her throat and tried again, speaking more clearly now, head high, trying to insist on her status, not only to the drunk in front of her but to the listening crowd. 'I worked for him as a clerk.'

He laughed. 'A clerk! A woman like you!' He spat. 'We all know there's only one thing a woman is good for and it ain't clerking, is it?'

'You interest me, sir.'

The voice came from behind Charlotte and she recognised it as Kit's instantly, though she had never heard it sound so cold and angry before. He stepped forward, moving her gently aside so that he was between her and the man. 'Perhaps you would like to tell me just how you think Miss Trevennan is employed?'

Relief made Charlotte's knees suddenly weak and she longed to lean against the wall to recover herself, but first she had to get Boy-John out of danger. She moved to the child. Already he was sitting up, rubbing his head, his eyes fixed in hero-worship on Kit. She pulled him to his feet, holding him against her, as much for her own reassurance as for his, as she watched Kit face the man.

He spoke again, his voice icy. 'You made an allegation, sir.' He was inches shorter than the other and much slighter. Charlotte felt her heart contract nervously. Kit mustn't fight him.

The stranger had no such qualms. He spread his feet further apart, leaning forward to thrust his face into Kit's. 'I said she was his mistress.'

Kit's right fist shot out with all the force of his body behind it, straight at the bully's Adam's apple. The man's eyes popped, his mouth gaped open. For a few seconds an excruciating sucking sound came from his throat as he gasped for air then his knees buckled and he collapsed writhing onto the ground.

Kit looked challengingly around at the crowd but they would not meet his blue stare and moved away in silence. He strode forward and stood over the man, fists clenched, ready to continue the fight if necessary. 'Who is he? Do you know?'

Boy-John edged forward. 'He's Big Rory, lives in the Barbican. He's a fisherman – when he's sober.'

'He is, is he?' Kit reached down and pulled the man to his feet. He hung in Kit's grasp, still struggling to get his breath back.

Kit gave him a rough shake to get his attention. 'Tell me, Big Rory, how would you like to work for me?'

Chapter Thirteen

'Mr Bates is here, sir.'

James Hargraves was suddenly still, his heart thumping erratically. News of Kit – it must be news of his son. But it never did any good to let your men know what you were feeling. He made himself check another column of figures and initialled the bottom of the page before he allowed himself to look up. 'I'm busy at the moment. Show him in in five minutes, will you.'

He kept his position at the mahogany desk until he heard the office door close and the footsteps move away from the other side, then he threw his pen down and ran his fingers through his greying curls.

If only the man had found Kit; if only he were well! James Hargraves rose to his feet, his emotions too strong to allow him to stay sitting any longer at his desk. Kit was all he had left now. If Kit were dead then his whole life was wasted, useless. The business he had built up, his position in society – what good were any of them to him if Kit weren't here to share it, to inherit it?

But Kit couldn't be dead, he told himself. Kit was strong, young, healthy. He had left because of a stupid argument, walked out because James had tried to run his life for him. It was the sort of thing he would have done himself at that age. He groaned, staring out of the window, across to the ships moored in the dock – *his* ships. The fleet he had spent a lifetime building up, the fleet he would leave to Kit.

Suddenly, he could wait no longer. He strode to the door, pulled it open. 'Bates.' His voice echoed through the great office and the clerks stared at him, but he did not care. As long as Kit was well, nothing mattered. As long as he was well, it would be a simple thing to make up their argument. Kit had his pride, but what did that matter? His father was willing to plead, to abase himself – anything as long as Kit came back.

James Hargraves moved back to his desk. Bates seemed a long time in coming and he was barely through the door before Hargraves' impatience got the better of him. 'Well?' he demanded. 'Have you found him? Have you any news?'

He knew. He knew before Bates had opened his mouth. He could tell by the way he turned before answering, making sure that the office door was firmly shut behind him. He could tell by the way the man twisted his hat round and round in his hands. He could tell by the look in his eyes even before he heard the fateful words.

'Your son shipped as a crew member on the *Isabelle;* and the *Isabelle* was sunk in a storm off the Scillies with all hands.'

'Mother, I've left my job.'

Bertha Trevennan's mouth opened in a silent 'O' of astonishment, then her face crumpled. 'No, Charlotte, you can't leave Polruans. You have to work there, you have to!' Her voice rose into a wail.

186

'Mother.' Charlotte moved forward, pushing her back into the old settle by the fire, its wood black with age and use. 'It's not owned by Mr Polruan now, remember. Frederick owns it and–' She paused. It was impossible to tell her mother that Frederick would have sacked her anyway, Bertha would never understand. 'And Frederick and I have never got on very well,' she ended.

'But he's Mr Polruan's son!' The older woman couldn't take this in. 'Mr Polruan said he'd look after me, that he'd look after all of us.'

'But that was the old Mr Polruan,' Charlotte insisted. 'The younger one is different.'

'But he's his *son.*'

Charlotte sighed. This should have been the easy part of the conversation; she had still to tell her mother of the difficult decision she had come to regarding the *Faith-Lily.* 'Mother,' she shook her gently, 'please listen to me. I know you're upset about it but it's too late. I cannot work at Polruans any more. And I have to find some way of getting in some money.'

Her mother's faded blue eyes fixed on her face. 'You're going to let your father sail your boat! Oh Charlotte, I'm so glad, so glad.' To Charlotte's horror tears began to course down her cheeks. 'It must have been what Mr Polruan meant when he left you the lugger; it must have been God's will.' Her thin arms reached out and caught Charlotte to her, sobs shaking the frail body. 'Thank God, oh, thank God.'

It hurt to do it. It hurt even more because Charlotte still wasn't sure that she was doing the right thing, but she had made her mind up. Now that she had lost her job at Polruans, the lugger was her only chance.

She pushed the woman away gently, until she could force her to meet her own, chastened gaze then she said slowly and deliberately, 'Mr Briars is going to sail my boat, Mother, and,' she took a deep breath, 'I am going to move into Granfer-John's cottage.'

Whatever reaction she had expected it wasn't this one. Bertha's face froze suddenly, the colour draining from it until it was grey with fear then she threw herself forwards, her arms clasping Charlotte in a desperate grip.

'No! No!' The voice rose hysterically. 'Don't do it! You mustn't do it! Don't go! Don't leave me here with him, alone.'

Charlotte stroked her mother's grey hair. 'I'm just going to see Granfer,' she said reassuringly. 'I'll be back in a few minutes, ma.'

The older woman scarcely moved. Charlotte wondered if she was so exhausted by the bout of hysteria that she wasn't aware that Charlotte had even spoken. She glanced worriedly at her mother. These attacks seemed to be getting more frequent lately, and her mother seemed less and less able to cope with life. Charlotte already knew that she spent many hours each day when her husband was out, at Mr Polruan's grave, as if the memory of her life before she was married was easier for her to bear than her present existence.

Charlotte had to tell Kit that she had made her mind up. She hurried quickly through the narrow streets, trying to ignore the sudden racing of her heart. But when she pushed open the door of the mean little cottage only Granfer-John and his grandson were there.

'Oh!' She had been so sure Kit would be there that she found herself lost for words. 'I – I wanted to say something to Mr Briars.'

Granfer-John puffed easily on his pipe; his shrewd blue eyes, she was sure, missed none of her discomfiture. 'Reckon he's out until late.'

Out until late! She could not stop herself. 'Out drinking and womanising again,' she said, and was horrified at the desolation in her voice.

Granfer-John smoked calmly. 'Reckon he might be, reckon he might not,' he said easily. ''Tes no point you getting in a proper boil about it. He's a young man who can run his own life, I reckon.' He puffed again. 'Well?' he queried. 'Are you going to leave a message with me or are you going to stand in the doorway all night looking like a bear with a sore head?'

'I – I wanted to say…' Knowing he was out, wondering where he was, her decision suddenly seemed wrong. But what else could she do? She had to get some money. She lifted her head proudly.

'Please tell Mr Briars that I have decided that he can captain the *Faith-Lily*. With you along, of course.'

It was stupid of her to expect thanks from Granfer-John. He just puffed away as if she had said nothing important. 'Reckon 'tes a good thing you've come down on that side,' he observed, calmly 'seeing as how Kit's over at the Barbican now, persuading a few men over there

189

to come and work on her.'

'The Barbican!' Her heart lurched then settled down to a nervous thudding. 'But they – they're dreadful people over there. Criminals.'

He looked at her. 'There's some around here as reckon I'm a criminal. Your da for one.'

But she had no time for levity. 'He might get hurt. They might *kill* him.'

He shrugged. 'He's tough as old Nick, that young un. He can manage them sort.'

'But why there?' she wailed, and then answered herself: 'Because nobody else would work on my boat.' She felt suddenly deflated and miserable.

He shrugged. 'There 'tes and can't be no tesser, they that can't get respectable men must make do with the rest, I say. But I reckon he'll get your crew for you.'

It was what she wanted, it was what she had decided but she felt empty and lost. 'And when will he put to sea?'

'Soon as maybe,' Granfer-John said, 'but not until I know that you'll stay with Boy-John.'

He looked at her. 'That's it, maid. We've done what we can, we two. 'Tes down to you now.'

The Barbican was dark – a fetid, dank darkness. Despite the fact that the warren of streets was only yards from the sea, the air was thick with the stench of filth. Under Kit's boots the narrow alley ran with unmentionable nastinesses while, overhead, the tenements leaned towards each other as if seeking comfort in their misery.

There was plenty of noise – the shouts and screams of humanity living out its existence on the edge of poverty, cries of anger, drunkenness, lust. There were places like this, Kit knew, in every town in England but somehow the close-ness of the sea and the countryside simply emphasised the squalor of such an existence.

In the darkness there was a patter and squelch of running feet, too quick and light to be an adult although, God knows, it was far too late for any child to be out. Kit waited until the steps had almost reached him before calling out, 'Want to earn a penny?'

The child stopped immediately. 'What've I got to do?' Greed and suspicion warred in the hoarse voice.

Kit reached out towards the half-seen figure in the gloom. 'Just tell me where Big Rory and his brothers live.' He tried to sound as reassuring as he could.

The boy had been well-trained in one respect at least. He spat. 'Fucking bailiffs. I ain't telling you nothing.'

Kit caught the boy by his thin jacket and lifted him until he was in front of his face. 'Just tell me, lad.'

High above the ground the boy was silent for a moment before he announced cautiously. 'I could pee in your face.'

'And I could hold your head under whatever rubbish I'm up to my ankles in.' Kit made sure that his voice gave no sign of the amusement he felt at the reply. 'Just tell me.'

It was a good thing his eyes were growing accustomed to the murk or he would have missed the brief inclination of the boy's head.

'Up them there stairs.'

'I'll give you the money when I've found them.' Kit lowered the child to the ground but kept a firm hold on his arm. 'Come on.'

He dragged the unwilling boy up a set of ramshackle stairs which ran up one side of a dimly-lit hovel. There was no rail on the outside and he clung harder to the struggling child, fearful that he would fall off the slimy steps in the dark. 'Rory? Are you there, Rory?'

'Who wants to know?' The door scraped open on uneven floorboards, hanging from one hinge, and the man he had recruited that afternoon scowled at him in the dim and evil-smelling light of a lamp burning pilchard oil.

Kit felt in his pockets and handed over a penny-piece to the boy, who escaped with a delighted gasp, then he stepped warily inside the hovel and pushed the door shut behind him. He smiled at the men inside, leaning negligently back against the wall. 'Your new captain,' he said.

'I'm sorry, old friend.'

James Hargraves lifted his head from his hands and squinted blearily at the dark figure across the table. 'Dick?'

Richard Robinson lowered himself into a seat at the side of the grand dinner table. The soft candlelight gleamed on the dark wood, sparkled in the cut glass of the decanter, lost itself in the dark folds of the newcomer's clothes.

Hargraves threw back the remainder of the brandy in his glass. 'I suppose–' despite the amount of alcohol he had drunk his voice was still unslurred – 'I suppose you've come to offer me the consolation of your religion.'

The other man shook his head. 'After a loss like yours, my friend, there can be no consolation.'

The very fact that he had said it was somehow more comforting to Hargraves than anything else could have been. He gestured down the long table, which stretched empty in front of him. 'We were a family once, Dick, a real family. Eliza, Sophie, Jonathan, Kit – all I wanted – all I ever wanted. And everything I ever did, I did for them.'

He poured more brandy then sat, swirling it round the glass, his eyes lost in the mists of the past. 'Eliza never came here, you know. She died before the house was finished, having little Sophie.' His voice grew bitter. 'She died happy, Dick – happy because we'd always wanted a little girl and if the price of having her was her own death, it was a price Eliza was happy to pay. And then Sophie died too. And then Jonathan. Now Kit...'

His voice broke and he gulped at the brandy to hide the sudden, unmanly tears that pricked at his eyes.

'A heavy burden, James, a heavy burden.'

'And heavier because it's my fault, Dick, all mine. If I hadn't pushed Kit, if I hadn't tried to make him marry that bloodless daughter of Harrington's, he'd still be here today. Instead he died on that bloody ship, that bloody *Cornish* ship.' The emotion was suddenly too much for him and he hurled the glass across the room. It flew, glinting in a rainbow of colours and

193

smashed against the far wall, leaving a wet smudge of brandy to disfigure the crimson brocade wall-hangings.

He dropped his face into his hands, hiding the tears that flowed freely now. 'My fault, Dick.'

'Here.' There was a sound of liquid being poured and another glass was pushed into his hands. 'Drink this.'

Surprise made him look up. 'You're encouraging me to drink? And you a rabid Methodist?' Laughter and sorrow fought in his voice so that it swooped out of control. 'Giving me brandy?'

'It's another gift of Our Lord, whatever some of my fellow Methodists say. And it can be a welcome gift – at times like this.'

Hargraves raised the glass to his lips with shaking hands. 'You don't have any hemlock on you, I suppose?'

Dick, shook his head. 'You'd never take that way out, James, you've too much pride.'

'Altogether too much pride.' He swallowed, feeling the pain inside him expand again. 'It was because of my pride...'

'It was because of *both* your prides,' Dick said gently. 'Do you think I didn't know Kit well enough to realise that, James? And whatever you say, he would have left here sometime. His pride would never have allowed him meekly to inherit what you had amassed. That wasn't his way.'

It was true, James knew it, and he felt the first, slight shred of comfort. Slowly, he reached out a shaking hand and put it over Richard's. 'He was a good boy, wasn't he, Dick? A good son.'

Dick grasped his hand in both his own. 'He was a *man*, James, a real man. And a good one.' He smiled slightly. 'He certainly wasn't a Methodist, for all I know, he may not even have been a Christian, but he was a good man, James.' His grasp tightened. 'If he saw injustice, he would fight it to the last of this strength; if he saw cruelty, he wouldn't rest until he had stopped it. A *real* man, James; a son to be proud of.'

Hargraves could feel the tears coursing down his cheeks now but he no longer cared. The eulogy had freed him to express his sorrow as nothing else could. He said brokenly, 'I'm glad you came, Dick, so glad.'

'I'm glad I could come. If this news had arrived just a little bit later I might not have been here.'

Shock brought Hargraves out of his misery. 'Why not? Where are you going?'

Dick Robinson smiled bitterly. 'To the place you hate so much, James. And unfortunately, to the place my son hates, too.' He sighed. 'Ever since the news came through he's been having those nightmares again. I thought he'd outgrown them at last but it's been every night this week.'

He nodded. 'I'm being posted to Cornwall.'

Chapter Fourteen

The earth was still black and raw, scarring the peaceful graveyard with its reminder of the tragedy of recent death. Charlotte guessed that once the earth had settled, the grave would be hidden under a granite mausoleum, erected by Mr Polruan's widow and son to trumpet their wealth and importance to every passer-by. But for now Charles Polruan lay in a simple grave, as he, himself, would probably have wished.

She knelt by the turned earth, her head bowed. Until he had gone she had never realised how much she needed Charles Polruan, how much she relied on his calm good sense, his good-natured cynical view of the world, so refreshingly different from her father's.

She needed his advice now. So many problems – and all stemming from his gift to her. He had wanted her to be happy, to be secure and to that end he had left her the *Faith-Lily*. An illogical wave of guilt washed over her, that what he had intended so well she had in some way perverted until it was a source of worry and concern.

Gently, she laid a hand on the black earth. 'I'm sorry,' she whispered softly, as if fearful of waking a sleeper. 'I'm so sorry.' She swallowed abruptly, forcing down the lump that rose in her throat.

The touch on her shoulder was light but it made her jump, swinging round with a startled intake of breath as Kit Briars lowered himself beside her. He stared sombrely at the recently turned earth. 'Mr Polruan?' His voice was as low as her own had been.

She nodded. 'He was – very good to me.' Just saying it seemed to emphasise the emptiness there had been in her life since his death and she turned her head away so that he shouldn't see the tears in her eyes.

'So everyone says.'

His voice was non-committal but she was instantly on the defensive. For some reason it was vitally important that he shouldn't believe the lies Big Rory had said about her.

She raised her head and stared at him. 'I wasn't his lover.' Her normally deep voice was suddenly high with tension.

Kit reached out and covered her hand with his. 'Of course not.' His blue eyes smiled down into hers with no condemnation in them at all. 'Do you think I don't know you better than that?'

'Other people say it.' Charlotte couldn't keep the bitterness from her voice. 'Other people who have known me longer than you have. Just because he left me the boat they think that there must have been something between us, but there wasn't.' Her hand clenched, the fingers digging into the soft soil. 'Really, there wasn't.'

'You don't have to convince me.' Kit reached out and took her hand, wiping the earth off it with his handkerchief. 'My father...' He stopped suddenly, and she felt his fingers pause for a second before he caught himself up and went on as if nothing had happened. 'My father employs

197

people. I know how he values a good worker.' He gave a harsh little laugh. 'More than a son, I've sometimes thought.'

'Your father?' It was the first time she had heard him speak of his family, speak of his life before the night she had found him fighting three men in the street. Curiosity got the better of her. 'Why don't you work for him, then, if he employs people?'

Kit laughed shortly. 'Because we don't get on, that's why.'

'Just like me and my father.' She felt a sudden kinship for him in their shared problems with their respective parents.

Her hand was as clean as he could get it. Kit stuffed the handkerchief back in his pocket but he had absentmindedly kept hold of her fingers and Charlotte felt it would seem rude to drag her hand away.

For a few seconds he was motionless, gazing into the distance at a sight only he could see, then he heaved a gusty sigh. 'Not like your father at all, thank God. He has his faults but he's not a bigoted, sermonising poseur.' He glanced down at her and Charlotte could see the contrition in his face. 'I'm sorry, sweeting, I shouldn't have said that about him.'

'Sweeting'! The term of endearment sent an electric shock through her, made her chest tight, her heart thump erratically. It was an effort to act normally, to pretend that she hadn't noticed the slip of the tongue.

'Mr Polruan often said the same about him,' she said swiftly, trying to hide her breathlessness.

198

'Mr Polruan.' He turned his attention back to the grave in front of him. 'It seems to me that he didn't do very well by you, however much he might have liked you.'

The words echoed her thoughts and she responded angrily, stung again by guilt. 'How can you say that?' she demanded, dragging her fingers from his. 'He was wonderful to me. Both my parents had worked for his family and he never forgot. He paid for me to have a good education, as well as employing me in his own firm.'

'And he isolated you from your community,' Kit said. He climbed to his feet, holding out a hand to help her up which she pointedly ignored. 'If you'd grown up amongst them the villagers would never had sided with your father against you and you'd have been married long ago, with a husband to protect you against him. As it is...' His voice tailed away as he gazed at her under frowning brows.

She climbed to her feet and shook out her creased skirts. 'As it is, what?' she asked furiously. 'As it is, he has given me a chance to get a better life, to own my own boat. How can that be bad?'

Kit's face lightened and he touched her arm. 'Polruan meant it all for the best, don't get me wrong. It's just the results that worry me. Because of this inheritance, you're at odds with your father and you've lost your job with one of the most important men in the district. And now I'm taking away your only real friend, Granfer. You'll have no one to turn to if there are problems. No one at all.'

Now? She was suddenly breathless. 'You've got a crew?'

'Of sorts.' He gave a harsh laugh. 'The good thing about them is that they are fishermen and they will sail on your boat. The bad thing...' he shrugged. 'Well, I wouldn't trust them as far as I could throw them – and I'm the one who is employing them.'

Her heart lurched. 'I didn't mean for you – I don't want you...'

His cold expression vanished instantly as he smiled down at her. 'Are you worried about me? You needn't be, you know. I'm sure I can keep on top of them – me and Granfer-John. But if you want him to sail–?'

'I do,' she said quickly. The thought of being without Kit, without Granfer, made her feel lonelier than ever but she *had* to have the money. With money she could be independent, she could face down her critics, she could help her mother, have a life. Without money she could barely exist. She would have to subjugate herself to her father, live from hand to mouth with nothing to look forward to, nothing to hope for.

'He must sail,' she insisted. 'To – to help you.'

'To help? Or to watch over your interests?' Under his quizzical stare she blushed and turned her head away, hating the fact that he had read her mind.

To her surprise he laughed again, kindly this time. 'Don't look so guilty. That boat is worth money. I'd think less of you if you didn't have some concern for your own interests.' His face became serious. 'But Granfer-John won't go unless you will stay with Boy-John. You know that?'

'Of course.' Charlotte swallowed. 'I – I haven't told my father yet…'

'But you will stay with him?'

She lifted her chin. 'I gave my word. And I do not go back on what I have promised.'

Kit took her hand again. 'I don't doubt it. You may not feel able to trust me but I trust you. To the ends of the earth.'

A pleasurable heat flooded her veins and when she spoke her voice was choked with emotion. 'When – when do you sail?'

'As soon as possible. With the crew I've picked, the sooner I can get them aboard the better. Wait too long and they'll probably all be in jail. On the boat they'll be under my control – I hope.'

Charlotte came to an abrupt halt. Suddenly, it was all too much. 'You're doing all this for me!' Her voice was almost a wail. 'You're having to go to sea with a load of criminals who'll probably rob you or even *kill* you – and it's all my fault!' She kicked furiously at the granite wall surrounding the churchyard. 'I wish I'd never inherited that boat! It's caused nothing but trouble.'

'Now, sweeting!' He put his arm round her shoulders and pulled her to him. His strength, his closeness, was overwhelming. He smiled down at her. 'Is this the brave woman who stopped three men attacking me? The woman who was going to risk her own life trying to save her boat in a storm?'

'That was my life,' Charlotte said mutinously. 'I

have no right to risk yours.'

'And no right to stop me risking mine, either, if I choose to.' He laughed and his arm tightened around her shoulders. 'This is a challenge, my love, and I never could resist a challenge.'

'Love'? She tried desperately to control her furiously beating heart, hoping that the shock and excitement that thrilled through her weren't showing on her face.

But he was glancing up at the clock on the church tower. 'Damnation! I have to meet my so-called crew in Newlyn in half an hour to sort out supplies.' He turned back to her and she was glad she had had time to get her expression under control.

'Don't worry about me,' he said, with a grin. 'My father always said I was born to hang. And don't regret the *Faith-Lily* either. Whatever problems she's caused, at least she was responsible for bringing us together.'

Another smile, a quick wave of his hand and he was gone, leaving Charlotte speechless and motionless, staring after his retreating figure with shining eyes.

Kit grinned to himself as his long legs ate up the road between Paul and Newlyn. She was a wonderful woman, wonderful. Her courage, her strength – even the quick anger that leaped in her eyes when he dared to criticise someone she loved – all enchanted him. Even her moment of sudden weakness was admirable, brought about, as it was, by concern for him.

To think that he had hated Cornwall, to think

that he had planned to leave as soon as possible, to find a way of making his fortune – well, he admitted to himself, making his fortune was still his plan. He would show his father he could survive without him, could *succeed* without him. And he couldn't do that in Cornwall; whatever Charlotte's attractions he would have to move on. But first he would help her solve her problems. And if that took some time, he certainly wouldn't object.

Lost in his thoughts, Kit was walking along the cliff at Newlyn before he was even aware of it. Only the sight of a group of figures, leaning over the rail, their heads together in discussion, brought him up short.

One was easy to identify. With his towering height and bright red hair, Big Rory could not be mistaken for anyone else and, next to him Kit could also recognise the smaller, slighter figures of his brothers.

It was the fourth member of the group that made him come to a sudden halt, muttering an expletive under his breath.

There was only one reason he could think of why Frederick Polruan should want to talk to his future crew.

Kit gnawed his bottom lip, wondering what to do for the best. It went against all his instincts to leave Charlotte here, alone, but with the *Faith-Lily* moored just offshore, Polruan had an easy way of getting back at both of them.

That boat was Charlotte's only chance. Without it, she would have lost her one hope of a better life, of escaping from her father.

So he had better go to sea as soon as possible. And take some precautions.

'Today?' Charlotte almost wailed the words. 'But you can't. It's – it's impossible.'

'We can.' Kit grinned down at her. The whitewashed kitchen of the Trevennans' cottage seemed homely and comfortable in the afternoon sunshine. Even the clomen cat on the hearth seemed to blink its earthenware eyes in the golden glow.

He leaned back in the settle and stretched his legs out in front of him. 'Now don't get so upset about it. You want the *Faith-Lily* out fishing. I've got a crew, nets, and Granfer-John. Just a few last-minute provisions to take on board and we can be away on the next tide.'

'But – but...' She knew it was ridiculous, but everything had happened so suddenly. One moment she had been thinking that the boat would never leave Mount's Bay and now, suddenly, everything had been arranged. Within a few hours Kit would be leaving on the boat – and she didn't want him to go.

'Look.' Kit leaned forward, suddenly serious. 'Every day that boat is moored, you're losing money. The sooner we sail, the better. But it all depends on you. Unless you move in with Boy-John, Granfer-John won't go. And without him I might as well stay home. Well?' His blue eyes challenged her. 'What are you going to do?'

Now that she had reached the point of no return, her heart suddenly failed her. 'But I haven't spoken to my father.' She twisted her

204

fingers together. 'Surely I ought to tell him first.'

Kit snorted. 'Tell him and he'll put the kybosh on everything. You're an adult; make your own decisions. How can you be a successful boat-owner if you can't even do that?'

She knew he was rushing her too fast but she could see the sense in his argument. Unwillingly, she said, 'Father's fishing up the Channel. He may not be back for several nights.'

'There you are then,' Kit said triumphantly. 'You can move out while he's not here. By the time he returns, it will be too late for him to stop you. After all, what can he do? He can hardly drag you back against your will.' His face creased in an unexpected smile. 'If you're really lucky he might wash his hands of you altogether.'

Her lips curved momentarily before her face became serious again. Bertha was still asleep, worn out by her attack of hysterics but Charlotte knew that when she woke she would be as opposed as ever to her daughter's moving out although it seemed, for some reason Charlotte could not understand, to be on her own account rather than on her daughter's.

But she had promised. She had to do it. She reached a decision. 'If you can get the boat out today I'll move in with Boy-John this evening. And when my father comes back...' she took a deep breath, not even wanting to think of the scene that there would be, 'well, at least I won't be living with him.'

He grinned at her. 'That's good enough for me. I'll trust you any time not to break your word.'

Despite the way her heart seemed to be

writing in her chest with nervousness, she could still bask in his approbation. 'But what about the money for provisions?'

'I'll come back for that,' Kit said easily. 'I'll go and get Granfer-John now. We need to work quickly if we're to be off on this tide.' He gave her a reassuring grin. 'It'll be all right, don't you worry,' then he ducked easily under the lintel and was gone.

Charlotte stared after him, feeling breathless. She had a hundred questions that she wanted to ask him; a thousand small but vital details raced around her head. And he had gone. His confidence in her was flattering but, at the same time, the responsibility was scary.

And there was no time. That was the most frightening thing of all. No time to have second thoughts, no time to argue. Only just enough time to do what she had to.

Money was the first necessity. She raced for the stairs and pulled out her secret cache of coins. He had better have it all – Granfer-John would make sure that she was not robbed. And the boat would be empty of everything after paying up – no fuel for cooking, no oil for the lights – nothing. She just had to hope that what she had would be enough.

'Lotty! Lotty!' Boy-John's shrill voice rang through the cottage. Back already. She ran a hand over her hair, smoothing it down, tucking in the stray ends as she hurried downstairs. Boy-John threw himself on her. 'You're coming to stay, Lotty!' His voice rose in an excited shriek. 'You're coming to stay with me!' He looked round the small kitchen, at the scrubbed table, the dresser and the range with its shining brass rail. 'It's not as good as here,' he said, his voice suddenly doubtful.

She hardly had time to attend to him; her eyes were on Kit, his sea boots on, a bag containing his clothes over one shoulder, his fair curls almost touching the low beams. 'It'll be all right, Boy-John. I know what to expect.'

She moved towards Kit, struggling to find the right thing to say but he was already smiling down at her. 'Lucky boy.'

'What?' she asked, mystified.

'I wouldn't mind you staying with me.'

Embarrassment coloured her face and took away her breath. 'I – I...' Words failed her. She swallowed, mutely holding out the money to him. He took her hand in his.

'You have to do your part too, you know.' The amusement had left his face and he was suddenly serious.

She made an effort to compose herself. 'I've got to look after Boy-John, I know.'

'Not just that.' His fingers were warm and hard, his touch took her breath away. 'We'll find the fish but it's up to you to sell them. And Polruan might try to stop you.'

She hadn't even thought that far ahead. Another problem. She opened her mouth but he forestalled her. His fingers tightened around hers. 'I wouldn't leave you like this if I wasn't sure you could cope.' His voice was so sympathetic that she glanced up at him and found herself caught in his bright gaze.

207

Slowly, gently, his mouth came down on hers, lightly caressing her lips, giving her the first real kiss she had ever had in her life.

She could not move, could not breathe. She had forgotten Boy-John, the room, everything. Her whole being was wrapped up in the pressure of his lips on hers, his closeness.

And suddenly the pressure increased. He moved forward and his hands slid around her waist, pulling her closer. She could feel his body hard against hers, smell the scent of clean, male flesh and the faint overlay of fish and tar which he had picked up from the boat. Her boat.

Under his hands, his lips, her body responded instinctively, softening under his touch, pressing against him as a thrill like a lightning flash ran through her being.

She gasped and he pulled back, breathing heavily. For long seconds their glances held then he moved, breaking the spell. A step back, a final lingering glance and he was gone.

Unable to move, unable to speak, she could only stare after him, her fingers touching her burning lips. She had never felt so alone in all her life.

Chapter Fifteen

Boy-John lay flat on top of the sea wall, peering over the side. Below him, sleek brown bodies twisted and spun in the sun-kissed waves. The sea-otters were out.

He craned further, bare toes digging into the unevenness of the great boulders that made up the quay, his eyes searching for the hole in the sea wall in which the otters made their nest. Untidy fair hair flopped around his face, hiding his view of everything that was not immediately beneath him. He wriggled forward another inch. Surely he could see it... Weren't they coming out of...

A shadow passed in front of his eyes and at the same time the otters were gone, disappearing with a twist of their gleaming bodies. Furious, he looked up, trying to peer through his mop of hair. Ahead of him he could make out the outline of a lugger, black against the sun-sparkled sea. He wriggled backwards into a safer position and pushed the hair out of his eyes, staring. It took only a glance to recognise the Mousehole-based boat and he swore softly to himself. William Trevennan was back.

His heart sank. Having Charlotte to look after him was an adventure and it promised to be better than living with Granfer-John, even if she had decided to clean the whole house as soon as she arrived. But if Trevennan put a stop to it she would have to go home, and the *Faith-Lily's* fishing trip would be called off.

Unless… He climbed to his feet and shaded his eyes against the sun, peering across the Bay. Three luggers were coming into sight from behind Penlee Point, the sea creaming around their bows as they headed for the Atlantic. Boy-John squinted. He didn't know the Newlyn boats as well as he knew the Mousehole ones, but surely…

The lead boat altered course slightly, heeling over in the wind and the sunlight glinted briefly on the white straike around her bows. Boy-John let out a whoop of delight, leaping up and down with excitement. The *Faith-Lily* was outward bound; whatever Trevennan did he was too late to stop Kit and Granfer-John from fishing.

Then his face became suddenly serious. Charlotte ought to be informed – she hadn't been expecting her da back for several days yet. His sturdy legs pumping, bare feet thudding on the uneven surface of the quay, Boy-John raced to warn her.

'Mother, he's landed.'

Bertha Trevennan's face twisted nervously and she clutched at her daughter's hands with icy fingers. 'You've got to come back, Charlotte, you've got to. If he finds out…When he learns…'

'It'll be all right, Mother,' Charlotte promised, trying to make her voice as soothing as possible although inside, her stomach was churning with nervous tension. Her father had made her an outcast merely for wanting the original captain to

210

sail the *Faith-Lily;* what would he do now when he learned the true enormity of her rebellion?

She swallowed, trying to bring some moisture back into her dry mouth. She was an adult, wasn't she? She had a right to decide how to run her own business, and where to live. But whatever her mind told her, her body refused to be comforted, and when the door of the cottage burst open she turned around with a jump.

'Peace be on this house.' William Trevennan's usual greeting rang hollower than ever but at least it covered his wife's frightened mew.

Charlotte licked her dry lips. When he learned what she had done... She cleared her throat. 'Good afternoon Father.' She was amazed that her voice sounded as calm as usual. 'We weren't expecting you back so soon.' She moved forward so that she was between her parents. 'I hope you had good fishing?'

'Alas, the Lord did not see fit to bless us.' He moved forward, tossing his hat onto the table and letting his bag of belongings slide from his shoulder onto the floor, then he caught sight of his wife and his face changed. 'And what's the matter with you this time?'

'Nothing, husband, nothing,' Bertha whispered in a shaking voice as she cast a beseeching glance at her daughter.

Charlotte moved forward again, interposing her body. 'Would you like some tea, Father? I know that it can be cold on the sea.'

He nodded. 'But not as cold as the heart of one's own family. Have you reached a decision yet about the boat?'

Charlotte stopped on her way to the fire. This was the moment. She gathered all of her courage and turned around to look her father straight in the face. 'I have given the command of the *Faith-Lily* to Mr Briars.'

The words fell like stones, seeming to reverberate in the sudden silence of the room. Even her mother's frightened gasps seemed to be stilled. There was an endless moment when time seemed suspended then Trevennan moved, spreading his feet further apart, lowering his head between his massive shoulders. '*What?*' The word was a whisper of disbelief.

Charlotte raised herself to her full height. 'I have chosen Mr Briars to sail my boat.'

'But – but you don't know him!' Her father seemed unable to accept the simple statement. 'He's a stranger; all he's ever done for you is paint the boat. What sort of qualification is *that* for being a captain?' He moved towards her, his voice rising. 'He might know *nothing* about boats.'

'He is a capable sailor,' Charlotte insisted quietly.

Her father was recovering. 'So he says,' he scoffed. 'And you believed him. With no evidence. Typical of the weak mind of a woman.'

'I have plenty of evidence.' Her nervousness was going now, being displaced by anger. 'I saw how he handled her on the night of the storm; I saw how he coped in a strange boat under dreadful conditions. I *know* he can sail her – and sail her well.'

'You – you saw!' His voice was suddenly harsh

and Charlotte realised, with a sinking heart, what she had just said. 'You were there, on the boat, with a man, all night!' He moved closer, catching her shoulders, shaking her. 'You lied to me!'

Guilt rose as it always did so easily when he accused her but she forced it down. 'Yes, I lied.' It took all her courage to stare him in the face. 'I lied because I was desperate for sleep, I lied because I knew what you would think if I told you the truth.'

He shook her so hard that her head jerked backwards and forwards. 'Of course I know what to think. I know what women are like, all the same, their loins burning with lust for a man, any man.'

'No.' Charlotte forced the word out through gritted teeth. Behind her she heard her mother's voice, rising in a wail: 'Sinful. Sinful. I shall burn in hell.'

With an effort she brought her fists up together between her father's arms, forcing his hands from her shoulders then stepped swiftly away from him, putting the table between them. 'You don't know what you're talking about,' she snapped. 'It was in the middle of a storm, for heaven's sake. If we hadn't fended her off from the other boats, kept the mooring lines taut, she would have sunk! We were busy all the time, with the sea breaking over us, and you–' it was almost laughable '–you think that we would have spent time indulging in passion. On a night like that!'

Her amusement seemed to disconcert him. 'There is a small cabin on a lugger,' he protested, but for the first time he seemed unsure of

213

himself. 'You could have gone there.'

'For goodness sake! The boat was empty. She was in the middle of paying up, with no ballast, in a storm.' Charlotte could not keep the quiver out of her voice. 'You must be a lot more passionate than I am even to think such a thing possible.'

He was on her in a flash. 'But an unmarried woman, a virgin, shouldn't think about such things, shouldn't even know about them.' He came closer, breathing heavily. 'Are you a virgin, Charlotte, are you pure? Or has that man,' his voice grew harsher, his breathing more ragged, 'has he had his way with you? Corrupted you?' His face flushed an unbecoming red. 'You can tell me, child, you can confess all to me.' He held out his arms. 'Tell me, Charlotte, tell me all.'

She ducked away from his embrace and moved further around the table. 'There's nothing to tell.' She was frightened though she did not understand why. 'I have done nothing to be ashamed of. At least...' Her wretched conscience threw up another confession she had to make.

'What? *What?*'

His eagerness sickened her and she made the announcement without any forewarning. 'I have employed Granfer-John on the *Faith-Lily* too.'

He stopped. 'That old reprobate.' He snorted, but to her relief he seemed to become a little calmer. 'It's a good thing I came home, Charlotte. As I thought, you don't know what you are doing. To employ a man like that, incapable of doing the hard work on a boat, shows how little you know.' The flush was fading

214

from his face now, and he smiled at her in almost his old superior way. 'You need to maximise your earnings from that boat, my dear. Especially now that you are no longer working for the Polruans. Now, when I am Captain–'

'Wait a moment,' she interrupted. She moved closer. 'What do you mean, "No longer working for Polruans"?'

He seemed embarrassed, unable to meet her eyes. 'Well, I assumed…'

'Yes?' She was quivering with suppressed fury.

'I mean – here you are in the middle of the day…' he flashed her a sudden, forgiving smile. For a second he looked like a kindly prophet and Charlotte suddenly wondered if he would have been so successful a preacher if his hair hadn't turned prematurely white. Would his moral authority have been less if he had still been the sandy-haired man she vaguely remembered from her youth? In her present state she found the thought comforting.

He wagged a finger at her playfully. 'Don't tell me, Charlotte, that you are playing truant, like a naughty schoolboy?'

Usually, she knew, such a suspicion would have roused his anger, led to a long discourse about dishonesty. His very good humour confirmed her suspicion. He already knew that she had been sacked.

But he had been at sea since it had happened.

Charlotte stared at him, her face growing whiter as the implications became clearer. She had always known that Frederick wanted to sack her, but he had never had the courage – until the

215

day of the procession. He had arrived that morning determined to get rid of her. The ridiculous search for long-lost files, the hunt for missing invoices – she had known at the time those were only a pretext. And, the night before he went out to sea, her father had been out very late, explaining that he had been with the Spargos since nine o'clock. But she had been with them then and there had been no sign of him.

He had been with Frederick Polruan, arranging for her dismissal.

For a few seconds, fury deprived her of the power to speak then the words came spewing out. 'You arranged it! You and Frederick Polruan arranged it between you.' She was sickened by his duplicity. 'Do you really believe that those were the actions of a Christian gentleman?'

Her words seemed to cut through the silence like a klaxon. Feet planted firmly apart she confronted her father, her silver-grey eyes stormy with anger while her fingers twisted damply in the ample folds of her skirt.

For a second or two he seemed to quail under her accusing gaze. A dull colour burned briefly in his cheeks then he rallied, moving towards her, his head lowered aggressively.

'You!' His deep voice rattled the plates on the rough dresser and vibrated in her stomach. 'You dare to accuse me! You, an undutiful child, a breaker of our God's Commandments, a *sinner!*'

The resonant tones were almost palpable and she instinctively took a step back before she could gather herself to attack him.

'You have betrayed me.' Charlotte's voice shook with the intensity of her anger. 'You have deliberately made me an object of contempt. *You,* who stand in the pulpit and preach that a woman's reputation is her greatest jewel – you have deprived me of mine. And not content with that, you have now lost me my job, the one chance I had of supporting myself, the one chance this family has of staying respectable.

'And for what?' she demanded, raising her voice as he tried to interrupt. 'So that you can gain by blackmail what you do not otherwise deserve, so that by putting me down you can build yourself up. So that you can achieve a position in the Methodist Church for which I begin to think you totally unsuitable!'

She leaned forward, staring him straight in the face. Her words had fuelled her anger, driving out any fear she had had. 'You,' she said, coldly and deliberately, 'are despicable.'

Her mother's faint mew of horror was obliterated by his roar. 'Sinner!' The word resonated through the house. 'Viper!' He pointed, his finger quivering with the force of his fury. 'Down on your knees and pray for forgiveness, or else–'

'Or else what?' she shouted over him, her clear voice ringing through the small room. 'What can you do to me that is worse than you have already done?'

She stared at him across the table, her breast heaving with the strength of her emotions, then, even as she watched, she saw his face change.

The antagonism was replaced by something

217

else, something that made her suddenly back away towards the door. But she was too late. He had caught her arm before she could undo the latch, jerking her towards him.

Charlotte was as tall as her father, but was no match for his strength. Holding her close against his body he dragged her across the room, throwing her face down over a chair.

She began to scream then, cursing, begging, but it was too late. With one broad hand he held her down while with the other he fumbled at his waist for his belt.

Frantically, she turned her head to him. 'You can't do this,' she shouted, struggling helplessly under his hand. 'I'm not a child. I'm not a naughty schoolgirl.'

But her words were muffled as he flung the voluminous skirts and petticoats over her head, exposing her legs and her naked buttocks.

Lost in the suffocating folds of material she retched, the humiliation, the immodesty of her position making her physically nauseous. She was a grown woman, he was a preacher; he couldn't act like this, he couldn't do this to her! Tears of anger and embarrassment stung her lids as she twisted and writhed under his hand.

Then the belt came whistling down, lashing across her tender flesh and her body jerked involuntarily as pain lanced through her. Again he struck, and again, and even through the folds of skirt over her head she could hear his breathing, harsh and strangely quick.

Charlotte brought her arm up to her mouth under the enfolding material, forcing back her cries by burying her teeth in her flesh. She could taste her own blood in her mouth as she sobbed silently under the cover of her skirts.

The belt fell again and again despite her struggles, lacerating her tender skin until she felt that the whole of her lower body was on fire. Once, maddened by the pain, she tried to kick him, but he merely brought the belt down a few times across her exposed thighs, expanding the throbbing sea of agony, until she stopped retaliating.

Drowning in a sea of torment and humiliation, only one thought stayed clearly in her mind; she would not give her father the satisfaction of hearing her cry out. She clenched her teeth harder in the flesh of her arm, stifling her cries as the belt fell again and again accompanied by his excited panting.

It seemed an age before his restraining hand fell away and the beating stopped. In the silence that followed, above her own ragged breathing she could hear her mother's quiet sobs and then her father's voice, hoarse and unfamiliar.

'I – I shall go out to the chapel. To pray.' Then hurried steps and the slam of the door behind him.

Slowly Charlotte slid back onto her knees and settled her skirts in their right position. Her face was wet with tears but they were tears of fury and confusion as much as pain.

How could he humiliate her like that? How could he treat her in such a way?

There had to be more to this than mere anger; there was something else, something she didn't understand. She had a confused feeling that in some way her father had enjoyed chastising her. The thought frightened her and she pushed it quickly away, unable to cope with it in her present state.

She only knew one thing: from now on it would be open war between them.

'What do you mean, you can't?' Frederick Polruan demanded angrily.

George Angarrack twisted his hat around in his hands. ''Tisn't that I don't want to be helpful, sir,' he said hastily. 'I'd burn that little bitch's boat for you, with pleasure.' A momentary gleam in his eyes indicated to Polruan that the man rather wished he'd thought of the idea himself.

'Then why won't you?' Frederick played with the paper-knife on his desk, watching the man carefully.

'Because the boat is gone from her moorings, sir.' Angarrack was almost contemptible in his eagerness to please. 'She sailed this afternoon, sir. With that brem gert chap what's been paying her up and Big Rory and his brothers on board.'

They had not known of their imminent sailing when he spoke to them this morning. For a second Frederick wondered if Briars had seen them together and guessed what he was planning. He gave a reluctant laugh. 'What a crew! Briars'll be lucky if he gets back alive. Those men will tip him over the side as soon as look at him.' He began to feel happier. It looked as if Charlotte had arranged her own downfall – and that of Kit Briars. 'Well, at any rate,' he said, more cheerfully, 'there's not much chance of them ever making any money out of that boat.'

Angarrack twisted his hat again, looking uncomfortable. 'I wouldn't say that, sir. They've got Granfer-John Jelbert on board too.'

'That old man!' Now Polruan did throw back his head and guffaw. 'He's so decrepit I wonder they managed to get him over the side.'

'But he's brem sharp still, sir. And he knows a lot about fishing. I wouldn't be surprised if they don't do well. As long as Big Rory doesn't throw them overboard, of course,' he added quickly, catching sight of the look on Polruan's face.

Frederick gripped the paper-knife until his knuckles were white then he stabbed it viciously into the top of his desk. It stood there, quivering.

'I don't care what they do,' he said, and his voice was suddenly bitter. 'I'll make sure that neither that damn man or the tart will ever sell a single fish around here. So let's see how much good they'll get from my father's boat then.'

Chapter Sixteen

The top bulb of the hourglass was almost empty; nearly time to hand over the watch.

The lugger was only partially decked and Kit had to move carefully as he went slowly round the boat, checking that all was well before handing over to a fresh watchman.

Across the black velvet of the sky the stars glittered, while below, he could see their earthly counterparts, the riding lights of other fishing boats, each well away from the other because of the mile-long wall of driftnets that floated out from the bows of each vessel. Further off, even in this light Kit could just make out the low-lying black humps of the Isles of Scilly, huddling against the horizon, so low that it seemed any storm would overwhelm them.

He checked the lines holding the nets. Pray God they had a good catch, for Charlotte's sake. Granfer had promised that they would, but even so...

Thank God for Granfer, he thought with a grin as he checked the sails, wrapped around their yards and stowed along the port side of the vessel together with the huge twenty-foot oars with which the lugger was manoeuvred in and out of harbour. Kit had known himself to be a good seaman but, without Granfer's help, he would never have got the *Faith-Lily* out of harbour, let alone to the Scillies. Even to change tack meant every crew member working together with never a fumble as the foresail was lowered and taken round the mast to the other side of the boat before being hoisted again. And as for fishing...

Back to the stern and check the punt, the small rowing boat also on the port side to balance the pull of the nets over the starboard bow. All secure, and the last of the sand had dribbled now into the bottom part of the hourglass. Time to change watch.

As long as all this helped Charlotte. She was so lovely, so brave. He could recognise the steely strength under her controlled demeanour, the love of life, of physical exertion, of freedom that her father had done his best to subdue. But it was still there, she was still fighting back, still struggling like a butterfly in a chrysalis towards a new world, a new freedom that she sensed but did not yet know.

Well, he would do his best to make sure that she reached the freedom she deserved. His body stirred as he remembered her lips under his, cool and controlled on the surface but underneath...

He moved forward and pulled open the sliding hatch in the bulkhead. Inside, in a small cuddy under the foredeck, the air was warm and fetid with the breaths and odours of four men sleeping in close quarters. In a boat this size there was no concern for the comfort of the crew; they bedded as they could, huddled together like animals. And it was not through lack of design, Kit had realised. The boat was beautifully designed and built, the holds for the nets, sails and fish laid out with care and forethought. It was just that the Cornish fishermen were hardy creatures who saw no profit in comfort.

He reached in and pulled at the bundled shape of Big Rory. 'Your watch,' he hissed quietly.

The big man stumbled blearily out, rubbing his eyes, his sea boots in his hands. 'What a bloody life.' He stretched, his great body arching backwards, hands thrust heavenwards. 'I need a drink.'

Kit nodded at the hollowed-out granite stone that served as a fireplace on board ship. A dull glow from the coals showed that the fire was still alive. 'Make yourself some tea. It will help to keep you awake.'

'Tea!' Big Rory snorted in derision. 'I meant a real drink.' He stuck his arm into his sea boot and pulled out a bottle. 'Brandy – nothing like it.'

The first challenge to his authority. Kit had known that it would come, it was impossible to have men like this as crew and not expect some challenge, but he hadn't anticipated it so soon. He took a firmer stance on the deck. 'I told you before we boarded, no alcohol.'

'Hark at the little goody-goody,' Big Rory jeered. 'Anyone would think you were a bleeding Methodist but you're no stranger to the booze, from all I hear. Just agin it for the lower classes, are ye?'

'I told you, no alcohol.' Kit moved swiftly, his hand shooting out and whipping the bottle from Big Rory's clasp before he knew what was happening. In a single movement Kit swung round and flung the bottle as far out to sea as he could. For a couple of seconds it seemed to hang in the air, glimmering in the starlight, then it sank with barely a splash and Big Rory was on him.

Huge hands gripped his round the throat, squeezing the breath out of him. Kit wheezed, fighting to stay conscious, his booted feet stamping on the deck as he resisted Big Rory's efforts to throttle him. The fisherman towered over him, using his weight so that, despite his efforts, Kit felt himself being forced backwards inch by inch.

The world was swimming in front of his eyes, his lungs were aching for air. Kit was only barely aware of the side of the boat stopping his remorseless backwards progress. His hands scrabbled uselessly at the great fingers that were squeezing out his life. This was it, he knew. If he was unconscious when he hit the water he wouldn't have a chance. The pressure increased and he felt his feet leave the deck and flail helplessly in midair.

'Let him go.'

For a few seconds Kit wondered whether the words were a figment of his imagination, then the pressure on his throat eased and he fell choking and gasping onto the deck of the *Faith-Lily*. He wiped his face with a shaking hand and looking up, saw Granfer-John standing on the foredeck with a revolver in his hands.

'Get up, boy,' the old man said. ''Tes no good you sitting down with the likes of he around.'

Kit struggled to his feet. 'Glad you arrived.' His voice was a grating whisper and he massaged his throat tenderly.

'Ah. Bin lucky to sleep, what with you two stamping and banging fit to wake the dead.' He gestured with the gun at Big Rory who was backed up against the mizzen mast, his face pale in the starlight. 'What shall we do with he?'

Each breath was agony to Kit's throat and he was shaking with reaction. It took a huge effort to say, 'Let him stand watch. That's what I got him up for.'

'And forget about what he just tried to do?' Granfer-John's voice rose in disbelief. 'You're off your head.'

'Not forget,' Kit grated. 'Just make sure he doesn't do it again.'

Granfer-John shook his head. 'Well, you're the cap'n but I d'reckon you're mad.'

Kit grinned painfully. 'That's what you said when I bought the gun and look how right I was then.' He limped across and picked up the sea boots which Big Rory had brought out with him and shook them upside down. A second bottle fell out of one and rolled noisily across the cover of the fish hold.

Kit picked it up. 'A man with forethought,' he noted. 'I must remember that.' Then he hurled it over the side before turning the hourglass over so that all the sand was in the top bulb. 'Your watch, Big Rory,' he said, and limped back to Granfer-John's side.

The old man looked at him compassionately. 'You were lucky there, my lad. Another minute and you'd have been a gonner, I reckon.' He clapped Kit on the shoulder. 'You get below and catch some sleep; I can stay up here and keep an

226

eye on things.'

The thought of going down into that stuffy atmosphere almost made Kit gag; he shook his head. 'It's a mild night. I'll be all right out here.' He wrapped himself in his warm, hooded fisherman's cloak and lay down on the foredeck. Above him, the stars shone as serenely as they had only a few short minutes ago, but now his mood was completely different.

He had been wrong to let himself relax, to think that he had left his troubles behind on land. Troubles were everywhere. And to forget that even for a few moments was to court disaster.

The chapel had always been a refuge for him, a place where he could revel in his power, his authority, but now he dared not enter it.

William Trevennan turned abruptly, leaning his head against the cliff-face that towered over him. 'Oh God!' His voice shook with internal anguish. 'God, help me.'

Behind him, on the rocky beach, the waves broke and frothed but all he could hear was Charlotte's bitten-off gasps as the belt fell again and again across her white skin. *'No!'* The word was almost a shout and he pressed the heels of his hands hard into his eyes to try to hide the vision of her, bent across the chair, vulnerable, open, her skirts above her head.

Sin. He had fought so hard against it, used the energy with which he fought it in himself to inspire his sermons. He had even used his one previous great sin to help him rise to greater heights of eloquence, transforming the self-hatred which consumed him as a result of that dreadful act into a whip with which to flagellate the villagers. And it had worked. He had achieved so much, converted so many. Sometimes he thought that it had been God's will that he had sinned that time, so that he could rise to these heights, so that he could use his hidden guilt to save others from the path of sin.

And now he was tempted again.

He groaned, pressing his hands harder against his eyes. Hadn't he done his best for the girl? Hadn't he raised her as his own, trained her to be a good woman, brought her up as a Christian?

Why should he be tempted like this?

His body was shaking with a mixture of despair and lust. His life, his planned, *Godly* life, was in ruins. How could he teach, how could he preach, with THIS hanging over him, consuming his thoughts, his ambitions, his beliefs until there was only one object of all his desires.

Charlotte's body.

'Dear God!' But he had to do something, he knew it. He couldn't commit the sin, the terrible sin, not like last time. Somehow, he would have to fight it.

Borlase's face came to mind, almost as if God had put it there and he sighed with relief, feeling his tension subside. He would go to the Superintendent; Borlase would help him. There was no need after all to actually tell him the whole truth, not every detail. Borlase probably wouldn't understand it anyway, so holy as he was and out of this world. But a generalised discussion – that might even improve Trevennan's position with the Superintendent, show that even though he was a good man he could still admit to weakness. And it would be a chance to make sure that Borlase had put forward his recommendation as he had promised he would. He was an old man, ill and failing fast – it wouldn't do for him to forget.

Trevennan was sure that a discussion about sin and the power to resist evil was all he needed. He *knew* that what he was feeling was wrong but his own strength wasn't enough to stop him. But let the Superintendent pray over him – let the Superintendent comfort and strengthen him with words of wisdom – and Trevennan was sure that he would be able to resist after all. Especially if he knew that Borlase had sent his recommendation off. NOTHING would stop him from achieving that ambition.

Already feeling happier, William Trevennan moved away from the cliff and began to stride the two miles to Newlyn.

The sea around the Isles of Scilly was an almost transparent turquoise. As he leaned over the rail on the quay at St Mary's, Kit could see fishes swimming and flashing across the Bay, turning instantly together like a flock of birds in an autumn sky. Everything around him was clean and perfect, with only the dirty smudge of smoke from the steamship from Penzance to show that they were living in the middle of the nineteenth century and not a hundred years earlier.

'Here, boy.' Granfer-John came up, limping heavily on the uneven stones of the quay, and thrust a bag into his hands. 'Twelve hundred fish at ten shillings a hundred. That used to be six quid when I were a lad.'

'When I was too.' Kit took the bag, tossing it up and down. 'But in Newlyn, mackerel were selling at twelve and six a hundred, once I saw fifteen shillings.'

Granfer-John spat. 'That's 'cos there weren't many, lad. If we'd been fishing around the Cornish coast we might have got a better price, I grant you, but we'd have been brem lucky to have brought in two hundred fish. You work it out. We've earned more here.'

'Perhaps.' Kit looked again at the smudge of black smoke on the horizon that showed the position of the steamship. 'What will the people who've bought the fish do – put them on the steamer?'

Granfer-John shrugged. 'What if they do?' He took out his pipe and fiddled with it, pointing the stem at Kit. 'What if they do make a bit of money out of it? That's business, isn't it? That's how they get their living.'

He seemed affronted by the suggestion, as though Kit were criticising him. 'I just meant,' Kit said hurriedly, 'that there's no reason why we shouldn't do that. We can put our fish on the steamer as well as anybody. And if the freight charges aren't too high, we'd make more money out of it.'

'Argh.' The old man spat again. 'That's providing you've got someone at the other end to meet up with your fish and sell them, boy. And we don't have that.'

'But we could have.' Kit was suddenly enthusiastic. 'If I write to Charlotte she can arrange it.' He could feel his pulse suddenly speeding up at the thought of writing to her. She had haunted his sleep these last few nights; her tall athletic figure had strode through his dreams. He realised suddenly that he wanted to impress her, to show her that he was a good custodian of her ship, worthy of the trust she had put in him. He glanced again at the smoke, closer now. 'I can get a letter on the ship when she sails.'

Granfer-John glanced at him. 'Seems to me,' he commented drily, 'that you take a brem interest in that young lady and her concerns.'

Kit turned away and stared concentratedly up at the bulk of the Star Castle that loomed over the small town of St Mary's. 'What rubbish,' he said.

The hand that Borlase stretched out to Trevennan was trembling and almost transparent. 'My boy,' he said shakily, 'it was good of you to come to see an old man.'

'It was the least I could do.' Inwardly, William Trevennan cursed his luck. The old man was ill, if not dying. Had he been able to write his recommendation? 'I am sorry to see you so weak.'

'It was the celebration in Penzance. I suppose I shouldn't have gone, though it was pleasant to meet your Charlotte and that young scamp, Boy-John.' The old man smiled and closed his eyes wearily.

And he hadn't even known she had been there!

Anger burned through Trevennan but he forced it down. There were more important considerations at the moment, more important even than his obsession with Charlotte and her strong white body. He sat beside the old man's bed, holding the thin, cold hand. 'It wasn't, perhaps, wise of you.' It took all his self-control to sound calm and concerned. 'Especially with all the work you have to do. You shouldn't have over-taxed your strength in that way.' He forced a smile. 'But I am sure you will be more careful in future.'

'My boy, there isn't going to be a future for me, not in this world at least.' Borlase opened crêpey eyelids and smiled tenderly at Trevennan. 'But you need not worry. I have done as I promised you, I have written your recommendation.'

The relief was so great that he dropped the hand he was holding; thank God for that at least! Then the dying man went on: 'But I won't be able to see it through, I am afraid. That will be the responsibility of the new Superintendent.'

'The new Superintendent?' Shock and horror made William's voice too loud for a sickroom and he was suddenly aware of the nurse peering inquisitively at him around the corner of the door.

Borlase moved weakly against his pillows. 'A good replacement, a good Christian and a hard worker. One, moreover, who knows the people of Cornwall.' He coughed painfully. 'That's important, you know. The Cornish – they're not like anyone else. They need someone who understands them.'

He began to cough again, his thin frame

shaking with the violence of the paroxysms. As the nurse came hurrying in he managed to get control of his breathing. 'A good man,' he gasped. 'He worked in this Circuit about nine years ago.'

Trevennan felt himself grow cold. A horrible certainty took hold of him. 'Do you mean–'

The nurse pushed him aside. 'I think you should go, sir. Mr Borlase is still very poorly.'

But he couldn't go, not until he knew the truth. 'It isn't – you don't mean...' The name refused to be said, cloying his mouth with hate and fury.

As the nurse gently lifted her patient on his pillows, Borlase said the name he dreaded to hear: 'Richard Robinson. A fine man with a young son. I believe you know him?'

Chapter Seventeen

'Sign here. You don't take no fish without a signature.'

George Angarrack took the pen, dipped it into the small travelling inkwell that the ship's officer held out to him and signed hastily, trying to give the impression that he had meant to do so all along. Damn it, he was the fisherman, not some blasted clerk. It was only because Polruans was in complete chaos these days, ever since Charlotte Trevennan had been sacked, that he had been pressed in to meet the steamship from the Isles of Scilly and collect the fish.

All around him the small quay at Penzance teemed with movement. Bags and boxes of fish and vegetables were being unloaded from the steamer, men and children were rushing to and fro trying to find relatives they were supposed to meet, and Islanders were standing bemused by all the noise after the peace of the Scillies. He stepped hastily aside as a pig was dragged along, squealing and shrieking with a small boy hanging onto its tail. 'Is it always like this?'

'Worse, usually.' The officer gave the unformed signature a sneering glance and folded the paper into a breast pocket. 'That's your fish over there.'

As Angarrack surveyed the wooden crates he asked, 'By the way, will you take a letter for one of the clerks at Polruans? It's addressed to a Miss

Trevennan at Mousehole but I was told she works with you.' The officer grinned broadly. 'Love letter, I expect – from some great tall fisherman. Not a local, that I can tell.'

'I know who you mean.' Angarrack barred his teeth in a wolfish smile. 'Certainly I'll take it.'

'Must be strange having a woman clerk.' The officer handed over a crumpled letter. 'Any good?'

'Not for clerking,' Angarrack said, 'but then, what can you expect?'

'Women are only good for one thing,' the officer agreed. 'They should stay in the house where they belong.' He sketched a brief salute and walked off.

Angarrack turned the letter over and over in his hands. It might be a love letter, of course – though it was difficult to imagine that anyone would find the great girl attractive, but it might be something else. He tapped it against his teeth, thinking deeply while he made up his mind then, turning his back on the departing officer, he split it open with a thick thumb.

'Stop that, Boy-John.' Charlotte reached out and slapped gently at the grimy hand that Boy-John was advancing across the table towards the thick slice of bread and butter. 'No food until you've washed your hands. I've told you before.'

'Oh, Lotty!' the child's voice rose in a wail. 'I'm brem leary.'

'Wash your hands and then you can have some supper.' She watched as he trailed slowly across the kitchen and struggled to pour water from the pail into the bowl as she had taught him. Looking at his dragging steps, weak from hunger, it was hard to believe that it was barely three hours since he had eaten a huge plate of grilled mackerel and potatoes. He swung round suddenly and she hastily wiped the affectionate smile off her lips.

'Is this clean enough?'

She inspected the small hands carefully. 'They'll do.' Only just, she decided, but at least the child would be quiet while he was eating. Sighing, she turned again to her accounts. How long could they last on the small amount of money she still had left?

Kit would need money initially to provision the boat. While fishing off the Scillies the men would sleep on board during the day and fish all night so the captain would have to provide food for them. How long before he felt he had enough spare money to send her some? And why hadn't she heard from him?

She gazed unseeingly out of the window. The *Faith-Lily* was valuable. Had she been stupid to let a strange man sail her away like that? It would be so easy to change her name, sail her to another port, then sell her. How could an old man like Granfer-John stop him?

But this was only her head thinking; her body just remembered his touch, his smile, her lips burned at the memory of his kiss. She woke in the night murmuring his name.

And she hadn't heard from him. That was her real concern. She had expected something, a letter to say that they had arrived, telling her of the voyage over, what the fishing was like … but she had heard nothing.

She moved uneasily on the hard wooden stool, its three legs mercifully steady on the uneven flagstones. Why hadn't she heard?

The knock on the door made her jump and even Boy-John stopped chewing to stare with his mouth open as Susan Spargo pushed the door open.

'Susan.' At the sight of the girl's pale face and red eyes Charlotte jumped to her feet. 'What's the matter?' She reached out to the girl. 'Is it your mother?'

Susan nodded. 'She's been and took to her bed.' The girl's voice broke. 'And I can't get her up, no matter what. And your da…' She stopped and both women turned to look at Boy-John who was staring at them, agog, as he chewed slowly at a piece of bread.

'Boy-John, eat that outside,' Charlotte said quickly. He stared at her, his mouth open, unwilling to miss anything interesting that was happening. 'I'm still hungry,' he protested.

She reached over and cut a thick slice of crusty bread from the loaf then handed over the piece of cheese she had been saving for tomorrow's lunch. 'Here. Now go.'

He ran off, a cheeky grin on his face and she knew that she had fallen yet again for his wiles. 'Young gannet,' she muttered to herself then turned to Susan. 'What about my father?'

'I don't know. I – I mean, he comes round to see Ma, and it's very kind of him and he talks to me…'

237

Charlotte's lips tightened but she made her voice as gentle as possible. 'What does he say?'

The girl's fingers twisted. 'Well – nothing, really, but he asks about Tom Matthews and what we do and, and... And he LOOKS at me, Charlotte.'

Charlotte nodded. She knew exactly what Susan meant. She, too, had been made uncomfortable by her father's looks, his eager questions, but she was his daughter; he had no such authority over Susan.

'You could refuse to answer,' she suggested.

'Oh, I couldn't. He's a preacher and all, soon to be made a proper preacher. I couldn't tell him anything like that.'

Charlotte drew idly with her finger on the table top. It was his position that made everything so difficult. He was a good man, everyone agreed that, yet somehow... 'What about Robert?' she asked.

'He's out most nights, playing cribbage down the Harbour Office. And if I told him...' her voice trailed away.

Charlotte knew what she meant. Robert was fiercely protective of his young sister. He might well over-react, and there was no real evidence that Trevennan was behaving other than as a concerned local preacher should.

Susan suddenly burst into tears. 'It's every night, Charlotte. He hasn't gone to sea like the other men. He's here all the time and I see him, when I'm doing the shopping, watching me.'

It was true. Charlotte had hoped to have a long talk with her mother but Trevennan was always about, and she knew that he would make Bertha suffer if he caught them together.

'You must get your mother up,' she decided. 'She's the right person to be with you, and it's bad for her, anyway, lying in bed all day. The longer she does it, the more difficult it will be to get her up again.'

She had only meant it as advice but Susan took it as an offer. 'Oh thank you, Charlotte. You can make her do it, I know. She likes you and you've got – you can persuade people.'

'I'm nobody's favourite at the moment,' Charlotte reminded her but the girl was already brighter, adjusting her bonnet, moving to the door. 'If we hurry, we can get her up before your father arrives.'

Well, the last thing Charlotte wanted was to meet her father face to face. Especially in these circumstances. She wasn't quite sure what was going on in William's mind but she had a suspicion that he would be angry at her interference.

'You can't stay here like this, old friend.' Dick Robinson laid a sympathetic hand on Hargraves' shoulder. 'Drinking and moping won't bring your son back.'

'Nor will staying sober.' Hargraves shrugged his friend's hand away. 'At least this way I can numb the pain.' He reached again for the half-empty decanter. 'What else is there to do?'

'Get away,' Robinson suggested. 'A change of scene, meeting other people…'

Hargraves' fist thudded onto the table top, making the liquid in his glass slop over the sides.

'My son is *dead,* Dick. Dead. Gone from me for ever.' His voice broke and he buried his face in his hands. 'For ever, Dick. And was only young. All his life – wasted...'

'Not wasted,' Robinson interrupted. 'He was a good man, James, he did a lot of good while he was on this earth and now he is with God.'

Hargraves choked. 'I don't think he even believed in God.' His voice was thick with grief.

'As long as God believed in him,' Robinson said softly. 'I always think that is the more important thing.'

'Oh,' Hargraves' voice was an ocean of despair, 'what shall I do? How can I go on?'

'You'll go on because you have to, because people need you – your employees, my son Mark...'

Dick Robinson moved away until he was staring out of the windows. Although darkness had fallen the crimson curtains had not been drawn and James could see his face reflected in the glass. It looked suddenly old and Hargraves noticed for the first time the way his old friend's hair was thinning, the dark strands pulled across the top of his head in an attempt to hide the ravages of time.

A sudden spasm of pity moved him. 'What is wrong with Mark?' He had to clear his throat twice before his words would come out.

Robinson shrugged. 'The old nightmares again. He had outgrown them but now we are to go back to Cornwall they have returned. It is every night now – sometimes two or three times in a night. Always the same dream – about a man murdering a woman and threatening to kill him, as far as I can tell. He shouts and talks freely enough in his sleep but when he wakes he can remember nothing.'

'But what can I do?' Hargraves demanded. 'I'm not a doctor.'

'No, but you reared two fine boys yourself and he is at that awkward age now – fourteen, nearly fifteen.' Robinson sighed. 'I think that perhaps a father is the worst person to have around at that age, especially if he is a minister. And when the mother is dead…'

'He's at school,' Hargraves protested.

'Not while he is having these nightmares. He is not happy there anyway and I feel that he needs reassurance while he is suffering like this. Anyway, I am hoping that the Cornish air will help his asthma. It's considered to be very good for invalids.'

It took Hargraves a second to put two and two together and then he was on his feet. 'You're asking me to go *there*, to Cornwall, with all those crooks and murderers who have taken my sons…'

'I am asking you to go there to help *my* son,' Robinson said quietly, 'to put his welfare above your own.'

'I won't do it!' He was shaking with fury now. 'Not there. Not even for you. I won't – I can't!'

Robinson gazed at him. 'Kit would have done it.' His voice was calm, reflective. 'Kit had courage enough for anything. Even as a young boy he would stand up for a friend of his, even if it meant fighting boys twice his size.' He smiled

241

faintly at Hargraves. 'Are you man enough to be a worthy father of your son?'

Charlotte heard the muffled sobs as soon as she opened the door. 'Boy-John!' She hurried to the huddled heap of misery, curled up on the black settle. 'What's the matter?'

Carefully, she sat herself beside him and lifted the child onto her lap. For a few seconds he lay, unresponsive, then his body softened and he threw his arms around her. 'I wish you were my ma, Lotty. I wish you were, then the boys wouldn't say...' His sobs grew louder, more uncontrollable.

'Say what, Boy-John?' Then she guessed. 'Have they been nasty to you because you don't have a father?'

He gulped and the arms he had flung around her neck tightened suffocatingly. 'They say she was a bad woman, a – whore?' He stumbled over the unfamiliar word.

She held him close, rocking him gently. 'Then they're wrong, Boy-John. I knew your mother and she was a very nice lady, very pretty and kind. But she wasn't...' she tried to think of a way of putting it that an eight-year-old would understand. 'She wasn't as clever as most people. Sometimes, it happens that someone is born not clever, and because of that – well, she was easy to lead astray. But if she did wrong it was only because she didn't know what she was doing, not because she was a naughty person.'

The sobs had slowed. She continued rocking, talking soothingly. 'And it doesn't mean that

242

you're not a good person, either. You're as good as anyone else. Understand?'

He was quiet for a few minutes. She could feel the wet patch on her shoulder where his tears had soaked through her dress and every few seconds they were both shaken by one of his huge sobs. Then he said, slowly, 'That means that my da were a bad man, then. He shouldn't have done what he did.'

Almost certainly, but she couldn't let him think that. 'He might not have realised how simple she was,' Charlotte said quietly. 'And perhaps it was all a mistake. Perhaps he meant to marry her but he was a fisherman and drowned. He might have been a very good man, really.'

The child was silent as if thinking this over. Charlotte let her head drop back against the settle, feeling drained. First Susan, then Mrs Spargo and now Boy-John – everyone seemed to need her strength, her influence but she felt tired as she had seldom felt tired, worn out by worry about her financial situation, about the boat, about Kit. Even walking through the village took an effort, knowing that she would be cold-shouldered, ignored, whispered about.

Boy-John raised his head. 'Do you know what, Lotty?'

'No, my love?' Despite her tiredness she made her voice as encouraging as possible. As he was opening his heart to her she was expecting almost anything. Be gentle with him, she reminded herself.

He sniffed. 'They say there's a dead whale floating in the Bay. D'you think it might have

243

eaten someone, like the whale in the Bible?' He wriggled round so that he could look at her face. 'If it did, they might still be in there. Wouldn't that be fun?'

Bertha was stretching as he entered the cottage, her slender figure was silhouetted against the oil lamps as she arched backwards to ease an ache in her back. For a second she was again the young woman he had married and he felt the ache in his groin deepen at the sight, then she was aware of him and straightened abruptly. 'You are home early, husband.'

'Mrs Spargo has left her bed.' William Trevennan knew that he should be thankful. It had been too pleasant these last few evenings, talking to Susan, her young body close to his, her downcast eyes and soft voice, the scent of young flesh. His conscience had screamed at him every time he went to the cottage but he had continued to go, telling himself that it was his duty to comfort the bereaved.

He knew it was the effect of worry, it always affected him the same way. Impulses that he could keep under control by the strength of his will under normal circumstances grew overwhelming when he was worried. It had been bad enough when he had become a local preacher; wondering whether he had been accepted, the nervousness that came over him when he had to preach ... it had been all the worry then that had led him to – he jerked his mind quickly away from that thought. That was long ago; it was past and done with. God would doubtless punish him after his death, but in this world, at least, there had been no repercussions.

But now it was worse, so much worse. The worry about being ordained, the change of Superintendent at this particular time, Charlotte's disobedience ... tension burned in him, building inexorably. Even prayer no longer helped.

Bertha had turned away. 'Dinner will be ready in a moment, husband.' She bent over the fire, stirring the savoury-smelling fish stew. Her full skirts outlined her slim waist, emphasised the swell of her hips. Above, the tight bodice followed the curve of her breasts and her white neck rose from it, almost too frail for the mass of coiled hair that in this light looked as blonde as it had been when he first knew her.

Suddenly the needs of his body were too great to be denied. In one step he was behind her, his arms folding around her waist, his face buried in her soft hair. 'Wife,' his voice was harsh with desire, 'Bertha, please, for God's sake...'

She whirled away, pulling herself loose with surprising strength. In two paces she had reached the table and snatched up the bread-knife. 'No!' Her voice was high and shrill. 'Don't touch me! You shan't touch me!'

'Please...' The need in his voice was palpable but she merely held the knife closer. 'I'll kill myself!' Hysteria rang in every tone. 'Come one step nearer and I'll kill myself.'

'Oh God.' He dropped his head into his hands. 'Bertha, please, we're man and wife. Please, after all this time...' His body throbbed and burned, lending a desperation to his words. 'Please, Bertha, *please*.'

'You promised!' Her voice echoed off the stone flags. 'When we were married you promised that you would not make me sin. You promised on your life, before God! You promised before HIM!'

'Not sin, Bertha,' he pleaded, as he had never pleaded before. 'Not when we're married. I've – I've been good to you all this time, Bertha, given you a home, raised your child.' His body was a pyre of agony, with him, a burning brand. 'He's dead now, Bertha, dead and gone. There's no sin – there CAN be no sin...'

Her hand moved, forcing the point of the knife against her chest. He could see the round shadow growing bigger as she increased the pressure. The knife was sharp, he knew that. It wouldn't take much to cut through the taut material and then–

'No!' The word was forced from him. He covered his face with his hands, fighting back tears of frustration and hurt. 'No, Bertha. Don't do it.' His voice was quieter but still it throbbed in time with his body – his treacherous, sinful body. 'It's all right. I won't – hurt you, I promise.' But he couldn't stay here, not with her standing there, so close, all he needed, all he couldn't have.

He pulled open the door, walking stiffly. 'Don't keep supper. I'm going to the chapel.' But praying wouldn't do any good, praying never did do any good. As he lurched uphill he was aware of a girlish giggle in the shadows, of two forms, half-seen, enclosed in each other's arms. And, beyond them, other female voices, female forms.

'Oh, God,' he groaned. 'God help me!' And turning his face away so that they should not see the tears, he hurried to the chapel.

Chapter Eighteen

George Angarrack signed for the fish. Above him, the steamship from the Isles of Scilly pulled at her mooring in the lively breeze. 'Here you are.' He handed the paper back to the officer.

'All cargo signed for now,' the man said cheerfully. 'Except for that lot.' He nodded his head at a pile of wicker baskets overflowing with fish. 'Not sure what I should do about that.'

'Whose are they?' Angarrack had to fight to keep the smile off his face. He would have put money on the answer.

'Oh, her!' he said casually, on hearing Charlotte's name. 'Don't you worry about her. She'll be along later.' He shrugged. 'You know women, never on time.'

And grinned as he remembered the letter he had taken, the letter that had warned Charlotte that her fish would be sent to Penzance, and which was still sitting on Polruan's desk, waiting for his return.

Robert Spargo leaned over the rails, watching the bustle of life in Mousehole Harbour.

It was the height of the mackerel season. Many of the luggers had moved away from Mounts Bay completely, fishing off the Scillies or the North Sea, others were out every night catching shoals of mackerel in their great driftnets. Each morning they would come to harbour and off-load their catches, then the crews would sleep during the afternoon before going back out for another night's fishing.

Even at this time of the year there was always something going on. Today, one of the boats had come in for a new suite of nets and they had just been barked, the local term for steeping the new nets in a concoction of oak bark that left them dark brown and made them more resistant to being rotted by sea water. Grateful for anything that could arouse his interest during the long boring days of his convalescence, Robert watched as the crew carried them from the barking shed on the cliff, and draped them like enormous lace curtains from the railings to dry. The smell made his nose tickle.

A heavy hand clapped him on the back. 'Enjoying your holiday, boy?'

Robert twisted round awkwardly on his crutches. 'Holiday?' He couldn't keep the bitterness out of his voice. 'I'll be fit for Bedlam at this rate, stuck at home with all the women and old men while the real work's done out at sea.'

'Must make you sick as a shag,' Oggy Gurnick agreed. He was one of the few village men who moved between the worlds of the fishermen and farmers, helping out with the harvests, catching moles and using his donkey and cart to transport goods when there was no other work on hand.

He glanced behind him now at the patient donkey standing in the shafts of a small cart, its long ears adroop. 'How'd you fancy a trip to

Penzance? I've got to collect stuff from a steamer but I can fit you in easy enough. You and your crutches.'

The chance was too good to miss. Anything was better than dawdling his way through another summer day. Robert swung himself cheerfully up onto the seat.

The driver clicked his tongue at the donkey and flapped the reins. 'Heard about that there whale, have you?' he asked as the animal ambled easily over the cobbles. 'Come ashore near Penlee.'

'Alive?' Whales sometimes beached themselves for no reason that anyone could see.

'Dead as a doornail! But a huge gert thing. You can see how one of they could have swallowed Jonah.'

Robert shifted awkwardly on the hard wooden seat. 'I'd pay to see that.'

'Not with your leg broke you won't. But she'll be there till next spring tides I reckon, so you may get to see it later on.'

The thought that his leg was growing strong cheered Robert until the other man added, after a pause, 'Preacher's been spending a brem lot of time round at your house these days, hasn't he?'

'No, you can't!' Charlotte said swiftly. 'It's a horrible idea.'

'Oh, Lotty. Lots of the men have been to see it. And – and it's eddicational really, 'cause of that man in the Bible and all.'

'You mean Jonah.' Charlotte ran her hand through her hair. However had Granfer-John managed? Keeping Boy-John out of mischief was a fulltime job. Even to try combining it with looking after the cottage seemed an impossible task. 'And speaking of education–'

'We can't afford it,' Boy-John interrupted. "Tis thruppence a week up Paul Lane and you said we need all the money we can get.'

Charlotte sighed. 'Well, when Kit and your grandfather start sending back the money they've earned, we'll think about it again.' When! How long would it be before she heard? She moved to the window, staring through the thick, uneven glass (cleaner than she had ever known it before) at the rough-hewn granite wall of the cottage the other side of the court.

Kit! The thought of him kept her awake at night, the memory of his mouth, his touch, haunted her sleep.

Should she write to him? But all she could do was send a letter to the Post office at St Mary's. Would they make an effort to find him, to tell him that there was a letter waiting? Was the boat even at St Mary's? It could be anywhere by now, either following the shoals of fish or... She forced that thought out of her head.

The fact that she had to hide her worries from Boy-John and even listen to his eulogies about Kit made it all the more difficult. And now the child was on about seeing the whale.

'Look, Boy-John.' She took a deep breath and turned back to him. 'That whale is dead and no one knows what it died of or how long ago. It isn't healthy to go near rotting things like that.'

'But it's only a fish,' the boy wailed. 'If dead fish were bad for you, everyone in Mousehole would be dead by now.'

'A whale isn't a fish.' She dragged up half-remembered facts from her years at Miss Chegwin's Seminary in Penzance. 'A whale breathes air, just like you and me.'

'So it can't do me any harm.'

The knock on the door was a welcome interruption. 'Robert!' She pulled the door wider. 'Sit down and rest your leg. Is your mother well?'

He tugged off his cap, hitching his crutches under one arm. 'A lot better. I never thought she'd leave her bed again but you got her up all right.'

Charlotte shrugged. 'Lying in bed, worrying and thinking about the past never does any good. Somehow, once you are on your feet again, things get back into perspective.' She smiled. 'Your problem was, you were too good a son, Robert. You should have got her up to cook your dinner. It would have been better for her.'

'Well,' he looked bashful at the compliment. 'I had Susan to do all that.' He felt silent, his face suddenly grave, twisting his cap in his hands. 'There's something I got to tell you, Charlotte.'

Her heart jumped awkwardly. 'About the *Faith-Lily?*' Suddenly she couldn't breathe. She stood motionless and Boy-John slipped from his chair and moved to her side, thrusting a cold grubby hand into hers.

He wouldn't meet her eyes. 'Well, sort of.' Robert Spargo fell silent again.

There was something blocking her throat. Charlotte had to cough twice to clear it before she could get the words out. 'She – she hasn't – sunk?' She felt Boy-John's hand grip hers more tightly, the small fingers clutching at hers as if to a lifeline.

'No, no, nothing like that,' Robert began and she relaxed with a sigh. 'At least – well, the thing is, Charlotte...' He took a deep breath. 'There's two gert piles of fish rotting on Penzance Quay with your name on them.'

'Stupid!' Frederick Polruan slammed his hand down on his desk.

'Sorry.' George Angarrack shifted uneasily from one leg to the other. 'I thought you'd want me to stop Charlotte getting that letter. And as you weren't here–'

'Not the letter!' Frederick resisted the urge to hit the man. How could he be so stupid?

'All you have done,' he explained, marshalling his patience with an effort, 'is stop the blasted female getting a load or two of fish. But she'll soon know what's happening. They'll send another letter or someone will tell her or something.'

'So, what should I have done?' George asked sulkily.

'Taken the fish when no one was looking, of course. That way, we'd have got the benefit of selling them and they wouldn't be rotting on the quay, inviting every busybody who goes past to see who they belong to.'

'And when she found out that she should have been having fish?'

'Where's the evidence?' Polruan demanded.

'One fish looks like another. She might suspect us but she couldn't prove anything. I'm a Magistrate, I know all about evidence.'

'Who's this Jonathan, then?' Granfer-John demanded. He adjusted the tiller slightly and the *Faith-Lily* heeled over, the sea creaming beneath her hull.

The question took Kit by surprise. He swung round, a gutted fish in his hand. 'What? What Jonathan?'

'That's what I've just been and asked you.' The old man puffed easily at his pipe but his faded eyes watched Kit carefully. 'You was shouting out his name all night, and kicking like a blamed mule.'

Kit threw the cleaned fish into a basket and reached for another, trying to decide what to do. He never spoke about Jonathan if he could avoid it, but Granfer-John had left his grandson to help him. To lie or to refuse to answer him seemed churlish in the circumstances. He stared down at the fish in his hand, the elastic body still iridescent from the sea, and tried to make up his mind.

'There's no one can hear you, lad.' The old man's voice was little more than a murmur. 'But, seeing how upset you was when you cried out his name, I thought it might ease your mind a bit to talk about him.'

The gutting knife ripped through the silver belly of the fish. His eyes on his work, Kit said slowly: 'He was my brother. He – died – a couple of years ago.'

Granfer-John puffed again. 'Drowned, did he?' Despite the casual tone Kit could hear the curiosity in his voice. He glanced up but the fisherman's eyes were fixed on the set of the sails.

'I suppose that was something else I said last night,' he muttered bitterly.

'One of the things, lad.' He puffed again. 'Why don't you tell me? Don't do no good keeping everything bottled up inside. That's when it all comes out in your sleep and then everyone knows.'

Automatically, Kit glanced at the three brothers gutting fish together nearer the bows. The screams of the gulls hovering over the ship, swooping on the guts as they were thrown overboard, covered all sound of their conversation. Perhaps it was better to get it out now, while they could not hear.

'We were out sailing,' he began, unwillingly, the words dragged out of him. 'In a yacht with a Cornish crew. We were foolhardy, I suppose, mucking around, daring each other to do stupid things.'

He stared sightlessly out across the blue waves, sparkling now in the early-morning sunshine, all trace of the clouds of the previous night blown away. A few miles ahead, the sea altered colour, the bright turquoise showing where the sandy sea bed lay only a little way under the surface of the sea. And in the midst of the turquoise, emeralds set in enamel, the Isles of Scilly lifted their green heads.

'One of the Cornishmen boasted how he had once fallen over the bows of a ship and caught at a trailing rope and climbed back on while she was still sailing. Jonathan said he could do that, he was a good swimmer – and he ran forward.'

Kit closed his eyes, trying to mask out the scene that was forever engraved on his brain. 'I shouted to him not to do it but he jumped. And the ship hit him.'

He swallowed. 'I went in after him while the others tried to get the boat around. There was a strong wind and it took them half an hour to get back to me.'

He fell silent. 'Was he badly hurt?' Granfer-John asked quietly.

'Just knocked out, I think. But he sank like a stone and there was weed there, under the surface.' Despite his iron control his voice wavered. 'I dived and dived but it was minutes before I could pull him free and when I finally got him up – well, if I could have got him on the boat at once we might have saved him, I suppose, but as it was...'

'And why do you blame yourself, lad? You did all you could.'

'I was the oldest,' Kit said bleakly. 'I should have stopped him, I should have saved him. And I failed.'

'I reckon you're in the right with heaven, though,' the old man said placidly.

'Right with heaven?' Kit snorted. 'What about right with my father? What about right with myself?'

A gull, tired of waiting, swooped down, catching the gutted fish carcase in its beak and whipped it out of his hand.

Kit stared after it for a second, then threw down the gutting knife with a curse.

'You can't come in here.'

George Angarrack moved swiftly from his desk to bar Charlotte's way as she threw open the door to Polruans offices.

'Can't I?' Charlotte was in no mood to let herself be ordered about. 'It'll take a better man than you to stop me, George Angarrack.' She waggled her finger in his face and he backed hastily away. Behind him she could see the startled faces of the clerks with whom she had worked for so many years, their mouths open with astonishment. Well, let them stare, she was no longer the paid employee, always polite and willing. She was her own woman now.

With a flick of her long skirts she moved past Angarrack and headed for Frederick Polruan's private office, throwing the door open with such force that it banged back against the wall.

Polruan was seated behind the desk and his pudgy face grew paler at the sight of her. 'Hoy, what do you think you're doing?' he blustered, struggling to his feet.

Charlotte reached out and pushed him so that he sat down abruptly again. Inside her, behind all the anger, she was conscious of a fierce joy. All her life she had apologised for being tall, for being active, for being strong; now, suddenly, she was aware that these were good qualities, qualities she could take advantage of. She leaned forward, resting her hands on the desk top, her furious grey eyes staring down into his. 'You stole my letter, you deprived me of my fish.' She spat the words out and he cringed back in his chair.

'You don't know that.' His voice was a weak bluster. 'You've no evidence.'

'Evidence!' She straightened swiftly. 'That answer is all the evidence I need. Is that the answer of an innocent man, a man who doesn't know what I am talking about?'

She stared down at him as he quailed under her anger. He was despicable, weak, mewling, not one tenth the man his father was. 'It's lucky for you that I don't have any real evidence,' she snapped. 'If I did, you would be up before your own bench in the Magistrates Court in Penzance. As it is...'

'As it is, you are trespassing.' Her admission that she did not have any proof had given him the courage to try to fight back. 'You may not be aware of this, my dear girl–'

'Don't you patronise me.' Her anger flared again. 'Treating me as if I were second-rate just because I am a woman, despising me when I am as good as you any day.'

'As good as me!' She was taken aback to discover that he found this genuinely funny. 'You! The semi-literate daughter of a common fisherman! You think you are as good as I am, just because you own one stupid little lugger.'

She could feel herself weakening under his scorn. 'A lugger you wanted for yourself,' she reminded him.

He ignored her. 'Suppose you had got those fish – do you really believe that you could have sold them?'

She stared. 'There's a market in Newlyn...' she began.

'A market means buyers and sellers. And who do you think would buy *your* fish?' he stood up, leaning forward so that his face was pushed against hers and she could smell his sour breath. 'No one here, my girl, I've made sure of that. And no one in the Scillies, either. I've put the word around. The name Polruan means something. The agents all know that if they annoy me...' He drew his hand across his throat in a cutting motion.

'You can't do that.' But even she could hear the uncertainty in her voice. Polruans was the biggest firm in Mounts Bay. It was just possible...

He must have read her thoughts. 'I can do it – with the important firms, anyway, the ones that will offer you good money. Oh, you'll find someone to buy the fish, eventually, at a low price – jousters, people like that. And because they know the situation they'll offer even less than they would have otherwise. How long do you think you can last like that? How long will you be able to run your beloved boat at a loss?' he laughed again. 'No, Miss stuck-up Trevennan, you're *not* as good as me, not by a long chalk – and it's time you knew it.'

'You don't own everyone.' It was hard to make herself continue the fight; only her self-respect prevented her from giving in to him there and then. 'There are other fishing grounds, other markets. The *Faith-Lily* can go to Ireland, the North Sea...'

'Not with that old man on board,' he sniggered,

'and without him, how many fish do you think that great lump you've got captaining her will catch?'

He snorted. 'A good-looking lad, I grant you, but you're not the only woman who's fallen for those broad shoulders and fair curls, and you're not the first that he's been making up to.' He leaned closer, lowering his voice. 'Do you know that tart, Peggy May, *Miss* Trevennan? No? I once caught him giving her money. But you are the one who's paying *him* and you think you're as good as me!' He threw his head back and laughed again, genuinely amused.

She was shaken but she would not let him see it. 'I'll find a way.' Her voice vibrated with determination. 'I'll find a way. Your father gave me that boat because he thought I could make a go of it, and I won't let him down. He was a good man, a far, far better man than you'll ever be,' and she turned and stormed out through the office, her head held high.

Outside, she leaned against the wall, her knees shaking with reaction. She had defied him, up until the end, but she knew, deep inside, that he held all the cards. Polruans was a respected firm, with a great deal of power, directly and indirectly. If he had put the word around...

The late-afternoon breeze cooled her burning cheeks. Around her, the noises of a fishing town rose on the summer air. With a sigh, she pushed herself away from the wall and walked slowly down to the bottom of Trewarveneth Street and peered over the drop to the shore below.

The tide was out and the sand was thronged.

Fish, laid out individually if they were special enough or in the wicker baskets known as pads, were displayed on the beach. Around them, the buyers crowded; jousters, cowels hung from their foreheads and their white aprons with huge pockets for carrying salt, bartered in loud, uncouth voices with fish agents and fishermen. Lobster pots were piled up in one place, and patient donkeys waited in their shafts, ears flopping, while their owners argued and bargained around them and all the while, overhead, the gulls wheeled and screeched, patterning the sky with their white wings.

Louder cries and shouts made her look up. A donkey cart, laden with ropes being taken to Mousehole for barking, was attempting to climb the steep slipway. To the accompaniment of shouts and jeers the driver galloped the beast along the hard sand, getting up enough speed to carry the laden cart to the top of the slip. As always she watched, her heart in her mouth as the little creature, dragging the heavy cart behind him, struggled up the slip. Slower, slower, and just when she thought that it wouldn't make it, that the cart would have to be unloaded and the contents carried to the top by hand, the small hooves found an extra bit of purchase, the straining hocks gave a final push and they were up on the level ground, passing her with a wave of the whip.

She had nothing to sell at the market and the *Little Western* wouldn't be making the trip from the Scillies until Monday, but now was as good a time as any to test Frederick Polruan's assertion.

261

Taking a deep breath she walked down the slip onto the firm sand.

'Good afternoon, Mr Tresize. I am likely to have some good quality fish...'

'Got all I need, thank 'ee.' The reply was accompanied by a nervous glance. 'I don't need no other suppliers.'

She tried again. 'On Monday...'

Even the jousters turned away from her although she knew that, in the end, it would be they who bought her fish – for a very low price.

It only confirmed what Polruan had told her. Disheartened, she turned away.

'Excuse me, miss.' Startled, she looked up at a stranger, English by his accent, middle-aged, balding. He pulled off his bowler, giving her an embarrassed smile. 'I couldn't help hearing you talk, miss, and the truth is...'

'Yes?' She raised her eyebrows, surprised.

'Well, the fact is, I'm making some enquiries. About a boat that came in here, the *Isabelle* – and I can't seem to get anyone to understand me. Nor I can't understand them,' he added with a sudden burst of honesty.

She guessed that it was mostly put on. The Cornish were not forthcoming to any stranger asking questions, and would often put on an incomprehensible accent rather than answer.

Well, after what had happened today she had no fellow feeling for them at all! Smiling, she said, 'I gather that you can understand *me?* But I am afraid I have no good news for you. The *Isabelle* was lost off the Scillies with all hands some weeks back.'

'I know that, miss, but my employer's son was on her and he's hoping against hope that he got off somewhere before she went down. It's a small chance, but do you know if the ship called in here? Some say she did and some say she didn't and I can't make head nor tail of it.'

Charlotte frowned, trying to remember. Polruans was always a hotbed of gossip where anything to do with the sea was concerned. Usually, she tried to close her ears to the talk, but some of it got through.

'I think she did,' she said slowly. 'But only to pick someone up. The brother of the captain or something. She wasn't here for any length of time.'

'And nobody got off?' he asked. 'The chap I'm looking for is a toff, a Mr Hargraves, only son of a rich shipowner in Hull.'

She shook her head. 'I've never heard of anyone disembarking and that name isn't familiar.' She sighed. 'Poor soul, his only son! No wonder he's clutching at straws. But the ship went down with all hands. We even lost a man from our village on her.'

'It's a dangerous life. Oh well,' he sighed, 'I'll just have to go back and tell him the boy's gone.' He glance down at the fish laid out all round him. 'They look good – and taste good, too. I had some for dinner in the Union Hotel last night and very delicious they were, too. And cheap, compared to London – cheaper even than you can get them in Billingsgate.'

She had never heard the name and he explained: 'It's a big fish-market in London

263

where I come from. Lovely fish they have there, but the cost! Two or three times what you pay here.'

Charlotte didn't want to hear about how much other people got for their fish; it simply brought back to her the trouble she was in. She had to make the boat pay, otherwise it would be a victory, a victory for Frederick Polruan and her father.

She had turned away when the thought occurred to her – Kit Briars could be described as a toff. She swung back. 'Sir–' But already common sense had reasserted itself. 'Son of a rich ship-owner'. Would a man like that be staying with Granfer-John in a small fishing village while he payed up a fishing boat for a pittance? Or even risking his life, sailing her fishing?

'I – I'm sorry.' It would be unkind to raise false hopes. No one had got off that ship. 'I just wanted to say, I hope you find him.'

'No chance of that now,' the man answered morosely. 'He didn't get off anywhere else and this was the *Isabelle's* last port of call. No,' he sighed, 'I'll have to go back tomorrow and tell him. If I get the early train I can be back in London by bedtime.'

Raising his greenish bowler, he bowed and moved away, leaving her alone with her worries.

Chapter Nineteen

'I bet Kit and Granfer John have caught more fish than anyone else in the whole of Cornwall, don't you, Lotty?'

'I'm sure they have.' She would not burden a child with her worries, but it was difficult even to sound enthusiastic. There they were, risking their lives to catch fish and she couldn't sell them. Not that she cared at all about Kit, she reminded herself. A man who would pay a prostitute was below contempt, but it was hard that Granfer-John was having to work on her boat for no proper reward.

She ran her hands distractedly through her hair. She had to think of something. A small hand touched her arm tentatively and she glanced up into Boy-John's worried eyes as he stood by her chair.

'Are you cross with me, Lotty? I didn't mean to upset you.' His grubby face was suddenly serious.

With an effort she laughed, ruffling his fair hair. 'Of course I'm not cross with you. Or, at least, only when you get into trouble.'

His blue eyes grew huge. 'When do I get into trouble?' he demanded indignantly.

She began to count, ticking off the occasions on her long fingers. 'When you fell over the cliff at Newlyn and tore your trousers, when you got

265

caught by Farmer Matthews and got a good hiding for trying to poach his rabbits, when you sneaked into the prayer meeting and let out a jar full of grasshoppers – and don't deny that because I saw it under your jumper as you went out. AND heard them!'

'Well,' he grinned engagingly at her. 'They're only little things.'

'And I've been here less than ten days,' she reminded him. 'By the way, what did you do today?'

'Nothing.'

The studied innocence of his face made her suspicious. 'You didn't go to see that whale? Because I told you–'

'Never went near it, Lotty.'

She sighed and got up from the table. Whatever it was, she would probably learn soon enough. 'Well,' she began, then stopped at a rap on the door.

She and Boy-John stared at each other. Except for the visits of Susan Spargo and her brother, no one had called at the cottage since she had been there. She raised her eyebrows at Boy-John. 'Is this anything to do with you?' she hissed.

He shook his head, looking baffled. Whatever he had done today, he obviously wasn't expecting anyone to have found out about it – yet.

Charlotte hurried to the door. She pulled it wide. 'Father?' Her voice rose with surprise and Boy-John ran quickly to the black settle and ducked behind it.

'Charlotte.' He doffed his black hat. 'May I come in?'

She stepped silently back, her heart thumping. They had never spoken since the time he had beaten her, although she had seen him step aside to avoid her when it had looked as if their paths might cross in the village. And now, he was here.

He crossed the threshold of the tiny cottage and she felt the atmosphere grow leaden. 'Where's that boy?'

She immediately thought of the guilty look on Boy-John's face when she had asked about today. If he had been annoying her father... 'He's not here,' she said quickly, turning her eyes away from the sight of a bare foot sticking out from behind the settle. 'What do you want him for?'

He snorted. 'Him? Why should I want–' He caught himself, lowering his voice, smiling at her. 'It's you I want, Charlotte.' His voice was soft, almost caressing. 'I wanted to ask you to forgive me, to come back home.'

She stared at him, wide-eyed. 'Why?' Her mind was racing.

He spread his hands, the thick fingers callused from fishing. 'Your mother needs you. If you are not around she becomes excitable, unreliable.' Under his busy white eyebrows his eyes burned with honesty. He stepped forward, reaching towards her. 'Come back to us, my dear.'

His voice cast its usual spell. It was an effort to drag her eyes away from him. Charlotte swallowed before she could get the words out. 'But – you were angry. You said...'

He moved closer. He seemed more like an Old Testament prophet than ever. 'It says in the Bible "Rejoice with me for I have found my sheep which was lost." And you, the child of my hearth – so much more precious…'

She wavered, struggling with herself. For so long this man had been her guide. While he was angry with her she could use that anger to buttress herself against him but now, coming as a supplicant, despite all her best intentions she felt herself weakening.

'Father,' her voice grated. 'Father…' She made an effort, stepped back, away from him. He had beaten her the last time they met, she reminded herself. Why should she be the one who had sinned?

'Come back, Charlotte. For all our sakes but mainly for the sake of your mother.' His voice dropped a half-octave. 'She needs you, she misses you. Misses your calming influence, your strength, even your humour.'

The word helped to break the spell. Humour? When had he ever allowed humour in the cottage? When had he ever allowed even common chatter? She narrowed her eyes, staring at him.

'And you, yourself, Charlotte.' She realised that he was as lost in the spell of his words as she had been. 'What will it mean to you, cutting yourself off from your family, living alone. What will people think but that you have lost your reputation, that you have been disowned?' His blue eyes crinkled in an understanding smile. 'I know you, Charlotte; I know that you are a God-fearing child. But for the sake of your reputation, for the sake of your mother, I beg you to come home.'

She stared at him. Inside she was aware of a

great fountain of anger and bitterness, a volcano of fury that threatened to erupt. Only twenty years' experience in controlling her temper helped her to keep it from boiling over. Every sentence sent another wave of anger rolling through her. Reputation? What right had he to talk of her 'reputation' when he had been instrumental in destroying it? What right had he to call her a child when it had been her wages that had kept the family from starving whenever he had stayed home from his work as a fisherman? She could feel her jaw aching with the effort of fighting back the flood of words that threatened to choke her.

'And you, Father?' Her voice shook slightly with the effort she was making to appear calm but he seemed not to notice. 'You said I should come back "for all our sakes". What is *your* reason for wanting me back?'

Had she just imagined the sudden quick look he gave her under his brows, a glance devoid of love or compassion? His mouth curved into a tender smile, the smile of a loving shepherd. 'I have a thousand reasons, Charlotte.' His voice resonated with love. 'The reasons I have given for your mother's sake, for your own – they are mine too, because I love you both.'

It would be so wonderful to believe him. Despite herself the thought slid into her brain. To live on good terms again, happily, at peace. 'But your own reasons?' Even in her own ears her voice sounded harsh as a corncrake's and she saw his brows drawn down.

'You want more? More than the fact that you

should be at home with your mother and myself?'
Under his lowered brows his bright blue eyes
stared at her, so different from the soft faded blue
of her mother's eyes.

'I want your reasons,' she insisted.

He shrugged. 'They are those of a good
Christian, of course. I want you home because
you should be at home, because, in my position,
the position I hope to fill when I am ordained, I
should be setting the example in the village, the
example of the Christian household, echoing, in
my poor way, the examples of Joseph and Mary,
even of our own dear Queen. But how can I set
an example when an unwed girl deserts my
hearth, deserts it to live in the house of a sinner,
a stone's throw from my own place?'

She could feel her fingers knotting together as
he went on, 'I have a greater concern even than
just our family, Charlotte. I have to have a
concern for the whole village, for all the souls in
it.' He spread his hands supplicatingly to her.
'Charlotte child, in this village there are sinners
who have come to believe in the Lord because of
me, men who once had no hope of redemption
but who now are saved – through the power that
God has given me. And I can save more,
Charlotte, hundreds, maybe thousands more.'

Lost now in the glory of his vision he turned
away from her, walking swiftly around the
kitchen, hammering one fist into the other palm
as he enumerated his plans, his future. 'If – *when*
I am ordained, I will have the time, the position,
the *authority* to convert more men to the grace of
God. I shall be able to save so many souls,

270

Charlotte, I know I shall.'

He swung round to stare at her. 'But I have to be ordained, Charlotte. I have to have that behind me or I shall only be doing a small part of the work that God has fitted me for. And there is so much against me. I am no longer a young man, I am uneducated. And now, I can no longer say that I am the head of a Christian family.'

He sighed heavily. 'What can I say, if the new Superintendent asks why you are living apart from us? What if that is the reason he refuses to put me forward for ordination? What will your conscience be like, child, if you know that hundreds, perhaps thousands, of souls will not be saved because of your actions?'

The old familiar guilt rose up inside her. It took an effort to say, 'And what of the sermon you preached against me, Father? What of the fact that you have denounced your only child as a sinner?'

He dismissed the question with a wave of his hand. 'It will do no harm. I have shown that I can see the beam in my own eye. What sort of preacher would I be if I ignored sin in my family but condemned it in others?' His chest swelled. 'Yes, indeed. I have shown that I shall support what is right and preach against what is wrong, wherever I find it. And that when there is repentance, I can forgive.'

'And – the *Faith-Lily?*'

He moved towards her, a kindly smile parting his lips under the full, white beard. 'You have had your rebellion, child. Now that you have seen the error of your ways I know that you will not fight me any more. Will you?'

He dropped his voice and reached for her, putting an arm around her waist. 'Let us kiss and make up, like good Christians, Charlotte. Then we can go home.'

She lifted her head. 'But Boy—' Her words were cut off. His mouth came down onto hers, cutting off the words before they could be spoken.

For a second, she was still, taken by surprise. Her mind was in a whirl. He had done a lot of good in the village, she knew it. There were men who were good fathers and hard workers who once had seemed to have no future but a drunkard's death and a pauper's grave. What if by her actions she really had prevented him from doing more good, saving more souls?

Lost in her thoughts, she didn't notice at first as his arm tightened around her waist. Then his lips pressed harder against hers and she felt the first stirrings of unease.

With an effort she pulled her head back. 'Father!' But his free hand moved behind her, his fingers twining into her thick, dark hair. 'Charlotte,' his voice was suddenly thick. 'If you knew how I've missed you, how empty the house has been without you. To lie there, at night, knowing that you are not in your virginal bed...' His mouth lowered again on hers, harder, more demanding.

Panic rose inside her. She began to struggle, wriggling in his grasp, jerking her head back. 'Father!' Her voice was high with nervousness. 'Father, stop.'

He caught at her again, pulling her tall body

hard against his. Although she was strong for a woman she was no match for his thick-set strength. 'Charlotte,' his usually controlled voice was suddenly rasping and he breathed as if he had been running. 'Charlotte, you must come home. I can't bear to have you away like this.' His mouth came down on hers again and now she could feel his tongue pressing at her lips.

She clamped her teeth shut and began to struggle in earnest, lashing out at him with feet and fists but he was too strong for her.

He laughed, jerkily, excitedly, and she was reminded of his strange uneven breathing when he had bent her over the chair and beaten her.

The memory galvanised her to greater efforts. One sharp jab caught him under the ribs and he loosened his grip for a second. It gave her the chance she needed. With a supreme effort she jerked herself back and broke from his grasp. For a second she reeled, stumbling over her long skirts, then she turned and ran for the door even as his hand shot out.

He missed her waist but caught a handful of her skirt. She threw herself towards the door, anxious only to get away from him, to get into the open where he would not dare to act so strangely – and the force of her movement was too much for the material.

The fastenings around the waist gave way, and the material parted along the seam with a loud ripping noise. In slow motion she felt her skirt begin to slide down over her petticoats. She knew what would happen but could not stop herself. Another step and she was treading on black wool, the material tangling round her feet and she was falling, falling.

She landed full-length on the flagstones with a thump that took her breath away for a couple of seconds, but it was all her father needed. She was aware of him, throwing himself onto her, his strange breathing heavier, more erratic than ever. Frantically she squirmed and lashed out but he was too heavy, too strong. The harsh male smell of tar and fish and old sweat caught at her nostrils.

Vaguely, through his gasps she was aware of words, strange, unfatherly words. 'Charlotte, darling, beauty...'

Horror twisted at her stomach. She had to get away, get help. Turning her face from his she forced out a scream, struggling to hold his hot, searching mouth from hers with all the strength in her arms. But he was too strong, she knew that – too strong, too determined. She could not escape without help.

Then, suddenly, she was aware that Boy-John was beside her. She heard his voice, shrill and furious. 'Let her go! You get off my Lotty!' And saw his bare feet by her head lashing out.

He was too small to do much harm to a man like William Trevennan. For a second the preacher turned his attention from Charlotte, raising himself on one elbow to strike at the child. 'Little bastard!' The voice was contorted with hate and fury. His fist shot out, thudded sickeningly against the child's thin chest.

Charlotte saw the small body fly backwards through the air and land heavily against the old wooden settle. The force of his landing made her wince but she knew that this was her only chance.

With a scream, half-terror, half-rage, she raised her knees, catching her father in the stomach. He jack-knifed with a gurgle and fell heavily onto his side.

She kicked herself free from the dead weight of his body and pulled herself gasping to her feet. Her knees shook so that she could hardly stand but she knew that she had to get away from here, get them both away. Leaving her torn skirt on the ground she leaned over Boy-John, pulling him frantically across the floor to the door.

She was dimly aware of her father, struggling for breath, beginning already to get to his feet. She had to get them both outside before he could stop them.

Gritting her teeth she heaved at the child, her fingers fumbling behind her for the door catch. Everything was moving in slow motion, her fingers heavy and shaking, struggling with the catch; Boy-John's body a dead weight at her feet and her father, like a mountain, rising slowly to his feet, taller than the sky, moving towards her with the inevitability of a giant wave.

Then the catch suddenly gave way; she pulled the door open, her breathing deafening in her own ears, and then they were both outside, outside in the cool darkness of the summer night and the child's body was sliding over the sea-rounded cobbles of the court and there were people around, faces peering out enquiringly, wondering at the screaming.

Reaction shook her. She fell with a bone-jarring thud to her knees, letting the boy's body sink to the ground. Behind her, she knew her father had struggled to his feet and she had a brief glimpse of his face, black with fury, as he stepped over her, stepped over both their bodies and then he was gone, disappearing around the corner without a word.

She was aware of the silence, aware that none of the faces were speaking. Her fear, her disgust overwhelmed her. Leaning over the gutter at the side of the court she vomited as if she wanted to rid herself of everything she had ever eaten in her life. Dimly, behind her, she knew that there were silent, watching faces but she did not care. If only she could empty herself of the seething emotions that churned inside her, if only she could be as innocent as she once was.

A voice spoke, chiding, haranguing. The faces quivered, left. There was only one face left. A soft, cool hand held her forehead, a gentle voice soothed her. Charlotte took a deep breath, blinking the tears from her eyes. 'Susan.' Her voice was a painful thread of sound.

'You'll feel better in a moment.' Susan knelt beside her. 'I'll help you inside when you've finished.' Her voice grew angry. 'Those stupid, small-minded–'

Charlotte reached up a shaking hand and caught at her sleeve. 'Susan. My father. Did he ever try ... to kiss you?'

She heard the girl's intake of breath, her sudden stillness. When Susan spoke it was in a voice as weak and small as Charlotte's own. 'He

276

said it was the habit amongst the Early Christians.'

Charlotte closed her eyes, tears of sickness and disgust running down her cheeks. 'Oh, dear God!'

And bent again over the gutter.

Chapter Twenty

'How can I help you, miss?'

Charlotte refused to let her nervousness show. Tossing restlessly through the night, struggling to come to terms with her father's behaviour and what it meant, she had reached one irrevocable decision; whatever happened, she could never return home. And this meant she was alone in the world, alone to sink or swim as her own efforts decided.

She was determined to swim.

She gripped the edge of the counter in an effort to stop her hands trembling. The Union Hotel was the best hotel in Penzance, the hotel where the Mail coaches stopped, where the rich ladies came to hear theatrical renderings and where the Freemasons met. It was not the place where a fisherman's daughter was likely to meet with a warm reception, especially in her present quest. She cleared her throat, trying to imitate the easy assurance of old Mr Polruan. 'You have – there is a gentleman staying here...'

The doorman's eyebrows rose. Charlotte knew what he must be thinking of her but she had to go on, she had to find out.

'A – a Londoner. With an accent.' She could feel her face burning with embarrassment.

'And his name?' No 'miss' this time. He must think she was a prostitute.

'I – I don't know.' Trying to ignore the disdain in his face she gave a brief description of the man with the bowler hat, but even as she spoke she knew that it was hopeless. The doorman would never let her speak to the man. If it weren't for the fact that she had left Boy-John behind, quite recovered from the knock on his head that he had received yesterday and swearing revenge on William Trevennan, she would simply have waited outside until the man emerged. But although she had extracted a promise from the boy that he would say nothing about yesterday's events, that he would not go near her father, she did not trust him. The sooner he was back under her eye the better.

The clerk obviously recognised the description she gave and a cold smile twisted on his lips. 'I'm afraid your charms did not work as strongly on the gentleman as his seem to have done on you. He has already left on the train.'

Her heart sank. She needed to speak to him. And now he was gone. Or was he? The train left at five minutes to ten. She glanced up at the large clock that dominate the entrance to the Union Hotel. It was not yet half-past nine; plenty of time to walk to the station and find the man.

And she would not let herself be intimidated by a trumped-up clerk. She was a businesswoman, she reminded herself. She had as much right to come here asking these questions as any man in Penzance. Ignoring her scarlet cheeks she forced herself to thank him gracefully and turned away. It was only as she reached the door that the thought struck her and she whirled around.

'Your clock – does it show London time or local time?'

The question would have been meaningless a couple of weeks ago. Noon was when the sun was at its highest, every fool knew that and every clock in the town had been adjusted to that time. But now that the railway line was opened, suddenly the old time was no longer right. Great Western Railways published timetables and expected their trains to run by them. And Great Western Railways used London time throughout.

Which was twenty minutes ahead of Cornish time.

The question startled him. 'Madam,' he pulled himself up to his full height and stared down at her in disdain. 'In *this* establishment we keep God's time.'

So she didn't have half an hour at all; the train would be leaving in ten minutes. She whirled around, snatching up her skirts and jumped down the front steps in one athletic leap. If she ran...

Market Jew Street was a mass of people, every one, it seemed to her, anxious to stop her in her tracks. Once past the Market House she gave up the crowded Terrace where the pedestrians walked safely above the traffic and took her risks with the horses and carts. She was aware that she was the subject of stares and comments and knew that some, at least, would get back to her father. Once that would have terrified her; now she did not care.

Out of breath, a stitch cramping in her side, she leapt the steps down to the platforms. The train

280

was still there, the engine puffing clouds of white steam, the brasswork shining.

'Ticket, miss?'

She shook her head, too out of breath to answer, and began to run along the platform. The line of brown-painted papier-mâché carriages seemed to stretch on for ever. Anxiously, she dashed on, peering through every carriage window. She could have only seconds left now. If she couldn't find him–'

And there he was! 'Mister! Mister!' She hammered her fists on the window, not caring that she was acting like a strumpet. 'Mister! About that fish!'

She saw the passengers in the carriage glance at her then look firmly away, their faces set in expressions of disgust. One woman whispered disparagingly in her husband's ear, and Charlotte's face grew even hotter as he looked her way and laughed. And then the man from the market recognised her.

He stood up, moving awkwardly over the passengers' feet towards the window, apologising, taking his time. Charlotte could have cried with vexation. Already she could hear the engine noise increasing; the smoke seemed thicker, the guard was standing back, eyeing the length of the train.

'Mister.' It wasn't the way she had been taught to speak at school or by Mr Polruan, but she had no time to impress anyone with her good manners. 'Mister – that market at Billingsgate. Who can I send my fish to?'

The whistle behind her blew, the engine noise was deafening. She saw his forehead crease with thought as the train began to move, slowly at first, then faster.

He said something but it was lost in the noise of the train. She began to run alongside, keeping pace. 'A name, mister, a name.'

The train was going faster now and she had no breath left, she would have to stop. Then he shouted it; *'Spencer & Greys!'*

'What?' She had to be sure she had got it right.

He shouted again: *'Spencer & Greys!'* There was more but the train was going too fast now, pulling away from her and she could not hear above the din of the engine, and the wheels.

She stopped, doubling over, sobbing for breath. The carriages pulled past, quicker, quicker, then there was silence and even the smell of the smoke began to clear and she could hear again the cry of gulls, shouts from the street, the sea lapping at the sea walls only feet away.

'Are you all right, miss? Did you want to get on the train?' Green corduroy trousers filled her vision. She raised her eyes. An elderly guard was bending down anxiously, trying to peer into her face.

Charlotte straightened, her hand pressed against her side. She was still panting and her hair had pulled loose from her bun but she did not care. She had found out what she needed.

'No, thank you. But I would like to know where I go to enquire about freight charges.'

William Trevennan walked swiftly from the village. He had to get away from people, he had to be able to think.

Last night – God, he must have been mad! To lose control like that, and with the boy there. He groaned out loud and a passing villager looked at him inquisitively. 'You all right, Mus Trevennan?'

He had to get away, away from people. But where? The villagers would be working in the fields, boys fishing along the beaches. Where?

The whale. The thought came out of the blue. It had been beached for days now, in hot weather and dead a long time before that. At first it had been an object of fascination and he had even used it in his last week's sermon – a discussion on Jonah and the whale; now it was given a wide berth, the smell of decaying flesh carrying inland on the breeze, and if he were to talk of it again in chapel it would be to pray for the foul-smelling corpse to be carried out on the tide. One thing was certain though; there would not be anyone around it.

Another certain thing, he knew beyond a doubt, was that if Charlotte and Boy-John spread the story of his actions last night he would never again preach in a chapel. And he had to! He could do so much good. God wanted him to, he was sure of it as he had never been sure of anything else in his life.

The wind blew in his face, bringing with it the stench of decaying whale; his lips twisted but he had to go on, he had to sort this out.

If God wanted him to continue – it was difficult to think straight with that smell in the air – then the Devil must want him *not* to. The thought spread through him like a benediction. That was it. It *hadn't* been his fault! He had been tempted.

Charlotte had been a handmaiden of the Devil, a siren to lure him from the ways of God. But right had prevailed. He hadn't, at the last, committed a sin. He had done nothing that he could not justify.

But if they described what had happened, if they connived to put the worst interpretation on what he had done, that would spell the end of his chance of ordination, the end of his hopes to be a fighter in the army of God.

It was the boy who was the trouble, he knew that. Charlotte alone – well, he didn't have the influence over her that he had once had, but he could have denied everything, put it down to hysteria – madness, even. Everybody knew she was too tall to be a proper woman and, doing a man's job as she had would very likely have over-heated her brains. But with the boy to back her up...

There was a sound of pebbles falling behind him and he swung round but there was no one there. Already, the great bulk of the whale was in sight, a grey bass on the blacker rocks, the tail awash in the sea, the huge mouth propped open on a length of driftwood by some brave soul. The smell was disgusting, but if he went past it, was upwind of the creature, he should not be bothered by the stench and he could think in peace.

Slowly, lost in his thoughts, William Trevennan walked on.

Behind him Boy-John crept, his tongue sticking out as he concentrated on not making a noise. He

284

still wasn't sure what he would do to William Trevennan, to pay him back for hurting Lotty last night, for making her cry, but it would be *awful*. His imagination played with pushing him over a cliff, of hitting him over the head with a stone. He was certain that when the opportunity came, he would recognise it.

Of course, he had promised Lotty that he wouldn't do any of this but that was just the sort of stupid promise grown-ups made you say. Getting his own back on William Trevennan was more important than that; it was almost a solemn obligation.

It was only when the great hulk of the whale came in sight that his determination wavered. He had made a promise to Lotty about this too, and she had made him repeat it so many times that it had almost stuck. But it wasn't as if he had come here deliberately, he told himself. He had always meant to keep his promise – but if William Trevennan came this way, what was he to do?

And now that he was here, it would be a pity to waste the chance. It would only take a second to examine the monster, to satisfy his curiosity, and then he could catch up with the preacher. He wouldn't stop for more than a couple of minutes at most.

Careless now of the noise he made, he scrambled down onto the pebbles and crunched his way towards the carcase. It was immense, towering over him, the skin blotched with lighter marks. Here and there great wounds gaped where the body had been torn against the rocks before being thrown onto this beach; some of the wounds, even Boy-John could recognise as having been made by the local men, possibly with the idea of obtaining meat or blubber from the rotting corpse.

He gazed wide-eyed at the animal, forgetting everything else in his fascination. Ignoring the smell, he slipped and clattered around to the other side of the creature.

Now the paler underside of the belly was towards him. Here, too, there were marks left by the locals. And he hadn't been the only one to think of the story of Jonah and the whale. Someone had used a piece of driftwood to prop open the creature's mouth so that he could see the conical teeth set in the lower jaw.

'Gosh!' he breathed. The mouth was enormous, easily big enough to swallow a man. But would he get any further? Granfer-John had told him once that whales only ate very small creatures.

He crept closer. Even though he knew the whale was dead there was still something strangely menacing about it. He could almost persuade himself that it was just playing dead, just lying there, ready to leap to life and snap at any human stupid enough to come near.

But that was silly, he told himself. Of course it was dead. Someone had even propped its mouth open, hadn't they? Closer still. Ahead of him was the dark secret mouth of the animal. The stench was stronger now. Even Boy-John was aware of it despite his interest, but he wasn't going to let a mere smell put him off.

He took another step forward. His heart was

thudding nervously, and he was half-poised to run if the creature should attempt to move, but it lay there, inert, dead.

No reason to be afraid, no reason at all. And now he was this close he would see for himself if it was possible for a man to go down into a whale's stomach. Just a quick peep, just to see if it looked possible.

Lost to everything but the whale, he laid a trembling hand on the great creature's skin. Nothing. Just cold roughness under his fingers, no sign of life.

He bent down, peering between the great jaws but it was impossible to see after the sunlight. But he would see, he would know. He took a last deep breath of fresh air and ducked down between the jaws, feeling his way in the sudden dimness. His hand brushed over scaly-feeling teeth then cold, damp tissues.

Still he didn't have an answer. He planted one bare foot on the animal's lower jaw and reached up ahead of him towards the darkness of the throat, desperate for the answer to his question. A further step. It was almost completely dark here, the smell sickening and there was an unpleasant sensation of soft, gristly tissues under his toes. Holding his breath he took another step.

And with a soft sighing sound the great mouth closed, leaving him alone in the vile-smelling blackness.

Chapter Twenty-One

'Have you seen Boy-John? Please, tell me!' Charlotte caught frantically at a neighbour's arm.

The older woman shook herself free from the grasp, and smoothed her sleeve with angry fingers. 'I don't know why you're bothering yourself with a young heathen like that,' she snapped. 'You should be at home with your father like a good Christian woman. No one would ever think you were the daughter of a fine man like that.'

But Charlotte was already running down the darkening street, her eyes alert for anyone she could ask.

She had scarcely exchanged a word with most of the villagers since that dreadful day when her father had denounced her from the pulpit, but now she did not care. Boy-John was missing, had been missing, as far as she knew, since just after she left for Penzance this morning. Something must have happened to him and she was determined to find him.

What did it matter that half the people she accosted turned from her in disgust; what did it matter if they tried to subject her to homilies on her undaughterly conduct? As long as she could find Boy-John, as long as he was all right she was willing to suffer anything.

The noise of crutches slipping on the cobblestones alerted her and she turned into the dark entrance to Duck Street. Here, the small cottages crowded so close that it was difficult to see even the rivulet that ran down beside the houses to debouch into the sea, and she could only identify Robert Spargo because of the sounds of his crutches. 'Have you found him? Has anyone seen him?'

'Not recently.' Robert sounded strangely reluctant to talk.

'But someone's seen him?' Charlotte caught at his arm and shook it. 'When? Where? Tell me!'

'Someone said they saw him early this morning.' Robert paused and Charlotte gritted her teeth to stop herself from hitting him. He had always been more likely than herself to get information from the villagers, but he was a man who took a while to think things through and hated being hurried.

Now he said slowly, 'He was going along the beach towards Tavis Vor.'

It was a cove just a little further from the village where the rocky beaches gave way to small pebbles, and was a favourite place for children to play. From the cliff top they had even set up a rope, slanting down to the shore, and would slide down it in an old fish-basket, landing on the pebbles with a teeth-jolting rattle and shrieks of laugher. She had already been there, calling for him but had had no response.

'He's not there,' she said impatiently. 'But someone must have seen him since then. That was hours ago.' Oh, why had she left him alone? Why hadn't she taken him with her?

Robert said reflectively, 'He'd go past Tavis Vor if he were going to look at that there whale.'

Her heart stood still. She hadn't thought of that. She had told Boy-John so often not to go there and so far he had obeyed. By now, she knew, the whale must be stinking. Surely even a small boy wouldn't succumb to the temptation now?

'Even if he went he'd have been back by now,' she objected. 'There are no cliffs that way that he's likely to fall from, and even a whale wouldn't keep him occupied for so long that he's late for dinner.'

Robert shrugged in the darkness. 'It were just a thought. I suppose he could have broken a leg or something.'

'He's like a cat,' she protested. 'He fell over the cliff at Newlyn the other day and just got some scratches and tore his clothes.'

'Well, he's somewhere. And if he's late for his dinner there's something wrong.'

She stood silently, gnawing her lower lip. 'No,' she said. 'He promised me faithfully that he wouldn't go to the whale. He must be somewhere else.' She could no longer suppress the worry that had been niggling at the back of her mind. This morning, Boy-John had been full of plans to get his own back on her father. Surely, after all she had told him, all her strict instructions, he hadn't tried to avenge her as he had threatened?

'You haven't – has anyone said that they've seen my father today?'

She could feel him staring at her through the gloom. 'I thought you and him weren't on speaking terms.' Then, realisation dawning, 'Susan said something about a bate at your house last night. Think Boy-John's gone after your da, do you?'

'I don't know.' She gripped his arm, the thick wool of his jersey rough under her fingers. 'Robert, please – ask if anyone has seen my father today. If *you* do it…'

'I'll get an answer.' He adjusted his crutches under his arms and swung off down the street. Despite the good weather, for once the Cliff was empty. Shrugging, he gave her a half-guilty grin over one shoulder and made his painful way into the Ship Inn, a few yards further along.

Anxiously, she hovered outside. He was renowned for his drinking but surely he wouldn't stay, not when he knew she was so worried? The windows of the inn glowed golden with the light of the pilchard-oil lamps and there was a noise of men's voices raised in happy conversation. It certainly didn't sound like the den of iniquity that her father had so often preached about, but she still felt guilty standing around outside, as if the demon drink could reach her even through the tightly closed windows.

To try to hide the fact that she was loitering outside a public house she moved along to the next building, known locally as Uncle Billy Burdo's cellar, and busied herself by staring at the barometer which the Board of Trade, in response to the fishermen's pleas, had erected the previous year.

'Your da was out past Tavis Vor this morning.'

She jumped around, her heart thumping.

291

'Before Boy-John went that way?'

'Reckon so.' He stared at her. 'You think your da had something to do with his disappearance?'

The question was too direct. She twisted her head away, staring out across the quiet harbour. 'What should I do?'

'You could ask your da,' Robert suggested. 'If they both went the same way...'

She shook her head. The thought of even seeing her father again after last night was enough to make her break out in a cold sweat. Besides, it would do no good. If he had had anything to do with the boy's disappearance...

But the suggestion had helped her to make up her mind. 'I'll go that way. It's the only lead we have.'

'We?' Robert Spargo pounded his fist against the grip of his crutch. 'If my leg was all right...'

'You'd have been at sea,' she said softly. She grasped his arm again. 'Without you, Robert, I wouldn't even have known as much as I do now.' Her face darkened, remembering the villagers who had snubbed her frantic enquiries. After all these years in the village, to be treated like that, and just because of her father...

She dragged her mind away from that line of thought; Boy-John was her first priority. She glanced up at Robert. 'If you should see the boy–'

'I'll give him a good hiding and tie him to the kitchen table so that he's there when you get back,' he promised. 'Mind yourself, Lotty. I don't want to have to get up another search-party.'

She gave him a quick smile and hurried back across the village. In the soft summer night it was not really dark but it was difficult to see her footing as she hurried over the uneven black rocks. In the end she cast modesty to the winds and bundled her skirts and petticoats up in one arm, in order to free her feet as she clambered as swiftly as she could using her free hand to help herself along.

'Boy-John! Boy-John!' But only the gurgle of the sea sucking against the rocks answered her. 'Boy-John!'

She could smell the whale long before she got to it. The tide was in now, the waves washing almost halfway up the black colossus of its huge body. If they had another storm it would get sucked back out to sea and the beach would be washed clean of its effluvium. Turning her head away from the sickening odour she hurried past, as far up the beach as possible, still calling, calling, but there was no answer.

Further on, she had to scramble over rocky headlands, the waves washing almost at her boots. But soon, even that was of no use. The incoming tide reached to the edge of the cliffs, cutting off the next cove completely.

But the cliffs here were neither high nor steep. Even if he had been cut off, Boy-John could have climbed them easily, escaping with nothing worse than scraped knuckles and a few scratches from the brambles that gathered around the cliff tops. Just in case, she shouted and called but there was no answer.

Slowly, Charlotte began to make her way back. The sea called and sighed but she would not let herself think about that. Boy-John was a good swimmer, but if he had fallen and struck his head... A phrase from the Bible came to mind. 'Sufficient unto the day is the evil thereof.' With a shiver she realised that she hadn't read her Bible or prayed once since she had left her parents' cottage, despite the fact that their whole life revolved around the word of God.

For a second she had an impulse to pray for Boy-John's safety but she repressed it. There was something nasty-minded about remembering God when you wanted something but forgetting Him all the rest of the time. She walked slowly back, the energy which had driven her here at top speed abated. She had looked for the child in the only likely place and he was not here.

With the wind coming from behind her she was on the whale almost before she realised it. Now that she was not so hurried she had time to appreciate its size, so amazing for a creature that lived on plankton. But this, she realised, was a sperm whale, the giant of the seas. The great mouth was closed but she could see the teeth in its lower jaw.

Fascinated, she moved nearer, pulling a handkerchief across her nose to keep out the sickly smell of putrefaction. She had learned about the creatures at school but nothing had prepared her for the immensity of the real carcase. She leaned closer.

And heard something.

She felt the hairs on the back of her neck rise and her heart suddenly gave a thump of superstitious terror.

Primeval instinct urged her to run, to get away

294

from this place. As if they moved by their own accord, her hands grasped at her skirts, lifting them to free her feet for flight.

She stopped herself. It took more courage than she had ever known that she possessed, but she stopped herself. In the confines of her corsets her lungs laboured for air and the world around her went brighter and darker with each thud of her heart but she stayed where she was. Her pulse hammered in her ears, almost drowning out even the noise of the sea, but she made herself stand still and tried to hear again the small, soft noise that had so frightened her.

Nothing.

She swallowed and the sound echoed in her head, then tried; 'Hello?'

Her voice was hardly louder than a whisper. She wiped sweating hands down the sides of her skirts and tried again. 'Hello?' Louder this time, but still no more than her normal speaking voice. She breathed in through her nostrils, forcing her lungs to expand, ignoring the creak of her laces, the stench of the carcase. She opened her mouth to shout—

And heard it.

A whimper, soft as a lost puppy's.

Let breath out softly, keep silent, *listen,* she told herself.

Nothing.

The sound of the sea.

The beating of her own heart.

Another whimper.

The whale? She felt her panic rise again and fought it down. Nothing that smelt like this could be alive. But the sound came from there.

She moved closer, trying to stop her boots scraping on the rocks, holding her skirts tight about her so that their soft rustling would not distract her. Her uneven breathing whistled hoarsely through her set teeth as she made herself approach the source of the sounds.

Another whimper. But this one was louder, closer – and she knew, she suddenly knew!

'Boy-John!'

The shout echoed off the rocks of the small cove as she threw herself forward, coming right up to the whale, not caring now about the smell, about anything but the child. 'Boy-John!'

'L-Lotty?'

The voice was muffled, tearful but close. But there was no sign of him. She called, 'Where are you?' but even as she said it, she knew.

In the whale.

'Lotty!'

No doubt about it being Boy-John now; she leaned against the whale, bending forward, closing her mind to the smell and feel of corruption. 'Boy-John, help me. How can I get you out?'

The child was sobbing now – loud, hysterical sobs, so different from the soft, despairing whimpers she had heard at first. She had to shout at him to make him listen to her, to make him answer properly.

'The mouth shut, Lotty. I can't get out! I can't get out!'

His childish voice rose in a litany of terror but there was no time to calm him down. Free him first, she could soothe him better afterwards. But she stared at the great mouth in horror. It took every ounce of willpower to put her hands on the rubbery lips and try to prise them apart, but she had no effect on the creature.

She stopped, wiping her hands down the sides of her skirts. 'How did you get in?'

She had to repeat the question three times, shouting, before the hysterical child answered. 'There was a stick holding the mouth open.' His sobs tore at her heart but she put them aside, concentrating on the business in hand.

There was no stick, now. There was no sign of it, even though the mouth of the whale was well above the present highwater mark. But his words had given her a clue. A stick would have been used to separate the great jawbones of the beast. There was no point in her trying to open the mouth of the creature by pulling at its lips; to open the mouth she, too, would have to lever the jaws apart. Without a stick.

She couldn't leave the child to get help; his sobs had turned to screams, now, their desperation ringing clearly even through the muffling body of the whale. She must get him out immediately.

Even the thought of what she had to do made her feel nauseous but she gritted her teeth and dropped to her hands and knees. She wriggled until she was close up against the animal's mouth, then forced her back up against its top jaw. She could feel the soft rubberiness of the lips and, as she pressed harder, the solidity of the creature's upper jaw.

She forced herself up harder. Her face was

against the stinking flesh now as she struggled to insinuate a shoulder between the two monstrous jaws. Something gave, a small movement but it lent her encouragement. She pressed hard, arching her back, her feet scrabbling against the rocks, using her own body as a lever to force the mouth open.

Once there was a small gap the work was easier. Now she could use her hands and feet against the animal's lower jaw, and the mouth began to gape.

'Boy-John!'

But there was no need to tell him. He was already scrabbling over her body, his bare feet slipping and sliding, his sobbing breaths hoarse in her ears and then he was out! He was out, and she rolled thankfully away from the monster as the great mouth closed with a soft sigh that sent a wave of stinking air rolling across the cove.

She reached for the boy, sucking in the cleaner air, gathering the frightened child to her, her own tears falling onto his bare head.

He stank! He stank even worse than the whale, his skin covered with an evil-smelling mixture of slime and liquid but she did not care. She did not care about anything now that she had him, alive and relatively unscathed.

Automatically, she stroked his matted hair, saying soothing words, holding the shaking body close to her with hands which also trembled uncontrollably. But even as she comforted him, even as she promised him that she would never let anything like that ever happen to him again, one thought ran incessantly through her mind.

Someone had knocked the stick away; someone

had trapped the child deliberately. And there was only one person who was likely to have done it.

Her father.

She could no longer be responsible for Boy-John's safety. Matters had got too bad for that.

No matter what it cost her, she had to get Granfer-John back again.

Chapter Twenty-Two

'You have to go.' Kit dropped a hand on the old man's shoulder. 'He's your grandson. His welfare must come first.'

Granfer-John leaned back against the sun-warmed sea wall of Hugh Town Harbour and stared out across the turquoise waters of the Scillies. Around him, small islands dotted the seas like scattered emeralds but he did not seem to see them. Crumpling the letter from Charlotte unconsciously in his arthritic hands, he said, 'She can cope with anything, that great maid! If she do be worried...'

'She's never had to look after a young boy before. And Boy-John can be a handful – you've told me that yourself.' Kit hoped that he sounded more confident than he felt.

'If only she'd said what the matter were.' Granfer dropped his eyes again to the crumpled letter.

'It doesn't matter what the reason is. Charlotte needs you back and you're going.' Kit glanced up at the sky, assessing the weather. 'We'll fish again tonight and get in early enough to put the catch on *Little Western*. You can travel back with the fish. That way you'll be home before tomorrow evening.'

'What? And pay for 'n?' Granfer-John was scandalised. 'I'll find a boat going back and work

300

my way. No point in wasting good money.'

'And not get home for days, perhaps a week?' Kit snorted. 'You're getting the steamer and I'm paying. Three and sixpence won't break the bank.' He glanced down at the old man. 'And what are you looking at me like that for?'

'I dunno as how I can't make you out.' There was a quizzical expression in Granfer's eyes that made Kit feel uncomfortable. 'One minute you're acting like you don't have no more money than the rest of us; the next you're throwing the stuff around like there was no tomorrow.'

Kit knew that it was true. Despite the best intentions he couldn't lose the attitude to money of a rich man. Money was to be used, if it saved time and effort; it wasn't to be hoarded against a rainy day. He had to make a conscious effort to remind himself that he was poor now, that he had cut himself off from his father and that there was no way that he would go back, crawling, again. But he still spent money like a rich man; he had sold his watch in Penzance but he had used the money to pay for the crew's rations and to pay the freight charges for sending the fish home. It was hard to get used to the idea that there wasn't an account that he could draw on in need.

And then there was Charlotte. She was the richer of the two of them by far; a boat owner, the owner of a seine fishery. He had left home intending to make his fortune, but her situation had called to him. He had had to help her. And now...

'What?' He glanced down at Granfer-John, suddenly aware that the old man had been

301

speaking to him.

'I said,' Granfer repeated, with heavy irony, 'this is the first letter I ever had in my life. And if it had been down to me, it'd have laid in that there Post Office till Kingdom Come. So, what did you go in there looking for?'

An awkward question. He was damned if he was going to admit that he had been hoping for a letter from Charlotte; even just a few words about how the fish sales were going would have been better than nothing. 'Well, unlike you, I am accustomed to getting letters.'

Always, when he was younger, his father had written to him. When he had learned his trade, sailing on the company's ships, there had been a letter for him at every port. Sometimes, he knew, his father must have sent them off even before he had left home, so that his son, living and working among strangers, had something to remind him of his homelife and the family he had left behind him. At the time he had thought it a ridiculous idea, the letters so full of good advice and homilies; he had skimmed through them, torn them up, ignored them. Now, for the first time, he realised the love and thoughtfulness that must have motivated his father. If only such love motivated Charlotte...

'I could always take a letter back with me,' Granfer suggested. Rheumy blue eyes stared up at him. 'I dunno why you haven't been writing to her all along. Not a very good way of courting, I reckon, sending her nothing but fish.'

He had often thought of it but, except for the first note which he had sent with the steward, he hadn't dared. She had so much and he was so poor. How could he court her when she was richer than he was? But to earn money, real money, he would have to get away from here and that would mean leaving Charlotte with all the problems she had had when he met her. No, if he really wanted to do what he could for her, then he was tied here as her employee, and that meant that he had to keep his feelings to himself.

And now she was in more trouble. The letter hadn't been specific but he could read between the lines. She would never have asked for Granfer-John to come home if there hadn't been a new problem, one that she felt unable to cope with herself. And, like Granfer, he had recognised the inner strength that ran through her like a tempered steel. If she felt unable to cope alone then she was in serious trouble.

'Perhaps – we could always sail the *Faith-Lily* back?' he suggested.

'And lose all that fishing?' Granfer-John was scandalised once again. 'You know half the Newlyn fleet has been turning up here these last few days. There's no fish in Mount's Bay for the moment. If you want fish you'll have to work the waters here or go to the North Sea or Ireland. No, lad, you stay on here and fish – as long as you can cope?' He suddenly sounded doubtful.

'Cope?' Lost in his thoughts of Charlotte and the impossibility of ever being able to woo her openly, Kit was lost for a moment then his face cleared. 'Oh, you mean Big Rory and his brothers?' He grinned. 'Don't worry about them. We've not had a peep out of them for weeks.

They've learned their lesson.'

He clapped Granfer-John on the back. 'And I've learned mine. I can fish without you now, you old salt. You've done a good job teaching me so much so quickly.'

'You're a fast learner.' The old man's voice was suddenly husky with emotion. 'Not but what you didn't know a brem bit of seamanship before you started. Still, I don't like leaving you, boy, and that's a fact.'

'You think I'll sail off with the *Faith-Lily* and sell her?' Kit's blue eyes met the old man's rheumy ones squarely. His mouth twisted into a wry smile. 'Oh, don't worry. I know that the thought was in your mind. And Charlotte's! That was the reason I asked you to come on board. She had to get money in and I knew that she wouldn't trust me with her boat without you.'

'Yes, lad, well...' Granfer's face was a study in conflicting emotions then suddenly he grinned. 'And I reckon I wouldn't have come along with you if I hadn't had a bit of a worry that way myself.'

'And now?' Kit asked.

One arthritic finger poked him in the chest. 'Now, I reckon you'll bring that boat home safe if it kills you. I've seen the way you look if I mention her name, aye, and the way you go all moony looking out towards Mounts Bay. Oh,' he wheezed with sudden laughter, 'you can look all in a proper boil, not knowing whether to blow nor strike, but I'm an old man, I am, and I've seen un all before. You've got a fancy for the maid and I don't know that I don't think she mightn't have a bit of a fancy for you, when all's said and done.'

Kit hoped that his face didn't show the full amount of his embarrassment. The old man seemed to have an uncanny knack of knowing thoughts and feelings he had believed that he had kept completely hidden. And this final comment put the seal on his discomfiture. Abruptly, he rose to his feet, digging his hands deep into his pockets.

'As long as you both trust me with the lugger, that's the main thing.' His voice was harsh with the effort to appear normal.

'Oh, I trust you with the boat.' Granfer-John had got his pipe lit now and puffed comfortably at it, though there was a twinkle in his eyes that told Kit he had noticed every nuance of the younger man's embarrassment. 'It's Big Rory I don't trust, him and his brothers. I wouldn't trust them as far as I could throw them.'

Kit snorted. 'I told you, they've given up. We got the better of them. They're like dogs. Now they know who's master they won't cause any more trouble.'

'I reckon you're forgetting something, lad.' The old man poked Kit in the chest with the stem of his pipe. 'Once I've gone you'll be alone with them, three against one.'

'Three against one with a revolver,' Kit corrected.

'Aye, and supposing they gets that off you, what then?'

Kit grinned and clapped the old man on the back. 'You're letting your imagination run away with you. There's no way I'll ever let that happen.'

'What are you going to do about the boat when Granfer comes home?' Robert Spargo rested his leg by easing his weight more onto the walking stick he had recently adopted and stared at Charlotte.

'Do?' Charlotte stared at him, puzzled. 'Nothing. What should I do?'

'You'll let a strange man you don't know nothing about sail her for you? And off the Scillies where he could be in France before you knew he'd skipped it?'

The thought had occurred to her but she had forced it down. She still clung to the memory of Kit, of his laughter, his kiss, the feeling he gave her when they were together. And Granfer-John surely wouldn't leave Kit with the boat if he had any doubts about him. 'Why should he steal the boat?' she demanded. 'Englishmen can be as honest as Cornishmen, can't they? More honest, probably,' she added, thinking of Frederick Polruan and her father and the way they had conspired against her.

He nodded. 'Your old boss, eh?' She blushed. She hadn't realised that the story of her sacking had got around, although in a village it was impossible to keep anything secret.

As if to prove her right, Robert said, 'Polruans isn't doing too well since you left, is it?'

'Isn't it?' She glanced up alertly. 'No one told me.'

He shrugged. 'You'd be the last to know. But

they say his customers are getting cross because their accounts are wrong – when they're not late, that is.'

It was only what she had expected. Charlotte had been responsible for much of the paperwork, taking it over from the men who often made a mess of it. Without her there she could imagine that the office would quickly sink into chaos.

'And you're not getting any fish either,' Robert remarked.

She stared at him, puzzled. 'Why do you say that?'

'Well, you've not been in Newlyn Market recently.' Robert saw the way her brows lowered over her grey eyes and said quickly, 'Not that there's nothing wrong with selling the fish over in the Scillies. Though I had heard tell that your old boss had thought of a way of stopping that.'

The news roused her temper. 'Has he?' she demanded bitterly. 'Then it's a good thing that the *Faith-Lily* isn't selling her fish there, isn't it?'

'So how are you selling it? Got some other boat to take it and pretend it's hers?'

She shook her head, glancing around the Cliff, but there was no one in hearing range. She leaned forward. 'Don't tell anyone,' she hissed, 'but I'm sending it to London.'

'To–?' he gaped at her. 'What for? My soul and body, it'll be fit for nothing by the time it gets there.'

She shook he head, her eyes sparkling. 'No, it's packed in ice, and now that the bridge has opened it gets to London in fourteen hours. It's off the steamer, packed and loaded in time to

307

reach Billingsgate the next morning.'

She gave another glance round and lowered her voice. 'The best of it is, no one even knows that it's my fish. I use these Jewish children from Penzance. I pay them and they buy the ice for me and load the fish onto the train. Their parents are happy that they are earning and they won't tell my father. Not that he'd ever speak to a Jew.'

She smiled in triumph as she thought of her cleverness. 'They are the only people I know who wouldn't give me away. I remembered one of his sermons once about how they had crucified Jesus and how we should hate all Jews. I thought at the time how unfair that was, how cruel, and I realised that they were the only people in the area who would have nothing to do with him and all those like him.'

She could see by the frown on his face that Robert was not happy with this and hurried on. 'I wrote to this firm in London and they told me how to send the fish to them. It was the only way I could get the better of my father and Mr Polruan.'

'Who are these people?' he demanded. 'How did you hear about them?'

'Oh, some stranger from upcountry told me so I thought I'd try it. After all,' she added bitterly, 'what had I got to lose? I couldn't sell my fish for enough to cover the cost of catching it down here.'

'But London!' He began to enumerate on his fingers. 'You've got the cost of the steamer, the ice, the children, the train. You'd have to make a brem good price to cover all that and make a profit. What are they paying you?'

She hesitated. 'I don't know yet. They said that they will send me a statement at the end of a fortnight and pay me once a month, and I haven't been doing it for long enough to learn.'

'You're mad!' he said brutally. 'I always knew women weren't no good at business but I thought you was different. Something to do with being so big, perhaps. But you're as daft as the rest of them. Going to all that expense to send your fish up to London to someone you don't even know, and expecting to get paid at the end of it! Even our Susan knows better than to do a thing like that!'

'Oh, phooey!' she snorted, with more confidence than she felt.

Chapter Twenty-Three

The train slowed down, the clackety-clack as the wheels rushed over the points becoming so slow that the rhythm was almost lost and then tall, grey pillars rose on either side, joined across the width of the river by the sweep of the suspension cables.

'Look, Mr Hargraves, look!'

Mark Robinson pressed his nose against the window of the first-class carriage. Below, far below, the River Tamar was crowded with boats, all facing up the river, bows to the current. Small fishing boats, great naval ships, all motionless at their moorings, no bigger than toys.

Slowly, the train crept further out across the bridge. Another couple of minutes, James knew, and they would be in Cornwall. Another couple of minutes before he was in the county of the men who had been responsible for the death of both his sons. Averting his eyes from the drop he forced himself to concentrate on the structure of the bridge itself. It was an unbelievable feat of engineering. No wonder Brunel had been driven there, almost from his deathbed, to see it completed. A work like that was a fitting monument to any man, a wonderful legacy to leave your sons. He put the thought out of his mind, don't think of sons, don't think of the dead, look to the living.

Not that he had much choice with Mark Robinson around. Already, the boy's thin, acned face was turned to him, taut with tension. 'You don't think the train will fall off, do you, Mr Hargraves?'

'Not a chance, lad.' James put all the confidence he could into his words. 'This is one of the miracles of modern science, the longest suspension bridge in the world.'

Strange that Dick should have such a nervous son, he mused as he made light conversation, talking about the *Great Eastern* – the largest iron ship in the world, another of Mr Brunel's creations – to take the boy's thoughts off the drop. It wasn't as if his mother had been a nervous woman. Dick blamed it all on the nightmares Mark had suffered as a child and which had come back with a vengeance these last few weeks. But a fourteen-year-old boy shouldn't be so nervy.

'It'll do you good to live in the country for a bit,' he said heartily. 'Lots of fresh air and good food and exercise – that's what you need.'

'Perhaps.' Embarrassed, the boy turned again to the window. Already the drop was smaller; the great cables that held up the bridge had soared up again out of sight. They were nearly on the Cornish bank. 'But I wish it weren't Cornwall. I – I keep having dreams, you see...'

'Dreams don't mean anything, lad.' As if he himself could forget those dreams he had, of Kit, of Jonathan.

'But I feel it even when I'm awake,' Mark protested. 'I feel that there's something awful

311

waiting for me in Cornwall, something horrible, that will do me harm.'

James Hargraves leaned his head back against the leather seat and closed his eyes, his jaw muscles tense. It would do the boy no good to be told that he felt the same.

With a click and a clatter the train ran off the bridge and onto Cornish soil.

'Granfer's leaving makes no difference to the way we work,' Kit said crisply. 'We'll all have to do more watches but that's all.'

The two younger O'Reardens said nothing but he was aware that they were watching Big Rory out of the corner of their eyes. He moved forward with a slight swagger, resting one hand on the mizzen mast.

'What about our shares? Now the old man's gone, we'll have more work to do.'

'You already get all the shares you're due,' Kit said. 'I was the one who paid Granfer from what I was due.'

'But we'll have to take more watches.' That was Gulger, always the weakest, whiniest of the brothers.

'Up until now you've done less than your share.' Kit's blue eyes surveyed them coldly. 'From now on, you do your full amount. Anyone who doesn't agree can leave this boat now.'

He stood tensely, waiting for their reaction. If they deserted him now there was no way that he could get another crew. But Big Rory simply shrugged. 'Oh, we wouldn't want that now, would we, boys?' There was a chorus of agreement before they turned and walked off to the bow, their heads together.

Kit stared after them. He had expected some argument about the allocation of watches now that Granfer was gone, and the recent exchange left him feeling uneasy. There had not been enough objections. Big Rory and his brothers would argue about everything, however unimportant; why had they given in so easily about something which might have been considered a real grievance?

His lips twisted. What was the matter with him today? He was seeing problems that weren't there. But the feeling of unease persisted. He glanced at the sun, hazy now behind low cloud. 'Gulger?'

The men were suddenly silent, swinging round to stare at him with unreadable expressions.

'Go and get some milk,' he ordered. 'We'll be bound in half an hour.' He was beginning to use the Cornish expressions, he realised as he watched the younger brother walk off before settling himself in the stern and pulling out a copy of the *Western Telegraph.*

Kit flicked quickly through the paper; advertisements for shops and hotels, local news.

He stopped, turned back as a name caught his eye.

'The body of a woman found floating in the River Tamar has been identified as that of Peggy May Pentreath, a woman of the streets, recently arrived in Plymouth from her home in Penzance. An investigation into her death has been held but there

are no clues as to the perpetrator of this heinous crime, nor is there any sign of the young girl who resided with the woman. Sad though this death is, it points up to women the dangers that follow from the loss of their most precious jewel of virtue and…'

Kit closed his eyes as despair washed over him. Why could he never do anything right? Why did everything he touch turn to dust? Peggy May, Jonathan, his father – all of them had trusted him and he had let them all down in one way or another. And look at him now, a young man, with all the benefits of a good education, a good home, barely scraping a living by acting as the master of a small fishing boat his father wouldn't sink to owning.

He might as well be dead, he decided bitterly. What good was he to anyone? He couldn't even give advice to a prostitute without her getting killed. And he had been wondering about how he could win Charlotte! Well, that was easily dealt with. If he really loved her, if he really wanted the best for her, then he should simply bring her boat back at the end of the season and leave.

Providing he was still alive, of course, he added to himself, eyeing Big Rory's back.

Charlotte stood on Penzance Quay, her shawl wrapped closely around her, staring out across the bay.

The good weather of the past few weeks had broken and, under grey skies, the sea was a mass of white horses. The waves slapped angrily against the quay so that even where she was

314

standing, she could feel the spray on her face and taste the salt on her lips.

There was no sign of the *Little Western*. Not surprising, really; even a steamer would not be able to make good headway in weather like this. But the train was due to leave soon and there was no way that she could get her fish on it.

She turned and walked back down the quay, staggering slightly as the winds caught at her full skirts. 'There's no sign of her, Joseph. No work today, I'm afraid.'

The child grinned. 'Tomorrow then. But you agreed with our da that we was to get some money if we had to turn up.'

Charlotte sighed and felt deep in the pocket she wore around her waist. 'Here you are, then.'

'See you tomorrow, miss.' He ran off, followed by a train of smaller children. More money gone. And now she had to pay for her lodgings as well. And there was Kit – Granfer-John had told her that he was buying the men's food and provisioning the boat. That meant that when he came home she would have to reimburse him.

If this weather lasted the steamer might be so late that it missed the train for days on end. And sending the fish tomorrow meant that it wouldn't be in such good condition and she wouldn't get much money for it.

If she ever *did* get paid! Robert Spargo's doubts came back to her and she ran a distracted hand over her hair. All these money worries. Would they never end?

On her way back to the lodgings she caught sight

of her father's back and stopped, her heart in her mouth, her pulses racing.

Since that dreadful night she had avoided him, although his presence haunted her dreams and she awoke, drenched with sweat and shaking. She longed to tell someone of his behaviour, longed to share her fears and worries with another person but the only one she could tell was her mother. After all, what had her father done? Kissed her? But he had done that all her life. He was respected, admired, a man of God. Perhaps what he had done was normal, perhaps it was all her fault. Instinct told her one thing, but the reserve, the cautious behaviour in which she had been brought up, urged another.

Her mother, weak reed though she was, was the only person she dare tell, but she could not visit her while her father was around. And her father always was around, now. All the other fishermen were away, but he was still here and she could guess that he had abandoned the fishing in the hope of persuading the new Superintendent that he should be ordained.

Her heart thumping nervously, Charlotte followed him until he entered the Superintendent's house then turned and hurried back to Mousehole. William Trevennan would spend as long as he could with the new Superintendent, trying to impress the man with his piety. It was one chance to see her mother, see how she was, tell her of her father's strange and brutal behaviour. With a last backward glance she turned and hurried to Mousehole.

But the cottage was empty. Charlotte pushed

316

the door open, called, but there was no reply. Just to make sure, she ran up the rickety stairs, peered into her parents' room. She felt uneasy, an intruder. It was hard to believe that only a few short weeks before, this had been her home. Now she was an alien presence and she could feel the cottage rejecting her.

Moved by a sense of loss she pushed open the door to her bedroom, the room she had occupied all her life, then stopped. Someone was using it. The worn black Bible by the bed belonged to her father, a new shelf had been put up to accommodate his religious books. He was sleeping in her room! Her sense of unease deepened.

She went again to the other bedroom. No doubt that her mother slept here. Her best dress hung behind the curtain, her combs were laid on the deep windowsill. Charlotte stood, wondering what this meant. Always, her parents had slept together. That was what poor people did. It was rumoured that the very rich had separate bedrooms, but the poor huddled together for warmth and were grateful if they had enough space to bed the children in a separate room.

Her mother could be at one of the village shops, she could be getting water from the chute, but somehow Charlotte doubted it. Seriously worried, she hurried outside. The villagers were still looking askance at her but she did not care. 'My mother? Have you seen my mother?'

Heads shaking. She hurried on. 'My mother?' Again, no helpful answer. 'My mother?' And finally, old Mrs Tresize, half-blind and doubled over, nodded.

''Tes only right you should be looking after her. I don't hold with what your pa says but you should be home with she, not gallivanting all over Penzance.' She shook an arthritic finger in Charlotte's face.

Charlotte controlled her impatience. 'I *am* trying to find her, Mrs Tresize. Have you seen her anywhere?'

'Her?' The old woman coughed. 'She'll be up Paul, if I d'know her. Mooning over that man's grave. And you shouldn't allow it, young woman. 'Tesn't good for her to be out in all weathers. Soft in the head they'll be calling her if this goes on.'

But Charlotte was already running back along the street. Mousehole was in the parish of Paul but that village was half a mile away, up the steep hill. Holding her skirts free of her feet, another hand keeping her shawl closed against the blustery wind, she hurried up the rough road. The sky was heavily overcast, now, with a spatter of rain being blown on the unseasonably cold wind. It was no weather for a frail woman like her mother to be out.

Panting with the effort of hurrying up the hill, Charlotte pushed into the small graveyard that surrounded the ancient church. Sure enough, her mother was there, kneeling over Mr Polruan's grave, her head bowed.

'Mother.' Forcing away the memory of the time she had met Kit here, Charlotte knelt beside her, trying to get her breath. 'Mother, I've been worried about you. Are you all right?'

The older woman glanced up and Charlotte was horrified to see tears in her eyes. 'All right?

How can I be all right? With all my sins, all the evil that I have done. I shall burn, burn for ever.' Her voice rose hysterically.

'Mother.' Charlotte fought down the horror that she felt and reached and hugged her. 'It's raining.' She made her voice sound as calm and ordinary as possible, trying to give no hint of the fear she felt inside. 'Mr Polruan would be glad that you remembered him, but he wouldn't have wanted you to catch your death of cold out here in this chilly weather.' Under her hands she could feel Bertha's shoulders, thinner than ever before. Hadn't she eaten since Charlotte had left home?

Bertha did not move; her eyes were fixed on the mound of earth. 'Mr Polruan.' Her voice dropped to a murmur. 'He was my master you know, my best, dearest master.'

'I know, Mother. You worked for him and his wife before you were married. But he wouldn't have wanted you to get cold like this.' Her mother's body was icy under her grasp. 'Please come.' Charlotte could hear the pleading in her voice. 'Please come home.'

'He's cold.' The woman ignored her, seeming lost in her own world. 'He's cold and in his grave but I shall burn in everlasting fire.'

'Come, Mother.' More worried than ever, Charlotte rose to her feet and pulled at Bertha's arm. She had always been excitable, inclined to chastise herself for imagined sins but never as bad as this. With an effort, Charlotte pulled the older woman to her feet and wrapped her own shawl around the thin shoulders. 'You need to get warm and dry, then you'll feel better.' She

319

paused, then said abruptly, 'I'm sorry, so sorry that I had to leave you. Now that you're alone with just Father–'

'I'm alone.' The older woman corrected violently. 'I'm all alone. I've always been alone. Alone with my sins. For years and years.'

Charlotte gnawed at her lower lip, guilt flooding through her. She had known what her mother was like, she shouldn't have left her alone with William, without the benefit of Charlotte's good sense. Her heart beat leadenly at the thought but she had to make the offer. 'Mother, shall I – if you want me to move back...'

'No!' For the first time that afternoon Bertha looked straight at her. 'No, don't come back, Charlotte. Not now. Don't ever come back.'

'But you–' Charlotte was almost in tears. 'I'm responsible for you being like this. If I were there to look after you...'

'Don't come back.' The thin body was trembling now with emotion. 'Stay away, Charlotte. If you love me, stay away.'

There seemed nothing to say. An arm round her shoulder, Charlotte led her mother slowly back to the road. For several minutes there was silence except for the soft sound of their boots on the damp earth then Charlotte spoke again. 'Father came to see me the other day.' She paused, struggling to find a way of passing on the information without hurting her mother, without alarming her. 'He asked me to come back, for your sake. He – he ... kissed me.'

Bertha spun round and her thin hands gripped Charlotte's arms painfully. 'No, Charlotte, no.'

320

Her voice rose hysterically. 'No kissing, Charlotte, no feeling, no love. It leads to sin, only to sin, to everlasting regret, to loneliness, to burning.' Her voice faltered and the energy that had activated her seemed to evaporate as suddenly as it had arrived. Her eyes went dull again and her hands fell to her sides. 'Burn, that's what I shall do. Burn in Hell, for ever and ever.'

Charlotte put an arm around her shoulders. 'Come on, Mother. I'm taking you home.' And the two women stumbled slowly down the hill in the gathering dusk.

Kit slid the hatch aside carefully, so as not to wake the men sleeping beside him, and eased his big body out onto the deck.

'Who's that?' Kit recognised the voice of Mick, the smallest of the brothers, a rat-like individual without Big Rory's courage or his violence.

'I came up to have a look at the weather.' Kit had set Big Rory on the first watch, knowing that he was the chief troublemaker, and had lain awake, the revolver close to his hand, until the watch had changed and Big Rory was snoring by this side. Then, Kit had dropped thankfully asleep, but the seaman's instinct had woken him, driving up to see for the safety of his vessel.

Even asleep in the hold he had been aware that the wind had risen and now, looking around, he saw that conditions were worse than he had thought. Thick mist swirled around the *Faith-Lily* so that it was impossible to see more than a hundred yards in any direction.

He moved swiftly aft to where Mick huddled in his cloak over the embers of the fire, contained in the hollowed granite stone. 'For heaven's sake, why haven't you got a flambeau lit?'

'I just refilled the lamp,' Mick protested. 'You didn't tell me about no flambeau.'

'You should have used your common sense.' Kit rummaged for the round tin then filled it half-full of oil, wrapping old rags around the iron rod which projected up through the middle. Once lit, it provided a good flare which could be seen much further away than the usual riding lights, and would warn other ships of their presence. In weather like this, the small lanterns would be invisible at more than a hundred yards but the *Faith-Lily* swung at the end of a mile-long series of floating nets.

To make matters even worse, they were in the line that the Atlantic clippers often took as they raced to get their cargoes home as quickly as possible. With their greater size and speed they could sink a fishing boat and never bother to check their frantic progress to their next port. The only evidence would be a small island of floating, broken wood and sometimes a punt, saved from the wreck, with just the name of the boat to tell who had suffered such a tragedy.

Kit paused before he lit the flambeau at the grate sniffing. A fruiterer could be smelled miles away, the fresh tang of oranges floating across the sea as a warning of her presence. Thank God, he could smell nothing now but sea and tar and fish, the usual smells of a fishing boat, but there were plenty of clippers that didn't carry fruit. Kit couldn't help a shiver of horror at the thought of a ship looming silently out of the night, the smash of timbers... He shook his head to drive out the thought and, lifting the flambeau high, he made a circuit of the deck, peering over the side, eyes straining into the darkness.

Nothing; although with the flambeau lit he should be visible much further away than he himself could see. He stared out, all his senses probing the darkness around him, but there was nothing to be seen, the odd white flash of a breaking wave, the cry of a sea bird, the occasional glow behind the clouds that showed that the moon was still riding high...

But sea birds seldom cried in the dark.

He hefted the flambeau higher, willing himself to see beyond its small circle of light. There again, a cry, weak, like that of a seagull, and a pale shape half-seen amongst the waves. Kit stared at it, but unlike the sight of a breaking wave it did not disappear but seemed to be moving slowly off the port side, moving slowly towards the stern.

Which would happen to a body, subject to the force of wind and tide and not slowed, as the boat was, by her huge curtain of nets.

'Mick!' Already he was stripping off his coat, kicking off the heavy boots that would weigh him down. 'Mick, man overboard!'

'You're raving!' But the other man came nearer, peering into the darkness. 'What can you see?'

'There.' Kit pointed. 'And listen.' Again the cry, faint, choked off. 'It's a man out there.'

Mick caught at his arm. 'You're mad. You don't

323

know that that's a man. It could be a bit of wood, a sick gull, anything.'

'It could be a man.' The second boot came free and Kit shook off his grasp. 'I can't risk it. I've got to make sure.'

He ran to the side then turned. 'Get the others up and pick us up in the punt.' Away from her own harbour as she was, they had fallen into the habit of keeping it floating behind the *Faith-Lily* in case they needed to land at one of the islands without a decent quay.

With a sudden leap he jumped onto the side of the boat and took off in a shallow dive, angling towards the pale glimmer, barely seen in the darkness.

'Bloody young fool!' but Mick ran to the sleeping quarters. 'Man overboard. Everybody up.'

'Who's overboard? What's all this bloody row?' Big Rory crawled out from the small cabin. 'What the bloody hell's the matter now?'

'Man overboard,' Mick said. He was leaning over the stern, the flambeau in his hand, peering into the darkness. He could see Kit as a flash of white arms against the dark sea, heard a shout, 'I've got him!' and turned back in relief.

'What man?' demanded Big Rory. 'Not flaming Briars!'

'And someone else,' said Mick excitedly. 'He's found a body. If we get the punt...'

'Bugger that!' A grin split his older brother's face. 'What do we want with the punt? We'll cut her free. With a bit of luck she'll be found and everyone will think we're sunk. Then we'll pull in the nets and sail for the mainland. Change the boat's name in a quiet cove somewhere and we're set up for life. Our own boat, to sail or sell as we think best. And no more bloody Briars!'

Chapter Twenty-Four

As he waited for Richard Robinson, the new Superintendent of the Circuit, to enter the room, William Trevennan felt his nervousness rising.

It was so important that he should make a good impression, so *vital* that he should be ordained. But, at the same time, he knew that he mustn't appear too eager. Nothing would ruin his chances more than a display of open ambition.

Restlessly, he walked around the office. The Methodist Church provided the building for the Superintendent to live in, and he had been here often to see old Mr Borlase. Robinson had only been here a week but already there were changes. Threadbare curtains had been replaced by new dark-green plush that completely cut off the noise of the worsening weather outside. The books on the shelves were no longer dog-eared but covered in soft leather that shone in the lamplight and there were different ornaments scattered around the room.

Trevennan's lips hardened. He remembered Robinson from the last time he was here, nine years ago. His fists clenched as he remembered the contrast between them. Everything had been so easy for Robinson. The son of a respected businessman, he had never had to struggle for his education, never had to worry about money or position. While William Trevennan had been taking the first tentative steps towards being a local preacher, Robinson, years younger, was already ordained, already respected.

The door to the room opened and he swung round and moved forward, hand outstretched. 'Mr Robinson, sir. Good to see you again. Praise be to God that the people of Penzance have such an upright and respected man to superintend the Circuit.'

'I hope you aren't implying that Mr Borlase wasn't upright and respected.' There was a humorous quirk to Robinson's eyebrows but Trevennan wasn't misled. The supercilious bastard hadn't changed one iota in the last nine years.

'No indeed!' He opened his eyes wide in pretended shock. 'Such a truly holy man, dear Mr Borlase, too good for this world.' He folded his hands together in a prayerful way. 'Too, too good, so willing to see only the best in men. He even thought fit to believe that a humble man such as myself might make a suitable candidate for ordination,' he added, getting straight to the heart of the matter.

'So I see.' Robinson seated himself behind his desk and motioned Trevennan to take the chair in front of it. 'And, as you have no doubt realised, Mr Trevennan, that is why I have asked you to come to see me today.'

Trevennan felt that the beating of his heart must be audible to the other man but he had schooled his face well. Nothing but humility showed as he lowered his glance to his interlaced fingers. 'Sir,' his voice was resonant with honesty. 'I realise well that I am unworthy. A rough man of the people such as myself, uneducated except by what I learned at evening classes as an adult.'

He rose to his feet. 'Say no more, I beg of you. Do not distress yourself by telling me that I am not suitable. No one could be more aware of it than I; no one except a true saint such as Mr Borlase could have considered the possibility even for a minute.'

He turned slowly away, head bowed, scarcely able to breathe. If that didn't push the swine into making a gesture of support...

'Sit down, Mr Trevennan.' The words came but they seemed to Trevennan to have a ring of impatience to them. 'I am not the sort of man to ignore the recommendations of my predecessor, especially when he was, as you have already pointed out, so much more holy and respectable than I am.'

The bastard was getting at him. Surely he hadn't given himself away? He could swear that every word, every nuance was right and yet... But he had achieved what he wanted. Allowing the humble expression to slip slightly, William Trevennan returned to his seat.

Robinson fiddled with some papers. 'But nor am I the sort who will simply take a recommendation at face value without making my own mind up.' As Trevennan sat, rigid with shock, he went on, 'I realise that you will want this settled one way or the other as soon as possible. I shall make every effort in the coming weeks to hear you preach, see you at work amongst the souls of your village, so that I can come to a decision as quickly as possible. I am sure you realise, better than anyone, how important it is that only the best, most suitable men, are called to the Ministry.'

And what did the swine mean by that? Trevennan wondered as he forced himself to express gratitude, humility, all the necessary emotions that would mark him as one of the suitable ones while all the time, deep inside, his anger blazed.

What right had this man to turn down Borlase's recommendation? Why couldn't God have given the old man another few months, weeks even? Possibly, another few days of health would have been enough for Borlase to have seen the matter through. It was almost as if God didn't want him to be ordained.

He pushed that thought aside. Of course, He did. Otherwise, why would He have given Trevennan his powers of preaching, his force for good? This was just another test of his faith, that was all. Pass this and the ordination was his.

As he rose to his feet he remembered that ministers were also expected to have certain social skills. Smiling, he said, 'I remember that you had a small son when you were last here. I look forward to making his acquaintance again, although I suppose he is at school at present.'

Robinson moved to open the door for his guest. 'Actually, he is rather unwell at the moment. A slight irritation of the nerves, but I felt that he would be better at home until he recovers from it. He is around the town at the moment,

329

showing it to an old friend of mine who is staying with us. They will be back soon, I expect. There is definitely a storm coming up.'

Damn! Everything was going wrong for him today. The least he could have expected was that the little pest should have been at school until after his father had reached his decision. If he ever remembered…

And then they were in the hallway, making polite conversation, saying goodbye and he was almost gone, was almost clear when…

'Hello, Father. There's a terrific storm brewing. It nearly blew me off my feet.'

He was unrecognisable, of course; nine years made a difference to a child that age. Then he had been a plump five-year-old with an insatiable curiosity; now he was fourteen, thin, unhealthy-looking. Even in the dim light of the hall where the servants had been late lighting the lamps, Trevennan could see the acne that marked his face.

'Shake hands with Mr Trevennan,' his father ordered and he did so, with no trace of consciousness, no sudden start, then it was an introduction to the older man who was with him and Trevennan was out, out in the wind that ruffled his white hair and turned his sweating brow icy.

He took a deep, uneven breath and mopped his forehead with shaking hands. One thing at least had gone well today. But now he had to look forward, prepare for Robinson's investigation into his affairs. He knew that one of the things the Superintendent would want to know was how respected he was, what the local people thought of him.

And he would find out about Charlotte.

Already, Trevennan knew, he was losing influence there. When he had first preached about her the villagers had been shocked, but now, the habits of a lifetime were reasserting themselves. Once, no one would talk to her; now he knew she talked to the Spargos, to Oggy. And the other villagers were growing less censorious, remembering how she had helped them, remembering her kindnesses. Even her rescue of that come-by-chance, Boy-John, was spoke of with admiration.

He had hoped her move to Penzance would have established her as immoral, beyond the pale, but it seemed to him as if public opinion was beginning to veer to her side. No one said anything to him, of course, but he was attuned to the feelings of the village and he knew. Behind his back, in whispers at the moment, only to their closest relatives, their very best friends, people were beginning to blame him for her actions. And then there was that scene in Granfer-John's house the other night, when Charlotte had overreacted so hysterically. Tongues were beginning to wag.

It was intolerable! If Robinson realised that Trevennan was being openly flouted by his own daughter, he would never be ordained.

Something would have to be done about Charlotte.

The noise of the storm hid it at first. Lying in his

331

warm bed, feeling the house shake under the onslaught of the wind, James Hargraves found himself carried back to the days of his youth, when he had sailed ships in storms like this, when his survival had depended on his skill and the skill of the men who had built the boat, feeling the wooden ribs creak and move, the hull bend, under the strain.

When he survived, when, against all the odds, he had prospered, he had seen it as a mark of God's favour – a sign that he would be the founder of a dynasty, to be carried on by his sons. And now they were dead. All his family, dead, and he was left alone, knowing the emptiness of success, the vanity of riches.

'Oh, God!' He turned in the bed, trying to cut out the noise of the wind, the waves that had been responsible for the death of his last son, of Kit – and heard it.

Soft, weak, high-pitched, the babbling cry of a child in terror.

Abruptly, he sat up. It was Mark, of course. Dick had warned him of the nightmares. Pulling off his nightcap, he lit his candle and pushed open the bedroom door. From down the stairs there was a glimmer of light. Dick was still working, trying to understand the ramifications of his new position, but closer, louder, James could hear the boy, formless words and frantic cries.

'Here, lad.' He pushed open the door, his voice deliberately calm and comforting. But Mark was past hearing. In the light of his candle James could see that all the sheets and blankets had been kicked to the floor. Crouched against the bedhead, his eyes wide and sightless with fear, Mark huddled behind the shelter of the bolster. Here, at the back of the house, the noise of the storm was less intrusive and the child's wheezing seemed to fill the room.

'Steady, lad. It's all right. There's nothing to be afraid of.' But the ears were deaf, the eyes fixed on something that James could not see.

'Don't kill me!' The breathing was faster now, the straining lungs scarcely able to force air through the vocal cords. 'I won't tell! I won't tell!' The voice rose to a frantic breathless scream.

'Of course you won't. Don't worry, no one will make you.' James sat at the side of the bed, pulling the thin, tense body close against him, stroking limp hair back from the damp forehead. But the boy was unresponsive in his arms, still lost in his own world of terror.

In the light of the candle, Mark's face was tinged with blue and his rasping breathing set James Hargraves' nerves on edge. No wonder Dick was so worried about the boy; an attack like this could kill him. He was preparing to shake the child awake when a memory of Kit's childhood came to him.

Kit had been a fearless child in general but for a time he had suffered from nightmares. Once, in terror like this, James had got him to describe what he was seeing. It was ridiculous, a picture of an elephant in a child's book which to adult eyes seemed completely harmless but somehow, Kit's young mind had turned it into a ravening monster.

Once he had known what was causing it, James had found it simple to talk to the child about elephants; he had shown him other pictures, emphasised the beasts' usefulness to man and the nightmares had disappeared. Could something like that be the cause of Mark's problems?

He supported the boy more comfortably, trying to find a position which did not hamper his effortful breathing. 'What can you see, lad? Who is trying to kill you?'

'A bad man.' The blank look in Mark's wide eyes made cold shivers run down James's spine. 'A big, bad man with yellow hair.' He was talking more simply than his fourteen years, relapsing in his terror to the speech of a small child. 'He hurt the doll, too.'

'Doll? What doll?'

'A big doll.' The breathing was faster, shallower. 'He's killed her. The doll is dead and he's killed her.' His voice rose. 'Don't kill me. I won't tell! I won't tell!'

'I won't let him get you.' The typical, meaningless nightmare of a child. James began to rock the thin body. 'Look, can you see me? I'm standing in front of you with a big stick. I'm stopping the bad man from getting to you.'

Was it his imagination or did the aching tension that sent spasms through the boy ease slightly? 'He's a bad man.' The child's voice had a note of doubt in it.

'And I'm a good man,' James said heartily. 'A good man with a big stick. Look, he's running away. He's frightened. More frightened of us than you are of him.'

'Running away.' The boy sighed. The air still whistled in his lungs but it was a deeper breath than he had taken for some time.

'Now he's gone. He's gone and you can wake up.' To his relief the staring eyes blinked, the unnerving fixed gaze waved and sank.

'I – what are you doing here?'

'You had an asthma attack. I heard you choking. Have you got any medicine?'

'On the table.' The boy leaned forward, exhausted, resting his elbows on raised knees. 'It's only honey and castor oil, it doesn't do any good.'

'Castor oil is good for everything,' James said confidently. 'And you're lucky to have honey in it.' He held out a spoonful of the liquid to the boy. 'Come on, swallow it like a man.'

The boy's nightshirt was soaked, his skin pale and clammy, but at least his breathing was easier. 'Stay where you are while I make your bed,' James commanded. He bustled around, stripping back the sheets and remaking the ruined bed from scratch, all the time keeping up a light-hearted chatter about nothing. By the time he had finished and found a fresh nightshirt, the boy was wheezing only faintly and James had hopes that he would soon fall asleep.

'Told you that castor oil was good,' he said, tucking the sheets in firmly. 'Anything else you need?'

Propped up on his pillows Mark smiled sleepily, his lids already drooping but as he left the room James Hargraves' face was unusually grim.

The boy could die from an attack like that. James had lost all his own family; he couldn't bear to think of Dick being in the same position.

A letter for Charlotte! From London! The news ran round Mousehole like wildfire.

'Maybe it *is* from they people up Lunnon she's bin and sent her fish to,' Robert confided to Oggy. 'P'raps she be going to get paid after all.'

'I'll go and tell her,' Oggy volunteered. 'She'll be wanting to know.'

'And,' Robert said thoughtfully, 'perhaps she'd better come and get that letter before preacher does.'

But William Trevennan was already on his way. The storm was worse today, the seas crashing against the quay, sending up huge fountains of spray that were carried right across the harbour and blighted the crops as far as Paul. No one willingly endured the lash of the rain, driven in rivulets by the wind under doors and round windowframes, bouncing back from the cobbles like spent shot. The women, on their necessary errands to buy food or to fetch water from the chutes, wore their husbands' old sou'westers and oilskins, hurrying with shoulders hunched against the rain. No one stopped to talk but still, by the magical osmosis of a village, the news spread. And Trevennan had heard it.

'You have a letter for my daughter.' Standing dripping in Betsy Trembath's small front room that served as the village Post Office, he knew that for once he was at a disadvantage. Unlike the rest of the village, Betsy was a Quaker and not

336

only immune to his influence but actively against it. And she was a redoubtable opponent. The villagers still told the story of how she had routed the novelist Anthony Trollope when he visited her in his position as a Post Office Surveyor.

'For thy daughter,' Betsy agreed calmly, 'but thy daughter doesna live with thee any more, not that I've heard.' She folded her hands in front of her and waited for him to make the next move.

'I am still her father.' He forced a reassuring smile. 'You can trust me to pass the letter on to her, I'm sure.'

She snorted. 'The Post Master General doesna give me my tuppence-farthing a day to trust people, even,' her faded blue eyes surveyed him satirically, 'if they have grown a gert white beard and go round pretending they're Moses come off the mountain. My tuppence-farthing is for getting the letters to their rightful owners, and so I shall, while the Lord gives me strength.'

'But she's my daughter,' Trevennan protested.

'And mebbe thee should have thought of that before thee threw her from thy door.' She took a firmer stance on the stone slabs that made up the floor, feet apart, hands on hips, the white cotton apron straining across her large bust. 'A young woman like that! Thee were happy enough to have her while she brought home her pay every week, but as soon as that were stopped, out thee threw her. 'Tis a disgrace, that's what it is! And thee a man of God!'

Trevennan's heart sank at the thought of what would happen if Richard Robinson heard that rumour. It had never occurred to him that the villagers might put that interpretation on his actions. He had been so concerned with becoming the master of the *Faith-Lily* that he had never considered that others would link the loss of Charlotte's salary and her leaving his protection – and blame him! The door opened and gust of cold wind spattered rain on the stone flags as another person entered the small room. A witness. Trevennan knew that he had to refute that story – and swiftly.

'Charlotte left of her own accord,' he said firmly. 'It was against my wishes. I even went to see her the other day and tried to persuade her to come home.'

'And she was so impressed by thy speaking that she ran out of the house, half-nekkid and screaming like a whitnick, from what I hear,' Betsy said sourly. 'If thy preaching is as good as thy persuading, 'tis a wonder that there's anyone left in the chapel to hear thee.'

He could feel a cold sweat trickling down between his shoulder-blades. What if his own congregation were talking like this about him? Betsy was an opponent of old but she got her news from the other villagers even if she did put her own gloss on it. And she was in an ideal position to spread her version of the story to the other villagers.

He took a deep breath. 'Now, listen my good woman, I could take you to court for saying things like this about me.'

'Court, is it?' Her voice rose in an outraged shriek. 'Good woman, am I? 'Tes not me that has ripped the clothes half off a poor, defenceless girl, nor 'tes not me that has cast her out – and all the time preaching like thee was some saint from a church window with a gert halo round thy head bright enough to read by. And now thee come here, trying to steal her letter, what's the first one she's ever had. But I'm wise to thee, Mr preacherman,' she wagged a thick finger under his nose. 'I'm wise to thee, and thee won't get thy girl's letter, not if I have to pay the Post Office tuppence-farthing a day myself to stop it.'

The door opened again but William Trevennan had had enough. Head down, he barged past the incoming woman who stared at him, affronted, and forced his way out into the wind and the rain.

That girl! That blasted Charlotte! She was ruining him, she was doing it deliberately! Everything she had done had been to thwart him, to show him up in a bad light, to stop him getting ordained.

He took a deep, labouring breath in through his nostrils, forcing his clenched fists to relax. He would be ordained, he would not let her win. There might be rumours but he knew the villagers, he knew his influence with them. They might talk amongst themselves but they wouldn't talk to an outsider. Richard Robinson had promised to make up his mind very quickly; all Trevennan had to do was to make sure that nothing happened to force the rumours out in the open.

'Look! Look!' Charlotte waved the paper gleefully in front of Granfer-John. 'Fourpence a fish! And seven pence for those hake that were included! Nearly three times the normal price. Down here I'd have been lucky to get fifteen shillings a hundred!' She caught Boy-John up in her arms and began to whirl around the small kitchen with him. 'I've made money! I can keep myself, pay for the *Faith-Lily!* I'm independent!'

'And I reckon 'tes about time you were, maid.' Granfer-John puffed at his pipe; the smell of cheap tobacco filled the room and the smoke billowed in the draught from the window as the storm rattled the panes. 'You bin too long under your da's thumb, that's what's the matter with you. You should a bin married to a good fisherman way back.'

Charlotte stooped abruptly and placed the child on the floor. 'No one will have me, Granfer,' she said sadly. 'I'm too tall, not womanly enough. But,' her face lit up, 'it doesn't matter now, anyway. The *Faith-Lily* will earn enough for me to be able to live as well as I could when I was with my father. Better!'

Boy-John reached out a grubby paw and slipped it into her hand. 'What are you going to buy, Lotty?'

She grinned, ruffling his untidy blond hair. 'After educating you, you mean?' She ignored his horrified wail of, 'Oh, Lotty!' and raced on. 'The boat first, of course. New sails, new ropes. They cost money and she can't sail without them, but after that...'

Her eyes glazed unseeingly across the small room. 'Clothes. Proper, nice clothes in pretty colours, not boring old black. A crinoline, so that

340

I can be as fashionable as anyone else. And,' her mouth quivered with amusement, 'a cat, to sit on my knee and welcome me when I get home.'

'But there's cats everywhere,' Boy-John said, aghast.

'But they're not mine. Father would never let me have one, said they ate food that we should have and that it wasn't right treating a cat like a human because it says in the Bible that animals are there to work for us, but I've always wanted a cat and I shall have one.' Her face softened. 'A tabby cat, to sit on my knee. I shall be a proper old spinster.'

Granfer-John puffed slowly. 'Reckon there's a man might make you change your mind about being a spinster and all.'

She knew immediately who he meant and turned away so that he shouldn't see the colour flaming in her face. 'You mean Kit? Just because I let him sail my boat...'

'Well, there's his side too,' Granfer said peaceably. 'He don't seem to me a man who would marry just 'cause some woman fancied it. But then, he don't seem averse to some woman I could mention.'

The memory of Frederick Polruan's taunts made her unusually snappy. 'The trouble with Mr Briars,' she said tartly, 'is that he isn't averse to *any* woman.'

There was a long silence broken only by the howl of the wind and the spatter of rain and spray against the window. Granfer-John raised his head. 'Well, for both your sakes, I hope he got that boat in safe moorings before this storm hit.'

Charlotte swung back. 'He might be out in this?' It was suddenly difficult to speak.

He shrugged. 'He's a brem good seaman but he don't know the area, and a storm like this, this time of the year, well, it could catch out even some of the locals.'

Boy-John pushed between them and caught at Granfer's hand, shaking it urgently. 'Kit's a good sailor! He's the best!' he protested.

'If he's out in this, he might *need* to be,' Granfer said soberly.

Chapter Twenty-Five

After the storm, the sun.

Charlotte hung over the rails at Mousehole, watching the busy scene. Men were swarming over the boats in the harbour, checking for damage. On the shore a line of carts stood, the donkeys and horses twitching their ears and flicking their tails against the plague of flies while their drivers loaded the seaweed, torn by the storm from the bottom of the Bay, onto their carts, to be taken away and used on the fields as fertiliser. Further out to sea she could see other luggers heading for shore, their brown sails dark against the glitter of the waves. She breathed the scent of sea and fish and tar, a scent that was a part of her childhood.

There would be no fish for several days. The steamer had been held up in Penzance Harbour, unable to make the forty-mile trip through the treacherous cross-currents around Lands End to the Isles of Scilly. Fishing boats had fled from the unseasonable storm, running for the shelter of safe harbours or huddling under the lee shore out of the force of the gale.

Even that had not always been enough. Although the boats here had escaped bad damage, protected from the force of the sea by two piers and the offshore island, two boats in Newlyn had sunk, unable to find shelter behind

343

its single, tiny quay. Her own spirits raised by the good weather and the knowledge that she had money due to her, Charlotte moved on towards the Jelberts' cottage.

'So why don't you trust him, Dick?' Hargraves had always found his friend almost too inclined to like people; his caution with regard to William Trevennan seemed out of character.

'I wish I knew.' Dick Robinson paced beside his friend up the granite Terrace that ran along one side of Penzance's main street. 'I never have trusted him, not even when I was here years ago. I was newly ordained then and he had just been appointed a local preacher, but somehow I couldn't take to him. Everyone else seemed impressed by him though.'

'Perhaps that was it,' Hargraves suggested. 'There you were – young, educated, probably really fancying yourself the way young men do, and there *he* was – older, simpler, but...' He paused, trying to phrase his comment so that he did not offend Robinson.

'But a man with more character and preaching ability than I will ever have,' Dick finished for him. 'You don't have to pussy-foot around the subject. The Lord knows I am not a great preacher and I never will be. And I have thought about this myself; I've prayed about it.' He turned to Hargraves, his tired face worried. 'I could never forgive myself if I denied a good man the right to serve God as he thinks best, just because I was jealous.'

'So you are going to recommend him, then?'

The face darkened. 'I don't know. They must know him down here better than I can, and everyone speaks well of him, but – I am still unsure. This is a cross that I just have to bear.' He glanced up and gave a little groan under his breath. 'And here comes another.'

Hargraves glanced at the thin, elderly lady rapidly approaching them, one mittened hand held out and her face contorted into a welcoming smile. 'My dear Mr Robinson. Such a pleasure, such a reason to thank God, that we should have you back amongst us again after the illness of poor Mr Borlase, but...' she hesitated coyly, 'I suppose after all this time that you have quite forgotten me?'

Robinson shook her hand but Hargraves could see that he was less thrilled by the meeting than the lady. 'How could I forget you, Miss Makepeace. Such a pillar of the Methodist Church. I would enquire after your health but you are in such looks that the question would be an impertinence.'

'Oooh, Mr Robinson!' The archness set Hargraves' teeth on edge. To avoid an introduction he hastily turned his back, pretending to be studying the window of the nearest shop while behind him the lady's voice ran on in high-pitched eulogies; of Mr Borlase, of Robinson himself and then, to Hargraves' secret amusement, of William Trevennan.

Well, here was one lady who had no doubts about the man's fitness to be ordained; John the Baptist would have had trouble getting a more glowing reference, and, of course, Dick would

345

recommend the man for ordination. His personal dislike of the man would make him even more inclined to support him; Dick would bend over backwards to avoid being prejudiced.

And still the eulogy went on. Bored by the woman's penetrating voice, Hargraves moved further away. Strange the items people would pawn, he decided, staring at a wooden leg and a baby's carved wooden cot, propped up in the window. But then, when you needed the money you would pawn anything. In his early married life, before he had made money, his wife would pawn her wedding ring and his Sunday clothes to buy them food for the week. Sometimes, in desperation, workers would even pawn the tools of their trade. He leaned forward, shadowing his eyes to see deeper into the window, trying to make out some of the smaller objects lurking mysteriously in the corners.

And saw it.

His first thought was: That ship looks just like my *Eliza Briars*, the pride of his fleet, named after his dead wife.

Then, disbelievingly, he knew. It WAS the *Eliza Briars*. Etched tiny on a watchcase, he still recognised her as he would have recognised the ship herself, seen at a distance, in fog, anywhere.

There was a feeling of pressure inside his head. His lungs refused to move, his heart was erratic, thumping, labouring.

The *Eliza Briars!*

He struggled to control himself, to think straight, to keep calm. The *Eliza Briars*. And he had had her engraved himself, by the best artist

346

in Hull. Engraved on two watchcases. One for himself.

And one for Kit.

Keep calm. His shaking fingers fumbled under his coat, pulled at the chain that anchored his watch. It was there, of course. He had placed it there only an hour ago but he had to be sure, he had to eliminate the possibility that it was his watch, stolen, already pawned, before he had noticed his loss.

His fingers found the watch and pulled it free. It lay in his shaking hand, twinkling up at the sun, identical to the one in the window.

'Sorry about that.' Dick's hand on his shoulder, his voice, came from a thousand miles away. 'She's a menace. I always imagined the wise virgins who kept their lamps filled with oil would be like her. Pity, really, darkness could only be an improvement.'

Then, noticing his silence, 'James, old friend, are you all right?'

He couldn't speak. In his trembling fingers the watch heliographed his agitation to the world. He could only point his free hand at the matching timepiece, his breath rasping unevenly in his throat.

'A similar watch?' Dick stared from the window to his friend and back again, uncomprehending.

'Kit.' It was only a whisper but it took all his energy to get the word out. 'That's Kit's watch.'

'But how...?' Dick stopped. 'You want to buy it back, is that what you mean?'

Hargraves shook his head. 'He got off the boat.' Why was it suddenly so difficult to speak? 'He

347

must have got off that boat.'

'Stay here.' Dick Robinson pushed open the door. Hargraves could see him, talking calmly, smiling, carrying on as if the world wasn't whirling around madly, as if the whole of life wasn't being tipped upside down.

He turned away, staring blindly across Market Jew Street, unable to bear the suspense. His fingers clenched around the watch in his hand. Kit had to be alive. Dear God, Kit had to be alive. Please.

Then Dick was back, his face puzzled. 'He said it was pawned a couple of weeks ago.' He stopped.

'Who by?' Hargraves swung round, gripping his lapels, almost lifting him off his feet in his urgency. 'In the name of God, who by?'

'A tall man, with fair curls.' Dick's voice seemed to come from a long way away. 'He got into a fight just afterwards, it seems. According to the records his name was Briars.'

'His mother's name.' The emotion was too great now. Ignoring the arm of his friend, the staring faces of passers-by, Hargraves buried his face in his hands to hide his flowing tears.

'But a new boat will cost three hundred pounds!' Granfer-John was scandalised. 'You can't think about spending that there sort of money.'

'Not yet, not this year. But this is the way to go forward. If one boat earns a good living, two will be better. And there are families here with two boats.'

'Not women,' Granfer-John objected. 'That's for men, that is.'

'You told me I should be more independent!' Charlotte wailed. 'When I try to be, you tell me I can't do it.'

He puffed on his pipe. 'I meant for 'ee to marry a nice young man; that's the sort of independent I meant. And you lay off they nicies, you young varmint,' he snapped at Boy-John, hitting the child's hand away from the paper of humbugs she had bought him. 'Clunking away like a toad, you do be.'

'But, Granfer. Marrying is just another sort of dependency.' Charlotte was beginning to get cross too, her happiness of the morning disappearing in the face of the old man's unexpected opposition. 'I thought you'd approve of me trying to expand.'

'You're a woman,' he insisted. 'One boat, left to you – well, that's fair enough. But to go round *buying* of them! 'Tes against the laws of nature.'

She opened her mouth to argue but the knock on the door cut her short. Boy-John dashed to answer it. Besides, what was the point of getting cross with Granfer-John? She'd make up her own mind. Now that she had money, everything was possible.

'Is Charlotte there?'

She turned round, smiling at Robert Spargo over her shoulder. 'Come in and help me, Robert. Granfer-John thinks I'm acting like a wanton.'

But there was no answering smile. He stood, head lowered in the doorway, staring at her, turning his greasy black hat round and round in his clumsy fingers. His silence warned her and

349

she straightened, staring at him. 'Something's wrong.' She began to move forward. 'My mother–'

''Taint your ma, Lotty.' He still wouldn't look her in the face. ''Tes something else altogether.'

And as she stared at him, struggling to understand, he said, 'Phil Trevelyan has just got back from the Scillies. He said...'

She reached behind her for the support of the table, hardly aware that Boy-John had come to her, gripping her skirt in a frantic grasp. 'What?' Her voice croaked. 'What did he say?'

He still couldn't meet her eyes. 'They found the punt of the *Faith-Lily*. She were stove in on some rocks off Samson.'

She tried to speak but couldn't. She could only stare dumbly at him as he finished, miserably: 'She's gone down, Lotty, that's the only explanation. She's gone down, lost with all hands.'

'No, you can't. No one can see her.'

She could hear Granfer's voice as she huddled further under the rough blankets, trying to hide herself away from reality. Despite the warmth of the weather and the hot brick at her feet she couldn't stop shivering. It was the room she had slept in while Granfer was – away (she couldn't think any closer to the subject than that), but it was alien now – a room from another world.

Her head ached, her jaw ached, her icy fingers crooked into the blankets ached but they were as nothing to the ache inside her, the all-encompassing agony of a broken heart.

350

Thumping, uneven footsteps on the creaking stairs and the old man was there. 'Here, maid, have a dish of tay. 'Twill do 'ee the world of good.'

But her fingers wouldn't unclench from the blankets, her jaw wouldn't open. She could only shake her head dumbly, knowing that if she spoke, if she once forced a sound past her tight throat, she would simply throw back her head and scream and scream and scream. Safety lay in silence, in keeping the agony within her, in holding her pain to her, huddling around it as if it were her most precious possession.

All hands. The words still echoed around the house. *Down with all hands.* With Kit, that was the bitterness, the root of her agony. Kit. Laughing Kit. Kit of the bright blue eyes and the echoing laugh. Kit who thought he could outface anybody. Kit who could find a way around any difficulty.

'Here, maid.' An arm around her shoulders, lifting her up in the rickety bed. A cup forced against her mouth.

She didn't want it, she wanted to be left alone, alone with her memories, with her memories of Kit. But the hot liquid burned her lips and she opened them and it flooded into her mouth and she swallowed.

The tea burned its way into her stomach, tea – and something else. She coughed and choked and he paused for her to recover before pressing the next mouthful on her. She tried to turn her face away, to push him off but he was stronger than he looked and his willpower was more

351

focused than hers. 'A bit of brandy. I dunno what your da would say but he's not here and I am, so drink it down.'

The next mouthful was easier; the warmth began to spread out from her stomach, easing her breathing and the knot in her throat. For the third mouthful she could even help, her hand over his, even though the cup clattered against her teeth. But it eased the tightness if not the agony. Suddenly, she found she could move again, could speak.

'Oh, Granfer.' Her voice rasped as if she hadn't used it for months. 'He's dead. Kit's dead. And I...'

'And you loved him.' He finished the sentence for her. 'Well, I dunno as it's much of a problem. He loved you too as far as I could tell.'

'Me?' Tears were coming now, first prickling painfully then suddenly falling – hot, scalding tears that ran down her face, trickled saltily into her mouth, tears she didn't even try to wipe away. 'He loved me?' Her voice rose in a wail. 'He loved me and I *killed* him! I sent him out on that boat and I *killed* him!'

He patted her gently on the shoulder. 'That's love, that is, maid. That's how you do know. There's no love without guilt like that. I buried parents, a wife and daughter and every time it was the same. A knife through the heart would hurt less.'

'But – but...' Her sobs were tearing at her, the words wouldn't come out. 'How can I bear it? How can I live with guilt like that? How can I live without *him?*'

'You jest keeps breathing and moving and it happens, maid. You don't have no say in the matter. No one ever died yet just 'cause they didn't want to live.'

He cocked his head at another rap on the door. 'Drat the thing. For someone no one's talking to, you got a brem lot of callers.' Thrusting the cup of tea into her hands he stumped painfully down the stairs.

Curled into a sobbing heap, Charlotte thought over what he had said and found no consolation there at all.

Chapter Twenty-Six

'Well?' James Hargraves was on his feet, the book he had been pretending to read dropping unnoticed from his hand. 'Have you any news?'

Dick Robinson ran a hand through his thinning hair. 'A lot of news, old friend, and quite interesting too.'

'He's alive?' That was all that really mattered, that Kit should be alive, that they could make up this stupid argument, be friends again.

'As far as I can tell. Whatever your detective said, he certainly seems to have left the *Isabelle*. He was in the area for over a week painting up a fishing boat before sailing off in her as her captain.'

'Kit?' Hargraves stared at his friend as though he were mad. 'Are you sure you've got the right man? Kit was a good sailor but I could never get him interested in the fleet or anything to do with it. And as for fishing – I'd as soon have expected him to work as a cook!'

'It's him all right. The description fits, and the habits. Likes a drink, inclined to get into the odd fracas – it's Kit all over. And there's one thing I haven't told you.'

'What?' Despite his delight that Kit was alive, the word came out in a half-groan. Hargraves was too well aware of his son's habits to doubt that something he wouldn't like was coming.

354

Dick gave him a wry smile. 'The owner of this fishing boat – it's a woman.'

'A woman!' Well, that explained everything. For the sake of a pretty woman Kit was quite likely to act out of character. 'I should have known!' James exclaimed bitterly. 'Some lightskirt, I presume.'

'Not at all.' Dick lowered himself into the chair on the other side of the fireplace and frowned at Hargraves. 'You say that Kit knew nothing about fishing?'

Hargraves shrugged. 'A bit, of course. I own a few fishing boats and as a boy he would go out in them, but as I said, he never showed any real inclination to get involved with the business, and once he was older I was more concerned that he understood the bigger ships and their problems. That's where we make most of our money.' Despite himself he couldn't help a note of pride creeping into his voice. 'Bigger ships!' Not bad for a man who started off with nothing.

'Then that makes it even stranger.' Robinson rubbed his hand over his balding head. 'I knew the owner of the boat years ago. She was still a child then but tall, intelligent, with plenty of character, but she gave no sign that she would ever be a real beauty.' He paused. 'She's the daughter of William Trevennan, the man I was telling you about.'

It took a few seconds for James to make the connection. 'But I thought you said that *he* was a fisherman?' he queried.

'Exactly. Interesting, isn't it? I wonder why she chose a man who knew nothing about fishing to

355

sail her boat rather than her own father.'

'"Do you good!"' Charlotte echoed bitterly.

She took Granfer's sock and bent again over the wooden washtub, rubbing it with the gritty soap, struggling to get a lather on the thick, oily wool. There was a hole in the heel but, whatever she owed Granfer-John, she wasn't going to darn these socks until they'd been washed. Preferably twice! From the evidence, he'd worn them since he set out on the boat.

The boat – she turned her mind away from the thought and from her bleak future. Yesterday, she had had hopes of making money, of getting a better life for herself, and her mother. Yesterday, the future had included at least the possibility of Kit.

And now there was nothing. He was dead, her boat was sunk, all hopes of being able to rise above the bone-grinding poverty of life as an unmarried woman in a small fishing village had vanished, leaving her only the shreds of dreams. If only she hadn't agreed that he should sail the boat to the Scillies, away from the comfort of local ports. If only she hadn't lost her nerve after the whale incident and recalled Granfer-John to help look after his grandson. With his experience the old man would have recognised that the storm brewing was no ordinary one. Whichever way she looked at it, Kit was dead – and it was her fault.

Tears pricked at her eyelids and she lowered her head, feeling in the murky water for the second sock. Keep occupied, that was the important thing. Don't think; don't feel; work.

'Lotty! Lotty!'

She sighed. Boy-John was the last person she felt like coping with. At eight he was incapable of really appreciating death. He was sorry about Kit, of course, but already his spirits were rising, already he was looking to the future. She had been relieved when Granfer had taken him off for a walk, but here he was, and far too soon.

'Lotty!' He rounded the sharp corner into the court at full speed, his untucked shirt-tails flapping in his wake. 'Lotty! Come quick! Granfer says there's pilchards. He can smell 'em. And see 'em. Royal purple, Lotty, royal purple!'

Royal purple! She knew what that meant. The presence of vast shoals of pilchards under the sea left a dark oily sheen on the surface of the water. The adjective 'royal' applied not only to the colour but to the riches under the surface. Royal purple!

For a second her heart leaped, then it sank again. A shoal of pilchards involved the whole village: men to man the boats, dragging the great nets out in a huge circle until the shoal was surrounded, then dragging it to shore or dipping the still-living pilchards from its clutches; boys to carry the pilchards to the cellar, women to salt the fish, which could sometimes be numbered in millions. It was work for the whole village.

And she had no one to help her.

Bitterness flooded through her. This was Fate's final blow. Ever since she had gained her inheritance, Fate had played this game with her, offering her a gift then snatching it away again, just as she thought that she had it in her grasp. The boat, riches, Kit – all had been shown her, all had been taken. And now this, a final, cruel joke; a huge shoal of pilchards, possibly the last that would ever come to Mousehole, and she could only stand and watch them sweep in and away, out of her sight, out of her grasp, for ever.

'Hurry, Lotty, hurry. There's no time! There's so much to do.'

There was nothing to do. Her father had seen to that. He had made sure that no one would help her, no one would even talk to her. And all because she had refused to let him sail the *Faith-Lily*. For the first time it occurred to her that all her troubles stemmed from that decision. If she had let him sail her boat...

If she had let him sail her boat then Kit would be alive today. Kit – young, laughing, kind. He might have left the area, he might not ever have been anything to her, but he would be alive.

But because of that decision, Kit was dead and William Trevennan alive. Alive to bully and slander, alive to hurt and corrupt. Alive to glory in her loss.

'No!'

The word broke from her lips with the force of an explosion, echoing round the court, ringing in her ears. Boy-John stopped, staring at her, his mouth open. 'No, Lotty?' he quavered.

'No!' She picked up the gritty yellow soap and hurled it across the court. It bounced off the opposite wall and skidded into a gutter. 'No!'

She would not give in to him like this. He was evil! Evil! Boy-John could have died in that whale. She had a right to make her own decisions, a right to decide how to live her own life. She spun on her heel and stalked out of the court, Boy-John running by her side to keep up. 'Where are we going, Lotty? What are you going to do?'

She ignored him, picking up her skirts and running down the narrow, twisting street that led to the harbour, the iron nails in her boots striking blue flashes as she ran.

The harbour was busy as always. The luggers were laid up for the day while their crews got a well-earned sleep before leaving again for the next night's fishing, but the quays were crowded as always by older men, leaning on the rails, watching, talking over the old days, warming their rheumatism in the sun. And the children were there, aping their elders, playing in the punts, swimming when the weather was hot enough.

Even women lingered there, away from their non-stop duties in the house, the constant washing and cooking, the toil of fetching water from the chutes, of cleaning and refilling the evil-smelling oil lamps, of emptying out the coals and relaying the cooking fires. On the rails they could get a breath of fresh air, using discussion about the boats in the harbour and the fishing prospects as an excuse for their absence from their dark cottages. If she wanted helpers, Charlotte knew that she had to go to the harbour.

'Excuse me.' She stopped abruptly outside the smithy, her boots skidding on the smooth sea-worn cobbles, and grabbed an old tyre-iron from a cart-wheel that was leaning against the wall.

Standing on the sea wall she began to beat the metal against the stone. 'Hevva! Hevva!' Her strong voice carried the traditional warning of the approach of pilchards out across the harbour. *'Hevva!'*

Tradition and instincts brought them, running, hobbling. As one the people on the quay turned and moved towards her. Further off, in the steep village streets, she could hear the clang of dropped pans, the pounding of running feet as men and women responded to the age-old cry, racing to the call that would unify the whole village in its fight to gather the riches of the sea. 'Hevva!' She couldn't believe it! They were coming! And there was such a need for hurry. At any time the pilchard shoal could turn away, head back out to sea where the seine boats could not reach them. And she had nothing prepared. The boats were still pulled high on the shore where they had been left safely last winter, the nets were in their loft above the fish cellar. So much to do, so little time. But with the village behind her she could accomplish it.

And then they stopped.

The leading runners stopped first as they realised who was calling them, realised the implications of her shout, remembering to whom the seine boats had been left. Behind them the late arrivals backed up, milling around. The voices, at first raised in excitement, died away into furtive mutterings. The rush towards her slowed, stopped, began to go into reverse.

They couldn't do it! They mustn't.

'No!' The word was forced out of her and to her surprise the drift away halted for a second.

They were here, they were listening. This was her chance, her only chance.

She had no time to think of what to say, of ways to appeal to them. The words came straight from her heart.

'The pilchards are here. For once, after the lean years they have come, they are near the village.'

She raised herself to her full height, staring out over them. 'This is work for all of us, men, women and children. The whole village is richer when the pilchards come. This year, at last, God has sent the fish to us.' She held out her hands to them, supplicating. 'Help me to gather them in. For all our sakes.'

There was a long pause. They stood, motionless, staring at her. But they weren't moving away, they were thinking it over. She had a chance.

She opened her mouth but before she could say anything more there was a disturbance at the edge of the crowd. His white hair shining in the sun, William Trevennan pushed his way through the silent crowd, climbed to stand at Charlotte's side.

'The Devil uses many ways to tempt us.' His rich voice reached easily to the furthest listeners. 'He will even use the name of Our Lord if he thinks that it will help him in his evil ways.'

He threw out a hand indicating Charlotte, standing speechless beside him. '"For all your sakes" she says, this woman who has already been found guilty of breaking at least one of the

Ten Commandments. "For all your sakes." But what about your souls, brethren?' His voice rang out louder, more confident, every word another sliver of ice in Charlotte's heart. 'What about your souls? God has sent the shoal, but is it so that you can follow a woman who refuses to honour her parents, who forsakes the home of her father, who sleeps in the house of a strange man, or is it so that you can prove yourselves as true Christians? So that you can show you are able to resist temptation?' His voice dropped again. 'What if you go out, brethren, out into the seas, following her lures and the fish are gone, have turned away from this village as surely as God will turn His face away if you follow the blandishments of this emissary of Satan?'

Charlotte felt as if he had punched her in the stomach. It had been hard enough when he had denounced her in chapel, but that had been personal; she had been a good individual who had sinned. Now he was talking about her as a temptress, sent by the Devil. She would never again be able to live in the village, in Cornwall, if she allowed this lie to be believed. He was just determined to punish her for disobeying him, and he was even willing to deprive the whole village of the desperately-needed money they would get from the pilchards if it gained him victory over her.

Anger gave her the courage she needed. She raised her head, proudly. 'People of Mousehole, you know me, you've known me since I was a baby. I have lived amongst you, worked with you. I have visited you when you were sick and comforted you when you were distressed. Do you *really* believe that I have been sent by the Devil?'

There was a low murmur, instantly quelled as her father interrupted. 'Comforted! Of course you have comforted.' He pointed a finger, quivering with fury. 'Your lugger, these very seine nets that you are asking the men of Mousehole to work, how did you get them? How much "comforting" did you do to your employer to persuade him to leave you these when he had a son of his own to inherit?'

Even through the shock of the unjust accusation Charlotte could feel the attention of the mass of people switch back to her. Behind the embarrassment and fury, she was dimly aware that the crowd was growing. More people had joined, caught by the sound of raised voices, by the sight of the unusual gathering. She could dimly recognise them, her mother, thinner and paler than ever, the smith those tyre-rim she had taken, the bonnet-maker and the post-mistress, the shop-keeper and the village cobbler – all stood around now, watching the scene, as though it wasn't her character, her life that was being destroyed before their eyes, as though this were just a play.

She swallowed, struggling to get air into her lungs. 'I did nothing!' she protested. 'It's not true.' Even in her own ears it sounded lame but how could she deny something so outrageous.

Trevennan knew it. He pressed his advantage. 'You have only to look at what has happened to her to see that God is angry. Nothing that she does prospers. She has lost her job, her boat has sunk, the crew has drowned–'

'No!' That he should use the deaths of those men, of Kit, for his own ends was unbearable. She turned to him, forgetting, for the first time, that they were fighting for the hearts and minds of the villagers. Suddenly, this was entirely personal. 'You cannot use that,' she said angrily. 'The Spargo boy drowned on the *Isabelle* but you did not say that was because he offended God. You even went to his house, to comfort his family.'

'Which is more than you did,' he retorted.

'I went there.'

'Once or twice,' he jeered. 'That was all. While I was there every day, every evening. Praying with them, comforting them.'

'Comforting Susan, you mean,' she snapped back. 'I've heard of what you did.'

'Me? A man of God?' He turned from her, staring out at the listening crowd, the crowd she had forgotten in the violence of her anger. 'My people, you know me, I am your preacher. Do I deserve such calumny thrown at me?' He paused and following his eyes, Charlotte saw Susan Spargo, standing in the crowd beside the tall young man who was Farmer Matthews' son. 'Susan. You will support me, I know,' he appealed to her. 'You are a virtuous and Christian maiden. Tell them that I did nothing to corrupt your modesty, that I always acted as a man of God should.'

As one the whole crowd turned to stare at Susan Spargo. She blushed furiously at their sudden attention, shrinking back against Tom

364

Matthews' side. Charlotte felt her heart sink. Whatever Susan had told her privately, there was no way that the girl would ever admit to it in public. Especially not with the whole village listening and Tom Matthews standing there, Tom Matthews who was Susan's best hope of marrying out of the cycle of poverty that entrapped her whole family.

Bitterly, Charlotte realised that she had been manipulated by William Trevennan into losing her temper. In her anger she had forgotten the listening crowd but he had been aware of them every single second. And now he had won. All it needed was for Susan to say nothing, to turn away, hide her blushes and he would claim a victory. He would denounce Charlotte as a liar and that would be the end of it. No pilchards. No future for her anywhere in Cornwall. She had been publicly branded a whore, a liar, a servant of the Devil. She was an outcast.

'See?' William Trevennan pointed at the girl. 'Her maidenly modesty is such that it supports my very point. Would a woman defiled, dishonoured, act like this? She has been defamed as much as I, and by the same evil woman.' He turned back to Charlotte and she took a deep breath, pressing back against the wall of the quay, ready for the fury of his denunciation.

'Wait a minute.' It was a different voice. Betsy Trembath thrust her way through the crowd, her short figure bustling busily between the taller men. 'Thee is going too fast for my liking. There's ways and ways of bearing witness, but I don't reckon silence is one of them.'

365

She reached Susan and lifted her chin with one brawny hand. 'Now, maid, tell the truth and shame the Devil. There's two stories going round and one of them must be wrong. Do thee open thy mouth like a good Christian and bear witness which one is the truth.'

The silence spread out from the two small figures like ripples in a pool. The girl swallowed and even over the intervening bodies Charlotte could hear the soft sound.

Trevennan moved impatiently. 'This is–' he began, but the post-mistress waved him quiet with one red hand.

'Well, maid?'

'I – he...' Susan swallowed again, her face now white instead of the fiery red it had been only half a minute ago. 'He kissed me.'

The words were quiet but they seemed to echo round the small harbour. Trevennan raised his voice in a shout. 'A holy kiss, such as the apostles gave each other.'

Susan raised her head. She was staring at Tom Matthews now, her face stricken, as she said, 'He put his tongue in my mouth.'

There was a second's silence then the uproar began. Dimly, Charlotte heard Robert Spargo's angry shout, 'Let me get at the bugger. I'll kill him, I will,' and she realised that she had won. But she felt no pleasure.

As if there were no other people in the world, she watched as Tom Matthews turned abruptly away, saw Susan reach out longing arms to him, saw him push away, through the crowd that parted to let him through and he was gone. She looked back at Susan, a small, shrunken heap, crying in the post-mistresses' arms.

'It's a lie.' William Trevennan had to shout above the uproar. 'You can never trust a woman. Their brains are too weak. Her recent grief has overset her.'

Charlotte lifted her head. 'He kissed me too.' She lofted her voice easily over the buzz of conversation. 'And he tried to do more.'

The talking started again. Parts of sentences drifted up to her. 'Her skirt – half pulled off.'

'Brem upset she were, too.' 'Her own father.'

Other voices took up the refrain. 'Her own father.'

'Hypocrite.' And then, unbelievably, 'Incest.'

Ignoring Trevennan, standing white-faced and silent beside her, ignoring the mounting tumult, Charlotte began to move forward. Her one thought was for Susan. The girl had supported her, but at what cost to herself? If she were to suffer because of William Trevennan's actions … Charlotte began to step down from her position on the wall when a familiar voice stopped her.

'No! No!' Even through the notes of hysteria she could recognise her mother's tones. 'No, not incest! Not that!'

The babel of voices around her rose and drowned her out, then her voice was heard again. 'No! It wasn't incest!'

'Bertha!' William Trevennan's roar cut across all the other voices. 'Woman. Be silent.'

But Bertha Trevennan was too far gone to hear. She was going up to men and women at random, clutching at their sleeves, begging them to listen. 'Not incest!' she kept repeating. 'Not incest!'

Someone had persuaded Robert Spargo to calm down. He touched her arm. ''Tes all right, Bertha. We do know it weren't Charlotte's fault.'

'But it's not incest!' Her hysterical voice rose above all the others. 'It can't be incest. He isn't her father.'

'Bertha!' But Trevennan's shout was meaningless. Struck motionless with shock Charlotte stood, staring down at her mother. Her mind was in a whirl. Her whole life, her whole existence was suddenly anchorless. She felt as if the harbour wall had disappeared from under her feet, as if the air had suddenly disappeared from the whole of the village.

'Who then?' The voice was anonymous but it asked the question everybody there wanted answered. 'If he isn't her father, who is?'

Bertha Trevennan gave a loud wail. 'It was Charles Polruan. I sinned with Charles Polruan and I have been paying for it the rest of my life.'

'Charles Polruan.' Robert Spargo dropped Bertha's arm and turned to stare at Charlotte. 'Then *that* were why he left her the boat and all. It weren't because she...' His voice choked. 'That lying bugger!' Suddenly he was moving towards William Trevennan again, his face burning with fury. 'If I can get my hands on he...'

'Never mind him.' Oggy pushed his way forward. 'What about they pilchards? They won't stay around for ever. Are we going to get they in, or aren't we?'

There was a sudden roar of approval and the

368

crowd moved as one. Within seconds the harbour was empty of all except the three Trevennans and Susan, sobbing silently into her apron.

Her legs didn't feel as if they belonged to her, but somehow Charlotte got them to move. Slowly, stiffly, she moved down to the lower level of the quay where Susan stood and put her arm round her. There was nothing to say, nothing she could say to any of them.

Gathering her mother to her with her free arm, Charlotte silently led them away, leaving William Trevennan alone.

Standing on the far quay where they had heard everything, Dick Robinson gave himself a shake. 'That poor man.' His voice was filled with sorrow. 'I must go to him.'

'Him?' James Hargraves stared at William Trevennan's motionless figure. 'A liar, a debaucher...'

'A man,' Dick corrected. 'Frail, as we all are.'

'He was a local preacher! He wanted to be ordained! And all the time...'

'He is a sinner,' Dick said gently. 'And he needs help, poor man.' He paused, his face dark with pain. 'To have those gifts, for preaching, for good, and to lose the chance of using them. How he must be suffering.'

'You're not going to ordain him now?'

'No. But I will still do what I can.' He began to move away. 'You'll go back to Penzance?'

'I think I'll stay and see a bit of the seine fishing,' Hargraves said. 'See if they get the shoal.'

Dick nodded and moved away then turned. 'By

the way, that girl.'

'The tall dark one?'

'She's the one who owns the boat your son is on.'

Chapter Twenty-Seven

The seine boats were almost hidden by the mass of people. As Hargraves approached he could see them bending low, heard the chorus 'One, two, three!' There was a sudden movement in the crowd and the largest of the seine boats suddenly appeared, rocking slightly from having been turned upright by the combined efforts of many men.

'Here!' More men, running, carried the rollers to put below her keel to slide her down into the water, and still more, their knees buckling under the weight of the huge piles of heavy, dark brown nets, hefted shoulder-high on the enormous sweeps the boat used.

The whole village was involved, he realised as the women appeared, cakes and pasties in their hands. The men struggled to get the thirty-foot seine boat into the water over the rollers while others righted the two smaller attendant boats.

'What's the hurry?' James asked an elderly man whose peg leg prevented him from joining in the more energetic of the activities.

He spat. 'They pilchards won't hang around. They could be off into deep water any minute.' He cupped his hands around his mouth. 'Take a boy with 'ee,' he yelled at the men in the seine boat. 'She'll leak like a sieve after being dry all winter.' One of the men lifted an acknowledging hand and a small boy of about nine years old climbed into the boat, flushed with pride, a bailer clasped to his chest.

'Why wasn't she in the water already?' James asked, his instincts as a boat-owner and seaman coming to the surface.

The old man looked embarrassed. 'Well...' he spat again. ''Tes the women, see. They don't tell 'ee nothing!'

'I see.' Already the men were salving their consciences by offloading the blame onto the women, but James guessed from what he had seen that if the girl had tried to get the boats down before, the men would have refused to help her. Another strand fell into place. Such a situation would certainly have appealed to Kit's quixotic chivalry.

'And how do they know where the pilchards are?'

'There'll be a huer on the cliffs. Granfer-John is there, so they tell me.' He glanced up, his eyes suddenly calculating. 'I could take 'ee out there, if you'd like a geek. 'Twouldn't cost 'ee much. I can't work the seines no more but I'm not out to grass yet.'

It was too good a chance to miss. 'Done!' Hargraves confirmed heartily.

'You go.' Susan wiped her tears with the back of her hand, struggling to regain her composure. 'You go, Charlotte. There are a thousand things for you to arrange at the cellars. I'll – I'll look after your ma.'

Charlotte hesitated. 'Susan, I ought to stay with

you. After what you did for me...'

The girl's face crumpled and fresh tears ran down her cheeks. 'I loved him, Charlotte. 'Twasn't just his money, I really did love him!'

'I know.' Charlotte felt her heart twist with anguish. Everything she did hurt the people around her. Susan, her only hope of a good marriage ruined by her support of Charlotte, and her own mother...

She turned to where Bertha Trevennan was sitting, her hands over her face, her thin body constantly rocking, rocking. Her voice rose in an eerie, keening moan. 'Guilty! I am a sinner. I deserve to die, to burn in Hell. Guilty! Guilty!'

'Should I get a doctor?' Charlotte hadn't realised that she had spoken her worry out loud.

'And what will they do but cost you money, supposing they bother to come to the likes of us?' Susan sniffed, brushing away her tears with the back of her hand. 'You go, Charlotte. You've got to get they pilchards bulked or else all this is in vain. You go.'

Still Charlotte hesitated. Susan turned to her, stamping her foot. 'You want your da to win after all?' She pointed at the door. 'Go!'

All three seine boats were in the water now, their huge twenty-foot oars driving them easily through the calm sea. Behind them, James Hargraves sat in the small punt being sculled by a single oar over the stern by the man he now knew as 'Stumpy Gurnick – father of Oggy.' It seemed that almost all the men had a nickname.

'See they gulls of Tater Dhu?' Stumpy nodded

at the shrieking flock, soaring and diving over a single patch of water. 'They pilchards be there for sure.' He redoubled his efforts, balancing easily on his peg leg.

'Your leg doesn't seem to bother you,' James commented.

'Not for this. Sometimes 'tis even a help – teeling tatties, for instance. It do make the planting holes something handsome.'

James couldn't tell if this was a joke or not. He turned quickly away. 'Who's the man on the cliff?'

Stumpy glanced round. 'Granfer-John. He's huer. See they furze bushes in his hands?' As they watched, the two yellow bushes came up, the right hand held high, the left hand outstretched to the side. 'Go west,' Stumpy interpreted. 'He's directing they seine boats.'

The big seine boat and a smaller boat, also carrying a net, moved onwards, close together now. James noticed that the crew weren't looking at the sea at all but at the man on the cliff, and he himself could see no sign of the fish except for the flock of gulls. Suddenly the bushes were brought down and swung round backwards. 'Towl roz!' Stumpy said excitedly. 'Towl roz!'

'What?'

'Cowl rooz they do call it in St Ives,' then seeing James was still baffled. 'He do mean cast nets.'

The men on the boats leaped into action. Both crews began paying out the dark brown nets, moving away from each other as they did so. Stumpy eyed the situation and sculled the boat round to the far side of the circle which the two boats were gradually creating, one eye all the time on the huer on the cliffs.

'What are you doing?' James demanded.

'Sometimes they fish do make a run for it, see? They can't get through the net so they try to get out of the open end before the two nets is joined. We'll be here to stop 'm if they do try that.'

The third, smaller seine boat was close to them now, her crew peering worriedly down into the water and up at the man on the cliffs. Although he was only a bystander, James still felt his heart in his mouth; the tension was palpable.

The two large boats were moving away from each other in a great circle, paying out nets as they went. Stumpy pointed. 'The net do go down to the sea bed. Once they ends is joined, the fish is caught unless there be a high tide. Then they can get out under the bottom.'

He leaned forward, peering through the clear water. Following his gaze Hargraves saw a flash of silver, then another.

'You buggers!' With a shout that made his passenger jump, Stumpy brought his oar down, smacking the water with the flat of the blade. From the boat beside them other shouts rang out, other oars beat the water. Caught up in the excitement James joined in, shouting with the others, smacking the surface of the water with the flat of his hand for lack of anything better. Through the clear water he saw another flash of silver swim forward, hesitate, then, with a flick of its tail it was gone, back into the area encircled by the nets.

Shouting, splashing, James watched the seine

boats come close together again with what seemed like agonising slowness until they met up. Behind them, a great circle of floating corks showed where the nets hung, an impenetrable wall, from surface to sea bed. And in the circle, leaping, swirling, was a mass of silver bodies. Success.

He gave a sigh of relief, feeling as proud as if he himself had organised the operation. Beside him Stumpy hit his good knee with his hand. '"Money, meat, light – all in one night",' he quoted gleefully.

The crews in the seine boats were finishing off their work, fastening the ends of the two nets together so that no fish could escape, and anchoring the nets so that they would not move. Other boats were approaching, smaller ones. As James watched, one boat carefully made its way over the edge of the seine net until it was inside the great circle whose circumference he estimated was more than a third of a mile. This boat cast another, smaller net.

'Tucking net,' Stumpy explained. 'They do catch the fish in that and they other boats, the dippers, do carry the fish ashore for curing.'

'Why don't you arrange for a way of pulling up the big net?' James asked. 'Or use smaller meshes so that the fish get caught in them.'

Stumpy looked at him with derision. 'You don't know how many fish there are in they shoals,' he said contemptuously. 'You can have one, two million fish in there and there's no way they can all be cured at once. No,' he went on, 'this way is best. This way all they pilchards will stay alive for

376

days until we have time to deal with them. As long as there ain't no storm.' He raised his head and eyed the sky carefully.

'And if there is a storm?' James asked.

Stumpy shrugged. 'They nets'll be breached and they pilchards off like a star shot.'

James eyed the sky in his turn. It would be terrible if, after all this, their efforts were wasted.

The women were already at the cellar, milling around in their white cotton aprons. Their clogs and boots clattered echoingly on the rounded sea pebbles that covered the open space between the pillars. Overhead, on the side nearest the street, the wooden floors of the nets lofts where the seine nets had been stored formed a ceiling over the front part of the cellar.

As Charlotte entered they all turned and looked at her, waiting for her instructions.

She swallowed nervously. She had worked in the cellar herself when she was younger and had accompanied Mr Polruan when he had come to oversee the pilchard catches. But it was a couple of years since the cellars had last been used and it had suddenly dawned on her that it was she who had to give the instructions now.

'I...' Her voice sounded shrill and thin in the large space between the walls. She stopped, clearing her throat, and tried again.

'We need salt.' Thank God Mr Polruan had mended and barked the seine nets and bought in more salt at the end of each season or she would have found herself with rotting nets and no salt or money to buy it. The bigger cellars had a salt room set in the middle of the floor for easy access but the salt room here was off to the back. She pointed. 'Salt, first. But don't spread it. Not until we know we have a catch.'

The atmosphere thickened with tension. The women talked together but now their voices were lowered, ears pricked for the first sign of hurrying feet that would tell them whether they had a good catch or a poor one – or even, no catch at all. Charlotte found herself alone but she realised that it wasn't because of her father's condemnation, but because she was the owner, the boss. The women were setting her apart from themselves, and this time there would be no way for her to get back on the old easy terms.

Charlotte folded her hands in front of her as she waited, trying to pretend to a calmness she didn't feel. Inside, her mind was spinning. To discover that you had been brought up all your life to live a lie, to discover the man you had always believed was your father wasn't and that Mr Polruan...

She took a deep breath. Mr Polruan. She should have guessed. All the clues were there. The way he had paid for her education, the way he had employed her in his firm. Even her name – Charlotte was only a feminine version of his own Christian name of Charles. And she had known nothing! Not even when he had left her the boat...

She turned her mind from that. That thought hurt too much. But that her father – William Trevennan, she corrected herself quickly – who must have known, had preached against her for not honouring her father when all along… The pain of her nails digging into the palms of her hands broke her thoughts.

Keep calm, she told herself. She couldn't allow herself to think of him, to think of anything except the hours in front of her. She ran through all that she would have to do if there was a catch; ensure that the fish were bulked correctly, order along more salt and fish as necessary, arrange for bread and cheese for the women's meals and for their glasses of brandy and their pay of threepence an hour – dear God, how could she pay for it all?

But she wasn't an ordinary woman now, she realised. She had a business. If she had to lay out this money it was because she had pilchards in store, pilchards that would be worth at least double what it would cost her to preserve them. Now, shops and banks would be falling over themselves to supply goods on credit or lend her money, knowing that she had good collateral.

Then there was a record to be kept of the hours the women worked, the pay for the men in the boats, each man in each boat earning an historically agreed proportion of the takings. In the old days she had kept some of these records herself; who could she find to do it now?

The noise of running feet. In the sudden silence Charlotte heard one of the women mutter the traditional prayer, 'Oh Lord, save our labour and send them in with a blessing.'

More running feet outside, heavier now, the sound of boots but it was Boy-John who first appeared in the doorway, his face red with effort.

'A big catch, Lotty,' he panted. 'A real sturt.'

She stared at him, heart pounding, wondering whether his hopes had misled him, then Oggy appeared. 'A gert catch, Miss Trevennan. They be tucking it now.'

A great catch! She swung round. 'Lay out the salt. A good thick layer.'

The women had all worked here before. The buckets of salt were emptied across the stone floor, smoothed flat with hasty hands. Each woman took up a position, a pile of salt beside her.

Charlotte turned to Oggy. 'You can count. You keep the records and names.'

He grinned at her, mouth open, delighted at the sudden responsibility. And then there was a distant noise of many feet coming up the street, the shrill cries of excited children. Charlotte took a deep breath and prepared herself for the onslaught.

'Here they come!'

James Hargraves leaned forward. In the circle of the great seine net the smaller tucking net was being pulled to the surface. This was the first indication the men would have as to the size of the catch. And there it was. Suddenly, the surface of the sea broke. A hundred, a thousand, silver bodies, scintillated in the afternoon light, leaping, dancing, falling.

The men made the net fast. From the other side of the seine net the dipper boats approached; men leaned forward, scooping up the pilchards from the tuck nets with wicker baskets and emptying them into the bottom of their own boats in a great silver flood. In seconds, it seemed to him, the dippers were filled almost to the gunnels, so that the rowers were sitting with fish up to their knees. And still they went on until it seemed that the boats would sink under the weight of the writhing, gleaming fish.

Only then did they pull for the shore, the heavily laden punts wallowing dangerously, but even as they pulled away another dipper moved forward to take its place.

'Seen enough?' Stumpy asked.

James looked at the seething mass of fish still in the tuck net. 'How long will this go on?'

Stumpy shrugged. 'Day and night until 'tis all finished,' he said. 'They got to be fresh, see.'

'And back at the village?'

'Ah!' Stumpy reached for his oar and slotted it into the half-moon cut out in the stern of the punt. 'Thought 'ee'd like to see that. 'Tes a fine sight. As long as 'ee don't mind the smell.'

In the cellar the women were tense, waiting. Under the continual soft chatter their ears were attuned to the sounds outside. Soon. Soon.

Unable to bear the tension, Charlotte walked outside, looking down the street. First came two men, one behind the other, each holding two handles like the shafts of a cart. Between them, piled high with fish, was a box, locally called a gurry, and around them, screaming, laughing, was a crowd of small children.

Every now and then a fish would slither from the heaped gurry and be leaped upon by small boys, to be secreted in their jerseys and taken home for Mother to cook or salt. Beside the men Boy-John ranged, a whippy stick in his hands with which he tried to fend off the other boys and throw the errant fish back onto the piled gurry.

Then the crowd was through the doors, the fish tumbled in a heap under the protection of the overhanging lofts. Women grabbed their sons, thrusting buckets and baskets into their hands. This work was as well organised as any factory line; each woman, each child had a part to play if they were to keep up with the constant flow of fresh fish from the seines.

'Fish!' And the boys dumped a pile of fish by each woman. Instantly, they were laid on the layer of salt that covered the floor of sea-rounded pebbles. Each woman worked on the area immediately in front of her laying fish side by side, all facing the same way, back against belly, until the salt was covered.

'Salt!' And more salt was brought, smoothed generously over the bottom layer of fish, then another layer of fish was laid, this time facing the other way, heads directly over the tails of those below.

And now the noise started. The tongues wagged as swiftly as the hands moved. Shouts and ribald comments were tossed from one woman to another. Gossip was spread, moving along the growing wall of fish, being repeated, amended, embroidered and passed back.

As Charlotte moved along the line of bulkers, checking that all was well, she was aware that the noise level would drop as she approached and knew that some of the stories were about her and her father – William Trevennan, she amended hastily. He was no relation of hers, thank the Lord.

More gurries arrived constantly, each bearing about a thousand fish. The noise of chatter was constantly split by shouts of 'Fish!' and 'Salt!' and the boys scurried to and fro, ensuring that the women had a regular supply.

The smell became overwhelming. Above the scent of more than fifty women, working flat out, there rose the stench of fish. The wall grew swiftly, and as each layer was added, the weight on the lower levels increased. Soon, a noisome ooze began to spread out from the bottom of the wall, moisture, drawn from the fish by the salt and oil, pressed from the bodies by the weight above them, trickled slowly between the stones on the floor, finding its way eventually into the gullies built to receive it. Charlotte checked that there was a barrel in the train pit. Later, the oil would be skimmed from the top and sold as 'train' oil, to light the village lamps during the coming winter, and the blood and salt, known as 'drugs' would be sold to farmers for manure. There was no waste from pilchards.

But she had to have money! All these people needed paying, feeding. And there were casks to buy, the hogshead in which the cured fish were exported to Portugal and Italy. She caught at the arm of one of the gurry-men. 'How is it going? What's the catch like?'

He grinned. 'The dippers say there's plenty more. They reckon it'll take days to empty that their seine.'

Days! That meant real money! And real costs! For every pound profit she made she had to reckon on a pound of costs.

'Oggy.' He was beginning to look bleary-eyed. He could read and write well but he was basically an outside man; keeping paperwork wasn't what he was used to. 'If I get someone to take over from you, can you drive me to Penzance? I need to get to Blacklock's Bank.' That would be the best one. She had been there often for old Mr Polruan – her father. She blessed him for the way he had trained her in the skills needed to run a business. At the time she had hated going to the bank – an object of curiosity in a place where women never went; now she thanked him. At least she knew the manager, she knew the staff, she knew the information they would need.

'Da will do it,' Oggy said. 'He's a brem scholar at book-learning.' Charlotte knew that this meant he was probably no more than adequate; the Cornish had low standards of scholarship but it would probably suffice. 'You'd better stop off at your lodgings and get some clean clothes on you,' he added.

Charlotte glanced down at herself. She was filthy, her dress streaked with blood and scales. Unlike the women bulkers she had not had time to get an apron to protect her.

She nodded. 'Where is your father?'

'He were off taking some toff out to see the seining but he's back now.' He glanced up. 'Look, there he is.'

Charlotte swung round. Two figures were outlined against the sunlight in the doorway. One was Oggy's father, Stumpy, easily recognised because of his peg leg, but the other...

She blinked, her heart suddenly thudding erratically in her chest. That tall, upright figure, the fair curls, the broad shoulders. It had to be Kit!

Chapter Twenty-Eight

'You do understand, don't you?' The compassion in Dick Robinson's voice merely served to infuriate William Trevennan further.

'Oh, I understand! I understand all right!' Normally, the harshness, the pain grating through his voice would have horrified Trevennan but now he didn't care. What was the use of the golden voice God had given him, the power to move people's souls, to bring them to Him? Gone. Gone. And all because of HER! His wife's bastard child – Charlotte. The cause of his ruin.

The Superintendent was still talking, talking. Strangely divorced from what was going on, William Trevennan examined him as he might look at an insect in his food. Thin, weak, no real man; all he had was his education, his background. What right had a man like that to be *his* superior? To pass judgement on *him?*

'Is there anywhere you can go? Do you have friends in another part of the country who can take you in until you can come to terms with all this?'

What a stupid question. As if the sort of people *he* knew could take in strangers, as if he even had enough money to go further than he could travel on his feet. Trevennan shifted his gaze past the Superintendent to stare at the harbour. It was bursting with activity but now this wasn't centred around the luggers, it was the small boats, the punts, in and out, in and out, ferrying the pilchards, living silver, to make money for *her*, to line *her* pockets.

He forced his voice, still hoarse with pain, to speak. 'I am to take evening service in Mousehole this Sunday.'

'My dear sir!' The horror in the Superintendent's voice was almost amusing. 'Haven't you been listening to what I have said? You cannot, *must* not preach again.' He paused. 'I will take that service for you and arrange for others to stand in for all the work that you do. But you – for your own sake, I beg you to go away, start again elsewhere. I will provide you with some sort of recommendation. And money, of course, if you need it.'

'If you need it.' He knew nothing, nothing! All this summer Trevennan hadn't worked as he should, and it was all for the church, in order to get ordained. 'If you need it!' What sort of man was there in his position who did not need money?

'I need nothing.' His voice still grated, as if God was punishing him by taking away His greatest gift. Would he ever get his golden voice back, rich, flexible, persuasive?

The Superintendent was moving uneasily from one foot to another, clearly upset by Trevennan's attitude. 'You won't – you won't do anything desperate?' He glanced at the sea beneath them.

Desperate? The fool really believed that he would try and drown himself! Though there was so much activity in the harbour now he was more likely to be able to cross from one quay to another, walking on boats, than to find a quiet place to drown himself. 'I won't drown myself,' Trevennan assured him in his new, rough voice. 'I still have things I want to do.'

Robinson looked relieved. 'Then, there are others I should see – your wife, your daugh – the other young women,' he corrected himself quickly. 'Do you know where they are likely to be?'

In his house or the Spargos'. Trevennen gave directions automatically, still amazed by the Superintendent's fears that he would commit suicide. Him? When he had so much to do, so much to live for?

Like making Charlotte suffer for all that he had lost.

'Kit! Kit!'

Charlotte ran towards the figure in the doorway. She seemed to be running in slow motion. All sound had suddenly stopped around her; all she could hear was the frantic racing of her pulse.

'Kit! Oh, Kit!'

The bright summer light, shining from behind the figure, shone in her eyes, blinding her. All she could see was the silhouette but she knew it, would know it anywhere.

'Kit!' And she was out in the light, was within an arm's length of him and – it wasn't Kit!

It was the same figure, the same fair, curly hair, the same smile, even the same face, but this face was older, more tired, heavier around the jowls, more wrinkled around the eyes.

'O-oh.'

Desolation swept over her; her loss was as achingly new as when she had first been told of it. She halted, arms by her sides, trying to take in the enormity of her mistake as the world reeled and shuddered under her feet.

And the man walked up to her, held out Kit's hand, said in Kit's voice, 'I had hoped my son was alive – and now I know it.'

'Can I do anything? See the young man, perhaps?'

Susan Spargo shook her head. 'Nothing.' Her face was pale with crying, all the prettiness washed away by the tears but she still had her pride. 'If he don't love me enough to forgive me, then I don't want nothing to do with he! Not that I done anything wrong,' she added fiercely. 'It were all *he*, that so-called preacher!' The scorn and hate in her voice were almost tangible.

'I am sorry that you have had to suffer because of what Trevennan did.' Robinson ran a harassed hand over his thinning hair. He had done his best to combine compassion with firmness in his talk with Trevennan, to love the sinner even while he was deploring the sin, but he knew that he had been unsuccessful. He had wanted to hammer his fists into the man's face, make him suffer as he had made others suffer; it had taken every ounce of willpower to try to remain calm and compassionate.

He hoped that Trevennan had not noticed the anger seething under his offers of help. Not that he seemed to. Except for a quiver that had run

389

through the thickset body when Robinson had told him that he could no longer be a local preacher, that he must take no more services, the man had seemed almost unaware of what was being said to him.

He forced Trevennan from his thoughts. 'There is his wife to consider.' He turned to where Bertha Trevennan sat, rocking, rocking. A thin, toneless wail rose constantly from her pale lips. 'A sinner. I am a sinner. I shall burn in Hell.'

'Should I get a doctor?'

'No, sir. She's often like this.' Susan patted the older woman tentatively on the shoulder but she didn't appear to notice. There was no break in her constant rocking and moaning.

Susan said hesitantly, 'Charlotte did ask me to try to keep an eye on her, after she'd left home, but it was brem difficult. I've my own ma to look after and she's still grieving for my brother.'

More heartache. Dear God. But at least the tall girl had got away from her father – her *putative* father, Robinson corrected himself. He knelt on the floor and chafed Bertha's cold hands but she still seemed unaware of him. 'She is often like this, you say?'

'Yes, sir. Especially since Charlotte left. I do think Lotty managed to keep her looking on the bright side, like. But once Charlotte did say to me...'

'Yes?'

The girl looked away, embarrassed at betraying a confidence. 'She did say that her father took a pleasure, like, in telling her ma what a sinner she was.'

390

Dear God, the harm that man had done; this girl, his wife, his daughter – and how many others? How long had he been corrupting the village, twisting it with the power of his warped mind? And maybe not only this village. The man had preached all over the Circuit. There might be other girls he had debauched, maybe worse than he had this girl. Robinson ran his hand over his thinning hair again, trying to get his priorities sorted out in his mind. 'Can you take this woman in for the night?'

'Well, sir, it may be that she'd rather go to her husband.' The girl sounded awkward. God in Heaven, did the man have that much influence over the poor woman, so that she couldn't be happy unless she was in his power?

'See if you can get her to stay here and...' he reached into his pocket for a coin. 'You've both had a shock. I think that brandy might help you get over it.'

'Liquor, sir!' Her eyes wide, she looked as shocked as if he had just made an improper suggestion. 'I couldn't do that, sir. Mr Trevennan was brem against any sort of liquor!'

'Consider it as medicine,' he said shortly. His anger burned in his stomach like a ball of fire. He wished Trevennan had accepted his offer of money. He would given a hundred pounds to get that spawn of Satan away from here, away from those whose lives he had ruined, whose hearts he had broken.

'What about the daughter?' he asked suddenly. 'Isn't she here? I saw her go with you.'

''Tes the pilchards,' Susan explained. 'She do

own the boats and the cellars, see. She had to go away and arrange about balking the pilchards.' She saw the look on his face and said comfortingly, 'She's a strong woman.'

A strong woman. He knew women like that. For some reason it always was women. They carried on, doing their duty, keeping the family together, when a man would have collapsed under the strain. He had known women who would go from one child's deathbed, dry-eyed although their heart was breaking, because they had to cook breakfast for their other children.

'Even so,' he said, 'to be accused by her father like that, in public. To learn that she wasn't even her father's daughter. That must have been a dreadful shock.'

'And 'twas only a day ago that she learned that her young man had drowned,' Susan added.

'I must go to her.' She had probably suffered more than anyone from that devil's machinations. Dick reached for his tall, black hat. 'Find someone to buy you that pint of brandy and make sure Mrs Trevennan has some – as much as you can get down her. It might give her some ease.'

At least there would be no difficulty finding the girl – what was her name again? Charlotte. Making a face against the all-pervading smell of pilchards, Robinson fell in behind the first gurry he met.

James Hargraves knew from the way her face changed.

With a sense of despair he saw her face whiten,

the corners of her mouth draw in as she struggled for control. This wasn't just the disappointment of finding that he was not his son but something deeper, crueller.

The anguish on her face tore at him. He reached out an unsteady hand, his happiness already replaced by bitter resignation. 'Tell me.'

She could only shake her head silently.

He had to help her. 'He's dead, isn't he?' The whole cellar was silent, the words fell like tombstones, echoing off the granite pillars, crashing leadenly on the stone floor.

She nodded. 'Drowned.' Her voice was a whisper, husky with unshed tears.

For a brief second hope flared. 'But he left the *Isabelle*–'

She shook her head. 'This week. In the storm. My fishing boat...'

He closed his eyes, shutting out the vision. He had been here, in Cornwall. He had known nothing.

Now that she had found her voice she could not stop. 'If I hadn't let him go... If I hadn't asked Granfer-John to come back...'

He could recognise the guilt in her voice. Hadn't he lashed himself in just the same way, tortured himself with a thousand 'if only's?

He gripped her hand in his. It was icy cold, the knuckles white under the taut skin. 'My dear.' His voice seemed to speak without his volition. 'What you did, it was all for the best, wasn't it?'

Her great grey eyes met his fully for the first time since she had realised that he wasn't Kit. 'But it's all gone wrong!' Her voice quivered with anguish. 'I did it for the best but it's all gone wrong!'

He squeezed her hand, trying through the hurt in his own heart to reach out and comfort her. 'That isn't your fault. As long as you did what you thought was right...'

He saw the tears of relief mist her eyes. 'I did.' She seemed to be trying to persuade herself as much as him. 'I truly did.'

He reached out and she was in his arms, the first woman he had held since the death of his wife. He could feel the sobs shaking her body, feel her tears wetting his neck. He patted her back, not caring that the women were all staring at him, not caring that there were muffled giggles from the small boys who stood, their buckets of fish and salt forgotten at their feet.

Inside him, a small, angry voice reminded him: *She's Cornish. The Cornish killed both your boys.* He ignored that too. He had seen the love in her eyes when she first came towards him, seen the agony of her loss. Somehow, it was a comfort to him to know that someone else grieved for Kit, to know that in his last days this woman had loved him even if he had felt alienated from his own father.

'Um, Lotty, Miss Trevennan.'

James raised his head and looked at the short, ugly man who stood nervously in front of him. 'What the hell do you want?'

But the girl had already freed herself from his arms, dried her tears. 'Oggy. I'm sorry.' She wiped a hand roughly across her face, turning to James.

'I have to go.' She paused, trying to find the

right words. 'About Kit, Mr Briars—'

'Hargraves,' he interrupted her. 'Briars was my wife's name.'

Hurt flashed across her face, then she composed herself, drew herself up to her full height. Despite the tears and her dirty dress, stained with scales and fish blood, she was oddly impressive. There was a dignity about her that he had noticed even when she was being traduced by her father on the quay. 'Mr Hargraves. Please believe me when I say that I have never been as grateful to anyone as I was to Kit. In these last few weeks he...' Her voice shook slightly but she got it under control again. 'He worked hard for me, supported me when no one else did and in the end, he died because of me...'

He patted her shoulder. 'My dear, now is not the time. Perhaps, when we are at leisure we can talk about him. You can tell me all about his last weeks.'

She nodded. 'I – I should like that.'

'Lotty!'

'All right, Oggy.' She turned back again. 'I'm sorry but it's the bank, you see. I have to borrow some money.'

'This catch isn't worth anything?' He was startled into the improper question.

'Oh, it's worth a great deal.' Her voice was suddenly tart. 'But the fish have to be kept in balk for at least two weeks, preferably four—'

'Six, bela, six!' They both swung round and Hargraves stared at the short, fat little man who was almost bouncing with agitation behind him. 'Six, bela, and I promise you the most monies of anyone in Cornwall.'

'Senhôr Da Silva!' The girl's grave face lit up with a sudden smile. 'You are back! And – and your wife?'

The little man kissed her hand, his quick brow reminding James of a sparrow. 'Well, at last. And all the little ones, but...' he was obviously not going to be diverted from the important matter by such irrelevances. 'The extra weeks, it makes all the difference. Two weeks in these walls, this balk, you call it, and half the hogsheads will be rotten before Lent. Four weeks – *phw!*' The extraordinary sound somehow conveyed his opinion of such a period. 'But six, bela, six weeks and if the hogsheads are well filled (and I know you – never do you do a bad work), I will pay you the most monies. They will be the best fairmaids in Portugal. And you get all the monies. I buy direct. Not through that great oaf of a Polruan.'

She actually laughed and James could see that the funny little man was a favourite with her. 'Your accounts wrong again?'

'Accounts! They are not accounts, they are fairy tales! They do not add up, they do not tell the truth. They are useless! "Where is my favourite," I ask, and they say you are gone away. Sacked! "So I will sack *you*," I tell them. And now I come here, bela, and here you are with lots of beautiful fairmaids. Providing you leave them for six weeks,' he added, fixing her with a dark, stern eye.

Charlotte turned to James. 'You see? And even then, there are the casks to be bought, and filled, and the fish must be pressed again. The fish are

396

worth a lot of money but it will take time for me to get paid.'

'There's no alternative?' he asked, concerned.

She shrugged. 'I could sell the fish as they are–'

'To some stupid Cornishman!' Da Silva was dancing on the spot with agitation. 'Who will put them in tubs in two weeks and spoil them all! No, no, no!'

'Then I'll try the bank.' She turned to the door. 'Come on, Oggy. We'll have to hurry to get there before they close.'

'Wait.' Hargraves reached into his pocket and pulled out a card case, scribbling rapidly on the back of one of the cards. 'Here. Use this if you need to.'

She read the scrawled message then stared at him. 'You'll guarantee the loan! But why? You hardly know me.'

What could he say? *Because you remind me of my dead wife? Because you loved Kit? Because I would have given anything to have you as daughter-in-law?*

They were all true but he couldn't say any of them. 'I – I'm a businessman,' he said weakly. 'I know a good risk when I see one.'

'You won't regret it, I promise you,' she said earnestly. And then she was gone.

Chapter Twenty-Nine

William Trevennan drifted along the empty streets like an angry ghost.

It wasn't right! This was his village, his chapel, his world and it had been taken away from him. Once he had been respected, looked up to, honoured. Wherever he went he had been greeted, deferred to. Yet even Miss Makepeace had turned from him when he spoke to her two days ago.

He moved on. No one was around. The villagers were at the chapel, the chapel where he should have been conducting the service. Instead, it was that milk-and-water Robinson. Where he would have thundered about sin, demanding, forcing the villagers to turn to God, the Superintendent was probably blathering meekly about thanks for the catch of pilchards, the pilchards put in Charlotte's cellars.

Her! His fists clenched automatically, fingers knotting until his nails carved into his palms. It was all her fault. If she had only let him sail her boat, none of this would have happened. Instead...

He stopped. As if subconsciously, his feet had led him to the cellars. There she had employed half the village for the last few days, getting the shoal of pilchards in, balking them up. If the snatches of conversation he had overheard were right, she had already got a buyer for them. She

398

had borrowed money but she would get it back, twice over. She would be a rich woman, successful, a force in the village while he...

His stomach twisted with rage and sour bile rose in his throat. He wanted to shout, hit, tear. He wanted to beat her, prove his superiority, humble her; but most of all he wanted to ruin her, as he had been ruined.

Those lies about him, about what he had done to her. As if she hadn't asked for it, standing there, kissing him; as if she shouldn't consider herself lucky that he had deigned to kiss a woman like her, so tall and unfeminine, so unlike her mother.

He felt the sweat break out under his arms at the thought of that night when he had been tempted – by her. When, for only the second time in his life, he had fallen. Other men gave into temptation but they were not pilloried like this. It wasn't his fault. If his marriage had been as he had expected, hoped, prayed for...

He had known about the pregnancy when he agreed to marry Bertha. The money Polruan had given him had helped, of course, but he would have done it anyway. Bertha had been so beautiful in those days, with her blonde hair and slender figure, dressing with an elegance that he had never seen in another woman of their station in life. He had married her, believing...

He had to stop thinking about it. The door of the cellar was shut but not locked. Trying to force the haunting memories from his mind he pushed it open, stepped into the quiet space.

Above him, supported on great granite pillars,

the net lofts thrust their raggedly thatched roofs to the evening sky. Before him, five feet high and four feet wide, the wall of salted pilchards stretched the whole length of the open cellar, just the tips of the noses and tails of the hundreds of thousands of pilchards showing through the grey pink of salt.

Riches. Riches that would never be his – and all because of Charlotte. Any other woman would have let him captain her boat, any other woman would have brought this money back into the family, would have shared it with her parents. Any other woman would have put the interests of her father first, not denounced him in front of his congregation, ruined his life, prevented him from doing God's work. And instead of being punished, she was rewarded for it. All this fish! How many hogshead were here? How much money?

He stared at the huge heap, the rows of fish stretching from one end to the other with almost mathematical exactness. Once, he knew, the fish had been smoked to preserve them for the long sea journey to Portugal and Italy, where the dictates of the Catholic Church led to a huge demand for fish. Now they were preserved in salt but...

But why shouldn't they still be smoked?

For the first time since the scene at the harbour William Trevennan began to smile.

James Hargraves moved uneasily, shifting his position slightly so that he could get a better look at Mark.

Ever since their dog cart had entered Mousehole the boy had been wheezy, coughing slightly, as if the smell of pilchards had set off his asthma. Dick Robinson had shrugged. 'Sitting quietly in chapel might help,' he had whispered as they walked to the small building set under the slope of Ragginis Hill, but it hadn't. In the quiet hall the boy's breathing was noisier, more laboured than before.

James looked around. The chapel was packed; it seemed as if the whole village had come to hear the new Superintendent preach. Amongst the women, sitting apart from the men on the far side of the chapel, James could easily pick out Charlotte's tall figure, see how she soothed and comforted her mother. On their side of the chapel the men congregated and, although they were wearing their Sunday clothes, the smell of strong tobacco and fish was overwhelming. No wonder Mark had trouble breathing.

James could see that he was trying to control it but that just made everything worse. The more he tried the more tense he got, his thin shoulders hunched with the effort and his breath rasping in his throat.

'Let us pray.' As the congregation rustled forward, covering their eyes with their hands, James hissed at the boy, 'Why don't you go out?'

Mark lifted startled eyes. 'But Father—'

'You go out.' James gave him a surreptitious push. 'The fresh air will do you good. We'll look for you afterwards.'

He watched as Mark, wheezing and rasping, walked awkwardly out through the praying

401

crowd. Being in here would do no good, he thought as he tried to turn his attention to Dick's prayer of thanks for the huge catch of pilchards. The boy would be far better off outside.

An investigation showed that his idea had possibilities. The train pit was almost full with a mixture of dregs and oil. It had to be emptied regularly; the bailer used for the purpose lay alongside, but on a Sunday people followed the instructions of the Scriptures and did as little work as possible.

The wooden floors of the lofts were of a wood so ancient that they seemed impervious to flame, but there were piles of old nets mouldering in the corners which he had no doubts about. And once the thatched roof caught, the whole place would collapse. He wondered briefly about the huge pile of fish. Pilchards were oily but he doubted if they would actually catch alight. But what did that matter? Once the burning roofs had collapsed on them, once they had been covered with ash and dirt, the salt washed off by the water used to try to contain the fire, it was unlikely that anyone would want to buy them for human consumption. Charlotte would be lucky if she could sell them as fish manure. And then there was all the money she had borrowed from the bank. She would never pay that back – and then what? A debtors' prison?

William Trevennan walked over to the brimming train pit and, using the bailer, carefully began scooping the yellow train oil from the top of the pit into a handy bucket, singing under his breath the lines by Charles Wesley.

'Life up your heart, lift up your voice;
Rejoice, again, I say, rejoice.'

Mark rested his folded arms on top of the railings, and leaned his chin on his arms, trying to catch his breath. In front of him the harbour scene was peaceful enough, ships pulling softly at their moorings, black hulls outlined against the yellow lichen on the old stone walls of the quay. He knew that he should be feeling easier, more relaxed, but instead his chest felt tighter than ever, and he was sweating with the effort to breathe.

He hated this village. He didn't know why, but even in the dog cart he had felt a great reluctance to come here. He knew that that was what had started off his asthma; usually he only got it at night, when he had *that* dream. He didn't like being alone here, either. The village was too deserted, as if he were the only person still alive, and the harbour was too full of movement, the boats shifting on their moorings, the slap of water against stone, of ropes against masts, the creak of wood. The noises would hide the sound of anyone creeping up behind him.

He swung round, his breath whistling in his lungs but there was no one there. He wished he could go back into chapel, where his father would protect him, next to Mr Hargraves' calm security, but he knew he would only get sent out again. A sea gull screamed overhead, making him jump nervously.

He had to get away from this harbour with its strange noises. He wanted to be with people, grown-ups, who could keep the ghosts that haunted his dreams away from him.

His lungs labouring, he started to walk back up the nearest street, watching the silent houses on either side with wide, frightened eyes.

The yellow train oil splashed over the nets, ran across the wooden floors, dripped through cracks in the warped boards to the cellar below.

Trevennan backed down through the trapdoor onto the rickety ladder, the empty bucket in his hand. Usually, anything heavy was lifted to the loft through the great double doors that overlooked the street using the hoist, but he dared not do that.

He stooped over the train pit again, filling the metal bailer with oil and emptying it into the bucket. He would hang some of the nets over the rafters, he decided. That should make sure that the flames reached the old thatched roof, and once that had caught the whole building would go. Other houses nearby might also catch fire; several of them were still thatched although the fashion for slate roofs was beginning to spread. Well, he wouldn't cry about that. The whole village had rejected him, spurned him; they all deserved to suffer.

The oil had all been taken from the train pit now, and he was down to the mess of blood and brine underneath. Surely he had enough?

Without thinking he tossed the bailer away as he bent to pick up the bucket. It clattered across the pebbles, rolling to and fro with a noise that echoed off the granite pillars like the tolling of a bell. Trevennan froze, the bucket of oil clasped to his chest. If anyone came...

But his straining ears could hear nothing from the street outside. No heavy fisherman's boots clomping urgently along to investigate the sound, no shouts.

Breathing more easily, he began to climb the ladder, the heavy bucket in his hand.

He was halfway up when the door of the cellar creaked slowly open.

Away from the strange noises of the harbour, the village felt less scary and Mark felt his breathing begin, slowly, to ease although he still disliked the feeling that he was all alone here. The villagers must all be at chapel and in that case he would see no one until the service was over. His father didn't make a habit of long sermons like some preachers, but he knew the service would go on for at least another hour.

Instinctively, he directed his steps towards the chapel. He would be able to hear the singing from outside, perhaps he would hear his father's voice. His breathing was better. If there was someone he could talk to, someone who would take his mind off his asthma, it would soon settle down; perhaps it would improve so much that he could go back into the chapel again with everyone else.

And then he heard it. A loud rattling crash from the old-looking building next to him. It obviously wasn't a house. He wondered if it were some sort of stable and one of the horses had kicked over a water bucket. If there were horses in there he could pass the time stroking them, plaiting their manes, talking to them. The thought of the warm, fuggy comfort of a stable was strangely attractive after the silent emptiness of the village.

He pushed open the door.

A witness.

This would be the end, Trevennan knew. If they could prove arson against him...

He let out a roar, jumping from the ladder to the cellar floor. His nailed boots clattered against the stones and the stinking oil slopped all over him but he did not care. He dared not let a witness escape.

As if he had read his mind, the boy in the doorway turned and fled, disappearing into the evening light, but not before Trevennan had caught a glimpse of the frightened face and recognised him.

Mark Robinson. Well!

This would really be killing two birds with one stone.

Mark glanced around. The chapel lay off to his right but the street was straight and the man would see him and could easily catch him before he reached sanctuary. In any straight race the man would catch him up before he could go more than a few yards. He turned and plunged up a narrow alleyway, praying that he had not chosen a dead end.

The path was scarcely wide enough for a man

to squeeze along, the top story of the house overhanging by at least half the width of the lane. Thankful for the light shoes on his feet Mark hurried, hearing behind him the scrape and clatter of the man's boots on the cobbles. The alley was only the length of four or five cottages, but there was no other exit apart from the far end. He forced himself onwards, half-frightened, half-amused. After all, he hadn't been doing anything wrong. He had only looked in through the door. The man was probably a bit funny in the head. Once he had lost sight of Mark he would give up, go back to whatever he was doing before. Mark breathed a sigh of relief as he reached the far end and found himself in a small square. He could get out another way, avoid the man, go back to the chapel.

He gave a last glance down the alley, to make sure that he was safe, and even as he peered back he saw the man's head, a black silhouette against the bright light of the street. Then his body appeared and Mark realised that he was still following.

Mark began to run in earnest now, his shoes pattering lightly over the uneven cobbles. There were plenty of places to hide; huge piles of nets, small mountains of lobster pots, even, here and there, a punt, upturned by the road or leaning against the side of a house, but Mark knew that first he had to get far enough away from the man to be able to pick a secure hiding place where his pursuer would not look for him.

He raced on. If he had been sure there were other people around he would have shouted but, in this lifeless village, it was more than likely that only his pursuer would hear. Mark swung round a corner into another narrow street and began to run down it, his eyes searching for a way out.

His breath was rasping again. The asthma had never really gone and exercise would always make him cough. Now, with the exertion and the fright, he could feel it clutching his chest with a vice-like grip. His lungs heaved and he could hear the air whistling as he breathed. Would the man hear it? Even if Mark could find a safe place to hide, all the man had to do was stand and listen.

Mark stopped, his head drooping. Over the noise of his laboured breathing he could hear the sound of shod feet coming closer, closer. He plunged on.

Where two streets diverged he paused, irresolute. One was straighter, wider, surely leading back to the safety of the chapel; the other twisted immediately but it sloped downhill and he knew that meant it led to the harbour.

The harbour, with its small, strange noises and constant movement, with the wide open spaces of the quays. He did not want to go to the harbour.

He struggled to catch his breath, straining his ears to hear above the sound of his wheezing lungs. The pursuing feet were closer, too close for him to risk the long, straight road. He plunged downhill.

This hunt had gone on too long. Something was wrong. Men didn't hunt boys like this, silently, not stopping. There was something here he didn't understand, something that made the hairs on his neck rise up in terror.

He ran on, his heaving gasps shaking his whole body. He had to find somebody soon; he couldn't go on much further. The street took a final twist and he was suddenly out in the open, as he had feared, out on the side of the harbour.

But here was rescue, here was safety. Moving slowly on the evening tide, her brown sails flapping limply, a black-hulled fishing boat edged her way in towards the nearest quay.

There were two men on her, one hauling down the last remaining sail, the other at the stern, steering by means of a great iron tiller.

He forced air into his lungs to shout for help.

And stopped.

The man at the tiller, his stance, the turn of his head, the fair curls on his head – he was familiar, known to Mark these ten years past.

It was Mr Hargraves' son, Kit.

The air escaped in a frantic gasp. Kit. But Kit was dead. Drowned. They had prayed for him at family prayers only this morning.

Suddenly Mark was cold; icy cold. A ghost. There was no other explanation. Kit was dead and he had come back.

A ghost!

With a mew of terror Mark swung round, away from the fearsome figure in the boat. Turned away–

And an arm caught him fiercely, a hand clamped over his mouth and a strange voice hissed in his ear: 'Got you, you little bastard.'

Chapter Thirty

'Did you just see something?' Kit stared around the small harbour. In the evening light Mouse-hole seemed completely deserted.

The other man looked up from the sail he was stowing. 'Like what?'

'A boy.' Kit frowned. It had looked just like young Mark Robinson. But that was ridiculous! What would *he* be doing in Cornwall?

'I didn't see anything. Perhaps you imagined it.'

It was a fine evening but the light was fading fast, always a time when it was easy to imagine things, to see things that weren't there. But why imagine Mark? Kit asked himself. Charlotte, yes – but a schoolboy he had known hundreds of miles from here? It was the very unlikelihood of it that made him suddenly worried.

'I'm going to look for him.' The words came without his volition.

The fisherman nodded. 'I can manage alone now, anyhow.' The *Faith-Lily* had come alongside a lugger, already moored at the quay and he jumped easily across on to the other boat, the painter in his hand. 'You carry on.'

Kit followed him, leaping lightly across the other boat and shinning quickly up the ladder that led to the top of the quay, his sense of unease growing. He hadn't felt like this since he had dived off the *Faith-Lily* in the storm.

Kit had alerted his position in the sea, supporting the rescued sailor with his left arm as he used his right to swing himself round.

Close by, the bulk of the *Faith-Lily* showed as a black silhouette against the dark sky. From sea-level she seemed enormous, looming over him as she wallowed at the end of her trail of nets. Wisps of mist gathered about her, creating haloes around the small lantern at the top of the mizzen mast and the brighter flambeau he had handed to Mick.

He could hear shouts and talking on the boat; the rest of the crew had obviously been roused and were awake.

A cold wave broke over his head and he submerged, coughing and choking. Stupid to stay here, he decided, he might as well get as close to the boat as possible. The seaman wasn't struggling now; he was lying still in Kit's grasp, exhausted by his struggle with the rising waves. Holding the rescued seaman with one arm and swimming with the other, Kit moved slowly towards the lugger.

'You can't do that!' Mick stared at his eldest brother in horror. 'You can't leave a man to drown.'

'Can't I?' Big Rory grinned. 'When it's Mr bleeding Briars I can. Ordering us around in his plummy voice when he do know less about fishing than we, laying down the law.' His voice took on an exaggeratedly English accent. 'Don't you drink, you're not good enough for pleasures

411

like what we gentlemen should have. Huh,' he snorted, his voice dropping to its normal register, 'he can drown and good luck to he.'

His two brothers looked at each other. 'But the other man?' Mick suggested diffidently. 'He's never done us no harm. We can't leave he to drown.'

'We don't even know if there *is* another man,' Rory said scornfully. 'And if there is, so what? He'd have drowned anyway, what difference do it make to him?'

A wave broke over the bows of the boat, making her shudder all along the keel. White water ran along the decks, creaming off into the scuppers. Tethered as she was by the drift nets, the *Faith-Lily* was less able to ride out the worsening weather.

'We'll get the nets in then make a run for it,' Rory decided. 'The wind's from the southwest anyway. If it gets up any more we'll be halfway up the Channel before daylight. And get rid of that damned flambeau. The less people who know we're here the better.'

He stepped forward and snatched the can from Mick's hands. For a second he held it aloft, his great figure and red hair gleaming in the light of the flame like some Ancient Briton, then he flung it far from him. It curved out over the sea, the flame streaming behind it, then sank with a hiss into the dark waves.

Big Rory grinned. 'We're on our way, brothers. Let's get those nets in. But first...' he moved forward to the pile of discarded clothes that Kit had left on the deck. '...I'll see if the bastard had the sense to leave that gun behind. It's one of they new ones, that were used in the Crimea. The way things are I'd feel happier with it in my hands.'

He scrabbled amongst the clothes, pushing aside the boots and coat, then gave a grunt of satisfaction. 'Here it is.' He pulled it from its holster. Even in the dim light it gleamed with a wicked sheen. Gloating, he admired the smooth metal, the weight of the weapon in his hand, the feeling of power it gave him. 'Got you at last, my beauty,' he murmured.

'And much good may it do you.'

With an oath, Big Rory swung round. Dripping, breathless, Kit sat astride the stern rail, one hand still on the trailing painter to which the punt had been tied.

The three brothers stared at him, startled by his sudden appearance. Big Rory was the first to recover. 'Get him,' he yelled, plunging back along the wet deck.

Mick hesitated. 'But–' he began.

'Get him,' Big Rory repeated, but it was already too late. Kit dropped onto the deck and began to move forward, and even in the dim light, there was something in his stance that made the two younger brothers back hastily away.

'For God's sake!' Big Rory shouldered his way past them. 'Are you bloody mice or what?' He stopped by the mizzen mast, his eyes gleaming in the darkness. 'I've waited all my life for a chance to get my hands on some easy money, and I'm not going to let anyone stop me now. Especially when I've got this.'

Slowly, he raised the revolver, pulling the hammer back with his thumb, and pointed it at the man in the stern. Kit stood silent, motionless apart from the heaving of his chest. In the dimness his fair hair and wet, white shirt gleamed like beacons. He did not try to move; there was nowhere for him to go. Head up, lips parted, he stood only feet away from Big Rory, staring down the barrel of the gun.

'Now!' Big Rory pulled the trigger, his eyes closing automatically in expectation of the shot. But there was no explosion. The hammer fell with a click that seemed to echo around the boat. Rory blinked in surprise – and Kit was on him.

With one hand he caught the big man's wrist, bending it backwards until the revolver fell from his grasp while he smashed his free hand into Big Rory's face. 'Bastard!' His voice was hoarse with effort and the sea water he had taken in. 'Leave two men to drown, would you? You–'

As he aimed another punch at Big Rory's face the other man recovered. Stepping closer he butted his head forward, catching Kit on the nose. Kit gasped, blinking away tears of pain then doubled over as another of Rory's punches caught him below the belt, winding him.

Then the two men were on the deck, hammering blows at each other, their faces inches apart, legs intertwined. Through the red fury that invigorated him Kit knew that he did not have much time. He was already exhausted with the swim and climb. Dragging a body through the waves, hauling himself up the trailing painter that had once held the punt, had taken all his strength. And there were the other two men. He had heard their horror at their brother's plans but that did not mean that they would not come in on Big Rory's side in a fight.

Another wave rose over the bows and ran along the deck, creaming around their fighting bodies, taking his breath away with its sudden coldness. Three against one. What chance did he have? But if he stopped fighting he had no chance, no chance at all and, worse, Charlotte would lose her boat, her one hope of getting free from the malevolent influence of her father.

The thought gave him fresh energy. He would not let her down. He had no hope of winning her, no hope of marrying her, but that did not matter. He loved her and he would not be responsible for ruining her life as well as his own.

The revolver was on the deck only inches from his hand. As a firearm it was useless but as a club... He reached for it, throwing himself sideways off Big Rory's body, hand outstretched for the weapon ... and realised too late that he had given Big Rory the chance he needed.

As Kit's weight was lifted the man's hand moved, quick as a viper, to his belt and Kit, still struggling to reach the discarded gun knew what he was doing. He was reaching for his knife.

Against a knife the empty gun was worthless but it was the only weapon he had. He threw himself further sideways, arms out, fingers grasping, then the boat rolled as another wave hit it and the gun skidded a few, precious inches sideways. Out of his reach.

Despairingly, fingers still trembling with the

effort Kit made a final lunge but even as he did so he knew that it was useless. Already he could see the glimmer of steel in Big Rory's hand, already he could sense another man, standing over their two bodies, leaning over them…

And then a voice he did not recognise commanded: 'Drop that knife.'

For a second both men were rigid with shock then Kit moved. Slowly, disbelievingly, he raised his head. A few feet away, halted as they hurried to help their brother, Mick and Gulger stood motionless, and even in the dim light Kit could see their eyes, wide with shock.

And standing over him, a viciously sharpened gutting knife held at Big Rory's throat, was the man he had rescued, the man he had left clinging frantically to the trailing painter.

Kit let his breath out in a long, slow sigh. 'You'll never know how glad I am to see you,' he said earnestly.

The other man laughed abruptly. 'Not as grateful as I was to see you.' He stepped carefully sideways so that Kit could get unsteadily to his feet, the knife still held against Big Rory's throat. 'You'd better get yourselves well back,' he advised the two brothers. 'You don't want me to get nervous. If my hand shakes…'

Mick and Gulger backed swiftly away. 'And your knife mate,' the stranger continued. Big Rory hesitated a second then the knife dropped from his hand and Kit stooped and picked it up.

Another wave broke over the bows. The wind was stronger than ever. A bad night, Kit decided; too bad to be hung onto the end of a mile of nets.

Granfer-John had said that the lugger could fish through a storm but Kit did not think he meant one like this. Every minute the wind was rising, the waves becoming more vicious. The best thing was to get the nets in, then run before the wind, up-Channel until the weather turned for the better.

Again the waves washed across the decks. The boat already seemed to be wallowing, appreciably lower in the water than she had been. Getting her pumped was another necessity. Kit grinned.

He moved towards the brothers who backed nervously away. 'Sound carries well over the sea.' Kit tried to keep all rancour out of his voice. 'I know that you didn't want to let me drown. But, under the circumstances, you can't expect me to let you keep your knives, can you?' He held out his hand. 'Give them to me. Now.'

Mick reached towards his belt but Gulger was made of sterner stuff. 'What are you going to do with us?'

'Do?' Kit was suddenly deathly tired. 'Nothing. I'll do nothing to you. But if we don't get those nets in the boat will sink and with no punt we'll go down with her. I expect you to carry on as before, but I'm not letting you keep the knives.'

As if to emphasise the point, from the corner of his eye Kit saw the stranger's hand move slightly and Rory let out a bellow of fright. Mick scrabbled frantically for his knife and threw it down. Gulger hesitated. 'And Rory? What are you going to do with him?'

'It would serve him right if I threw him over the

side and let him swim back to the Scillies.' Kit couldn't keep the bitterness out of his voice. Then he grimaced. He'd never do it, why pretend. Wearily, he said, 'Rory can work the pump. I'll tie him up with the padlock and chains we use for securing the holds in harbour. If he pumps, he'll be as safe as we are. If he doesn't...' Kit shrugged. If the weather got any worse they might none of them survive the night.

But already the weather was too bad to get the nets in. Even with the four of them on the capstan they made slow work of it and all the time the weather worsened, the *Faith-Lily* wallowed lower in the water.

Cut the nets. It was their only hope. But without her nets, the *Faith-Lily* was useless. Some had come with the boat and belonged to Charlotte but the others he had paid for with his own money, the money he received from pawning his watch. It was gone now, spent. If Charlotte hadn't made money from the fish...

But at least she would have the boat. Closing his mind to the loss he slashed at the ropes as they ran out over the starboard bow. 'Gulger, take the tiller. Mick, start trying to get a sail up.' Without the nets holding the bows to the wind there was a danger the boat would swing sideways and be swamped.

But already the stranger was struggling with the sails. Kit cut the last of the ropes and as the boat was freed she swung round, wallowing dangerously, the wind and seas catching her broadsides. For a second Kit thought she would overturn as waves reached up her sides, thrusting

418

greedy hands at the deck; she heeled dangerously, then the wind caught at the sails and the
rudder took hold. With a shudder the lugger
swung further round and began to run before the
wind.

'Not too much sail.' They might even be better
with bare poles now that they had got her under-
way.

''Strewth,' the stranger grinned as Kit took a
place by his side. 'Albert Corin, here, alive thanks
to you. Though I thought for a while there I was
going to find myself back in that blamed water
again and I didn't want that. Being cut in half by
a bloody clipper was enough for one night.'

'It may still happen,' Kit pointed out. 'If we hit
anything in this weather...' He brushed wet hair
out of his eyes. 'And if we're talking about saving
lives...'

Albert Corin glanced at Big Rory and his
brothers. 'Fine crew you've got yourself.'

'A fine crew,' Kit agreed tersely, 'but not for
long. Once we're out of this weather I'm
dumping the lot of them if I have to row the
damn boat all the way home by myself.'

He glanced at the stranger. 'If we survive this,
I'll have to go back to Cornwall, explain to the
owner, try to get a new crew, more nets.' He
paused. 'They say,' he began hesitantly, 'they say
that a man and a boy can sail one of these luggers
if necessary.' He paused. 'What about you? Are
you willing to give it a try?'

'I'm with you, mate.' The stranger glanced up
at the sky above them, black as sin. 'If we get out
of this alive.'

Kit nodded. 'It'll be a long night,' he agreed.

'And this storm won't die with the morning, either,' the stranger answered.

'Portsmouth!' Kit stretched and laughed. 'Who'd have thought we'd have had to get to blasted Portsmouth before we could get rid of that lot.'

'From what I saw of them, it would have been worth going to Jerico,' Albert said. 'They were trouble whichever way you look at it. Whatever made you take on a crew like that anyway?'

'Needs must.' Kit spoke more lightly than he felt. While Big Rory and his brothers had been on board it had been impossible to relax, and the storm, pounding in from the Atlantic, had been too dangerous to fight. They had run before it with the minimum of sail for the best part of three days and in all that time, preoccupied with the necessity of keeping the *Faith-Lily* afloat and with controlling the O'Rearden brothers, Kit had snatched only moments of sleep.

Now that he could relax, the enormity of his failure weighed him down. He had been so confident that he could solve Charlotte's problems, find her a crew, make her enough money to free her from the despotism of her father. He had imagined himself sailing home in triumph, imagined her throwing herself into his arms, full of gratitude.

And here he was, miles from the fishing grounds, no crew, no fish, no nets. Instead of sailing home in triumph he was a failure, creeping back with his tail between his legs. His lips twisted. It was all hopeless anyway. What could he offer her? He was poor, cut off from his family. He had left home full of plans to make his fortune and now he had showed that he wasn't even capable of managing a small fishing boat.

Well, all he could do was sail back to Mousehole, confess his failures, let her find another master. By now she had probably become reconciled with her father and would have no problem getting a decent crew. His lips twisted in self-disgust.

'What about you?' he asked Albert abruptly. 'Are you going ashore here?'

'I thought we were going to sail her back, just the two of us.' The older man ran his hand through his thinning hair. 'I was looking forward to it, like. There are always arguments about whether the west coast or east coast luggers are better; I thought this was my chance to find out.'

'It'll be dangerous,' Kit pointed out. 'There are just the two of us and these are busy waters.'

'I bin run down once.' A grin split his weatherbeaten face. 'I don't reckon I'm due for drowning. Thanks to you.'

'Thanks to you'. The words seemed to echo round Kit's head. 'Thanks to you'. The man hadn't drowned. And it was because of him. He felt suddenly breathless, his chest tight with emotion.

'What about family?' he asked, and his voice was unusually gruff. 'Is anyone likely to be missing you?'

'No one. My ma'll expect me when she sees me. She doesn't like letters, not since she got one saying my younger brother had drowned. Now she just prefers to live in hope.'

He strolled over to where Kit stood by the bows and clapped him on the shoulder. 'Yes, I reckon you'll be remembered in Ma's prayers for the rest of her life. My brother John's death nearly killed her. She'll be some glad you saved me like that.'

'John!' Kit closed his eyes. The last sight of his brother flashed across his mind, the drowning boy, his useless struggles to rescue him. And now, here was another man, alive, because of what he had done, a mother, contented because he had saved her son.

It didn't make up for Jonathan's death, nothing could do that, but it was something to set in the scales, something to balance that ultimate failure.

Suddenly feeling lighter, he grinned at Albert. 'I want to get back to Cornwall as soon as possible. Do you object to sailing on a Sunday?'

'Sunday?' the man scoffed. 'Course I don't! What do you think I am, some sort of blasted Methodist?'

Kit moved to the stern and took the tiller. 'Then let's get going,' he said cheerfully.

Now the small cottages were silent and dark in the fast-fading light as Kit made his way through Mousehole. It was always like this on a Sunday, he remembered. Not everyone went to chapel but those who didn't lay low so that the whole village appeared deserted.

Charlotte's cottage was just in front of him. For a second, he hesitated, remembering the last time he had been here, the way he had said goodbye to her, the kiss they had shared. Should he go to her? She might not be at chapel.

But there was the boy. The more he thought about it, the stranger it seemed. Even if it *had* been Mark Robinson, why would he turn and run like that, as if the very sight of Kit had frightened him? Perhaps he was a figment of his imagination. He had invented the child as a way of putting off his visit to Charlotte, the confessions of incompetence he must make.

The road in front of him, the street the boy had run into, was empty. But surely he could hear footsteps ahead? Making up his mind, Kit began to walk quickly up the narrow street, his own steps echoing off the silent, empty houses.

The streets were too twisting and narrow for him to see far ahead but the steps were still there, ahead of him, leading him on. He followed, half-amused, half-annoyed at himself. He could probably hear the footfalls of some respectable villager who had been taking an evening stroll while everyone one else was at chapel and who didn't want to be found out.

It was getting darker now and the steps had suddenly ceased but he knew where he was; in the street where Boy-John had showed him Charlotte's fish cellar. He moved forward and noticed that the door was slightly open. It had caused him a problem on his visit, he remembered. The door had dropped slightly on its hinges and protested as you pushed it the last few inches shut.

Curiously, he opened it further and glanced inside. The huge wall of pilchards made his eyes open and he grinned. Good for Charlotte!

423

Something, at least, had gone well for her. He might have failed her but she was still succeeding on her own. Not that it did him any good. It set her more out of his reach than ever.

He was turning away when he heard a noise from the net loft upstairs. It was barely audible but he recognised it – the sound of asthmatic breathing. So it *was* Mark. How strange! He grinned, pleased that he would be seeing the youngster again. Maybe there'd be news of home. 'Mark? Is that you?'

No answer. Not so much as a creak of a floorboard. He climbed the ladder. 'Mark?'

It was dark in the net loft. The two small windows let in only a minimum of light but it was enough for him to see the huddled figure lying on a pile of nets in the corner. The laboured wheezing made him want to cough himself in sympathy.

'Mark? Are you all right?'

The breathing seemed to grow more frenzied and, seriously worried, Kit climbed through the trapdoor and stepped up into the dark loft.

Then something hit him across the back of the head with a crushing blow, and the floor came up to meet him.

Chapter Thirty-One

'God has promised us forgiveness for all our sins.'

He wasn't as good a preacher as her father – as William Trevennan, Charlotte quickly corrected herself. Dick Robinson appealed to the minds of the listeners but Trevennan had appealed to their hearts.

Beside her, Bertha's gentle, continuous rocking became more frenzied; her voice rose from a constant low mutter to an audible shriek. 'I am a sinner. I shall burn, burn in Hell, for ever and ever.'

'Hush, Mother.' Charlotte took her hands, stroking, soothing. 'You are a good woman, a good mother. God will bless you for it.'

For a second the rocking stopped and there was a brief glimmer of intelligence in the dull eyes. 'You think so, Charlotte, you really think so?'

'I am sure of it.' Charlotte tightened her grip on the cold thin hands. 'Now listen to the Super-intendent, Mother. He's preaching.'

But her mother had already sunk back into her normal state, rocking and muttering to herself. Charlotte forced herself to appear as if she were listening to the sermon, but inside her thoughts were very different.

No matter what Mr Robinson preached, what Trevennan had done to her mother was unforgivable. He had ruined her life, her health, her mind. Charlotte knew that she herself could recover from the harm he had inflicted but there was no such hope for her mother. She would suffer until the day she died.

Under the shadow of her best bonnet her grey eyes blazed. 'Damn you for ever, William Trevennan,' she muttered under her breath. 'Damn you to Hell.'

William Trevennan laid down the wooden bar with which he had knocked out Kit. He bent and heaved at the unconscious man, moving him further away from the trapdoor in the floor.

For a second, when he had first seen the *Faith-Lily* and Kit, his heart had sunk. It seemed an omen, a sign that he would fail, but now he knew better. God was making sure that he succeeded, succeeded beyond his wildest dreams.

The wooden bar had originally held the double doors over the street shut. Trevennan slotted it back into its two holders then turned his attention to Kit. He was young and strong, his fair hair thick and curly; there was no telling how long the blow would keep him unconscious.

The loft, like all such places, was a repository for odds and ends for which no one could find a use, but which they were unwilling to throw away. He rooted through the piles of rotting sails until he found a length of rope, still relatively strong. With a grunt of satisfaction he leaned over Kit, dragging his arms up behind him before pinioning them with the rope.

The wheezing gasp made him look up. Mark,

huddled and bound on top of a pile of old nets, was staring at him, the whites of his eyes luminous in the dusky light of the loft.

'The bad man!' His tortured breathing could scarcely make the words audible. 'You're the bad man I saw with the doll!'

Damnation! Trevennan felt a cold shudder run down his spine. The boy had remembered! After all this time...

But it wasn't his problem. He took a hold of himself, forcing himself to think clearly. It needn't change his plans at all, just made them even more necessary.

The boy was trying to scream now, writhing impotently against the ropes that tied him, but all he could get out was a thin keening noise. It wouldn't carry to the street, but even so—

Trevennan reached him, slapped him sharply across the cheek. 'Shut up, you little bastard.'

The boy's mouth opened with shock and Trevennan forced his handkerchief inside, binding it in place with his own neck-scarf. The noise was cut off and the preacher realised that Mark was finding it even harder to breathe now that his mouth was stopped. Well, if he passed out it might even be a blessing. At least he wouldn't be alive when the flames reached him.

A groan from Kit made him drop the boy and hurry over to his other prisoner. He definitely couldn't take any chances with this one. He gagged him swiftly, using Kit's own handkerchief and neck-scarf, then checked his bonds. He had tied Kit's arms and legs separately, using the best pieces of rope he could find. Unless the man was

427

a circus strong man there was no way he could break his way out.

Trevennan bent and caught Kit under the arms and began to drag him up onto the nets. Kit was tall and well-built and it took all Trevennan's strength to haul him up the pile of nets which slithered and moved under his feet. But he had to be there. The nets would catch fire first and he needed these bodies to be not only dead, but so badly burned that all traces of their bonds would be destroyed. Panting and struggling, his ears pricked for the sound of anyone approaching, he heaved the body further up the pile of nets.

Kit's eyelids fluttered and Trevennan felt a thrill, half-fear, half-delight. This man had stolen the boat that should have been his, had turned Charlotte against him. Trevennan had no regrets if *this* one was awake when the flames reached him.

But it was time to go. The place must be well alight by the time the service was over. And he had to get himself an alibi. It was difficult because most of the village could be at chapel but he knew better than anyone those who would be absent. Betsy Trembath and Granfer-John were two; they would almost certainly be at home – and the fact that they both heartily disliked him only added to their value as witnesses. He found the thought amusing.

He had it all planned. Some oil-soaked cord led from the trapdoor to the pile of nets Mark and Kit were lying on. He would make sure the cord was burning well then leave, shutting the trapdoor behind him. By the time the nets caught alight and the flames had spread to the thatched roof he could be away, talking to his witness, as innocent as a newborn babe. And if they ever found the bodies – well, it must have been they who had set fire to the loft. He thought of the scurrilous rumours he could spread about the bodies of a young man and a boy being found in a loft together, and actually laughed. Bloody Robinson wouldn't hold his head up so high when he knew what was being said about his darling son.

He moved to the trapdoor and climbed partway down the ladder then lit the end of the rope with his tinder box. The old cord sputtered a little then glowed as the flame took hold. He watched it for a second to make sure that it wouldn't go out then slid quickly down the ladder, pulling the trapdoor back into place. He'd move the ladder, too, he decided. Just in case.

As he carried the ladder to one side his foot knocked against the bucket of train oil that he had dropped in his hurry to chase after the boy and it tipped, the yellow oil spreading in a pool across the cobbled floor. No time to do anything about it now; already he could smell the characteristic odour of burning train oil from upstairs. It would just drain back into the train pit.

He peered through the open door to make sure that no one was around and stepped out into the empty street, pulling the door shut behind him.

'Nnh?'

Kit groaned. Something was wrong. His head

429

was thudding as if he had a dozen Cornish miners inside it, each with a fifteen-pound hammer, his mouth felt dry and stiff, strange. His eyes squeezed shut against the pain in his head, he tried to touch his head, to see if there was a bump but his hands wouldn't move. And there was a sound – frantic, asthmatic wheezing.

Mark Robinson. Memory came back with a rush and Kit's eyes flew open. He was in the net loft, Charlotte's net loft, lying on a pile of smelly nets, his mouth gagged, his arms and legs bound. To one side he could hear Mark. Painfully, he turned his head, peering through the dusk. Above him, higher up the pile of nets, the boy lay, bound and gagged, as he was. His thin chest heaved painfully as he struggled for breath and above the dark band of his gag the whites of his eyes showed as he stared, eyes big with terror, at something on the far side of Kit.

With an effort, wincing at the pain, Kit turned his head to follow the boy's gaze. In the gloom of the loft the small flame was a dagger of brightness that seared into his brain as, smoking and spitting, it made its way along the cord to the pile of nets.

'Here! What are you doing on that boat?'

Boy-John stared down belligerently at the older man who sat peaceably on the bows of the *Faith-Lily*.

The strange fisherman looked up from the pipe he was lighting. 'Smoking,' he said calmly. 'And making sure young heathens like you don't do any harm.'

430

'It's not your boat.' Boy-John knew all the sailors around here and this wasn't one of them. If he had stolen the boat, the boat Boy-John himself had helped to paint, he'd soon know about it. The child's hands clenched into fists.

'I never said she were,' the man answered. 'But I'm looking after her till the captain gets back.'

'The captain?' Boy-John could feel the tension rising inside him. Just suppose... 'Who's the captain?' he demanded.

The fisherman snorted. 'This boat comes from round here. If you don't know that...' A sudden thought struck him. 'You aren't the boy that Kit chased off after, just now, are you?'

'Kit!' The sudden surge of happiness made him feel as if he would burst. Kit! He wasn't dead! All the time the grown-ups had been shaking their heads and crying he hadn't believed it, not really, not deep in his heart. Kit had been too strong, too big, too clever to be drowned. And now he was right! Boy-John beamed. Lotty would be really happy.

But Kit had gone off after some boy. Strange. 'What boy?' he wondered.

The seaman shrugged. 'I never saw him. Just thought it might be you, that's all.'

'Well, it weren't.' Boy-John scowled, rubbing at a patch of yellow lichen with his foot. All the other children went to chapel, so who was this mysterious boy Kit had seen?

He cast another suspicious look at the stranger in case he had been lying to him, but the man seemed oblivious, puffing easily at his pipe. He didn't look the way Boy-John thought a boat

431

thief would look.

He swung round and began running back up through the village, his bare feet pounding on the cobbles.

Once the flame reached the pile of nets Kit knew that the whole lot would burst into flames. He had to get free. Ignoring the pain in his head, he began to struggle against the ropes that bound him. If his hands were free, even his legs, he could stamp on the flame, pull the cord away from the nets, do something that would save their lives. He hunched his shoulders, feeling the veins stand out on his forehead as he struggled to force his hands apart, break the rope, but it was too strong and the knots too tight for him to pull his hands out.

He had only seconds. The flame seemed to be racing along the cord towards him. Somehow he had to put that flame out.

In desperation, he straightened his body, wriggling until he began, slowly, to roll down the hill of nets. It was difficult to control the direction of his movement on the yielding, uneven mound, but it was their only chance. If he could land on the cord he could use his body to extinguish the flame.

It was there below him, snaking inexorably along the cord. Kit gave a final wriggle and lurch, praying as he had never prayed before...

And the final small hillock of nets slid away from the main mound, taking him with it and dumping him on the floor with the burning cord two impossible feet from his head.

'Mm? What is it?'

Granfer-John woke with a start. He couldn't have been asleep for long, for it was not yet dark, but then, he didn't need to be asleep long for Boy-John to get himself into mischief.

The knock on the door that had awakened him was repeated. Swearing softly to himself, Granfer struggled stiffly to his feet. Drat that boy. What had he done now? 'I'm coming. Hold yer horses.'

But the door was pushed open before he could reach it and the white-haired figure of William Trevennan, his hat held respectfully in his hand, his hair shining in the deepening twilight, appeared before him.

Granfer grunted. He had never liked the man and liked him even less after the recent revelations. 'What do you want?'

Trevennan turned his hat respectfully round in his hands. 'I knew that you would not be at chapel and, feeling in need of someone to talk to while my wife is there–'

'Oh, ah?' Granfer spat. 'Never saw fit to come and have a chinwag with me afore now, did 'ee?'

At least the man could have looked embarrassed, he thought, but Trevennan seemed impervious. He simply smiled in a friendly fashion, as if he and Granfer had been friends for ever, and leaned against the doorpost. 'In the past,' he said easily, 'I was a man lost in the paths of my own ambition; I did not appreciate the good that there is in simple, honest people. But now God has opened my eyes and I see...'

So he hasn't changed, Granfer thought. Only

the message. It used to be: 'I have seen the light.' Now it's: 'I used to be a sinner but now I have seen the light.' Or was that always his message and only the dates have changed?

Anyway, one thing stayed the same. The man was willing to run on if you let him. Granfer lit a small lamp called a chill and sat down again to braid his nets while Trevennan's voice flowed meaninglessly over him.

All the same, he couldn't help wondering what the man was after.

Two feet. No distance normally. Impossible to make it in the time, bound as he was. In only seconds the flame would reach the nets and the whole lot would go up. As he rolled down Kit had been aware, even through the gap, that the heap had been soaked in train oil.

Who the hell could have done it? That was what was worrying him. Why should anyone want to burn down the cellars? And why tie him and Mark up, deliberately murder them in this dreadful way? If only he had caught a glimpse of the man who had hit him.

He forced the thought from his mind. Get out of here, that was the first thing. And Mark was still lying on the mound of nets, staring as if hypnotised at the approaching flame. Kit knew that they wouldn't survive unless they could get out of this loft; once the nets had caught, the flames would lick the roof and with the thatch on fire the whole place would be an inferno in no time. But if he could get the boy off the nets he would have bought him a few, precious minutes.

'Nngh.' With the gag in his mouth he could only make a grunting noise through his nose. He repeated it, trying to catch the boy's attention. 'Nngh.'

His desperation must have got through. He saw the fixed gaze on the speeding flame waver, transfer itself to him. 'Nngh.' He jerked his head, trying to indicate that the boy should roll down the heap as he had done. 'Nngh!'

It was amazing how difficult it was to get even a simple message across when you couldn't speak or move your arms. He jerked his whole body, frantically, ignoring the stabs of pain in his head. *'Nngh!'*

And at last the boy realised what he was trying to convey. Kit saw him wriggle his thin body, trying to make himself roll. He glanced at the flame. It was inches from the nets now, gathering speed as it met a smear of oil that had soaked through the pile. He grunted more frantically. Mark didn't have much time.

And then the thin body began the long descent. It seemed easier for Mark than Kit had found it, perhaps because his lighter weight did not compress the nets so much. But it would be a close-run thing.

The boy was rolling faster now, but still too slowly. The flame reached the pile of nets, seemed to hesitate a fraction, then lapped at them greedily. Flames flickered up, climbing the heap.

And then the same thing happened to Mark as had happened to Kit. The last bastion of nets slid away from the pile, bringing Mark with it. For

435

one horrifying second the boy seemed to fall straight onto the rising flames, then he was on the wooden floor, rolling clear.

Wriggling frantically, Kit made his painful way over to him. They had managed to buy themselves a few more minutes of time.

Or had they only postponed the inevitable.

Boy-John mooched along the empty streets. Who was this boy Kit had run after? *He* was the only youngster Kit really knew in Mousehole. He had no right to run after other children, especially when everyone thought he was dead. He should have come to Granfer's first, or Lotty's and told them, not gone disappearing off after some stranger.

Well, he'd had enough. If Kit didn't want to see him, then he wasn't going to chase round after Kit. He'd go back to Granfer. At least he'd be able to tell him the news.

He turned around then stopped, sniffing.

His nostrils caught the smoky smell of a newly-lit fire. But no one would light a fire at this time of a Sunday, not in hot weather. They'd have cooked their dinner this morning, then let the fire either go out or at least die down so that it didn't make the cottage unbearably hot.

He glanced up at the roofs, wondering who had done it, but no plumes of black smoke billowed out of any chimney into the still evening air. Then something caught his eye; something that wasn't quite right.

He stared again at the roofs but they were as they always had been, some covered with slates, others thatched. He lowered his eyes and saw it.

A red gleam behind windows that should have been dark.

Even as he stared at it, it flickered, grew brighter. Fire. And in Charlotte's net loft.

Then he was running, breathless, his bare heels thrumming on the cobbles. Help! He had to get help! And quickly.

He had never been into the chapel before, but he did not hesitate. He jumped up the steps and pushed open the heavy doors to the lobby and then pelted through them into the main part of the building.

The place was full, everyone in their best clothes, listening to the new Superintendent, the one who had given Lotty's da the sack. As the doors burst open they all swung round, silently staring at him. Even the preacher, up in his special place in front of everyone else, stopped what he was saying.

For once Boy-John was aware of his untidy hair, his bare feet and cutdown trousers, then he rallied. This was important.

'Fire.' He was so out of breath that he could only gasp out the words. 'Fire in Lotty's cellars.'

'Fire!'

The word rippled through the congregation, flowing out from him as if he had been a stone thrown into a pool and then they were standing, moving, the whole room surging towards him in a silent, concentrated rush.

He stepped back, suddenly frightened of this mass of people he had known all his life and they were past him, pushing through the doors, into the open air, men, women and children – each, as they got outside, running, running. And all in the same direction.

He forced himself into the rush, ignoring the booted feet that trod on his bare toes, then he was running with them.

He could only have been a minute at the most. No one could have been quicker. But already the thatch was alight, flames licking to quiet sky, brilliant against the darkness. The flames reflected off the other houses, lighting them with an eerie glow that reminded Boy-John of a once-heard description of Hell.

'They pilchards!' A woman's voice rose frantically. 'We must save they pilchards. I worked brem hard on they.'

There were shouts of agreement, a flow of bodies towards the door of the cellar when suddenly they were pushed aside. Charlotte stood in front of them, her face white under her best Sunday bonnet, her arms outstretched, barring the way.

'No.'

The single word stopped them in their tracks. They stared at her, angry, excited, muttering, but she stood firm.

'No,' she repeated. 'Let it burn. You can do nothing to save the cellar now and the pilchards must take their chance. No fish is worth the life of a human being. Let the cellar burn.'

Chapter Thirty-Two

There was a roar of disapproval. 'Don't be a fool!' 'All they fish!'

Charlotte stood alone, her head high, but inside she was crying. This had been her last chance, her last hope of making something of herself, of cutting herself and her mother free from the tentacles of poverty. And now this too had been snatched away. All she had left was the knowledge of the money she had borrowed from the bank against the security of these pilchards, money she had already spent out, paying the women threepence an hour for their work and providing them with bread and cheese and brandy, the traditional recompense for such labour.

She tried to make them understand. 'Thatch is made so that water runs off it. You won't be able to put the fire out by pouring water from above. And the floor of the loft is wood; it can collapse at any minute. It's just too dangerous.'

'But they fish?'

The anguish in the voice echoed the agony in her heart but she could not let any of them risk their lives. 'If you want to help,' her voice sounded strangled and she had to clear her throat, 'if you really want to help, wet the thatch on the houses around. The cellars are done for, we must save the houses.'

The crowd in front of her churned, separated.

Men ran for buckets, for ladders, women chattered and called, children ran, screaming with excitement, all lit by the eerie leaping flames, flames that were destroying her life. Dry-eyed, beyond crying now, Charlotte blinked as a heavy hand fell on her shoulder.

'Life goes on.' It was Kit's father, his voice leaden.

She did not glance round. 'It's so hard.'

She felt his grasp tighten as he understood her unspoken words. 'Dick Robinson always says that we are not given any trials we are not capable of bearing.'

Charlotte turned then, pulling herself away from his grip. 'What would he know about it?' she demanded, and walked back to where her mother was standing, rocking gently, amidst the seething mass of villagers.

'What's that there noise?'

Granfer-John cocked his head on one side, holding up a hand for silence.

William Trevennan cursed under his breath. There was only one thing it could be – someone had discovered the fire. But he hadn't expected it to happen so soon. If the man and boy survived...

'Something's up. Come on.' Granfer limped painfully to the door and Trevennan followed, praying as he had never prayed before in his life. They mustn't be rescued, dear God, let them be dead. Please, let them be dead.

As Kit had expected, once the fuse met the pile

of oil-soaked nets they flared up in seconds. Flames leaped from one part of the nets to another, first flickering on the surface as the oil caught then dancing up as the nets themselves began to burn.

By the uncertain light Kit made a quick assessment of his surroundings. The ancient floorboards wouldn't burn – for a few minutes, at least. But the gaps between their warped and twisted lengths were acting like a fire grate, allowing the fire to suck up fresh oxygen from the open cellar below to fuel itself, driving the flames high into the air so that already they were licking at the underside of the thatch.

Thick, choking smoke rolled down from the nets, as big a danger as the fire itself. He lifted his head. Mark was lying on the floor nearby, for the moment away from the flames, but in the red light Kit could see his contorted face as he fought for oxygen.

It was amazingly difficult to move with legs tied together and arms pinioned behind one's back. Kit jack-knifed himself across to the boy.

Close to, he could hear the boy's desperate wheezing, see the terrified whites of his eyes. Mark had to have air, that was the first priority. Using his legs, Kit levered the boy over onto his face and pushed him until his nose was above a gap in the floorboards. The smoke rolled through the loft in great clouds, but there was a small layer just above the floor where the air was relatively clear, and there was still fresh air coming up from the open cellar below. Kit knew that at best he had bought the boy only a few more minutes of life. They would both die soon unless he could get them out of here.

Every movement of his body took a tremendous toll. He was panting and sweating with effort, struggling for breath around the sickening barrier of the gap. But every breath now drew more smoke into his lungs, making him want to choke and cough. Closing his mind to the fear of death and the agony in his chest, Kit struggled across the uneven floorboards to the closed trapdoor and began to try to lever it up with fingers that were already going numb.

It only took one glance to see that they weren't even trying to save the cellar. Trevennan let out his breath in a satisfied sigh. He glanced around the noisy crowd. It hadn't even been necessary to gag the pair; no one would have heard their shouts from inside the building with all this racket going on. In the whole group only Charlotte and Bertha were silent; Bertha because she seemed almost unaware of what was happening and Charlotte, he guessed, because she knew all too well that her last asset was literally going up in smoke.

But it wasn't, Trevennan suddenly realised. He had got rid of that blasted Kit but she still had the *Faith-Lily*, even if she didn't know it yet. Behind him, Robinson was talking quietly with his tall, fair friend. He wouldn't be around for long, Trevennan gloated. Not once he found his precious son was dead. And then there'd be a new Superintendent...

The plan came instantly to mind. So simple, so

442

easy. It would take time, of course, but once Robinson was gone, as long as he had the people on his side there was still a chance. Perhaps he would never become ordained, but he could still remain a local preacher. Robinson might put in a report to Conference about him, but if the people were behind him...

'My wife, Bertha.' He shouldered his way through the crowd to where she stood, rocking slightly from one foot to another, Charlotte's protecting arm around her waist. 'And my daughter.' He extended his arms and the people around him edged away, giving him the space he needed, falling silent. He could feel their eyes on him and it invigorated him. He was a preacher, always and for ever a preacher. He had the power to move armies if he so wanted.

Charlotte raised her head. Her grey eyes shone eerily in the light of the flames. 'You're not my father.' Her voice shook with fury. 'You have no right to call me Daughter!'

'The right of a man who has reared you and cherished you.' His voice rolled out across the crowd, silent now, listening. Against the background crackle and roar of the fire his words seemed to soar, carried on the hot wind. He reached out towards her, gently, understandingly. 'Do not despair, my child. Do not give in to desperation. God may be punishing you now for the lies you spoke against me, the hurt you did me. But I have forgiven you, my child, and God too, will forgive you. When you repent.'

Behind him, the flames reached hungry hands to the darkening skies.

443

The trapdoor was designed to be opened from below. From above, it fitted snugly into its hole and Kit could not get a grasp on it. Coughing, choking, he rolled onto his side, narrowing his eyes against the black smoke that curled and billowed through the loft.

The roof was alight, now. Small lumps of burning straw came loose and dropped to the floor, smouldering amongst a pile of old ropes in one corner. The heat was intense. Mark was still face down, breathing in fresh air that rose through the floor, sucked up by the heat of the fire, but that wouldn't last for long. Soon, the floor would collapse, or the burning roof would fall on them. Soon, the heat would grow unbearable.

Eyes streaming, Kit peered around him, desperately trying to find a way out.

Hargraves caught Robinson's arm. 'Can you hear what that bastard is trying to do?'

But Robinson wasn't listening. Face pale, he stared round the crowd. 'Mark.' His voice was high with worry. 'I can't see my son anywhere.'

'Never mind Mark,' Hargraves said impatiently. 'He'll be all right. He's probably down at the harbour. But that bastard Trevennan—'

'He'd be here,' Robinson broke in. 'This fire must be visible all over the village. No boy would stay away. So, where is he?' His voice rose frantically.

Hargraves stared upwards. In the still air the flames were like a beacon. On surrounding roofs, men were busy, emptying buckets of water over the thatch or sitting astride the ridges with brooms in their hands, ready to beat out any sparks that tried to gain a hold. Never mind the village, this fire could be seen right across the Bay. So where *was* the boy?

Robinson swung round, staring at the cellar. The upstairs floor was well ablaze now but, although there were drifts of smoke feeling their way under the doors, it looked as if the lower floor was not yet on fire. 'He's in there. I know he is. He's in there!'

He made a run for the cellar but Hargraves reached out, caught his arm in a brutal grasp and pulled him back.

'Don't be a fool. Why would he go in there? He's got asthma, damn it, hasn't he? He's just sitting somewhere, feeling unwell, trying to get his breath. That's why he's not here.'

As he spoke, a part of the roof caved in and flames leaped higher with a mighty roar.

Why was no one coming? Kit wondered dizzily as he tried to find a way out. Surely, someone would come to attend to the fire. He could hear voices outside, even over the noise of the flames, but no one came, no one helped.

The smoke was getting to him, he knew. Soon, he would be unconscious and then... But there was Mark. He was breathing clean air, he would still be conscious when the flames reached him. Kit groaned through the gag, struggling to gain control of his reeling mind. He had to save him somehow.

His body was a mass of pain now. Sparks fell around him, smouldering in his clothes, burning his skin. The agony of the burns even eclipsed that of the wound in his head. He gritted his teeth, holding onto consciousness by willpower alone.

He forced his streaming eyes open once more, jack-knifing his aching body round as he gave the burning loft a final survey.

Trevennan raised his voice so that it carried even to the men on the roofs. 'The loss of a cellar full of fish – why should God give them to you and then take them away if not as a punishment? If not so that the roaring flames can remind you of the burning Hell that awaits all sinners who do not repent?'

He could feel the villagers listening, silent, wondering. He knew the way their minds worked. He knew what they would think – as long as he showed them the way, as long as he pushed their minds in the right direction.

He glanced across at Robinson but the man wasn't even listening to him; he seemed to be having an argument with Hargraves. Trevennan felt contempt thrill through him. They were having a battle for the hearts and minds of the villagers and the fool didn't even know it! Just because Trevennan had lost one battle, the Superintendent thought the war had been won – that he had been completely vanquished, but he hadn't. He'd win this next battle. And then he'd show them.

Bertha was mumbling again, rocking from foot

to foot more violently. 'A sinner. I'm a sinner,' she droned. 'I deserve to burn in Hell.'

He raised his voice, easily overpowering her. 'Charlotte, my daughter.' He held out caring arms to her, bared his teeth in a caressing smile. 'Come to me, dearest. Admit that you lied. And let God take you once again into His loving heart.'

The silence was complete apart from the greedy work of the fire. All around him he could feel the villagers holding their breath, staring at the poignant tableau in front of them. He could hear his words, loving, kindly words, echoing in their minds.

And Charlotte moved. Slowly, gently, she took her arm from around her mother and stood alone. In the flaring light of the flames her face was pale, downcast. Slowly, she lifted her head until she was looking at him; slowly, she moved towards him, one step, then another.

He had done it! His heart exulted in the thought. He had won. And once she gave way to him, how could the villagers hold out? And Robinson, he would be leaving soon, when he found out about the boy, when he knew that he had been wrong.

She was in front of him now, her face white and set. A soft buzz of conversation broke out behind him and Trevennan quelled it with an impatient gesture. He wanted them all to hear this.

She spoke. Her voice was husky with emotion and grief but the words carried clearly across the hushed crowd.

'You are evil, William Trevennan. Evil through

447

and through. You try to subvert God for your own ends but He does not work like that.'

She lifted her head, faced the crowd. 'I did not lie. I did nothing wrong. If my cellars are alight it is the work of man, not God!'

The smoke was too thick to see through but the memory of his previous visit to the cellars came to Kit. He closed his eyes, trying to remember. There had been Boy-John, laughing, playing around, telling him about the cellars. And there had been, surely, doors in the net loft, doors that overlooked the street.

There had to be. His seaman's brain clicked into gear. Nets were long and heavy – and who would know that better than he, after these last weeks at sea? They would be stored here, and there would be doors to load and unload them – probably some sort of derrick to lift them to the loft for storage at the end of the season.

If he just could get to them... He oriented himself. Over there – surely they were over there?

He made his painful way through the choking smoke, over smouldering floorboards. A pile of partly burned nets was in the way; still alight. Setting his teeth he rolled over them, gasping then coughing at the pain as he did so. The doors must be somewhere here...

And there they were. Forcing his eyes open against the blinding smoke, Kit saw them in the light of the flames. High, double doors, held shut at waist-height by a wooden bar dropped into two catches. If he could kick the catch free...

His head was whirling, his body felt like lead.

Every movement was an effort but he had to do it. For Mark's sake.

Wriggling close to the door he kicked his bound legs up together, as high as he could reach. His foot grazed the bar but that was all. He tried again. And again. The bar was only about two inches thick, held against the wood of the door by its supports. His feet thudded into the door again and again. Could they hear him down below? But even if they could, they would be unable to open the doors. Unless they were opened from the inside it would need an axe to get through them.

Choking, gasping, he prepared to try again. And heard something.

At first he thought it was outside then he realised it came from Mark.

Wearily, achingly slowly, he manoeuvred himself round until he could see the boy. Even through the smoke-filled loft he could see the mortal fear on his young face. But he wasn't looking at Kit, he was staring at the roof above him.

Kit looked up. The whole roof was on fire now, the burning thatch falling away in lumps. And one flaming lump, dangling from nothing, was hanging right above him.

Instinct moved him, rolling and jack-knifing away. With agonising slowness he worked his way back from the doors that meant salvation and with agonising slowness the thatch fell, landing just where he had been lying.

The bitterness of failure rose in his throat. He had done all he could and he had failed. There was no way out now. No hope. Not for him or for Mark. All he could do for the boy now was to keep him company during the last few minutes of his life before the flames enveloped them.

He worked his painful way back to where the boy was lying. He had moved from the airspace Kit had found for him and was pressed, wide-eyed with terror, against the inside wall of the loft. Kit rolled beside him, wondering if there was anything he could do for the boy, to ease his dying.

There was a roar and another part of the roof fell in. Instinctively, Kit rolled his body over the boy's, trying to protect him from the raging flames.

Then with a groan the ancient floor collapsed and they were falling, falling...

Chapter Thirty-Three

Boy-John was bored.

He'd been expecting excitement, fun. He'd run to the chapel anticipating the wild race to the cellars, but now it had all calmed down. The houses around didn't seem to be catching fire and no one was doing anything about the cellars at all. He'd thought people would be running in and out, carrying fish, pouring water on the roof, but they were just standing around talking. It wasn't his idea of a fire.

At first that big Mr Hargraves had been standing in front of the doors to the cellar, telling everyone to keep out but he'd moved away now, talking to the new Superintendent. No one was watching the doors at all.

After a quick glance around to make sure no one was watching him, Boy-John pushed open the doors and slipped inside.

Charlotte was shaking with fury. She knew what Trevennan was trying to do; she had had a life-time's experience of the way he could manipulate people and events for his own benefit. And now he was trying to rehabilitate himself in the villagers' eyes – and using her misfortunes as a weapon.

Briefly she closed her eyes. She was tired, so very tired. Ever since Mr Polruan's death she had been fighting; fighting for her reputation, her livelihood, even her mother's sanity. She had lost so much already, the *Faith-Lily*, Kit... She forced the thought of him from her mind, afraid that the memory would weaken her.

This cellar, the fish it contained, were her only hope and now they were gone. And, next, it would be her reputation again. She would be back to being a moral leper, stared at, ignored. And all because of William Trevennan. Dear God, would it never end?

But she had to carry on fighting. It was all she could do. She opened her eyes...

And saw Boy-John's small figure squeezing hurriedly around the edge of the door into the burning building.

'Boy-John!'

Even as she shouted his name she was running, forcing aside the bodies in her way. 'Boy-John!'

She flung the door wide. The cellar looked like a scene from Hell. The thatched roofs which surrounded the open space in the middle were all alight. Sparks and wisps of burning straw dropped to the ground and flared briefly as they touched the thin layer of oil running across the pebbles. The huge heap of fish was already charring in the intense heat, a black mound in the eerie, red inferno. Against the flames Boy-John's small figure looked like a two-dimensional silhouette, black but oh, so fragile.

'Boy-John!'

Ignoring the heat, the danger, she ran forward, caught at him. 'Come out of there.'

He struggled against her but she was winning.

One step she dragged him back, two steps.

Then with a crack and a roar the floor of the net loft above them fell in.

'Oh, dear God!'

Hargraves spun round at the sound and raced forward. 'Keep everybody out,' he shouted at Robinson as he ducked his head to enter the burning cellar.

The floor of the net loft stretched above the full width of the front of the cellars, making a long, low ceiling, already alight in several places.

The part immediately in front of the door had collapsed, filling the cellar with a blinding, choking fog of smoke and dust, whirling and roiling in the uncertain draughts that filled the open courtyard.

Coughing, using his hand to shield his eyes, Hargraves moved forwards. It was impossible to see, impossible to breathe. Then his foot stepped ono something yielding, round. A human arm.

'Charlotte?' He bent down, peering through streaming eyes. 'Charlotte?' He caught at the arm, pulled.

She was still coughing, but she was still alive. He backed away, dragging at her, trying to get her out of the inferno, but she shook him off.

'Boy-John.' She could barely gasp the words out between coughs. 'I must find him.'

But already the courtyard was clearing of smoke. The draught from the open door was sucked up by the flames, taking the smoke and dust with it. The child was lying a little way past her. Hargraves reached down to lift him up...

And stopped.

Beyond the boy the floor of the loft had demolished part of the wall of pilchards. Ancient black boards and silver fish spewed across the cellar floor in an avalanche of destruction. And something else.

Half-hidden by the mounds of fish but black against their silver he could see, unbelievably, a man's feet.

He wiped his smarting eyes. It was impossible! The uncertain light threw dancing shadows on the fallen heap – but this shadow remained steady.

It was real.

Beside him, he was aware of Charlotte reaching for Boy-John but he himself moved forward, pulled at the feet.

They both moved together, unnaturally, and the movement disturbed the pile of fish. The pilchards flowed away, slithering in a mass of salt and blood, to spread further out across the sea-rounded pebbles, and the body appeared.

Tied.

He stared disbelieving at the sight. The man's face was black with soot, his shirt stained with blood and ash, but his feet were bound. And his hands. And there was a gag.

There was a roar, and another part of the floor above fell, burning. Hargraves threw up his hands to protect his face while his mind reeled. But he knew he had to get the body. Someone had wanted to kill this man. The fire was arson.

He lunged forward, dragging again at the feet and now the body slid completely down the pile of fish and revealed another body, smaller but also tied. A body not yet full grown. Dear God.

Then Charlotte was beside him, reaching for the smaller body, and he pulled and dragged at the other. A tall man, well-built. What trick, what treachery had been used to lure him here, to tie him up like this?

Then there were other hands, other arms. The weight was taken from him. Eyes streaming, retching, he was led back from the raging heat and glare of the cellar, out to the comparative calm of the night outside.

The two bodies were laid out on the ground, surrounded by silent, horrified villagers. Already one of the men, with an instinctive feeling for decency, was cutting the ropes that tied their hands, untying the gags.

And as the material fell away Hargraves saw the face of the man for the first time.

Kit.

When he saw Charlotte enter the cellar after Boy-John, when he heard the roof fall, Trevennan had closed his eyes briefly, offering up a prayer of thanksgiving.

God was on his side. He had never doubted it, never wavered in his faith for a second. Everything was working out even better than he had planned. He lowered his face into his hands, thanking his Saviour, feeling the silence grow around him and knowing that the villagers thought he was praying for the lives of Charlotte and Boy-John.

How could he lose? If they were saved it

showed the power of this prayer, and if they died in there he would not grieve. The girl had become a thorn in his flesh, a centre of rebellion against him. Her death could only help.

Opening his eyes he saw Hargraves run through into the cellar. Let him go.

'Friends.' He raised his voice. Now was the time to reassert his power; now, while that weak fool of a Superintendent was standing there looking worried and bewildered, he would show his strength of mind, his powers of oratory, his leadership. 'Let us pray. Let us ask God to watch over that child and these two brave people who have risked their lives to save him.'

Most bowed their heads but a couple of men moved through the doors, into the cellars. No matter. He lifted his head, feeling the heat of the flames beat on his closed eyelids, feeling the certainty of his power as his words, strong, powerful, surged forth without conscious thought.

A swirl of movement and, opening one eye, he saw Boy-John brought out, coughing, beginning to struggle in the arms of the man who carried him. Then another body, taller, limper – and his voice quavered then died.

Around him the crowd turned, staring. A third body, smaller.

This wasn't meant to happen. This wasn't the way he had planned things. They should not have been found until tomorrow at the earliest. They should have been discovered badly burned, the ropes and gags consumed by fire. They should have been almost unrecognisable.

'Mark.' Dick Robinson threw himself onto the

body of his son. 'Mark.' His voice was harsh with grief. 'Oh, my God, Mark.'

Act, Trevennan's mind told him. Take the lead, assert your authority. Make the crowd see things your way. He took a deep breath...

And Mark coughed.

The small sound seemed to echo through the street. Trevennan felt it reverberate in every cell of his body. *No!* The word blazed silently through his brain. No, it's not true, it can't happen!

'He's alive?' He whispered the words, slowly, disbelievingly, and equally slowly, equally disbelievingly, Robinson raised his head and echoed them. 'He's alive?'

The boy coughed again and the street erupted into action. Before Trevennan's horrified gaze, rough hands pulled the incredulous father from his son's body, lifted the boy up, thumped him on the back.

Trevennan saw Charlotte and Hargraves throw a swift look at each other then hurl themselves on Kit's body. 'A bellows,' Charlotte yelled. 'Get a bellows.'

It was the traditional way of trying to save a drowning man, Trevennan knew, but would it work here? A woman raced into one of the nearest houses but already Charlotte had realised that she could not wait. She threw herself across the motionless body, mouth clamped to mouth, breathing in air, using her lungs instead of the traditional bellows, while Hargraves pushed at the man's chest, again and again.

Leave, a small sane voice somewhere in Trevennan's head told him. *Leave. Now. Before they find out. Go away. For ever.*

But he couldn't move, couldn't speak. In front of him his whole life crashed into ruins; his hopes, his plans, his faith...

In the enormity of his disaster he watched, detached, as the boy gained strength after a coughing fit and began to croak out words. In the depths of his despair he was unmoved when Kit groaned, raising a swollen hand to his blood-stained head. He was alone. He was cold, cold through and through. He was dead. Nothing would ever touch him again.

Then a sudden cry. Susan Spargo's voice, shrill with fear. 'Mrs Trevennan!'

Still coldly, from far away, he watched Charlotte raise her head from her lover, climb to her feet, search through the crowd with her eyes. 'Mother!'

And Trevennan saw her. Stepping through the open doors of the cellar, black against the red flames, thin, alone, moving into the flames of Hell.

'NO!'

His shout drowned out Charlotte's. He saw her turn to run after her mother, but Kit's hand caught at her ankle, Hargraves' arm held her back, Granfer-John's body barred her way.

But no one stopped *him.*

'Bertha!' He thrust his way through the bemused onlookers. 'Bertha, come back.'

He could hear her voice, soft, monotonous. 'I am a sinner. I have sinned. I shall burn in Hell.'

'No!' He could feel tears on his cheeks, now. He threw himself through the door after her, into the raging inferno inside. 'Bertha, no. Come back. Come back.'

She stood, motionless in the heat and smoke. 'A sinner.' Her voice was merely accepting. 'I am a sinner.'

'No.'

He tried to reach her but she moved ahead, her long Sunday skirts sweeping the ground. Bits of burning thatch fell from the roof, lit the running oil into tiny flares, licked at her skirts.

'Bertha.' He was pleading, crying. 'Not you too, Bertha. Don't you leave me.'

'A sinner.' She drifted onwards, into the courtyard. The flames around the hem of her skirt jumped higher.

'Bertha!' He caught her, swinging her around, trying to pull her away from this place of death and danger. 'Please, Bertha!'

And saw her full, flaming skirts swing wide, saw them sway, with majestic slowness, over the pit of train oil, the train oil already heated almost to flashpoint by the fires around.

'No.' He threw himself against her, clutched her in his arms, pulled her to him, close, close...

And the oil exploded.

Above the roar, above the flames and the agony, he heard the wail of anguish. 'A sinner!' and held her to him, comforting her with his body as she would never let him during their marriage...

And their flesh melted together into death.

Morning.

Cool, fresh air blew in through the window, stroked burned skin with gentle fingers, scented the air with roses.

'So,' James Hargraves said, pretending to ignore Kit and Charlotte's entwined fingers under the breakfast table. 'You expect me to set you up here, buy you God knows how many boats—'

'Build,' Kit interposed swiftly. 'The *Faith-Lily* is beautifully designed but she's not built for speed. We,' he cast a quick smiling glance at Charlotte, 'need boats that can do a night's fishing and still make it in to catch the steamer or the train. And an ice-works,' he added. 'Shipping bits of glaciers here from Norway isn't really ideal.'

'And leave you down here, to run it all yourself?'

Kit gave him an affectionate smile. 'Be honest, Father, it's the perfect answer. You always told me you wanted me to take an interest in the business, and this way you'll have me – *us*,' he corrected himself, 'down here, where we won't interfere with your side of things.'

'As if I'd let you…' Hargraves growled.

He broke off as Robinson came wearily into the room. 'How is he, Dick? What does the doctor say?'

'He'll be fine. He just needs to rest and keep quiet for a few days until the burns heal,' Robinson ran his fingers through his hair and glanced warily at Charlotte. 'There was one thing, though.' His voice was uncertain. 'It's about your stepfather, my dear. Do you feel up to talking about it?'

She took a deep breath. 'I'd rather get everything over and done with as soon as possible.'

Kit's fingers stroked her palm, and she squeezed his hand in return. It was wrong to feel so happy when there was so much evil in the world but she could not help herself. 'What is it?'

'Mark's been having nightmares for years, ever since we were down here last. Always the same nightmare, about a man and a doll.'

He looked at her, his kind face clouded with worry. 'Now he says that it's because of your stepfather. He's remembered that he saw Trevennan hurting a young woman, a girl with black hair and red cheeks, like a doll, according to Mark.'

Charlotte pulled her hand from Kit's. They were too close now, he seemed to be able to read her mind. And she did not want him to know this.

Abruptly, she rose and moved to the window and stood, looking out across the roses. In the distance the Bay sparkled, sending diamond flashes to the sky. It was a perfect day. And here was more evil.

Sarah Jelbert. She had been just like a doll, with her pink cheeks and black hair and sweet, meaningless smile. Sarah Jelbert, simple-minded and innocent, who had escaped Granfer-John's watchful eye one day and ended up pregnant with Boy-John. Sarah Jelbert who died in childbirth, never knowing what she had done or what was happening to her.

Charlotte swallowed the lump in her throat. 'What are you asking me?'

'Could it be true?' The Superintendent's voice was very gentle. 'You've lived in the village all your life. Is there yet more harm that man has done?'

461

Boy-John's face flashed in front of her. Boy-John with his untidy hair, his missing front tooth, his face alive with mischief and intelligence. He was already despised for his illegitimate birth; what would people say if they knew who his true father was?

She swung round, her grey eyes steady and clear. 'I've never heard of any such incident,' she said calmly.

She wouldn't look at Kit, staring at her, his blue eyes still bloodshot from the smoke yesterday, his hair and eyebrows singed and face covered with small burns. This was her business, hers and Granfer's. She'd tell him; he had a right to know, but that was that. Even Kit would never know this secret.

Robinson sighed. 'Thank God for that, at least. I'd hate to think that there was some other dreadful secret about Trevennan.'

Kit moved painfully, trying to find a position where his burns did not hurt him, and Robinson said worriedly, 'I wish you'd let the doctor have a look at you while he's here, Kit. Perhaps he can give you something for those burns.'

Kit grinned, reaching out a hand to Charlotte. 'I asked my fiancée here about local remedies for burns, but I rather went off the one she knew.'

Robinson looked surprised. 'Why? Local remedies are often very good. What was this one, Charlotte?'

She took Kit's hand in both of hers, smiling into the blue eyes she had never expected to see again.

'Train oil,' she answered.

The publishers hope that this book has given you enjoyable reading. Large Print Books are especially designed to be as easy to see and hold as possible. If you wish a complete list of our books please ask at your local library or write directly to:

Magna Large Print Books
Magna House, Long Preston,
Skipton, North Yorkshire.
BD23 4ND

This Large Print Book for the partially sighted, who cannot read normal print, is published under the auspices of

THE ULVERSCROFT FOUNDATION